Take a Chance on Me

Debbie Flint

Where heroes are like chocolate – irresistible!

FSC
www.fsc.org

MIX
Paper from
responsible sources
FSC® C020471

To all at Choc Lit, and also to Simon, who knows who he is, for taking a chance on me.

Acknowledgements

With the utmost gratitude and big hugs to all the lovely friends, relations and Facebook contacts who helped me during this 'first novel-writing journey'. From the initial concept and painful early versions back in 2010, through to the final, widely varied versions, all carefully considered by my patient beta-readers group. To the Ladies of Posara, my Tuscany writing group, where this book began. To the Debbie's Readers group on Facebook, without whom it might have been another three years before I finished this book, and particularly to Sharon Harvey, who runs the group, for being the most supportive pal anyone could hope for. And of course to my family and those closest to me, who have seen this achievement of a lifetime come finally to fruition, after decades of saying 'when I'm a grown up I want to be a writer ...' Which is still true, by the way. Thanks to you all.

Thanks to Choc Lit Tasting panel members: Robyn, Rosie, Sammi, Purabi, Linda Sy, Olivia, Liz R, Caroline & Jane O for giving the novel their approval.

Chapter One

She nearly did it. In that split second, she nearly did it. After all, if throwing a mobile phone into the sea could magically take *all* her troubles away, Ms Sadie Turner (PhD) would instantly be a stone lighter, debt-free and not in the mood for killing somebody. Well, one body in particular – the one explaining light-heartedly that he couldn't have the girls at the weekend – again. Something had 'cropped up' – *again*. But this time, Sadie had a way out. This time, the deal of a lifetime was within reach, and this time, nothing could stand in her way. Least of all the waste of space she used to call husband – because tomorrow she had a business meeting with a billionaire, and, with his investment, everything could change. A way to be finally free of the painfully thin string that was holding her hostage to her past.

She had just thirty days to make it happen.

'Aw come on, sweetie, let your mum have them for me. She did it for you last month when you went swanning off to play aloha halfway round the world.'

'She's my mum, Stuart. And it was business,' Sadie replied. At that moment a ship sounded its horn offshore, and Sadie jumped, as did a hundred seabirds who took off, filling the air with their cawing and flapping. Not quite the Mediterranean 'breeze' she had in mind.

'Anyway, where are you? On another cheapo jaunt? Some European jolly, sweetie?' said the voice on speakerphone.

'Don't call me sweetie,' she replied. 'It's not a jolly. And they flew me here Club Class, if you must know.'

'Oo-ooo, sorry, sugar-lips.'

'And don't call me sugar-lips! Or babe, or cutie-pie, or anything – in fact, don't call me at all when I'm away on business!'

'Is it proper business?'

'*Yes, of course it's proper business!*' Sadie snapped a little too loud for her opulent surroundings. She heard a 'tut' from somewhere nearby and looked around but couldn't see anyone, just a group of glamorous people a little further down the jetty, queuing to board one of the executive yachts.

She adjusted her jacket, lowered her voice, and banished her demons.

'No more of your sob stories, Stuart. And I'll tell you something – if you don't take your daughters somewhere nice this weekend, then your latest "girlfriend" – *girl* being the operative word – will be mysteriously *twittered* about how old you really are.'

'It's tweeted.'

'I don't care if it's *twatted*, don't let your children down again.'

She made a mental note to tell her kids later about this latest heated debate with their dad – it would make them smile. He had stopped being their fourth musketeer years ago, but it could be worse – he could be worse.

'But there's no way I can miss my …' he began, but at that moment her call waiting bleep sounded.

'Hold on a sec, Stuart,' she said as she jabbed at her phone sharply. 'Good afternoon, Sadie Turner speaking.'

It was an update on her lost luggage. It was still lost. A few more hours in the business suit then.

Sadie swapped calls again, and let out a big sigh.

'Was that one of your big sighs?' her ex-husband asked.

She rolled her eyes at the phone.

'And I bet you're rolling your eyes?' *Damn the man.* 'So I saw the local paper – who'd have thought it, my Sadie winning a marketing award and a trip to Hawaii to pick up some trophy.'

'I'm not your Sadie. Not any more.'

'Something happen when you were out there?' he

continued, ignoring her comment. 'No sooner are you back than I try to call and get yet another foreign ringtone. What's that all about then?' He gabbled straight on, not waiting for her reply – like he used to do when he had a bee in his bonnet. 'Most unlike my workaholic Sadie. Have you met someone?' he asked, an edge to his voice. *Ah, there it was.*

She took a moment to compose herself, then mentally squeezed him out from under her skin like a great big spot. *Satisfying.*

'That's none of your concern, is it?' she replied triumphantly, stretching her neck to left and right. 'Not any more. Got to go, Stuart, people to see, things to do. And don't forget – be there on Saturday. It's your turn. Bye.'

She hung up before he could reply. That felt good. She exhaled and closed her eyes. Things to do indeed – *like wasting time waiting for my suitcase to turn up*. She started to walk along the jetty.

Lost luggage – today of all days.

A long blonde tendril escaped in the breeze and blew onto her face, so she stopped walking to fix it. Her handbag was heavy and she put it down at her feet. She'd brought the shiny glass trophy along so she could look at it every now and then as a kind of talisman, a good luck charm. And maybe if she rubbed it enough her luck would continue. She'd need it because palpitations hit her chest like a freight train every time she thought about the make or break presentation she had to give tomorrow morning. Was it any wonder, with the challenge she was facing? Could she do it? Could *anyone* do it?

Just thirty days to find an investor and sign the contract – certainly not your run-of-the-mill business deal. But then Sadie Samantha Turner was 'not your run-of-the-mill business woman'. At least that's what her fridge magnet said.

She pulled a little tube of high protection sun cream from her jacket pocket. It smelled wonderfully exotic and felt soothing as she dabbed some onto her glowing cheeks. Then she shoved the wayward hair back into the once-smart 'up-do' that had become more 'do' than 'up'.

Picking up her weighty handbag again, she set off, carefully clip-clopping along the cobblestones as fast as her five-inch stilettos would allow. *Ouch* – not so fast – she nearly twisted an ankle.

She wasn't expecting cobblestones. Why cobblestones and not wood? Well, the boats were huge. Goodness only knows how wealthy you had to be to own one of these beauties. She remembered the conversations amongst the plane passengers on the way over, two of whom were having an in-depth debate about which stars were docked here for the Grand Prix. She'd been so fascinated by their conversations, and so clearly out of her depth in Club Class, that they'd taken pity on her and regaled her with stories of the glitterati in Monaco. 'Here,' one of them had said, 'take this ticket – if you don't mind pretending you're on the guest list. It's for an Open Day for a yacht that's for sale – not on our agenda, darling, not this trip. But you are welcome to go – you've certainly got the shoes for it.'

She'd hesitated. *What would it be like … imagine the view from the deck … just to get one photo on board, to see the girls' faces when they saw it …* She'd heard about the famous marina and wanted to see how the other half lived – play a bit of make-believe. But now cold feet had set in. Maybe just seeing the outside of the *Nomusa* – the massive blue yacht pictured on the ticket – would be enough. Maybe it would be best not to try to pass herself off as someone she wasn't, considering her inappropriate business attire and dishevelled hair. But as she got closer to these amazing craft it was hard to ignore the pull of curiosity to find out more. Yet the nearer she got, the colder her feet became.

No, it's no good – I just don't belong.

She couldn't do it. She'd just have a look from the outside.

And maybe find some interior images later online. Ever the stickler for detail, she took out a tiny notebook and pen, and looked around her on the dock, jotting down one or two of the other yachts' names to Google later. Two very glamorous people passed her by and looked at her quite strangely, so she smiled and quickly popped her notebook back in her bag. Then she walked off, head in the clouds, allowing herself a little daydream.

Several feet above Sadie, on the deck of one of the biggest yachts in the marina, a seaman called Mac was distracted. Sadie's slightly raised voice and mad gesticulating had caught his attention. Then her voluptuous curves had kept it, despite her tetchy manner. So who was this woman in the tight blue business skirt? No tourist dressed like that, plus she'd been taking notes. Maybe this was the harbour inspection the Captain had warned the crew about. But in those shoes ...? *Hmmm.* Mac stopped his chores, rested an elbow on the end of his mop handle, and took in the sight of Sadie's backside swaggering away up the jetty in her towering heels.

He pondered, taking out a handkerchief – white-linen and monogrammed – to dab the sweat from his tanned forehead and chiselled face. Then the corners of his mouth quirked as, several yards away, Sadie tripped a tiny bit, and glanced around to check that no one had seen her.

Smiling and shaking his head, Mac tucked the hanky away in the shortest of shorts, and kept one eye on Sadie while he went back to mopping the deck.

Sadie was completely oblivious to being watched. She meandered down the jetty, approaching the queue of people near the *Nomusa*, trying to pretend she belonged. She was, however, much better at sticking out like a sore thumb. Sadie drew level with the group of supercilious fashionistas standing in line, all hoping for a spare invite. As she got nearer her heart pounded knowing she had what they desired – the magic ticket tucked tidily inside her bag. Could she do it?

Nope, no way am I going on there, she thought, as the glamorous group of girls nudged each other and glared at Sadie. She took a deep breath, and strutted straight by, sticking her chin in the air. Just then, several tresses of Sadie's hair suddenly freed themselves and dramatically flopped onto her face, blocking her view completely, and the group giggled. She simply tossed her head back, and continued walking by, peering out from underneath the hair at a funny angle, just till she passed the end of their queue. She cursed under her breath and stopped to rummage around in her bulging bag, removing things one by one.

'Where's that damn brush …?' she muttered to herself. *Ahh, there it is, underneath everything else, naturally.*

Looking around she spotted a low post nearby and deposited her things on it, while she fixed her hair. In the bright sunshine, if she held the glass trophy at the right angle, she could just about see her reflection in it. Stupid hairdo. *It might be newly blonde, but it's definitely getting another cut when I get home.* A business-bob, yes, that would suit her new executive image.

Absent-mindedly she started placing her things back in her bag. With an effort, she began to close the zip, then stopped. The last thing she'd stuffed inside was the colourful invite, with gold-embossed lettering in French. She took it out again, and gazed at it, thoughtfully, completely unaware that a pushy salesman, holding a clipboard, had spotted the invite and was coming her way. Suddenly a pair of very smart brogues were right in front of Sadie and she looked up, holding the ticket. The gaggle of yacht groupies behind her fell silent, and she felt their eyes piercing through her back.

'Ah, the final latecomer,' he said, with a strong French accent. Then he thrust a glossy brochure into her hand and took the ticket from her before she could say a word. 'Do come on board. You are just in time. And I believe I know who you are,' he said. Sadie's heart began to pound as the man continued. 'Mr Clooney said to look out for ze heels! Ha-ha. Welcome to the tour, Miss ...'

'Turner,' Sadie replied. 'And it's Ms.'

'Merzzz?'

'Yes, Ms. As in *not-Miss* but *not-Missus*.' The man merely raised an eyebrow then started looking down a list of names on his clipboard.

'Oh, but you won't find me on any list of Mr Clooney's,' she said.

'You won't be the first woman to say that,' he said. 'Or the last.' Shaking his head slightly, he gave up looking at his list. With another glance at her heels, and at her, he shrugged, closed his clipboard and put away his pen. He took her ticket, then her elbow and guided her to the walkway.

'We are about to commence. Straight up the gangplank there, but stay on the red carpet. Champagne awaits you at the top.'

Sadie opened her mouth to explain, and then stopped, looked up at the plush, luxurious red carpet leading onto the yacht, and the buzzing hubbub taking place on deck. Jealous eyes burned into her back from the queue behind her. A massive, full-headlights beam spread right across her glowing face as mischief crossed her mind, and she held her arm out graciously to accept his offer to help her onto the gangplank.

Why not? Why the hell not! About time, lady luck ... Before she knew it she had joined a tour of a very large vessel that apparently was having an Open Day for a certain Mr Clooney.

Half an hour, a few nibbles and two small glasses of Cristal champagne later, Sadie was back on the jetty, having learned that Mr 'Alistair' Clooney was no relation to any film stars, married or otherwise, and not at all partial to gatecrashers.

But hey, she thought, fanning herself with the glossy brochure she'd been allowed to keep by the amused French salesman, it would make a nice little story to tell her girls when she got back. And she'd got the prized photo on her phone – which she began uploading to her cloud storage straight away, while she wandered distractedly back down the jetty once more. It had been worth it, pretending to be someone else, even if only briefly. And no one would know, would they?

Time to chase the luggage again. But there was still no news. She could only hope and pray it would turn up at her hotel by this evening, as her laptop and back-up were in there with everything she needed for the meeting tomorrow. *Oooo more palpitations.* The meeting tomorrow, everything depended upon it. Her little health food store back home in Surrey, the girls' education – everything. This opportunity was what she'd been praying for and it simply had to be a success. And if it wasn't …

She shuddered at the alternatives, all too dismal to contemplate, each of them meaning she would still have to lean on pain-in-the-butt Stuart.

Sadie took a moment to catch her breath and looked out at the amazing view on the other side of the jetty. In front of her was the bluest sky she'd ever witnessed, and the most luxurious harbour. She felt like she was on one of those travel programmes and expected Judith Chalmers to come creeping out from a yacht with a microphone, looking all orange and shiny. Sadie was old enough to remember Judith Chalmers' travel shows, another fact that bothered her slightly – she wasn't getting any younger. She caught herself mid-thought. *No! No negativity. Come on, Sadie, think positive.*

One minute and some serious focus work later, she was allowing herself to feel a little elation. After all, she, Sadie Samantha Turner, had made it this far. *Who would have 'thunk it'* as her girls were fond of saying.

Not her critics, who kept telling her she'd never amount to anything, especially Stuart – and his mother.

This time, they would see that this wasn't 'just another hare-brained scheme' as her old boss had called it, when, post-divorce, the newly single Sadie had left the university research lab to strike out on her own – in more ways than one.

This time it was Sadie doing it by herself. And if she could only pull off this multi-million pound negotiation, the commission would be incredible. *Then* let's see them laugh on the other sides of their faces.

And in her ex-mother-in-law's case, that would be at least two.

The mobile phone in her bag rang and snapped Sadie out of her stupor. She squeaked in surprise, retrieved it and checked the screen before straightening up and answering in her best voice.

'Hello? … Oh, thank goodness.' She continued walking as she talked. 'So, where did you find it? … But *how* could my suitcase end up in Milan? … What time "later"? … Well, it will *have* to do, won't it? And I'll just boil in my business suit till then … Yes, I know you're doing your best. It's not your fault, I'm just having a bad …' She stopped herself.

Don't say it, Sadie, think positive. Always think positive.

'It's … unfortunate,' she continued. 'I've got an important meeting first thing in the morning so I sincerely hope it *will* arrive this evening … Yes, that's my hotel. Thanks for letting me know. Bye.'

Heaving her bulging bag from her shoulder, she put the phone safely back inside and zipped up the top. She straightened, overbalanced slightly as her heel caught on a cobble again, and the glossy brochure slipped from under her arm and smacked to the ground. She stared at it, hands on hips.

Bending down to pick anything up in this tight business

skirt was not going to be easy – it needed some thought and preparation. She angled her legs awkwardly, and hoisted the hem a smidgen, then stretched and stretched until she managed to bend low enough to pinch the corner of the brochure between finger and thumb.

Pleased with having retrieved it, she wafted herself with its glossy pages a little. Then, huffing and puffing, she gave her heavy handbag a hoist onto her shoulder, the weight of it almost swinging her round like an unstable clothes airer on a windy day. *Oh, heck.*

'Why me?' she said out loud. 'Why is it always me?'

'Because you *believe* it's always you,' ventured a nearby voice.

A deep voice.

What the …?

Startled, Sadie swung round to see a man silhouetted against the sunshine slightly above her on the deck of a huge yacht that was even bigger than the *Nomusa*. She squinted up to try to see him more clearly. She could hear metal against metal, and smell engine oil and soapsuds … was he fixing something?

'I'm sorry? What?' She shielded her eyes with her hand but still couldn't see more than an outline. The outline of an athlete, whoever he was.

'I was watching you.'

'And listening in on my conversation too?'

'Yes, and some of the earlier one. Couldn't help it, you were talking so loud.'

'I was …?' said Sadie. 'I—'

'You asked "why me?",' he interrupted. 'I'm guessing something always upsets your plans, right? Well, it always will if you always expect it to. The trick is to hope for the best, but plan for the worst.' He had a London accent. She hadn't expected that, although his accent was a bit broader than hers, which she took a certain amount of comfort from.

She felt out of place amongst all this opulence, but finding someone with a background not dissimilar to her own ...

Maybe it wasn't all toffs and tiaras here on the Riviera.

She found herself responding, intrigued. 'Yes, but it's probably just my bad luck, this time.'

'Some people say we make our *own* luck.' There was an unmistakeable smile in his voice. '*Every* time.'

'Hey – it's usually *me* preaching positivity and no-such-thing-as-coincidence!' she said. Who *was* this guy?

'Well, in that case, why be so negative today?' he continued. 'I was watching you earlier, being all humpy.'

'Eavesdropper!'

'Whatever. Look, we've got sunshine, fresh air, clothes on our backs and shoes on our feet. Some people say that's all we need.'

'Well, *some people* ought to try being in my shoes for a while – they hurt.'

He seemed to be looking down at her feet, but the sun was still in the wrong place to see his face properly. *Was he old? Young? Sane? An axe murderer?*

'Nah, I wouldn't wear *those* shoes if you paid me,' he said, then laughed. 'Except on Sundays.'

Oh, he's such a smart alec.

'Bikinis, sarongs, pedal-pushers and pumps at most – that's the de rigueur dress code for these yachts.'

Yes, a smart alec who's making me feel stupid. 'I know that!' Sadie said, pulling her jacket down smartly. 'But there's a reason I'm dressed like this, *actually*.'

'A reason ...? Oh, I've got it! You're here for Mario's birthday today, aren't you! But I thought we ordered a policewoman.'

'I am *not* a strippergram!'

'I was teasing you. His birthday's not till Friday.'

A very smart alec indeed. Much as she didn't want to, Sadie had to smile. 'Oh. Good one,' she said, shifting on her painful feet.

'So, what *are* you doing here?' he asked. 'You don't look like the usual posh yacht people.'

'You saying I don't belong? Huh! So says *you*, with the conspicuous London accent,' she replied. She could hear a little chuckle. *Got him.* 'Exactly what do the usual posh yacht people look like then?'

'Oh, I don't know. Stuffy, stuck-up, boring as hell and seriously, seriously unattractive. You're none of those.'

Okay, this man is the devil. He had to be. Every time she was about to get angry with him, he took the wind right out of her sails.

'Really?' She almost cooed like a teenager. 'So you think I'm—'

'Not stuffy. Yes.' Trampling right over her moment of glory and he knew it. 'And anyway,' he added, 'you didn't answer my question. What're you here for?'

Sadie looked up at him and for a brief moment she wondered, *yes, what* am *I doing here exactly?* Making a right royal mess-up of being away on my own, that's what.

She winced as she remembered her plane journey – feeling stupid for thinking you have to travel smart in Club Class. No one else had – scruffy-chic was more the order of the day. And then losing her luggage and accepting a lift to the quay from the kind ladies on the plane. It was their fault she'd become curious enough to go party-crashing. And her own fault for doing it. Another awkward situation. And now she'd been sucked into a surreal conversation with some strange deckhand who obviously thought she was a bit of an idiot. Perhaps he was right.

'Actually, I think I'm just lost,' she said, eventually.

'In life? Or just today?' He stepped down the gangplank towards her.

Sadie's usual laser-sharp retort evaporated on her lips at the sight that came into focus. He was tall – tall and lean. Attractive in a rugged sort of way – if you like them rough and ready. And Sadie did. The problem was her pounding heart forgot she was on a 'Man-Ban'.

He was wearing shorts. *Just* shorts. All that stood between them was a pair of oily cut-offs and a spanner.

'*Uh-oh,*' she murmured. She wished she hadn't, but it happened all of its own accord. *Uh-oh.* There it was again.

This man was gorgeous. She fanned herself faster with the brochure. He spotted it.

'Ahh, I see you're viewing today? Well, you're not *very* lost at all. This is the *Nomad*. The *Nomusa* is a few berths down.' He wiped his hands on a dirty cloth hanging from his pocket and smiled. By now Sadie was in a complete trance.

Hot Boat Guy waited for her answer, but it didn't come, so he smiled a bigger smile.

'Oh,' she replied eventually. 'You mean the *blue boat* down there. Yes, I've just been round it, actually.' He waited as if wanting her to say more. '*Nomusa* means *merciful* you know,' she added.

'And ...'

'And?' She had no clue what he was asking. Did he know she was chucked off?

'And what did you think of it? The "blue boat"?'

Good grief is he seriously going to quiz me on it? I can't say I wasn't supposed to be there, I just wanted a nose-round and a free glass of champagne. 'Actually, it's ... not quite what I was looking for,' she said with a cheesy grin.

When he replied his voice almost purred. 'Why? Not *big* enough?'

The corner of his mouth curled and Sadie felt like a rabbit in the headlights. Her blush attack began in earnest, as he took another step towards her down the gangplank.

'Did you want something bigger?' he asked. The shorts were dangerously near now. His thighs getting closer. Eye-level thighs.

Oh my lord. *He's talking about his crotch. Is he talking about his crotch?*

After all, there was only about two feet and a layer of denim in between it and her ... what should she say? What *could* she say? The first thing she should *do* is stop looking at it. She quickly averted her eyes to the right.

It looks plenty big enough, she thought to herself, as she struggled not to look back but couldn't help it. After all, it had been so long since she'd actually seen a naked man ...

Stop it, Sadie, she told herself. *Being six hundred miles from home might mean you can go 'pretend shopping' for a boat, but you cannot go home with a member of crew rolled up and tucked under your arm like the rug you bought in Turkey.*

Turkey, that was the first time she'd been abroad alone after the break-up with Stuart. Goodness, was that really four years ago?

She blinked. The whole marina seemed just a little out of focus. She'd better not be getting ill. Damn travel tablets on an empty stomach. And damn the tiny canapés – rich people at boat viewings obviously don't eat. And damn the expensive perfumes wafting through the air, mixed with coconut sun cream and decadence – a world away from her normal life. And Sadie was rapidly becoming a world away from her normal self.

'It's *big* enough,' she said, finally, unable to stop the words coming out – what *was* it about this man? And then, there it was. 'It's just not *long* enough.'

Why, Sadie? Why did you say that? You know you're just teasing him. Was this her cobweb-covered alter ego coming out to play?

Oh, it was there all right, it had happened before. One night a good-looking policeman had knocked on her door to ask if she'd seen anything suspicious because a neighbour's house had been broken into. What did she do? She invited him in and asked to see his truncheon.

With Hot Boat Guy standing there just a few feet away, Sadie felt 'single-girl mischief' rising up in her belly, stirring memories that felt alien but so, so delicious.

And then it hit her.

I'll never see him again, so what the heck.

She smirked. It didn't go unnoticed by Hot Boat Guy. His eyebrow raised, the corner of his mouth flickered, and a slow, languorous grin spread across his face.

Sadie was captivated by his face. It looked lived-in, but with an air of intrigue. Tanned, no doubt from working at sea, but what stories could it tell? Deep blue eyes and thick blondish hair. In another life, another lifestyle, he could have been a Bond guy. With better cheekbones …

She snapped herself out of her musing as the importance of this trip came ricocheting back and smacked her between the eyes. Sadly, there could be no renaissance for her neglected libido – not on this trip. In fact, not on *any* trip till after the girls had gone to uni. Not until she'd proved to herself and everyone else that she could make it on her own. That's what Sensible Sadie told her she should do. Or her mother did, frequently.

'So …'

'So?' he asked.

'So, which way do I go to get out?' There was a change in her tone, and he looked like he noticed it.

'Same way as you came in.'

'Okay, thanks. Nice to meet you! Bye then.' Sadie walked off – and that was that.

What a wasted opportunity, what a shame, she thought to herself. *Maybe if I come back tomorrow after the meeting, he might still be here. Or he'll have sailed away on the morning tide.* She looked back and he was still smiling – just smiling – and watching. No, nothing for it but to keep walking.

And walking.

And a bit more with the walking. Until …

Ooops.

Until she realised she was going the wrong way and had to turn around and go right back again.

'That wasn't the way I came in, was it?' she said, sheepishly, when she reached him.

'No,' he said, trying hard not to laugh. 'It's down there.'

'You could have told me,' she replied.

'I was enjoying the view.'

'Are you always this cheesy?' she asked, and now it was Sadie's turn to suppress a giggle.

'Only with my own kind,' he said, catching her off guard, and she inhaled a sharp breath. *My own kind ... Uh-oh!* Even more reason to get the heck out of here.

'I have to go. I really do. Honestly. I've got a big meeting tomorrow,' Sadie said, looking into eyes that just didn't believe her. Then, as if on cue, her phone started ringing again in her bag. 'Excuse me a sec,' she said, and turned away to dig out her mobile and answer the call.

Mac was by now well and truly enchanted. And bemused. He wandered back up the gangplank, picked up the dirty rag again, and resumed cleaning a piece of shiny metal, watching Sadie totter out of earshot to take the call. A flicker of amusement ran across his face as he watched her juggling the bag and the phone. *What is it with women and huge handbags?*

He thought about her accent and tried to place it – he was good with voices. And hers being closer to home made it easier than most. South London, perhaps – Surrey, probably. No, she definitely wasn't a yacht person, but now he was intrigued – if she wasn't a harbour inspector, what was she taking notes for? Was she on a recce? Perhaps she was film crew. Neither did she look like any business person he'd ever met, not in those heels.

Mac pondered, and pulled up a deckchair to sit himself

down, ran his fingers through his hair and swigged from his bottle of water. On the distant hill something glinted, and caught his eye, but he couldn't make out what it was. Instead, the view close-by was much more interesting. He sat watching this strange woman, wondering what on earth she was getting so animated about.

'But, Mr Rosebery, believe me, salvation is truly just around the corner,' Sadie was saying under her breath, several yards away. 'No, of course I'm not winding you up ... Oh, you saw the article too, did you? ... No, it was indeed all-expenses paid. Didn't cost me a penny – it was my prize ... Well, actually, Hawaii *was* hard work, really it was. Very hot and very pressurised, especially once they offered me this deal ... Well, you see that guy presenting me with the award, on the left in the picture? He's Bill Galloway and he produces this water called Frish in Maui. And they want me to help with their international marketing and ... oh, of course, yes I'll hold.'

This is all I need. If only her bank manager wasn't one of her mother's exes. Then maybe he'd stop acting like her guardian and leave her alone. She wasn't that far over the overdraft surely? And why would they bounce a payment for £40 and charge you £30 for doing so? None of it made sense. She began working out a calculation on her fingers and as she did so, she glanced up. Hot Boat Guy raised his bottle towards her as if to say 'cheers'. *Weirdo.*

She smiled and raised a hand to acknowledge him, and her bag slipped off her shoulder an inch or two. She turned her back to him and leaned on a railing. Funnily enough, now she knew he was sitting watching her, she found it most comfortable to lean down on the railing and stick her bottom out ever so slightly – just for balance, of course.

'Oh, hi,' she continued her phone call. 'Yes, of course ... I'll let you know as soon as things change.' The bank manager was being pushy – more pushy than usual, which meant she was in more trouble than usual. She swallowed, and tried to act confident.

'Yes, it must be … *Very* inconvenient … but in thirty days it could all be over, you see and then you won't have to keep calling me. For which I apologise most profusely … yes, again.'

Awkward …

The mobile was throbbing now, she swore it was throbbing – or else her head was. *One final tactic*, she thought, when the voice just wouldn't shut up.

'Mr Rosebery, how about this? I could always send in my mother to give you the full low down on this new deal. You know how much she enjoyed seeing you last time, and … No? Oh. Okay then, if you say so … Oh, did she? … Oh dear, I'm sorry to hear that. Have you tried removing it with bleach?' *What else has the woman been up to and not told me?* Sadie thought. *Change the subject, fast.*

'So how's the new Mrs Rosebery? … Good … No, there's still no one for me. It's all about the business now … Yes, it *is* proper business! In fact I'm finding …' Sadie caught herself, and decided to take the plunge. *Think positive.* 'I've already *found* an investor for the Frish company, and they're paying me a lot of money to help seal the deal and do the follow-up. That's why it could all be over in thirty days. It's, er … it's all being confirmed tomorrow.' Sadie was glad he couldn't see her crossing her fingers behind her back. 'Soon. Yes, in my account soon. The money won't take long to transfer. It'll tie in perfectly with my next lot of debits, won't it? Ha-ha. Isn't it funny how the universe works in mysterious ways?'

Sadie cringed – she hated lying, one of her big things was honesty. Usually. But not on this trip, apparently.

It wasn't totally a lie though – the deal *was* on the table after all, and the billionaire investor *was* meeting her tomorrow. And it *could* indeed happen in thirty days. Couldn't it?

What's more, as she explained to a suddenly much more genial Mr Rosebery, *time was indeed of the essence.* What she didn't tell him was that otherwise the Frish Company – FrishCo – would accept an alternative offer from a competitor. It was a very short deadline for normal people. But even her pompous bank manager – and ex-almost-stepfather – had to agree there was nothing normal about Sadie. Including refusing to call him by his first name once he'd split up with her mother. *Formality is good in business,* she thought to herself. Unless you're travelling Club Class.

'Yes, Mr Rosebery,' she concluded, 'I'll see what I can do to get some funds in the account for now. But I can assure you, nothing – and I mean nothing – can get in the way of this deal.' He seemed to accept the certainty in her voice, *thank God.*

Grateful for the reprieve, Sadie hung up and put the phone away once more and hoisted her heavy bag. She was getting tired – and not just today. In truth, it was nice to have a break from the shop – and her routine – and the day-to-day burden of running her own business, solo. To escape from it all – even if only for one night. In any case, the babysitting credits, and the loans from Bank of Mum were fast running out.

Sadie smiled, then walked over to say goodbye – again – to Hot Boat Guy. Time to get back to real life.

'Why leave so soon? Got more "boats" to see?' he asked, wandering back down towards her. 'I guess you agents usually see several in one trip, don't you?'

'I'm not an agent,' she replied. 'Double, secret, provocateur or otherwise.'

'Okay then, maybe you're a sales exec for his competition?' he said, nodding towards the *Nomusa.* 'Are you with Rigby's?'

'No.'

'Geller and Geller?'

'No, actually ...' she hesitated. *No point in explaining – where would I even begin?* 'Look, I really have to go. Nice to meet you. And don't worry – someone else will be along in a while and you can eavesdrop on them instead!'

He just grinned in reply. Feeling the thrill of flirtation fluttering through her body, she gave a superior shrug, and swung her handbag slightly, trying her hardest to look confident. But the cobbles underfoot did their best to prove otherwise, toying with the high heels of the borrowed Jimmy Choos – they were her sister's redundancy money treat, so 'scuff them and die'. Sadie skipped a little, to avoid damaging them on the rounded stones. Again he looked amused. Or condescending, she couldn't quite work out which.

'Sorry – not the best choice of footwear, is it?' she said.

He looked down at her feet, thoughtfully. 'Oh, I wouldn't say that.' Then their eyes met, meaningfully, and the air sizzled between them in the silence.

'Nice to meet you, then,' she said again, and held out her hand as if to shake his, but his dirty mitts just waved the oily rag, as if to say *bad idea*.

'You too,' he said. 'See you next Open Day. And don't forget the shore is that way.' Sadie's look said it all. 'Oh, and good luck finding your *dream boat*,' he added with a wink.

Can he mind read?

Sadie hoisted her handbag again, and the brochure once more dropped to the jetty. Bending down to pick it up, even more awkwardly now she was being watched, she then dropped her sister's expensive sunglasses. *What a klutz,* she thought.

Immediately and before she could say anything, the man nimbly sprang down and picked them up for her. This time she noticed he was barefoot. Without a word, just a smile, he handed them back to her. His fingers touched hers and a spark of electricity raced through her.

'Thank you.'

Close up now, she could see the tiny sprinkle of silver at

his temples, making him all the more interesting. Striking azure-blue eyes, like the ocean, twinkling with anticipation. And as for the way he was looking at her …

Wonder what he kisses like.

Sadie!

But her body was rebelling. Maybe – just maybe – playing along some more might be fun, so far from home. Who's to know? Maybe it would bring back a bit of that supreme Student Sadie confidence she'd had at uni, all those years ago. Just over a decade and a half ago, in fact. Yes, a bit of confidence boosting sure wouldn't go amiss ahead of the scary boardroom at nine a.m. tomorrow – it'd be better than wine. And maybe, just once, it would be good not to be the sensible one. Just once not to have to obey every rule. Just, for once, not to be … herself.

What do they say? What happens in Monaco stays in Monaco?

Suddenly another voice broke the tension.

'Mac, are you finishing up? I'm heading ashore soon.' An older, distinguished man appeared in a uniform. He raised his eyebrow when he saw Sadie.

'Aye, aye, Cap'n!' Mac replied.

The older man rolled his eyes, and then ducked back inside, mumbling to himself.

Sadie snapped out of the daydream. 'Sorry, you really mustn't let me keep you from your work,' she said. 'Wouldn't want you to get in trouble with your boss.'

'Actually, I'm the boss,' he replied, grinning. Sadie eyed up his frayed shorts and oily hands and smiled. Along with the London accent, it didn't convince her. She knew a wind-up when she saw one.

'Hmmm, *sure* you are,' she said. Mac was looking at her strangely. 'Seriously, he looks like he runs a tight ship. You wouldn't want to cross him. I'm guessing he's the Captain? The boss of your boat, right?'

Mac hesitated, and then laughed. 'Well, yes, he's the "boss of the boat".'

'Well, then.'

'And no, you're right – you definitely wouldn't want to cross our Captain Wiltshire. You wouldn't like him when he's angry – he's a real slave driver to us mere deckhands and no mistake. In fact, when he's in the mood, he'll make you walk the plank as soon as look at you!'

'Well, before he splices your mainbrace, you'd better get on with scrubbing the deck, or … shipping ahoy, or … whatever.' Her clichés dried up along with her courage, and she was starting to feel a little weak beneath the piercing, inquisitive gaze of those eyes.

'Wow, sounds like you're right at home with all the ship talk. No wonder you had your eye on a cruiser.'

'A what?'

'Sunseeker … cruiser … that "boat" on your brochure – theirs is a cruiser.'

'Ahh,' replied Sadie with a grin. 'And what is this? The *Nomad*, you said?'

'Yes, *this* is the *Nomad*,' he said, puffing up proudly. 'She's a superyacht. A Ferretti Custom Line 124.'

'Ohh, ri-i-i-ght, a "super" yacht.' She nodded, not sure if he was still winding her up or if that was a real term. In any case, it was time to own up. Being footloose on the French Riviera with all its colour and character was making her more carefree than she could recall – taking the edge off her inhibitions. But freedom and champagne were a fatal combination – Sadie always got 'honest' before she got drunk.

She leaned in towards him. 'Actually, can I tell you a secret?'

'Only if you don't have to kill me after.'

'I'm really *not* buying a boat … er, cruiser. I was just killing time. The sales guy thought I was someone else, you see. So – promise you won't tell anyone – I gatecrashed.'

'You *didn't*!' Mac leaned in. So close now she could smell his heady fresh male odour.

'I did. I couldn't tell him the only boat I've ever owned is a gravy boat.'

He laughed, the warm, throaty sound reverberating in the air. He had a great laugh.

'But I'll tell you something,' she went on, aware she was rambling but unable to stop. 'When I get my next million, I'll definitely bear it in mind.'

'Ahh, so you're one of those landlubbers who comes to all the viewings, but never signs on the dotted line!'

'What can I say – so many boats, so little time.'

'I thought that was men.'

'Nope – no time for men, unless they're rich!' Sadie giggled.

Mac didn't.

Out of nowhere the Captain's head suddenly reappeared. 'Mac, can I have a word?' he said, making Sadie jump slightly.

'Can't it wait? I'm a bit … busy,' Mac replied.

'Best if it's now,' the Captain said, and he disappeared inside again with a '*harrumph*'.

Mac hesitated, turned to go, then turned back and touched Sadie's arm.

'Stay here a sec, will you?' he asked. 'I have a question for you.'

'Er … okay,' Sadie replied before she had time to think about it.

'In fact, come up and make yourself comfy on the lounger over there – but take off your shoes before you board.'

'You're kidding me, right?'

'No, it's protocol. If you're going to be a rich yacht owner you'd better get used to it!' And he disappeared up the gangplank and inside.

Sadie was left standing there, fighting a losing battle with her conscience. A feeling of foreboding was being beaten by a buoyant thrill of flirtation. She rubbed her chest. It was filled with palpitations again, as she forced herself to think of tomorrow's make-or-break presentation and a boardroom full of grown-ups. One deep breath later, she was clutching her shoes and walking slowly up the gangplank, holding tightly onto the rail.

What am I doing?

The young Sadie wouldn't have hesitated to let off steam with a very wild night out, but the older Sadie had packed her away years ago. Along with the short skirts and crop tops, and the belly button piercing she'd never quite managed to re-insert after the instructor at Center Parcs wouldn't let her abseil unless she took it out. Years ago.

I'm not that person any more.

I don't belong here.

She shook her head and turned to leave, but just then Mac reappeared at the door. He was smiling but appeared to have been duly reprimanded, and was called back to the doorway briefly by the Captain, who muttered something under his breath then hovered a while before shaking his head and turning away. Mac rolled his eyes and skipped back over.

'Sorry about that. Where were we?' he said.

'About to say goodbye, I'm afraid. Good luck with your power-yacht.'

'Superyacht.'

'Is that really a thing?'

'Yes, it's really a "thing".'

'Well, that then. Now I've really got to go.' She stood up and went to put her shoes back on.

'Oh – not on here,' he said, reaching out an arm and stopping her. 'The Captain will kill you if you make any marks on his precious deck that I've spent the last hour scrubbing.'

Sadie paused with her high heel half on, half off and the

whole world went into slow motion. To her utter dismay, her leg went one way and her heel went the other. She swayed unsteadily, nearly toppled over the side, and then lurched straight forward – right into his open arms.

Her precious designer bag, however, made a bid for freedom. It swung loose, and before she could react, it was in the air, over the railings and down the side of the hull, making a small plop as it fell into the sea, yards below.

'Oh my God! It's sinking, it's sinking!' she cried, making a bid for the edge.

'Hold on, Trouble!' He pulled her back.

'My life's in that bag!'

'Well, we'd better get it back then, hadn't we? Allow me.' In one smooth movement, he launched himself over the side. Sadie was speechless. She felt her knees going weak, and stumbled further along, trying to get a better view. She squinted her eyes, breathed deeply, and waited for him to reappear. *Please God let him bring it back.*

Her mind went into overdrive, playing out various 'no mobile' scenarios, and struggled to even remember her home number. The seconds ticked by and Sadie looked up and down, left and right. Shoeless, on the deck of a multi-million pound yacht, everything suddenly felt terribly, terribly wrong. She should have left earlier, while the going was good. Before the doofus inside her came out to play.

Why is it always me?

Moments later there was a tap on her foot and a massive squelch. There, by her feet in all its waterlogged glory, was her best posh bag.

Or, more accurately, her only posh bag.

It didn't matter that it had been half price in the sale, it was her pride and joy – a combined gift from her mum, sister, and two daughters for Christmas and Mothers' Day all rolled into one.

Thank goodness it wasn't leather.

Two hundred pounds worth of Lulu Guinness bright red designer vinyl was unique enough with its cameo queen's head on one side. Now the PVC queen had a green seaweedy beard. Sadie watched in a daze as her gallant hero hauled himself up onto the deck, cascades of water running in rivulets over his shoulders, past his neck chain, down his chest and across his washboard stomach before cascading down the little shorts and over his bronzed thighs. He raised his arms above his head and pushed his hair back from his eyes.

He's a Chippendale, he's actually a Chippendale, thought Sadie, transfixed.

Then he bent down and gallantly pulled off the slimy plant, tilted the bag and grinned as a dribble of the Mediterranean came out through the zip onto the deck. Then he handed it back.

'Thank you,' she croaked, looking up at him standing there, dripping but triumphant.

He bowed. 'It was my pleasure, m'lady, to rescue your life for you.'

She beamed. 'You've no idea how long I've waited for someone to say that.' Then she surprised them both by throwing her arms around his still wet neck and kissing him on the cheek.

'Mmmmwah! That was to say *thank you,*' she said, unsteadily. But instead of letting her pull away, he slid his arm around her waist, and drew her towards him, till his lips were almost touching hers.

She gasped.

'And this is to say *you're welcome,*' he said. Then he bent towards her, but at the last minute planted a lingering kiss on her cheek, just grazing the very tip of her mouth. Sadie's most sensitive bit. Her knees buckled slightly under the powerful jolts of desire darting around her body. When it ended and he brushed against her lips again as he pulled back slightly, she didn't back away.

Standing there virtually nose-to-nose, she felt her heart pounding and knew she should leave, but his mouth was mesmerising her – his full mouth – the mouth that had just almost kissed hers. The zing was still coursing through her traitorous body. *More, more.* He stood his ground, looking deep into her eyes, so close she could almost taste him. She certainly wanted to.

For the longest moment, they were motionless, her arms around his neck, his arms around her waist. He was dripping wet and half-naked and this felt good.

The temptation to feel those lips again was overpowering. But she was not the sort of girl to start something she knew she couldn't finish. So with a sigh she stepped away.

'Long time since I've been given a thank you like that,' he said.

'Long time since I've needed to give one,' she replied, and felt her cheeks flush.

He looked thoughtful. 'Actually, I was thinking there's another way you could thank me.' He suddenly seemed almost bashful. 'I meant to ask … Why don't you meet me ashore this evening? If you're free? It's my last night here – the *Nomad* sets sail tomorrow.'

'Oh, the old "one night of pleasure"' ploy,' Sadie said, trying to play it cool. If he couldn't hear her heart before, he must surely be able to now.

He just smiled back, and raised his eyebrows. An air of vulnerability had washed over him, waiting for her verdict. *How endearing.*

'I, em …' Sensible Sadie was tugging at her conscience – *refuse, young lady. Get out of here.* But Fun Sadie was winning the battle. Right now she should be heading back to a computer file full of facts and figures, budgets and cash flow forecasts. But she felt magnetised to the spot. The epitome of torn.

But you know every word already. Every page, every projection.

Maybe a little 'R & R' tonight would help her get centred for tomorrow – help her go all-out to impress the investor, the top man himself. All she had to do was make him like her and want to invest in her. And who didn't like Sadie? This Mac guy certainly did – she'd felt it in his body, seen it in his eyes.

'I'm not sure. I've got people to see—'

'Places to go, yes I know,' he added. 'But I'm still asking.'

A loud 'fairy tale' alert was ringing in her ears. The thought of getting up close and personal with this sexy stranger was like her purest fantasy. But this wasn't a fantasy – it was real life. Although, come to think of it, the whole of the last month had been something of a dream ... so why break the spell now? Winning a competition, jetting off to far-flung corners of the earth to pick up her prize, and beginning the helter-skelter business ride she was now clinging onto by her fingertips. So why not add a fling? *No one would know.* And if she didn't do it now, it might be months – years – before she got another chance for a no-strings encounter like this. If indeed that was what he was offering.

'Well?' he asked.

'A-are you always such a quick worker?' she gasped.

'Only with anyone in a tight navy suit and very inappropriate footwear.'

'Even the women?'

He laughed.

'Mac – I need you – now, please!' came the Captain's voice again.

'With you in a sec, Cap'n. Just finishing up here.' He turned to Sadie. 'Or have we just started?'

She smiled.

He beamed back, he genuinely glowed, and Sadie felt a thrill of awareness, a rush of adrenalin. And an overpowering urge to dance a little.

'So you'll come?' His pleasure was so youthful, so exuberant. But romantic interludes had definitely not been on the agenda this trip.

Oh hell ... She frowned.

'Look,' he said, 'if you're too busy, or you don't want to, then just say. I'm a bit out of practice at all this asking out stuff. It's just that you happen to be very attractive,' to which Sadie looked down before she started blushing, 'and fun. Plus I happen to be celebrating the end of an era, so I'd like very much for you to join me. If you'd like to. Unless you have other plans ...'

'It's not that.'

'Or maybe you've already got someone.'

'It's not that either ...'

'So?'

'Well, I would *like* to meet you this evening—' she replied.

'I sense a "but".'

'But, well ...' She bit her tongue. Her usual response was so nearly out of her mouth – *but I have to get back to my children.* But for once, she didn't. Not for precisely twenty-two hours.

She took a deep breath.

'*But*, it would mean interrupting my very tight itinerary and rescheduling my commitments. And as for asking my "staff" to entertain themselves at dinner tonight – they won't like it, won't like it at all.' He hung on her every word. There were no staff, nor any elaborate plans for dinner, but she was enjoying playing along. And it had been ages since she'd been out on the town. '*But* ... it's not impossible ...'

He brightened.

'... In fact, I suppose it wouldn't hurt to take some time out from yet another packed business trip.' She waved an arm elaborately.

'My thoughts entirely,' he said, looking like a puppy.

'You can't imagine how tiring it can be for us international business executives.' Again with the arm, this time melodramatically draped across her forehead.

'Oh, I can easily imagine,' he said.

'Monaco today, London tomorrow. Hawaii before that. Busy, busy, busy!' Sadie was really getting into the role play now.

'Hawaii? Really?' he asked. 'We were in Hawaii too, last month.'

'You sure you're not stalking me, in your "power" yacht?'

'Ha-ha! No, just some charity work, and it's a *superyacht*, remember?' he said as he reached up and fiddled with his chain – a gold and silver St Christopher, she noticed. *He wasn't nervous, surely?* If he was, it made him all the more endearing. 'And anyway,' he said, changing the subject, 'you stumbled on *my* deck, remember?'

'Literally.'

'So? What do you say?'

'So ...'

'You're milking this a bit, you know that don't you.'

'So ...' she teased, putting her finger on her lips, thinking. 'So – one word of warning. At the stroke of midnight I turn into a pumpkin, so I can't stay late.'

'Fine by me, I've got an early start too. And anyway,' he said, looking knowingly into her eyes, 'I quite like pumpkin.'

'I mean it! And it's one night only, right? I mean don't make *too* many "plans", eh?' She raised an eyebrow at him.

'Well, Mrs Businesswoman, you'll be pleased to know I gave up making those sorts of "plans" a long time ago – specially not with someone I've just met.'

'Makes two of us,' she replied.

'Kindred spirits then,' he said. 'Perfect. Great minds think alike. Or ...'

' ... fools seldom differ!' they chorused together.

Sadie laughed aloud and it made him chuckle too.

'So, sevenish okay? Shall I pick you up?' he asked.

'No. Let's meet wherever we are going.' *Best not to let him know which hotel I'm in just in case he turns out to be a weirdo.*

'Okay, how about the Buddha Bar up in Monte Carlo. Do you know it?' he asked.

'Yes,' she said, recalling the handful of leaflets she'd taken from the cab that dropped her off at this jetty. *Fate and destiny.*

He stepped back and took her hand – then kissed it – without taking his eyes off hers. A shiver shot down her spine. 'It's a date,' he said.

A date!

One night of fun with Hot Boat Guy. One night of being someone else. Someone desired. *Someone that's not boring old Sadie Samantha Turner.*

She grabbed her waterlogged bag and leaned up to plant a kiss on his cheek, pulling away before he could respond. 'See you later then.'

'Haven't you forgotten something?' he said as he walked her down the gangplank.

'What?' she said, her eyes wide. 'Oh, you want this?' and she handed him the glossy brochure. 'I know you'd like to buy one of these when you're a grown-up. But for now, just stick the pictures on your wall – it might help you make your own luck.'

'Ha-ha. No, I mean your name,' he said. 'You forgot to tell me your name and I didn't quite catch it from your loud phone calls. I'm Mac. Pleased to meet you, Miss ...' He did a mock bow and held out his hand.

'It's *Ms*,' she said, wagging her finger at him. 'And it's a pleasure to meet you too, Mac. My name is Sss ...' but as soon as Sadie heard her own name in her head, she instantly felt less adventurous. Instantly 'life' flooded back in and brought a whole load of humdrum with it. In a split second, she knew what to say.

'Samantha.' Pretending not to be herself had been very enjoyable so far, so she might as well go the whole hog. 'But you can call me Sam. And Mac,' she said as she turned to walk away. 'No more spying on people. Deal?'

'We've got a deal.' He shook her hand formally. 'Okay, Sam, see you at seven.'

Mac watched her sashaying off into the distance, until she had disappeared amongst the sightseers on the shore. *What the hell just happened?* He hated lying at the best of times – although he had often done it at the worst of times. Times when lying came with the territory, especially in the early years, where women were concerned. But anyone can change, right?

What an interesting last day this had been. *And it wasn't over yet.*

Mac finished tidying away his work, and trotted off with a spring in his step, completely oblivious to the occasional glints flashing away in the distance once more, way up on the hillside above him.

Because Mac wasn't the only one doing the spying. High above the harbour, a pair of binoculars was lowered. A mobile phone raised, a window closed, and a silver Mercedes SLK convertible pulled away in the direction of Monte Carlo.

Chapter Two

Mac felt like a kid again. He pondered what the hell had just happened to make Mr Cool and Sophisticated disappear into the ocean along with the voluptuous woman's handbag. Toying with his neck chain, he recalled her rear-view clip-clopping back along the jetty. He mentally chastised himself. Where was his usual reserve? Where was his normal *play it cool, no matter who* philosophy?

'What the hell happened there, boss?' said an olive-skinned man in chef's whites who was waiting for him inside a doorway on the deck. He handed Mac a fluffy white towel. As he took it to dry himself down, a dozen or so faces – all peering through nearby windows and round corners – instantly scattered.

'Beats me, Mario.'

'She say no? I can't wait to tell the boys if she say no. *Tell* me she said no.'

'She *nearly* said no.'

'Which means she still said yes – goddam, playboy rich kid from the wrong side of the tracks.'

Mac slapped him hard on the shoulder, and he cursed.

'Now, you slumming it with us for dinner tonight?' Mario's voice went all sing-song. 'It's your last night in resi-dennnnce ... I'm cooking your favour-eeet?'

'Leave me a plate. I'm not sure how the evening will turn out.'

'Mamma mia. *You* might not be, but *we* are – *very* sure. It will turn out just as it always does.'

'Always did, Mario, always did.'

'Leopards, spots, leopards, spots,' said the chef as they both disappeared inside. 'Maybe the spots get smaller – but they're still there.'

Mac left him and passed down a corridor full of photos of himself meeting various dignitaries and celebrities, with Mario's words ringing in his ears. His image had changed. Quite a lot through the years, actually.

New kid on the block.

Property developer.

Playboy property developer.

Playboy billionaire.

Philanthropist, entrepreneur, Midas-touch investor – there were various paparazzi terms now used for him but he never framed the headlines, only the images.

A line of chronological pictures on the wall punctuated most of his major achievements. At one end a shot of him in a hard hat topping off, or finishing, his first office building project; less grey, less tanned, less wrinkled. At the other end a photo from a couple of years ago that had made every financial publication – marking a deal that had truly put him on the map internationally, and earned his place amongst the high-flying venture capitalists – *amongst the big fish*. There weren't many in that sought-after clique, and he'd worked hard to get there. That's what had made a single life worthwhile throughout those years. *Wasn't it?*

That was the deal which had made him. And made him some enemies. Including the man who'd been pictured next to Mac in one of the earlier photographs – Philip Tremain. Mac walked back to look at his wiry face, gaunt, a decade older than Mac, and nearly a foot shorter. Stupid man. He'd tried and failed to oust Mac from one business deal too many, to take control of the cartel of investors who worked together to share risk. It had split the group, leaving Mac with his staunch ally, BJ McKowsky, on their own, and Tremain had been chasing Mac's deals ever since. He leaned in closer to peer at the next photo of just himself and BJ, with an attractive blonde standing in the background. Mac raised a finger to the glass and touched his face from five years previous, clean-shaven and almost unrecognisable from the stubbly chin and unwaxed hair he was now running his hands over. Thank goodness for loyal friends, thought Mac.

This was his own private corridor, untouched when the yacht was rented out for hospitality. Full of photos his office regularly worked hard to bury amongst Internet searches. Privacy could still be afforded with enough Internet know-how, the right connections, and enough money. But these photos gave away too much. He scrubbed at his chin while he looked at them. Maybe his date wouldn't even come back to the yacht tonight, let alone take a tour down this corridor. But he wasn't going to leave it to chance. He knew he shouldn't deceive her but the thrill of her thinking he was a deckhand was too much to resist.

It didn't take too long to remove all the photos, one by one. They needed cleaning anyway. He looked at each as he took it down – yes, the carefully cultivated playboy image had come off a treat including a beautiful woman often pictured close by. He tried but failed to remember all of their names. They'd usually made a play for him at some function or other, and who was he to pass up the offer of an evening with a pretty girl? Although it was just that – an 'evening', rarely a night. In the last few photos, the most recent, the women had gone. So tonight really was an unusual occasion for him – in more ways than one.

Mario appeared again.

'We been talking, and we think maybe you lost your moves, boss.'

Mac merely smiled and handed him the box of pictures. 'See you later, chef.'

'Aha – the photos come off the walls, maybe the pants come off tonight.'

'Kitchen!' said Mac, 'and ask Miguel to give those a wipe over?' The chef ambled up the corridor chuckling and Mac walked to his cabin wondering what destiny would bring.

He opened the door to the master suite and took off his diver's watch and began to undress. First, work out how to play tonight.

For sure her body had filled him with the most powerful charge he'd felt for years. Still feeling it. Either that or the air con was too low in here.

Unbuttoning his shorts, he realised the thought of her was still affecting him now. If only he wasn't such a fan of a challenge.

Too competitive, that's your trouble he told his reflection in the mirror.

Hesitating, then taking off the chain from around his neck, he shook his head. *One night.* She'd made that clear, that was her choice, so to hell with reserve. Tomorrow he'd be gone – like he always was. And anyway, this Sam seemed like someone who could take care of herself, independent and feisty and not likely to turn 'bunny-boiler' anytime soon. Charming too, even if she was as clumsy as any girl he'd ever met. But if it was just a date, why was he feeling all jittery?

Feeling nervous about a date hadn't been on Mac's agenda for years. Maybe because this Sam had reminded him of his first crush, it made him feel seventeen once more. She *did* have the same incredible green eyes and tousled blonde hair, high cheekbones and voluptuous curves, but it didn't mean he had to act like a jock on prom night.

He carefully removed his shorts and went to turn on the shower. Something unexpected had definitely happened today – and it felt so real, so refreshing. Even if she did think he was only a deckhand.

In truth, perhaps that was why all this felt so delicious …

The hot water felt good. So did his body with all the training he'd been doing. It'd better pay off. Mac never did anything without an end in mind. Business deals, extreme sports events … dates. Well, he could always make an exception – he had absolutely no idea how tonight would end. He only knew it would be fun. In any case, with all the stresses of recent events, he needed to get lost in a woman – truly lost. And if that afternoon was anything to go by, with *this* woman he appeared to have a direct route deep into the forest with no white pebbles to find a way home.

A little while later Mac was standing in just a towel, perspiring in the steamy bathroom but hotter still from thinking about his earlier encounter with Sam. He wiped the mirror, looked at his face and wondered if she'd noticed.

Running his finger across one of the scars on his chin he examined the deep marks, right across his jawline. They were disguised more than usual by the five-day stubble he grew on the rare occasion when he finally took time out to train and just be himself, with only the crew for company. He picked up an expensive-looking tube and squeezed out the thick, skin-coloured camouflage cream – one of many unusual lotions and expensive potions on the shelf nearby – till a big blob filled his finger. He looked at it, then at his face.

They never usually mentioned it – the women – they wouldn't dare.

Would this one?

He put a swipe of it over one scar, rubbed a little window into the steamed up mirror, and smiled at what he saw – actually, the stubble was already doing just as good a job of disguise. Maybe it should be his new look. Captain Jim would no doubt approve. He started wiping the cream off again with a tissue.

A sudden banging on the door interrupted his thoughts. *Talk of the devil.* The Captain appeared, red-faced and puffing, wafting his hand through the steam and coughing.

'You should let Giorgio in here afterwards to help steam his acne.' Then he spotted the coloured cream on the sink, and frowned.

'You know what you should do about those scars, don't you?'

Mac shook his head. 'Don't start,' he said, wiping the remainder of the cream onto the tissue and throwing it into a bin.

'Don't you think it might be time to pay attention to your weaknesses, for once?' said the Captain, concern in his eyes. 'Take the plunge? It's not like you haven't got the money.' Mac raised an eyebrow at him but he didn't stop. 'You know that I'll just keep bugging you until you do what I say,' boasted the old man. 'That usually works.'

'I let you think it does.'

The Captain waved a dismissive hand. 'I'll have a word with Simon Leadbetter and get him to book you in the next time you're in LA.'

'Leave it, Jim.'

'What happened to *Cap'n*? All for show, was it? All for "Mrs Buy-me-a-Boat"?'

'It's *Ms*,' said Mac.

'Yeh, and knowing you it'll stay that way.'

Mac threw a damp towel across the room and it landed right over the old man's cap. 'We're only going for drinks,' Mac protested, and began to wash his face again.

'Are you now? Is that why the whole crew's been given shore leave till midnight?' The eyebrow was quivering mischievously but Mac didn't take the bait.

James Wiltshire simply fanned himself in the steam. 'Anyway, I just wanted to find out if you're joining us all at Mimi's tonight and I guess I've got my reply.' He turned towards the doorway.

'Get the crew a few rounds for me anyway, will you? And tell Mimi I'll, er, I'll pop down later to settle the account personally.'

'I bet you don't!'

'Okay, well take the credit card and sort it for me, would

you? It's out there on the dresser. And don't lose it like you "lost" that supermodel's phone number you were supposed to give me last month.'

The Captain didn't need asking twice, trotting along behind Mac like a puppy, a slight waft of Old Spice aftershave exiting the bathroom with him. He picked up a black American Express card, and held it gingerly, almost with reverence. 'Yes, boss.'

'Oh, and buy Mario a bottle of Cristal. He and the galley staff have excelled themselves. None of the Grand Prix party had a word of complaint at this year's gala dinner – unusual for bankers.'

'Yes, but did you hear? They still cancelled for next year. Everyone seems to be feeling the crunch.'

'Or else they've been poached by Tremain,' Mac said.

'He's not at the foot of every bit of skulduggery you come across, you know.' Mac looked doubtful. 'Really – that was years ago. Time you two healed your rift, isn't it?' Mac replied by rolling his eyes. 'No,' continued the Captain. 'It's another "rift" you've got your eyes on tonight ...'

Mac ignored him. 'You never know with Tremain what he's trying to elbow in on.'

'Well, a couple of the other skippers have said their bookings are down for next year too, so maybe you'd better get a downgrade on this?' The Captain waved the hallowed black card in the air. 'Curb your spending like the rest of us have had to? Make some cutbacks if bookings are going to be down?' he teased.

'Maybe I should go the whole hog and just sell the *Nomad* – would that do you?'

'You wouldn't! You've only had her a year.' The old man looked suspicious. 'Is this new attitude to do with that woman, or with you know, your *plan*?'

'Who knows, Jim boy, who knows. If my plans come off maybe I'll be a million miles away from Monaco and freeloading bankers.'

'Well, I still think you're making a mistake, but you're the boss.'

Mac didn't reply, just disappeared into a walk-in wardrobe.

The Captain knew a lost cause when he saw one. 'So ...' he said, seizing his moment. 'Just the *one* bottle of Cristal, you say?' A very cheesy, very toothy, expectant grin peeped round the door at Mac, who couldn't resist his old friend.

'What the hell, make it two! But I want every man back around midnight! No later.'

'And no earlier, either. Right, lover boy?' said the Captain, winking.

'Midnight's *fine*.'

'Bibbidy-bobbidy-boo,' said the old man, watching with a curious look on his face, as Mac pulled on a plain white T-shirt. 'Eh? What's all this? You not getting all Armani'd up as usual tonight then?'

'Nope.'

'No "whiff me at ten paces"?'

'Nope.'

'No "baby's-bum" face? Hang on, you've even taken off Shauny's chain? You must be planning some pretty impressive bedroom gymnastics with stiletto woman.'

Mac's reply was to whisk the damp towel from around his waist and fling it, this time scoring a direct hit across the old man's face.

'Gaaah. Less insubordination from the crew!' the Captain said, rolling his eyes. Then he shook the towel, folded it perfectly in half and hung it over a rail, looking thoughtful. 'Seriously, Mac—'

'I *hate* it when you say that.'

'*Seriously*, Mac, that's why I called you inside earlier – because I heard the warning signs. Remember what happened the last time you veered off course for a woman with dollar signs in her eyes?'

'It's taken me a decade *not* to remember, James. I'll leave a key under the gangplank for you, now naff off and go pickle yourself.'

'Less of yer lip! One day you'll come back and I'll have taken the *Nomad* as a reward for my years of service. I'll have sailed off into the sunset without you, landlubber!'

'Well, you'll be sailing off into the *sunrise* without me tomorrow, won't you? Just don't forget my early morning swim – I can't miss it. Mess with my training schedule and I'll be sorry in a month's time.'

'Just as long as you're not sorry in a few hours' time.' The Captain looked defiant. 'Anyway, the boys are lining up a bottle of Jack with my name on it, so I can't hang around here listening to your nonsense.'

'Give Mimi my love.'

'Too busy giving her my own,' he called from the doorway. 'Oh, and be careful, Mac. I'm not sure I can cope with another lovelorn socialite with her eyes on the prize. I'd just got used to you being celibate. Just make sure it's not *me* clearing up the tears again this time. Or hers.' And with that, he left, in a waft of Old Spice.

'She's not like that,' Mac said to himself in the mirror. '*Is* she … *deckhand.*'

He practised a smile briefly, but then it faded and he chewed his cheek. It *had* been a long time. Nothing – and no one – had been tempting enough. None of the business deals, none of the rich men's gadgets, and none of the eligible women Simon Leadbetter kept insisting he meet. Even the extreme sports barely filled the gap. And they were getting more and more extreme. And the gap was getting wider and wider.

Maybe this was what he'd been waiting for – maybe *she* was what he'd been waiting for. A challenge, yes, that must be it, and so different to all the others. He certainly felt different in his body.

Well, let's make it a 'one night only' to remember.

Incognito. Designer stubble, and tousled hair untouched by gel nor coiffed by professionals. Old denims and a plain T-shirt. No expensive watches or telltale bespoke stuff tonight – no cufflinks or statement rings. No lobster, no champagne. He'd have beer, common-sense food, and no-nonsense company – he couldn't wait.

Mac the billionaire was officially off-duty.

There was a 'message waiting' light flashing when Sadie finally checked in to her hotel room. She sighed with relief when she saw her missing luggage dutifully delivered and marvelled at the decadent suite that she'd been booked into by the advisor who had arranged her meeting with the billionaire guy. Her heart skipped a beat again. Sixteen hours to go. What if she got tongue-tied? What if she botched the presentation completely? What if he said no ... *Stop it.* Taking off her jacket and tight skirt, she went straight to the huge bathroom and dumped her sodden bag in the shower tray. Marvelling at the splendour of the decor, she briefly toyed with the 'his and hers' expensive toiletries by the 'his and hers' sinks in a bathroom that was almost the size of her lounge back home. The towels were impossibly white and supremely fluffy, the lighting was plentiful and flattering and she pondered whether to run the bath or take a shower. In the end she decided to run a bath anyway and make her mind up afterwards. She poured almost a whole small bottle of bath soak into the running water and sat wrapped in the pristine bathrobe breathing in the aroma. Her worries were starting to wear off. Rubbing her temples, she went out to the mini bar and glugged a whole bottle of water in one, then pressed a few buttons to listen to the answerphone message.

Beep. 'Mum, Georgia's taken my jeggings again, and, no, this time I'm not going to be calm. Oh, and good luck for tomorrow.'

Sadie slumped down on the bed and smiled a mother's

half-smile, the one you give when your kids drive you mad but you love them anyway. The machine carried on.

Beep. 'Mum, Nana started it. She told me I can wear Abi's jeggings to the sleepover 'cos they were in the washing basket so she can't need them, can she? And anyway they make me look like Kate Moss. *And* she's only jealous 'cos my legs are longer than hers 'cos I take after Dad's side and she doesn't. And talking of Dad, he's cancelled yet another visit, by the way. And Nana put the phone down on him – it was well dramatic! So ... em ... anyway, hope you're having a nice time and good luck with the billionaire guy.'

Beep. 'Mum, Georgia may have Dad's legs but she's got your bum, so if she stretches my jeggings again, she's buying me new ones this time.'

Beep. 'Darling, it's your mother. Go away, Georgia, and finish your Greek. Okay German, whatever, it all sounds the same to me. Take no notice of the girls, my love, and I'm sorry they found your hotel number but your mobile wasn't answering. I said not to worry you with arguments about *jeggings* as you're probably preparing for tomorrow. So, if you are, don't worry about calling us back. I told them Mummy needs to concentrate so leave her alone tonight. Hang on. *What*, Georgia? ... Yes, yes, *Mum* not *Mummy* ... Anyway, my lovely, call me tomorrow after you knock 'em dead, okay? We'll survive till then. Well, I will, but poor Herb's stressing out about the bowls match tonight. Greta is a poor substitute apparently. Oh, well, nice to know I'm missed. Bye.'

Sadie started undressing as the machine continued to play.

Beep. 'Oh, I forgot – this might please you – it's your mother again, by the way. There's been a bit in the *Guildford Gazette* about you winning that competition – a big write-up like that hunky journalist promised. Do you remember the nice young blond guy with the big shoulders? The one who was so impressed that someone from our little village had

43

won something so big? I told you he quite liked you. He's used a big photo of you accepting your marketing award in Hawaii on page five! You'd think that PR company would have issued a better one though. You can't see your face very well actually, but it's an impressive award they gave you, isn't it? Don't know if it'll fit in that spot in the shop where you wanted to put it – we might have to move the mung beans as well as the alfalfa. Erm, what else? Your hair definitely looks better now it's blonde. And … No, Georgia, I'm not telling her about your father now, the machine's just beeped at me and I think it's going to cut me—'

Beep. 'Sorry, darling. Damned machines. Just quickly, something to make you smile. Takings were up today – quite a bit, actually. That bit of PR seems to have helped. But I might as well tell you, I've got my final thousand to put into the bank account – Tom Rosebery's secretary let me know you needed it or they'd bounce stuff. I don't know why the silly man can't talk to me himself. But after this last transfer I'm afraid that's me done, my darling. It's all gone. You've had yours and Helen's had hers – well, most of it. Her nutritionist's course wasn't anywhere near as much as I've given you, but she'd just had her redundancy money even if she did blow it on those silly Jimmy Shoes … yes, Georgia, Jimmy Choos, whatever. Go away, I'm talking to your mother – well, her machine anyway – and it'll cut me off in a minute if I'm not quick. So anyway, sweetheart,' and here the voice got faster, 'at least you don't have to worry while you're away and anyway if this deal comes off we won't have to worry at all, right? And Sadie – you know you can do it. Good luck tomorrow, love. Sleep well. Nighty-n—'
Beeeeeeep.

Sadie threw herself backwards onto the bed and sighed a massive sigh. What would she do without her mother? And her sister, Helen. She wouldn't have survived the last four years of Single Mothers R Us, that's for sure. Long hours at her shop to make it a success, to keep paying the bills – just. And to keep the girls at the local village school, with its must-have school uniforms and must-go educational trips, in spite of what her stingy ex-husband had tried to make her do.

Without her sister, who was to thank for Hawaii in the first place, ironically, but who was *persona non-grata* at the moment because of the way it had happened. Helen needed to learn not to take Sadie for granted, so was getting the silent treatment for a few weeks. That was in spite of Helen having forced Sadie into a life-changing situation in Tuscany a couple of months ago, one which she'd never have ventured into on her own – an amazing adventure involving two very hot Italians. But a bit of space would teach Helen not to take liberties next time.

And, of course, without her mother Sadie definitely wouldn't have been able to drop everything when the amazing offer had landed in her lap in Hawaii. To help pull off the deal of the century with a product that couldn't be more up her street. It was truly fate.

And if there was anything Sadie believed in, it was fate.
Fate and destiny.

She hauled herself off the bed and walked back into the bathroom to turn off the bath. Flicking on the wrong light, she got a reality check. In the harsh brightness of spotlights around the mirror, she found her mother looking back. Eurgh! Sadie flinched and turned away. Then looked back and tried pulling her cheeks back towards her ears, giving a slight lifting effect. Then she gave up, shook her head and picked up her sodden handbag.

The whole soggy contents came tumbling out into the shower tray, and she sifted through, separating her precious documents and placing them onto a towel to dry. Then she held the bag up, pulled off a speck of seaweed and smiled, transported back to that moment on the deck. She closed her eyes as her fingers found her cheek, remembering that toe-tingling kiss, then her lips. Then she grimaced as she removed the piece of seaweed that had made its way onto her mouth, and sighed.

'Why is it always me, indeed,' she mused out loud.

Careful Sadie, keep your feet on the ground. One night, remember – no Prince Charming, no white charger. But, hey, the way she was feeling, a jester on a pony would have sufficed.

Beats being at home making organic chilli con quinoa for three.

She tested the water in the bath, nodded her head, then went to sort out her newly-delivered luggage – covered with stickers and battered from its journey via Milan. Thank goodness she'd packed a suitable dress. It wasn't expensive but it would do. She was just thankful to finally be out of the tight business suit, and into something more comfortable for the evening ahead.

She also thanked her lucky stars that both her vital laptop, iPad – in need of charging – and backup USB stick had been safely packed in her suitcase, not in her submarine-bag.

She couldn't resist. Opening the all-important presentation for the hundredth time in the last two days, she instantly got heart-stoppingly nervous once more, thinking about tomorrow's meeting. Especially about the mountainous task she'd been given. She perused the document.

Thirty days to find an investor, they'd said, and earn herself a huge bumper commission. Debts solved. Bank of Mum repaid. Ex-husband's alimony a mere formality. And be part of a new worldwide product distribution team that would take the international health food market by storm.

It was all happening so fast – perhaps those 'laws of attraction' books really did work, and all that 'ohmming' and manifesting and visualisation was beginning to pay off. Or maybe she was just in the right place at the right time to have come across the money men chasing down a deal that was quickly circulating amongst the exclusive clique of venture capitalists? The advisor had explained to her that that was how it all worked, amongst the super-rich. With their 'superyachts.'

Putting feelers out amongst her old university research department contacts had returned a very swiftly interested team of scientists eager to be involved in this exciting new power water called Frish. Some had even heard of Bill Galloway, the inventor, and were really impressed when she told them about her offer. Maybe now they wouldn't laugh at her and her high hopes.

She was going off in pursuit of her dream – to help improve the health of the nation. So what if it was only the health of Godalming, her little village near Guildford? She had to start somewhere, but admittedly so far it had been a bit of a struggle. The good folks of Surrey might have *heard* of manuka honey and acai berry, but they weren't rushing to buy it just yet. Still, maybe this new Frish performance water would be her salvation – in more ways than one.

Sadie finished checking her presentation and turned off her iPad, then pulled off the bathrobe and the rest of her clothes including the big knickers that helped her get into the skirt. Her belly-pooch sighed in relief and she squidged it. It had been with her as long as her youngest daughter had, and was her weak spot. Another reason why she'd been happily devoting her life to work. And so what if it had cost her a social life? It had all been worth it, hadn't it? If her last attempt at a relationship was anything to go by, she wasn't missing much. Damian had been like having another big kid in the house. Mind you, his stupid shiny red Ferrari had cheesed off the girls' dad so much it was almost worth it just to see it wipe the smug look off his face.

She smiled to herself at the memory of that last awful session in the bedroom, kinked her little pinky finger and wiggled it, remembering it was true what they say about 'little' men and flashy cars. Another reason why he didn't last long. *In any sense.*

Good job really that he'd gone – the girls could do without yet another bad male role model in their lives. Her mother brought enough of those to visit as it was, bless her hippy cotton socks.

Sadie looked at the photo of her girls on the side table by the hotel bed. They were chalk and cheese – but her finest hour. There was a handmade good luck card underneath the photo, and Sadie pulled it out like a talisman.

'*Go get 'em Supermum*' was from Abi, and '*Bring home the Bacon*' from Georgia – which was funny considering her youngest had been veggie for a good seven years now, since she was ... oh, four, and cried when she found out sausages were made of Babe. Sadie shook her head. They were growing up so fast, her two very own musketeers. She was so lucky to have them, and she was so determined not to let them down.

Yes, this venture couldn't have come at a better time.

Sadie rubbed her feet. She made a dutiful call home, but no one answered so as usual she left a message.

'Hi, guys. What an amazing hotel. What an amazing day ...' *and what an amazing man* she thought to herself as she finished her message and hung up. She checked her watch. Plenty of time.

One hour and three minutes later, freshly scrubbed and glamorously made up, Sadie was almost ready. Twenty minutes until she was due to meet Hot Boat Guy. Actually, twenty-five – she should tarnish her perfect punctuality record, and aim to be five minutes late – *don't want to look too keen,* or God forbid, arrive *before* her date. No, it was good form to arrive just after, wasn't it? Weren't they still *The Rules*? Damned if Sadie knew any more.

She felt her butterflies kick in with a vengeance. Having set up a five year exclusion zone in her personal life – Tuscany notwithstanding – it felt strange to be dressing to impress once more. Time for one last check in the full-length mirror.

Hmmm …

Hair – blonde, bit tousled, fresh 'up-do' – good.

Make-up – glam, sexy, not tarty – good.

Shoes – ahhh, *very good.*

Dress – kind to curves and cut just above the knee, showing off the best bits of her legs before the thighs went lateral.

Wide neckline – nice and stretchy – she pulled it down slightly – better off one shoulder.

No – off two shoulders.

Oooo, no – off one.

She posed sideways and inhaled, then frowned at her tummy in the mirror. The dress was empire-line – cut-in just below the bust, enhancing her hourglass shape, and skimming over the part that let her down. Her tummy always let her down. But according to that infomercial she'd watched a while ago – *'just a phone call away, there's an instant, no-surgery solution!'* And needing some retail therapy, and a way of fitting into her old suit, she'd made that phone call! And it was a twin pack, so another pair left to wear. Time for the pivotal, shape-changing decision of the night, then.

Slimming Magic knickers? Or no *Slimming Magic* knickers?

Disappointment now? Or disappointment later?

Dangling the offending garment in her fingers, she raised an eyebrow. *Come on, mirror, what do you think?* The mirror responded and she could swear she heard the wicked queen's voice. *Not bad. But not great either.*

However, on the 'plus' side – as some of her clothes would be if she didn't stop missing her power-walking class – she already knew Mac approved. He must like 'em cuddly – *there is a God*! And the way he'd held her meant he appreciated her curves. Unlike some men – unlike the slick tycoon she was meeting tomorrow, whom you could barely Google without seeing some skinny supermodel draped all over him. Slicked back hair, huge designer sunglasses, dark suit – sharp, prickly. YUK. Luckily she wouldn't need to do much more than make her presentation, according to his advisor, the kindly older gent she'd been dealing with. When Sadie had told him about the deal, the advisor had been absolutely insistent that he had a client who was already interested in the product, and could meet the thirty day turnaround. He'd emphasised how unusual that was in business, but she would still read the small print carefully – no one was going to rip Sadie Samantha Turner off, not now she was a bona fide businesswoman. But she was impressed at how fast they'd responded and how quickly they'd arranged this meeting on the back of her Hawaii trip. *Time really was of the essence.*

So back to the pants, still hanging there.

Nah, disappointment now. Shrugging, she launched the parachute pants onto the bed, opting for her black lace ones instead. Then she picked up her posh toiletries bag – smart enough to double as a clutch bag – and made her way to The Buddha Bar for her date. For her 'just one night' with the Hottest Boat Guy she'd ever known.

Chapter Three

Sadie hovered outside the front entrance to the bar, unsure what to do. She bit her lip. Through the window she couldn't see anyone in the foyer who looked remotely like the man she thought she'd met this afternoon. *Damn. Do I go in and act nonchalant? Or do I wait here till I spot him? What if he doesn't show? What if ...*

'Hi, seen any good boats lately?'

'Oh, hi!' Sadie relaxed the tension in her stomach. Then immediately sucked it back in again, remembering she didn't have her Bridget Jones knickers on.

'No, I haven't. Nor cruisers. Nor power-yachts!'

'Superyachts!' he corrected.

'The difference obviously matters to you, so *superyachts*.'

'That's better. Coming inside? I've taken the liberty of ordering already.'

'Ordering what?' she asked, a bit taken aback.

'Wait and see,' he said, and showed her to their table – a side booth, relatively private, subdued lighting, but music blaring a bit too loud. They shuffled close, to hear each other.

On the table in front of Sadie were a beer, a water, a juice and a cocktail.

'*Four* drinks? That must cost an arm and a leg in here,' Sadie said.

'Sorry – it's an old habit. Saves time standing at the bar, and ... Can I tell you a secret? It usually impresses the "laydeez" if you guess their drink.'

'And what if *none* of them are right, Mr Moneybags?' she teased.

'Well, are they?' he winced.

'Actually, I could murder the juice! All that window-shopping and sea air's built up a thirst.'

'Phew! Thought I was losing my touch. I always used to be able to guess what a girl drinks, back when I was in college.'

'You must have a long memory.'

He poked her arm for being cheeky and slid the juice over to her with its garish umbrella and half a glacier of ice.

'Here you go, Sam. Cheers.' For a split second Sadie wondered whom he was talking to, then remembered what she'd told him this afternoon. *Game on. 'Samantha' it is.* It was only one date, after all.

'So what brings you to Monaco then – apart from the yacht crawl?'

'Big meeting.'

'Right. What kind of business?'

Sadie was mid-sip and hesitated. She looked away. Even telling him the short answer would bring on nervous palpitations. She downed the lovely cool juice in one, looked him in the eye, and leaned closer.

'Mac, can I ask you something?' she said, huge doe eyes looking up at him from under long, dark lashes.

'Mmm, you smell delicious. What?'

'A favour? Would you do me a really big favour?'

'Depends if it involves getting wet,' he joked, but a flash of unease had crossed his face.

'Don't worry, it's nothing like that. It's this …'

He furrowed his brow, awaiting her next words.

'Tonight,' she said, 'can we please *not* talk about work? At all?'

'Oh, sure! 'Course, no problem.' He let out the breath he'd been holding. 'It's just that, for a minute there, when you said a favour, I thought you meant money.'

'What?'

'I mean—'

'What kind of girl do you take me for, buster?'

'No, I mean … favours. When people ask me for favours it's usually money.'

'What the ...!'

'Erm ... Not you, though – obviously.' Trying to change the subject, he back-pedalled. 'You know – sponsor me for this, lend me that, or asking me to buy your silence in return for not reporting me ... to the snog police.'

She looked thoughtful, then laughed, shaking her head incredulously. 'Idiot!'

Mac laughed too, and also took a sip of his drink, turning his head away from Sadie. She didn't see him mouth to himself in disgust – '*the snog police!*'.

'The thing is,' she explained. 'You see, this is the thing.'

'What's the thing?'

'It's all been really intense lately, and ... I'd rather have a night off from thinking about business.'

'That's the thing?'

'That's the thing.' Sadie looked at him hopefully. It would mean she could totally forget about everything else and just let her hair down – literally and metaphorically. She tossed her hair and her blonde silky tresses played over her bare shoulder.

'Mmm, well, I'm not sure,' he replied. She felt a flash of nerves, wondering if he was going to quiz her all night long about her trip. 'After all, that's my whole repertoire gone if I can't do my "a funny thing happened at the office" routine!' he said.

Sadie nudged him playfully.

'No, seriously,' he continued, picking up his drink. 'Great idea. *Wonderful* idea. Deal. No job talk, then. No moans. No anything relating to the daily grind. Tonight we can be whoever we want to be.'

'Yes, absolutely!' She beamed, picking up the iced water.

'In fact, let's go the whole hog. No last names. Just Sam and Mac. And one night in Monaco. How 'bout it?'

'Well, mystery can be very exciting.' She smiled at his enthusiasm for her suggestion to make it all incognito. *It's like he understood her ...*

'Mystery, eh. Sure, why not. Cheers to mystery!' he said, and raised his glass.

Mystery it is, she thought, *right down to the mystery of whether I'll be strong enough to end this 'one night' early enough to be fresh for tomorrow.*

'Cheers!' she said, clinking glasses. Then she sipped through the straw and smiled.

If Mac's plan tonight was to get lost in her, he was already halfway into the forest. He swallowed, realising the implications of what he was setting up. No telling her who he really was. Was that a good thing, or a bad thing? She seemed to think it was a very good thing. Maybe she had secrets too …

God her mouth was so kissable.

Seeing her tongue toying with the straw while she watched him, he felt his pulse quicken a little.

He was enjoying the anonymity – buying ordinary drinks, paying for them in cash, being in 'mufti' clothing, and not having to sit in the fenced-off VIP area being ogled, and occasionally approached for photographs. Keeping totally incognito would make this a night to remember – and a bit of a fantasy. An inverted fairy tale, where it was more fun to be poor than rich. And he was more like Shrek than Cinderella.

'Cheers to mystery, romance and adventure!' He raised his beer glass again, and this time she lifted the cocktail glass. 'Here,' he said, linking his arm through hers, as they brought the glasses to their mouths. Their faces were just inches apart.

'Chin, chin!' She laughed, her face beaming.

Never a sweeter sound than that laughter, he thought. She was enchanting. Ordinarily he'd opt for safe, disposable arm candy with absolutely no chance of reeling him in. But there was something so refreshing about her realness, her womanliness. Her authenticity. It was filling the heart of him with a yearning to get closer. They relaxed back into their seats together.

'And what else are we drinking to? End of an era you said earlier?'

'Oh, it's nothing much,' he said. 'Just a decision I've been toying with for ages about ... a job.'

'You got a new job? Won't the Captain be mortified?'

'No – he'd be going, too. But not even he knows that yet. So that's all I can tell you, or we'll break our pact before we've even begun!'

'Well, cheers to new directions!'

They linked arms again and this time the straw got in the way and flicked a little of the cocktail onto her cheek. She giggled and he wiped it off, and then licked his finger. She blushed slightly then reached into her makeshift clutch for a tissue.

'Did the other bag survive its swim?' he asked.

'Bag will live, but can't say the same for the phone! Strange being without it. My mother will think I've run off with some weird man!'

'Not yet, but the night is young.' He relaxed back on the bench.

'It wouldn't matter – she's a bit weird too,' she said, looking up at him expectantly. 'Yours probably thinks the sun shines out of you.'

'Actually, I never really knew my mum,' he replied. She made a 'poor you' face. 'Oops, sorry, we said no personal details, didn't we?' he added. 'It's sweet that yours cares so much though. Bet she misses you while you're away.'

'Yes and my daugh ...' Sadie stopped herself mid-sentence. She corrected herself quickly. *No personal info.* 'My door ... key – I lost it. Mum might have been needing to ring me to tell me she ... found it.'

'Rrright. Well, you'd better remember to pack your "waterproof mobile" next time.'

'Thanks so much for rescuing my bag for me. Are you always such a hero?'

'Of course! *Drowning handbags*, run of the mill. *Damsels in distress*, a speciality!'

'Well, if I'm ever in distress, I'll give you a call!'

'Dis-dress, dat-dress, you look good whatever,' he said, then cringed. Bad joke. Old habit. He really was stepping back in time tonight.

She whacked his arm. 'Ha-ha, funny man. Well, thanks anyway. I'm glad you were there or it'd have been *me* needing waterproofs.'

'That's okay. You were the best thing to walk down my gangplank all day.'

'I'll bet you say that to all the girls.'

'Listen, just 'cos I'm a sailor doesn't mean I have a girl in every port.'

'Hmmm,' said Sadie, smiling up at him while sipping her drink.

'Seriously – too busy – been there done that. You know how it is at our age – you start to want different things. Time to move on.'

'To a new era.'

'To a new era.' They toasted again.

'And to making your own luck.'

'And to making your own luck, Samantha Businesswoman.'

They paused mid-toast, and the air sizzled between them. 'I hope I didn't disturb you too much today. Did you finish your ... erm ... What were you doing anyway?'

'Oh, just a spot of maintenance. Pump problems.'

'And did you finish mending your pump ... thing?'

'No, my pump thing has had to be replaced. It's seen too much action in recent years.'

She raised her eyebrows. '*Has* it now?!'

He laughed and leaned nearer to her on the soft seat to continue the banter.

An hour flew by. Quips about Monaco – the place, the people, her opinions about the Grand Prix – or the 'car race' as she called it with *'rich posers flocking in to watch expensive lumps of tin go round and round in circles'*. She'd get on famously with Captain Wiltshire, for sure. Favourite foods, sports, pastimes and, of all things, he was surprised to find out they were both board game fans – traditional games, none of the new digital stuff. She shared his love of nostalgia – Boggle, Rummikub, Monopoly. She even seemed genuinely interested in the history behind his precious Tank watch. He'd replaced his usual Rolex with an inter-war, leather-strapped, rectangular timepiece. Battered and unassuming, you wouldn't realise it was an antique.

'You should get it valued,' she joked. 'You might be a millionaire!'

'I did,' he said. 'And one thing's for sure – I'm not a millionaire.'

She made a big deal of fake-tutting. 'Well, seems I'll have to go find somebody else's gangplank to walk down then, won't I?' She laughed.

He smiled awkwardly. *One night,* he thought to himself, *it's just for one night.* 'What would you do if you couldn't find another "gangplank"?'

'Seriously? Honey, I walk my own,' she said, sincerely. 'I'd make my own, just like luck.'

That was the correct answer, he thought, and he found himself relaxing more than he'd done with a woman in a very, very long time.

A second hour was spent in easy repartee, with more philosophical musing about life in general and a debate about the old-fashioned version of Scrabble versus the new. The old won, naturally.

Mac could feel himself getting progressively turned on by her feather-light touches, glancing across his arm, his knee. He returned the compliment by putting his arm along the back of the bench-seat, touching the skin on the back of her one bare shoulder every so often and pulling her close every time she had a story to tell.

They ate a little dinner, his treat, but she insisted they took it in turns to buy the drinks – a revelation for Mac. The last time he'd allowed a woman to pay was back in college when he was skint. He'd since made it a principle that if *he* extended the invite, *he* picked up the tab. Over the years the party numbers had grown inordinately, but his principle had remained the same. Champagne by the magnum had eventually become the norm. Sure, he got it back in spades when his rich patrons stumped up with stratospheric charity donations, but sometimes his bar bills ran into tens of thousands. Tonight he doubted it would hit a couple of *hundred* euros – even including a big tip. But somehow, in a way Mac was scared to admit, it meant a whole lot more.

When it came to another round of drinks, Sadie asked to switch to juice instead, and Mac found himself surprisingly pleased.

'Good idea,' he told her. 'I've got an early start too so I need to stay sharp.'

'And I've got my business meeting. PowerPoints and pina coladas don't mix too well, do they?'

Mac laughed.

The banter was distinctly more witty, more fun, and definitely more memorable without the 'affluence of incohol'.

What a revelation.

After one particularly cheesy joke, at which Sadie laughed out loud, a genuine, hearty laugh, Mac felt his body completely relax. He realised his shoulders were loose, at ease, and in the last two hours he'd also laughed more in a woman's company than he'd done in the last ten years. He felt rejuvenated. A little of the old Mac was creeping in – he started to feel a bit more like himself. And he was definitely wanting to feel a bit more of Sadie.

As the night progressed, Sadie also found herself feeling more and more relaxed as she snuggled next to Mac. She was chuffed that after a long drought, she was proving to herself that she could still drink her fill of fun with a man. Or maybe *this* man.

'It's really weird, you know,' she said. 'I'm surprised at how natural this feels. Like I've known you for years. Are you sure we haven't met before somewhere?'

'Not unless you've been Internet stalking me already?' he said.

'Ptchah! Sure! With a name like Mac? Too many pages about computers or burgers to find anything to do with odd deckhands!'

'So you tried then?'

'Don't flatter yourself! No time, sonny boy. Looking this naturally beautiful takes many hours. It's an art.'

'Well, I'd pin you on the wall in *my* gallery anytime.'

'Creep!'

'Ahh, welcome back, dear high school nickname, it's been a long time. How I have missed thee.' And he took off an imaginary feathered hat and twirled it round in the air as if bowing to her.

'You're a nutter.'

'Ooh, say I'm a loser too, and that completes the set.'

Sadie felt good. Good to be flirting again. Good to be on a date with such a hot man. And maybe because tonight she wasn't being Sadie, she was being 'Sam'...

She liked the way she fitted under his arm. And the way the pressure was off. No high expectations from tonight. It was what it was. And he was what he was – a simple deckhand, and he seemed very proud of it. Unlike some of the chancers she'd dated before she got married – all full of themselves, striving to be someone, to get somewhere, and failing miserably. This man was so different. Even more relaxed around her than her ex-husband Stuart had been. Two children too late, she'd found out that his carefree attitude was only because he was a man who couldn't give a monkey's about anyone but himself.

Unlike her Hot Boat Guy, who didn't seem to be bothered about his looks at all. He hadn't even shaved for tonight.

Unlike Sadie.

Unusually, Sadie didn't mind Mac's designer stubble. In fact she liked it – a lot. She liked *him* – a lot.

As she listened to another one of his funny 'life at sea' anecdotes, she wondered who else had felt the same about Mac through the years. There must have been a broken heart somewhere down the line, perhaps that's when he stopped making 'those plans'. But she just couldn't see him as a player. It was simple, honest attraction, with no games, no holding back and no deception, just the way she liked it. 'Honesty' wasn't tattooed in Chinese on her lower back for nothing. Well, apart from the little white lie about her name.

But he'd never know, would he.

She smiled as they spoke, aware that he couldn't take his eyes off her mouth, or his arm off her shoulder. He'd even angled himself completely away from the rest of the room – everyone else could only see his back – he was giving her his total attention. In fact, much of the night, his gaze never left her face, apart from the occasional look over his shoulder and a scan of the crowd in a way Sadie found curious. Maybe he expected to see someone from the boat ...

Mac was on the lookout. Old habit. Just in case anyone saw him – anyone he had to avoid. Usually female. There was a close call when a group of glamorous model-types stumbled past on their way to the VIP area on the other side of the bar, just as Mac turned round. One of them, in a tight red dress, did a double-take. Mac dipped his head quickly, but not before she'd taken a step towards him. When she spotted Sadie, however, she halted, looked quizzical then walked on with her friends, her quip in French, just audible to Mac's straining ears.

'Can't be, not dressed like that. Anyway, he usually has a

young cover girl on his arm, not someone like her. Probably just looks a bit like the playboy billionaire, that's all.'

Mac froze. How dare they insult his companion like that? If he wasn't 'undercover', he'd have taken great pleasure in telling them that she was more beautiful than any cover girl.

Then he realised with a jolt that the insult was really for him. He felt shallow, superficial. *Was he really a cliché?*

Suddenly a sledgehammer blow caught him in the gut, bringing with it the sad realisation that that was precisely what he was.

He'd never been amidst raw public opinion before, not in this way – hearing sheer honesty, rather than the sanitised, filtered version the *über rich* usually got told by their minions. How sad that this playboy persona was all he boiled down to in their eyes. And they'd been right – his arm candy *was* usually a carefully groomed size zero – with a personality to match. No wonder he'd stopped finding them attractive.

And as for his playboy image?

Well, let's see if the new plans would finally change all that.

His companion was regaling him with some information about a health food product she'd recently tried, animated and enthusiastic, and he watched her red lips pouting and pursing as she spoke. He wasn't really listening.

Would *she* care about what other people thought? Probably not.

The topic of discussion had got to the stage where those red lips were adamantly advocating that the scientific press should 'grow some'. She was enchanting. Then the music slowed down, so he asked Sadie if she danced.

'You mean am I capable of it? Or would I like to?' She chuckled.

'Come on, come dance with me. I'm not very good but let's give it a go.' *Hmm, still the self-doubt creeping in.* Why was it so important to him to make a good impression on her?

She certainly was unlike any of the others he'd been with – ever. But still he shrugged – *that's simply what happens when you spend too long away from women …*

Sadie felt completely happy. She'd laughed a lot, her body felt energised, as only sexual heat can make you feel, and she hadn't thought about the big meeting once. She looked up at this strapping guy, holding his hand out hopefully towards her. How lucky was she? Taking his hand and feeling its warmth, she followed him out to the middle of the floor, mingling anonymously amongst the other swaying couples.

A humid, heavy heat lay in the air and a bubbling anticipation began to rise between them, as they brought their bodies together. Hands, arms, chests all touched, then lower down the same thing happened.

The sudden physical contact made Sadie gasp. He was *sooo* hot. So strong, rock solid. She shook her head. He looked perturbed.

'What?'

'Nothing, it's just … it's you.'

'Makes a change from *it's not you, it's me*.'

She laughed and looked away. He continued. 'Anyway what *about* me? Did I tread on your toes already?'

'No,' she said with a laugh. 'You're doing fine, just fine.'

'Fine. Well, *fine's* better than *not fine*, I suppose! Dancing never was my strong point.'

'Never mine either, not in these shoes.'

'Aww … Don't make me think about the shoes! I was trying not to think about the shoes.' He pretended to fan himself approvingly at her high, high heels. She blushed.

Another frisson passed between them, and his hands slipped around her waist, pulling her closer. She looked up – he was a good six inches taller than her, even in her highest high heels. Chiselled features, sexy designer stubble.

He was truly magnificent – looking for all the world like he'd made no effort, but the pressed T-shirt and intoxicating freshly-showered aroma gave him away. Reaching his face, half-illuminated in the dim lights, she was struck by his expression. Intense – eyes barely showing any blue now, they were so black with desire.

'You're beautiful, Sam.'

She went to reply but he was lowering his head towards her. Sadie watched him come closer, savouring the moment. She closed her eyes at the last possible second, inhaling deeply as their lips met for the first time.

Slowly at first, then more passionately his mouth explored hers. Sharp darts of desire shot through her, as his tongue nudged between her lips, finding *her* tongue and infiltrating her senses. This kiss was even more powerful than she'd expected.

He smelled so intensely male, tasted so exotic and rare, that he made her body tingle as he tenderly kissed his way from her lips across to her cheekbones and ears, then back to her lips, cupping her face in his hands, just the way she liked it. His hard body felt so powerful against her soft curves that she immediately wanted more of him. She felt like she was acting out a romance novel – the kind she'd lived and breathed for the last few years to get her fix of schmaltz. Tales in which he would have swept her off her feet, and away to a remote castle on a mountainside, in a horse-drawn carriage, and she would have been powerless to resist.

Her imagination was running riot.

So were his hands.

They were in her hair, touching her neck, along her shoulders, down her arms, cupping her face and kissing her intently and Sadie loved every second of it.

In that moment, all that existed was a powerful bond, and she didn't want to break the spell as they moved together, slowly swaying to the music, turning, kissing all the while.

He felt like the happy ending she'd been waiting for her whole life.

But this wouldn't be like a romance novel, Sadie thought, bringing herself back to earth with a bump. This was a 'one night only'. 'Sam' today, Sadie tomorrow – *don't forget that. Don't get carried away.*

There would be no crimson sunset to disappear into – he'll be the one that's doing the disappearing when he hoists anchor tomorrow and sets sail in his power boat. Superyacht. What*ever*.

With his kiss deepening, she allowed herself the luxury of surrendering to the simple excitement of seduction. *But* she made sure to detach her blossoming emotions, neatly storing them away in the 'for future reference, but not now' section of her brain. Because, as inevitable as his departure would be, she also guessed how the rest of the night was likely to play out, and she found herself eager for the next step.

So she kissed him back.

Hard.

His reaction was equally fervent, and she felt him raise his own game. Their arms wound around each other, more frantic, more fevered. Mac's hands found her hair, released the rest of her up-do and pulled her face towards him. Running his fingers through her tousled blonde locks, his tongue showing her mouth exactly what he'd like to be doing to her body. And it didn't escape the attention of nearby couples.

'Vous voulez une chambre à l'hôtel?' a fellow dancer asked and giggled.

'She said, "get a room",' Mac explained, as he and Sadie unclamped themselves from each other.

'Pardonnez-moi,' Sadie said, and the dancer smiled.

'You speak French?' Mac asked

'About four sentences.'

'What are the others?'

'You don't want to know.'

Things were getting a bit too hot on the dance floor, and with a couple of pointing fingers aiming his way, this was definitely not the way to remain incognito. Holding her hand, he led her back towards the booth.

As he reached the table and slid in next to her, his eyes were drawn across the other side of the bar. There, by the door, two of his crew innocently stood watching them, making a thumbs-up sign.

He shook his head, warning them off.

Sadie saw none of it.

'So, I was thinking,' he said as they both finished off their drinks and he grabbed his jacket. 'Ever seen inside a superyacht?'

'No. Only a Sunseeker Cruiser.'

'You're learning.'

'I was *wondering* if you'd be offering me a tour.'

'Well, only if you think your sea legs can stand it without throwing something else overboard. I've had my swim for the day,' he said.

'I'd say my legs are capable of lots of things,' she replied, and then giggled realising what she'd said.

Mac chivalrously picked up her jacket and as he placed it on her shoulders he saw her bite her lip slightly.

'Although,' Sadie continued, 'I do have a busy day tomorrow.'

'I've got an early start too so no problem. A quick tour and a nightcap to round the evening off?'

'Walk me outside and I'll think about it.'

A woman like this in my arms and I'm wanting a quick tour and an early night? I'm losing my touch, thought Mac.

The lights were twinkling in Port Hercule as they walked outside. The sky was clear and the silence of the night air was broken periodically by a tinkling of mismatched music as they passed the various bars in silence. From time to time, Sadie glanced up at him, admiringly, then looked away quickly when he turned to see what she was looking at. Finally they reached the quay.

'Well, are you going to come back?' he said, taking her in his arms, playing with her hair and looking expectantly into her eyes.

Sadie was thinking.

It'd been a lovely night. Should she risk ruining the magical memory by going further? Or risk ruining it by saying no? Miss out on a scintillating night of passion? Or miss out on a potential disaster? She shuddered, remembering the last one-night stand she'd had. In Tuscany. And the one before that with a date she'd met on the Internet. 'Tragically funny', was how she'd described it. She'd vowed never to do that to herself again. *Not without love*, she'd told herself. After all, being feisty with her clothes on was one thing – keeping men at a distance was her specialty. But when it was all stripped back – literally – the vulnerability scared her.

So full of the backchat, so lacking in confidence in her post-baby body. Yuk – tragically funny all right. That's why it had been easy to set up a five-year exclusion zone. Then when her business was sorted and the kids were grown up enough not to need so much of her time – then she'd hit the gym and find a man. She blamed sister Helen for what had happened in Tuscany, and anyway, that wasn't real life. And neither was this.

But looking up at Mac, she saw how different tonight had been – how easy she was in his company, for one thing. And for another, how much she fancied him – totally unlike a one-night stand guy. Or Damian the big kid. Or Stuart the domineering ex-husband. Mac was gorgeous and she could tell he was totally attracted to her too. She surprised herself – suddenly she was imagining the look on Stuart's face if she turned up with Mac by her side – and it was too much. A pang of longing passed through her and she knew in a heartbeat there could only be one possible answer.

Ten minutes later Mac closed the stateroom door, not quite sure how he'd ended up there – alone.

Alone.

He took a deep breath. What was he doing? *Messed that one up completely.* And what was this alien feeling? Fretting? Disappointment? Failure? *Surely not ...*

It had all seemed so promising.

'Thank you for a lovely evening,' she'd said. Then she'd kissed him with all the passion and promise he usually received at the end of a successful night out, usually followed by a successful night in. But that was it – she'd gone off in a taxi, and he'd gone off to consult with his old friend Mr Jack Daniels. Mac swigged the whisky he'd poured himself and grimaced at it – *nope, not working.* Then he started undressing, removing his belt, and throwing it onto the floor in frustration.

'You certainly didn't see that one coming, Mac my boy,' he said to his reflection in the mirror. *First time for everything,* he thought.

Still hot from his earlier encounters, he relived the scintillating kisses over and over again. She'd certainly left him shaken – and stirred. He thrilled at the memory of her curves. Real curves.

But something was niggling him. And it wasn't just being turned down for the first time in years. It was his own behaviour, that's what.

Mac sat himself down on his bed and started untying his shoes. The more he thought about it, the more he became wracked with guilt.

Why did he let her think he was a deckhand?

He paused and rasped his fingers across the stubble on his

face. Because she joked about being into rich men? Because that's when his alarm bell had rung, an alarm bell that chimed with the clang of ancient history?

He clinked more ice into his glass and it too gave a clang. He downed it in one. *Go on, punish yourself and ruin your training tomorrow, yeh, good move, loser.*

Whatever, it wouldn't make any difference 'cos now she was gone. And whether he'd intentionally lied or not, now he'd never be able to tell her the truth.

Which was what? Exactly?

He held his head in his hands and rubbed his temples. *Think.*

Point one, 'Mac the deckhand' wasn't likely to be rich, but she'd agreed to meet him anyway.

Point two, even *she* had suggested it was going to be just a brief liaison, so don't stress about it.

Point three, she seemed keen on him too – she hadn't pushed him away when he'd kissed her. In fact, she'd kissed him back, hard and full.

But even that had particular significance. For most men, that would be quite normal. But for Mac, a billionaire, it was rare to know for sure whether a woman wanted him for himself – or for his wallet. No wonder he'd been too easily tempted to play along. The way she'd reacted to him, even though she thought he was mere crew, meant more to him than any of his usual encounters.

No, there had been something altogether more ... primal ... about this voluptuous woman called Sam. And he'd been curious, that's all, to see what would happen if he stayed incognito. Yes, that was it. Curiosity. That was all it was.

Then he realised *point four* – the most reassuring thought of all – a killer fact: telling her he was rich at the end of the night – specifically to find out if it would make her act differently, to even stoop as low as to see if it would change

68

her mind about coming on board, that would have been far, far worse.

Lose lose.

It didn't matter now, she'd gone. But he couldn't get her out of his mind.

He rubbed his scarred face. *She didn't even say anything about this.*

What a woman.

He remembered the feel of her luscious lips and the press of her hips, and felt the familiar stirring. Again. God she was sexy. He adjusted himself and picked up his shoes.

Obviously she had a good brain on her to match her generous curves, if she was here on business. And he'd always had a weakness for intelligent women with curves. Sadly, that combination was rare amongst the lettuce-munching Barbie dolls everyone expected a billionaire like him to have on his arm.

Mac stopped what he was doing and paused for one second to think about that description. He stared into space like a statue, contemplating. Then threw his shoes into the corner.

Billionaire. On paper at least.

It brought him happiness, it brought him trouble. He'd earned every penny of it and nowadays he'd found ways of spending that resonated with who he'd become.

This yacht had brought him the best kind of happiness – it had been a hard-won prize – unique, admired. It made him feel part of the select group of people rich enough to not only afford to buy it, but to maintain it, crew and all. A carefully chosen crew, genial and full of camaraderie – some of whom had known him since he was a rookie property developer and began taking weekend sailing courses. It meant a lot that they treated him with no airs and graces – at least when no outsiders were around.

Yes, he could totally be himself here, cocooned away from

the glare of publicity and other people's expectations, when it wasn't being rented out. Which was of course partly why he'd bought it.

Mac took out his smartphone and checked through the calendar – hired out to capacity and paid for months in advance – no more nights for him here till the end of the summer. *Dammit.* Sucks for him, but it'd be a busy season for the crew. This year, at least. A pang of concern about the lack of bookings for next year sprang up but he parked that thought in the same silo as 'check-up on Philip Tremain'.

Mac picked up the only photo frame on show now in his elegant VIP stateroom. Mac and Captain James Wiltshire, plus financial advisor and old friend, Simon Leadbetter, all standing at the helm of the *Nomad*, on the day he bought it, early the previous year. No BJ McKowski money needed for this venture. And Tremain outbid. Hence it had meant so much to Mac. He smiled, remembering the look on his old adversary's face when he discovered he'd been beaten to the post by Mac.

Touching the photo frame, he saw the Captain's burly chest puffed out so far you almost couldn't see the slight, suited, serious figure of distinguished gent Simon, raising a glass beside him. And Mac with his usual slicked back hair and designer shades.

Almost as rewarding as owning the craft was seeing the Captain's beaming face taking the helm of the vessel that day – his new 'baby' was twice the size of Mac's previous yacht.

Mac's mouth quirked into a wry smile, remembering the satisfaction he'd felt to be placed at the top of the wait-list, despite, or rather because of, Tremain's foolish attempts to bribe the selling agent. *Stupid man,* thought Mac.

A great photograph. A great day. It had made him very, very happy.

Then Mac frowned when he thought about what was kept safely behind the yacht photo, inside the frame.

Sure, that had been a good day. But sometimes a day starts off well, but ends badly. He felt a pang of regret. He'd certainly had his fill of bad days too. And the biggest reminder of one of his worst mistakes was millimetres away from his fingers inside the back cover. He turned it over, hesitated, but then went ahead and flipped open the back of the frame and pulled out a small snapshot hidden inside. He held it up and blinked at it.

He was looking at himself, a few years ago, holding the hand of a small child. *Yes, it still hurt.* He looked at it blankly. Pain coursed through his heart as it always did. A great photograph, a nice moment, but the day had ended up really, really bad.

But it provided a watershed. From then on he obeyed a very important business rule. One that he now lived his life by, and based every decision on, one he was renowned for amongst his colleagues and competitors.

'Never mix business with pleasure – or children.'

Fool me once, shame on you. Fool me twice, shame on me.

Mac's brow creased. How old would the boy be now? The whole experience had been alien. He'd spent most of his life getting as far away from children as he could. And then that debacle had happened, and reminded him why. But it wasn't the kid's fault.

He moved it towards the rubbish bin in the corner of his room, then changed his mind and slid the small photo back into the rear of the frame, and put it back on the shelf.

End of another era.

Still, onwards and upwards. Suddenly he felt very weary. Time for a change – time for a new chapter.

Mac picked up his belt and sneakers and entered his walk-in closet full of expensive designer clothes, row after row of pristine jackets and trousers, plus shoes, belts, ties, and cufflinks. At the end there were a dozen expensive suit bags containing whole outfits – complete with little Polaroids stuck to the front of each.

Easier for Mac to choose the outfits for a valet to pack when he was in a rush. The final photo made him stop in his tracks and laugh out loud. Instead of a slick suit ensemble, someone had put a picture of some shabby old tramp, and stuck Mac's face on it. *Banter, there was always banter.*

He reached below that suit bag to his favourite chest of old clothing and replaced his worn belt inside it. He also replaced the shabby pair of loafers – his first pair of Tod's – a natural choice for tonight as they were a super-expensive brand but with no obvious designer label on show. Tidying up the fifteen-year-old frayed laces, he felt the frisson of *first-date* excitement again – the one she'd rekindled. The one he hadn't felt in years. He stared at the shoes, remembering.

Until tonight, he'd forgotten what his life used to be like out of the spotlight. To go out for an evening on shore and just be treated like a normal man.

Not to be kowtowed to.

Not to be surrounded by sycophants.

Not to be treated like royalty wherever he went. Just to be ordinary. To be Mac. Well, tonight, thanks to this gorgeous woman, he'd had a trip down memory lane, and loved every minute. For the right reasons, or wrong ones, money hadn't even got a mention.

So often, having so much of it made it meaningless. He ran his fingers along the row of handmade suits – navies, blacks, charcoals. Each silk tie cost more than the average family's weekly shopping basket. He shrugged. Reaching the end of the row, he walked back out and closed the closet door behind him. Sure, wealth was a blessing, but it was also, undeniably, a curse.

And anyway, lately, just lately, there'd been that gaping hole – something missing, something important, something money couldn't buy.

And if it *could* buy it, it couldn't keep it.

Deep down, Mac knew exactly what that something was,

but tried hard to ignore it. He had everything else, everything he'd ever wanted to own and that would have to do, right?

Sadly the answer was as clear as day – to anyone else. To Mac, it was a gnawing feeling that crept over him when he closed his eyes at night, and opened them in the morning. He shook himself often to chase it away. But no matter – he was certain the brand new venture he was planning would help take the edge off the emptiness, and take him in a new direction. Yes, *a change was as good as a rest.*

But some things never change, he realised as he topped up his drink. Even though this lady had reached parts of him none of the others had, lately, it had still been his plan to let her walk away. And maybe Sam deserved better than that, so perhaps it was a good thing he'd not got his way tonight.

It was so hard to learn new tricks – he truly was an old dog.

Taking one final look in the mirror, he shrugged. *An old dog, that's for sure.* She'd probably say he looked 'weathered'. Too much time in bright sunshine. His private trainer, private doctor and his personal health expert all told him to use factor 50 whenever he went skiing or mountain climbing, but in truth he knew he wouldn't bother. He still scrubbed up pretty well. He'd never give George Clooney a run for his money, but hell, George Hamilton better watch out.

And the scars … well, he'd deserved them. One day maybe he'd succumb to the Captain's suggestion of laser surgery, but for now he used the camouflage creams. Except tonight. The disguise – the covering up who he really was – was for other nights, to provide the mask, to complete the shroud of formality, the uniform of a billionaire. But tonight he'd been free of it all.

Yes, tonight had been a good night.

Mac took his drink and made his way back up to the deck, barefoot on the smooth polished wood once more. He felt the cool boards beneath his feet – that'd help take some of the heat away. He gazed out over the bay into the distance at the sea wall and the dark sky, a vague smell from an on board barbecue floating somewhere in the breeze. The gentle night air cooled his heated body, and beckoned him to his new life beyond. Ironic that having made his first fortune in property, big executive penthouses and sprawling ranches all over the US, he would be moving into the next phase of his career on a glorified mobile home. A home that didn't have a woman. Any woman. Even a woman like Sam. Especially a woman like Sam.

On the breeze, he could swear he smelled her fragrance and his heart began to pound again the same way it had that afternoon when she'd walked along the jetty. Blonde hair falling out of her up-do. Curves, confidence and an air of being comfortable in her own skin. So refreshing. Plus the rare thrill of the backchat. The high cheekbones and her beautiful green eyes had helped too. And that walk. And those shoes. And the noise they made on the cobblestones. In fact, he could hear it right now.

Mac shook his head, rubbed his eyes and looked at his drink, then looked back again along the jetty. He couldn't believe what he saw.

'Ahoy there shipmate. Is it too late for a tour?'

Chapter Four

Sadie's heart was pounding thirteen to the dozen but from the moment she'd bid him goodbye, there'd been a pull in her chest like she'd never felt before. So much so, that as soon as the taxi had arrived back at the hotel, she knew she had to ask the driver to turn right round again. Then when they'd reached the quay, she'd changed her mind and asked him to about-turn once more. But when the hotel was again in sight, Sadie had finally changed her mind for the last time, and headed back to the jetty, telling herself it was 'now or never'.

It was a philosophy that had embraced her, rather than her embracing it – but 'now or never' it was. Whether it was the exotic location going to her head, or being intoxicated by the magic of that night, or just telling herself she simply wanted to see inside a 'superyacht' then leave, Sadie had felt a magnetic pull too hard to resist. She had to return. Exactly what for, she didn't know. But she hoped she'd soon find out.

And there he was, looking amazed to see her again, and hurrying down the gangplank to greet her. *Thank God.* For Sadie, it was win-win either way – if it turned out to be literally a tour and a nightcap, then she'd at least have pictures of the inside of a superyacht to show the girls. And if it became another soulless one-night stand, then hey-ho, at least physically it'd prove she'd still got it, and it would probably be the last steamy session before the months – maybe years – of abstinence to come. And if by chance any potential encounter turned out to be filled with more than that, more feeling, and the same sort of connection she'd had since she laid eyes on him, then this night might even inspire her to be a bit less cynical about finding a good man – when the time came. Plus, she was a big girl – and actually, she rather felt like having a close encounter of the physical kind while there was very little chance of anyone knowing about it. So, all well and good. Whatever happened from here on in, this would be a trip to remember.

Mac greeted her with a huge kiss.

'Hey, you,' she said.

'Hi, Trouble.'

'I decided if I'm going to own a "Ferretti Custom blah blah" one day, I should really take advantage of a private tour if it's offered to me,' she joked.

'Glad to hear it. Ferretti Custom Line 124.'

'Yes, that. And if that nightcap is still on offer ...'

'It most certainly is. This way for the grand tour.'

Ten minutes later, they were back in the expensively decorated salon, having completed a brief lap of the vessel, avoiding any nooks and crannies where anything would have given him away. Hopefully no clues, no questions.

'So, is the owner in that other bedroom we avoided?'

Spoke too soon.

'He's off duty tonight. Went ashore.'

'Shame – looks like I'll have to slum it with the paid help, then.'

Before he could reply, she took his face in her hands and kissed him hard and long. He returned the favour and lifted her in the air. Her little squeak of surprise amused him. He deposited her effortlessly on the expansive c-shaped sofa in the lounge area.

'Wow, you're strong,' she said.

He responded by swinging into an Atlas pose, with one fist on his forehead and the other on his hip. Wanting to make her laugh came so easily. Then picking up a remote control he poised it like a baton in the air.

'Music ...?'

'... maestro, please,' she quipped.

He dramatically flicked the remote, having already picked

the music earlier that evening, and the speakers sprung to life, filling the room with the sensual sound of soul music.

'You certainly know your way around, don't you?'

'So I'm told.'

He slumped down beside her on the sofa and went to kiss her again, but a look of trepidation crossed her face and he cocked his head to the side.

'What?'

'Mac, I ...' she paused. 'I don't usually—'

'Neither do I.'

'No, seriously, it's ... been a while. That sounds crass, doesn't it?'

He paused, softened, felt a flicker of concern show on his features. 'Samantha Businesswoman really is all work and no play, huh?' She nodded, apologetically. Leaning down on his elbow he kissed her in reply, gently, tenderly. She smiled gratefully and took a deep breath.

'Can I get you anything to drink?'

She shook her head.

'Eat?'

'No, thanks. Game of Scrabble?'

He laughed. 'I'd prefer some other games, if you don't mind ... Or else we can just lie here for a while.'

He surprised himself. Since when was he the New Man? Sadie responded by pulling him towards her by his T-shirt.

'Just lie here? Next to *this* body? The hell we will ... I was just warning you, that's all. I'm a bit out of practice.' And with that, he pulled her down next to him, and she sank back onto the sofa beneath his heated kisses.

'Well, with what I've got in mind, you won't need to worry about having many skills at all.'

Sadie was surprised to find herself relax completely beneath his tender kiss. Without leaving her lips once, he moved her arms above her head, and caressed down the sides of her body and back up again, making her shiver with anticipation. Then he looked into her eyes, searching once more, then kissed her delicately, from her mouth, down to her neck, over her collarbone, sensuous on her sensitive skin, making her body quake a little with every move. It felt so good.

'Mmmm ...' she murmured. 'Looks like I'm in the hands of a master.'

He responded by moving across on top of her slightly, his knee rising up between her thighs, taking her hemline up with it.

She gripped his powerful leg, feeling the roughness of his jeans on her bare thighs. Tantalisingly trapped beneath his bodyweight, her arms still pinned above her, she responded by rubbing her body against him gently. He groaned. All the while she could feel his lips and tongue exploring her skin. His fingers traced a path back down the inside of her arm. She could feel her pulse beginning to race and her breath begin to quicken.

Mac paused ever so briefly, giving himself time to feel the full impact of getting intimate with Sadie's amazing body at last, having wanted her all night. He watched her voluptuous breasts heaving, her face flushed, struggling to retain her composure. Caught in the dim light of the salon, she looked alluring, and sexy as hell in the full throes of being turned on. He moved up to her face, looked deep into her eyes.

'Give me your tongue,' he said.

Sadie poked it out at him cheekily, retracting it just as he made a little lunge for it.

'Give me it. Just the tip.'

She extended her tongue slightly between her parted lips until it was just peeping out between her teeth. He ran his tongue around it, flicked it delicately, then sucked it gently, and her sharp intake of breath told him she knew exactly what he meant by it. Then, without his eyes leaving hers, he moved back down towards her breast. Using his chin to tantalisingly pull down the stretch fabric of her dress just a millimetre at a time, he bared her skin, lower and lower, stopping just before he reached her skimpy bra. The enticing mound rose towards his mouth as she panted, the curves exactly as he'd imagined they would be, hoped they would be.

'If only you knew how much I've been wanting to do this,' he whispered, as he darted his tongue below the laciness of her bra, down towards her achingly hard nipple. His tongue just skimmed the tip of it. She gasped. Pausing, barely touching, tantalising and teasing her, she bucked beneath him.

'If only you knew how much I've been *wanting you* to do that,' she replied.

So he did it again, with the other nipple this time, but still oh so slowly. He brought his head back up to her, pushed a tendril of hair back from her face, and kissed her lips softly and tenderly, as she caught her breath, then suddenly kissed her deeply, his tongue thrusting inside her mouth.

Sadie felt the overwhelming need to have him inside her, as he continued to make love to her mouth, and tease her with his tongue. She freed one of her hands – she couldn't resist – to caress his face, then his neck, shoulders, and down his back, feeling his rippling muscles hard beneath his shirt, his back tapering into a smaller waist. *Mmmm – runner's stomach, swimmer's arms, well-defined thighs –* the man certainly kept himself in good shape.

Her hand went down and down, found the rounded muscles of his rear, and caressed firmly, before moving around to the front. Rubbing up and down as she moved slowly across, nearer and nearer, but not quite touching the hard ridge beneath the zip, she thrilled at his reaction as his breathing sped up to match hers. He caught her hand again, just before she moved the final inch. *She hadn't lost her touch.*

'Sam, you're a tease,' he groaned, stopping her just in time. 'A stunning tease.' Then he raised her arm back up above her head. She tried to bring her lips up to his chest instead.

'Uh-uh!' he said, pushing her back down. 'You first, this is all about you.'

'You're a dream come true,' she said with a sigh, unable to remember the last time a guy had said that to her, and relaxed back onto the sofa, eyes closed, in rapture.

'Watch,' he whispered, and she opened them again.

Parting his lips, he lowered his head slowly, a wry smile quirking the corner of his mouth, his fingers nimbly pulling her dress down further, hungrily revealing her breasts still encased in their lacy prison, until her fullness was revealed for the first time.

'Beautiful.'

Cupping both in his hands, his tongue flickered from one side to the other. Not once did his eyes leave hers, deliberately making her watch what he was doing.

Driving her crazy was what he was doing.

Then he was done with teasing. He reached around and undid her bra, pulling her clothes looser for easy access. Then his mouth was upon her. Enveloping one nipple through the lace, he sucked her gently at first, then nipped slightly. She let out a little cry.

'Sorry, I hope they can't hear me on the Sunseeker!'

'I hope they can,' he said, mischievously. 'Bad girl,' he said, sucking her breast and again nipping her gently through the fabric.

Sadie cried out once more. He paused, and kneeled up over her.

'Getting hot in here, isn't it?' He smiled, and in one smooth movement, lifted his arms and pulled the white T-shirt off over his head, and paused, half-naked before her. Sadie just looked. And looked.

That afternoon on the boat, he was off limits. Now he was presenting himself for her pleasure. She scrutinised every inch of the body just a foot away, feasting her eyes upon the Adonis before her. *Utterly amazing.* She drank in every contour – well-defined pecs, six-pack stomach, big shoulders.

'I need to touch ...'

She brought her hands onto his chest, then downwards, but when she reached his waistband he wagged his forefinger at her. *No.* Obediently she put her arms back up over her head. Then he began his own more intimate exploration.

She wanted him. Her nipples – pert and hard in all their glory – gave away how much. She noticed how hard he had become and felt a thrill of satisfaction that she could be doing this to him. Then he upped the ante. Circling his thumbs across the lacy peaks, tormenting both, he lowered his head, his teasing gaze fixed on her face.

'Now, time for this to come down.'

He pulled her arms clear of her dress, then further and further he pushed the lace of her bra down until her nipple was completely clear, then her whole breast. Then the other, till her magnificence was completely on show. She felt exposed, but there was none of her usual self-consciousness – not in the hands of this guy. She could be proud of her ample bosom. Her dress pooled into an elaborate toga further down, around her belly, and she sighed with anticipation, his hands cradling her voluptuousness and his mouth so close she could feel his breath against her skin.

Then he teased her nipple till she writhed, drawing her breast into his mouth, and sucked and licked and nipped.

It felt so good – like he was pulling on the very soul of her. She clutched the back of his head, but he wanted to do it his way.

'Keep ... your arms ... *up*,' he said, taking his tantalising tongue towards the other breast, and repeating the process, even more slowly, even more hot.

By now, Sadie's breasts were well aroused, and she arched her back against his caresses as they intensified. Just as she thought she couldn't take any more, he stopped.

Suddenly his face was deadly serious, and his eyes had become deep dark pools, watching her intently. Sadie felt a flash of passion course through her veins, as he began trailing a path downwards towards her legs.

His hand slowly skimmed to her hemline, then he raised the dress further up. His fingers set her skin on fire, slowly circling around closer and closer towards her hot centre. She was moist, she was ready and she was yearning. Caressing her inner thigh, then upwards, teasing all the way, soon he'd pulled the dress up almost to her hips, and he looked down to feast his eyes upon matching black lace underwear.

Thank goodness she hadn't worn the big pants.

He shifted his body downwards. Her mound was clearly on show through the see-through lace, and Sadie wondered if it was obvious how wet she was already. She groaned and moved her hips slightly.

'Stay there, I like to … take my time,' he said.

Unable to move, restrained by a make-believe binding, she just relaxed and felt his fingers do the talking. Starting again at her knee, and then tracing a path upwards, they promised the most exquisite pleasure. Sadie tossed her head and moaned, but he refused to let her do anything but lie back and think of fingers – around the edges of her, above, below, across, electricity zapping through her body at every slight stroke, every light touch.

His face was now only inches from her warmth, and she felt his breath through the thin fabric of her panties as his mouth closed in on her. He shut his eyes as he brought his mouth down and exhaled through the fabric – a long, hot breath – directly onto her core.

'Ohhhh ...' She couldn't stop herself screaming a little, and writhed in pleasure beneath his touch, mouth open and eyes screwed tightly with passion, trying not to lose it completely.

'Sam, look at me,' he said.

As she opened her eyes, the sight that greeted her was his tongue tracing a path across the top of her panties from one side to the other, then down, across her thigh to the material now barely covering her pulsating centre. He licked his lips slightly as he looked at her, and slowly, teasingly, his tongue pushed the fabric into her folds. The roughness of the lace against her nub had her shuddering with pleasure. He did it again, harder this time, licking up and down along her creases, then sucking in earnest, her wetness seeping through and making him moan too.

'God, you taste so good.'

'Mac, what are you doing to me!'

'Told you – what I've wanted to do all day. And this ...' he whispered hoarsely, as he roughly pulled her pants aside, to gaze upon her quivering sex. 'Beautiful.'

His breath was hot on her skin and she bucked up towards him, groaning.

Then he gave her exactly what she wanted – his mouth touched her body, and she felt his hot tongue slip inside her. She struggled to keep herself still as he drove her crazy – kissing at first, and then sucking and nibbling.

She bucked, then her hands finally came down onto his head, gripping his hair, pushing him further into her. His tongue slid downwards, into her depths, and she cried out and lifted her hips to drive him deeper. Then he brought his thumb up to her throbbing peak and hastened her journey towards complete abandonment, while he kept on sucking then plunging his tongue deep, sucking then plunging, obviously loving the taste of her and moaning as she moved against him, his mouth, his tongue and his thumb.

I truly am in the hands of an expert, she thought.

Sadie was losing herself completely now, as he continued pleasuring her with his mouth.

Then he gave her a wicked half-smile as he inserted his two fingers inside her, and slowed the pace to an excruciating ecstasy. Every area became super-sensitive, and she watched him take all of her into his mouth, then start sucking, while flicking his tongue around her, sucking all the while, and stroking his fingers in and out. He seemed to unleash a connection to her soul, with these skilful movements, and those mesmerising eyes of his watching her, his body working in perfect unison with her body's needs.

Without the connection she felt to him, it would have been a pretty stunning session, but *with* this undeniable connection, she began to feel a little tremor, a quivery feeling deep inside, aware that a door was opening that she'd find hard to close again when it was all over. In that moment, she knew that all the other lovers she'd ever had were just a preliminary flirtation with real lovemaking, and this was finally, overwhelmingly, the real thing.

Before she could consider it further, she felt her body go into overdrive, racing to a crescendo, stoked by his artful motions, and she came in a shuddering wave that seemed to go on and on, as he stroked in and out, up and down, cradling her as she rose, then slowly fell back down to earth. Somewhere in the distance, someone was crying out in ecstasy, and she realised it was her.

Panting, Sadie gasped, breathless, 'Incredible. Absolutely incredible …'

A half-smile crossed his lips. His eyes were black with desire.

'God, you're so wet,' he said, sucking his fingers, and then inserting them back inside her slowly, tenderly and delicately as her body's spasms slowly subsided. One finger, then two, stroking against her gently, while he freed himself, with his other hand, then produced a small rustling packet. A few moments later, he was proudly erect before her, sheathed, and she gazed at him in awe.

Stunning. Utterly, utterly stunning.

'Are you ready for me now?' he asked.

'Now,' she replied, and realised she'd never wanted anyone more in her whole life. With a passion, she pulled him down on top of her, and with one smooth motion he was at the edge of her, their faces only inches apart, gazing deeply into each other's eyes as inch by inch he entered her, and their bodies became one.

'Ohhhh …' The feeling of being filled so completely, and finding a fit she never thought possible, took Sadie to a place where the gentle motion of the yacht ceased to exist. It was replaced by an urgency, a building flame, that made her feel alive and panicked that it'd all be over too soon. Passion overwhelmed her as he gained momentum, rising towards his own climax, and taking her with him.

Together they exploded, falling into the abyss, and hearing each other's cries of passion – distant, then coming nearer, until their breaths were synchronised, grounded once more, satiated, spent.

'That … was … incredible, absolutely incredible,' he said, echoing her words playfully, and kissing her once again full on the mouth, with a tenderness that took her breath away.

This didn't feel like a 'one night only'.

Stop it, Sadie, he probably has this effect on all the girls.

'You were amazing,' she replied, 'and this tongue …' she pulled it into her mouth as she kissed him deeply. 'This tongue should be licensed. It's dangerous.'

He smiled, warmly, and turned over, disposing of the evidence of their lovemaking into a nearby bin. Then he returned and laid his head on her breasts, his fingers entwining with hers, stroking her palm fondly.

For the longest time, neither spoke. It was as though no

words were needed, their bodies had connected so thoroughly and said all there was to say. For Sadie, whose other previous partners amounted to a couple of college fumbles or one-night stands, the errant husband and the last psycho ex, this felt like she'd always known it *should* feel.

And she'd only ever get this one night. *Dammit.*

Still, what a night.

Years ago, Sadie would have become upset at this point, dwelling on what might have been, mourning. But nowadays *this* Sadie was more worldly, more pragmatic. Besides, tonight she was Sam.

A wry smile curled at her lips, feeling very content and pleased with life. And it had got her through this evening without having to stress about tomorrow once. Staring at the ceiling, she was filled with a warmth, a buzzing happiness, the throbbing afterglow still bubbling through her body.

'Penny for them,' he said, raising his head.

'Nothing much, just … everything.' She smiled and bent down, placing a tender kiss on his nose. 'Mind-blowing.'

'I was, wasn't I?' he teased.

She smiled and stretched languorously. 'Not bad for a beginner.'

He laughed and reached up to kiss her lips.

'I've got to say I won't forget these in a hurry,' he said, tapping on her stiletto heels, still firmly in place on her feet, despite the rest of her attire being in a heap around her middle. She'd wondered why he'd insisted she put them back on again when they got into the salon after their tour.

'I haven't got the energy to reach down and take them off.'

'Don't – I like them. Even if I have got puncture marks on my bum.'

She laughed and snuggled down a little.

They lay there in silence for a time, semi-clothed on the cushions that were now on the floor. Sadie replayed the whole experience in her mind, biting her tongue in case she said anything more meaningful.

Mac was particularly intrigued by the emotions coursing through his veins. He'd reached his peak quickly – speedier than he'd known it for a long time. Which surprised him – she was obviously ringing bells inside him, this irresistible woman.

'It's pretty breathtaking, isn't it?' Sadie said after a time.

'Incredible, breathtaking, keep them coming.'

'No, I mean this boat.'

'Superyacht.'

'Superyacht.' She smiled, shaking her head. 'I mean, not just the size. Sure it's the biggest one I've ever experienced, but when you get below decks, it's magnificent too.'

'You sure you're not talking about me?' he joked.

She laughed and elbowed him. Back in familiar jovial territory. This felt safer.

'Whoever owns it has great taste. It's done out so well – in a sophisticated but understated elegance.'

'Have you swallowed that brochure?' he teased.

But she'd said it in genuine awe, and it made him fill with pride, taking it as a personal compliment. He nodded appreciatively and tenderly kissed her lips, then laid his head back, sighing and looking upwards.

'Just think, Mac,' she continued. 'How fabulous would it be to live a life like this. Can you imagine?'

'Em, I can … yes.'

'What's it called again?'

'A Ferretti Custom "blah blah" – you got it right earlier on.'

'Tell me.'

'A Custom Line 124 from Ferretti. Wait-list as long as your arm. It was a real buzz the day it was delivered.'

'You were here then?'

'Er, yes.'

'Bet the owner was overjoyed.'

'You could say that.'

'How it must feel to own something like this ... The likes of us, we only glimpse it – well, you more than me, you being around them all the time.'

Slightly phased, Mac just nodded.

She went on, 'But to have that kind of wealth – not to have to worry about money – ever. The daily grind, bills and all that. No problems, just cruising, in the lap of luxury.'

He wasn't replying.

'Just rescuing the odd handbag from the deep blue sea,' she said. 'Hey, maybe I'll hang around to see if the Captain will introduce me to the owner, eh?'

Ouch.

She was joking, he knew that, but he frowned. Both for deceiving her, and for the gut reaction of suspicion that he felt when she said those words. After all, he still didn't know her, not even her full name for goodness sake, and she could be playing him along.

But it all feels so genuine, so different from last time.

Mentally chastising himself for being cynical, he took a deep breath. Almost exactly at the same time, she did too.

'What a lovely life it would be. Ahhh, one day.' She sighed, and propped herself up against the opulent sofa, so his head rested on her tummy.

'Yes,' he agreed. 'One day. And one amazing night ...'

Her hands stroked the suede of the sofa, and the furry cushion, and she had a far-away look in her eyes.

Mac turned his face slightly so she couldn't see that his brow had furrowed, his eyes narrowed, and he bit his lip.

Should he own up?

If he wasn't leaving tomorrow, things might be different, but everything that had happened tonight had played out so successfully – possibly *because* they'd kept it all so anonymous. And anyway she'd practically insisted. Maybe she had a partner already? He didn't think so, but you never know with some women. Which type was she? He'd probably never find out.

And it had been a good night. To confess right now would break the spell.

'Too bad we couldn't have made it two nights, but I'm due back in London tomorrow,' she said.

That decides that one. She's obviously making a point. One night it is then. Better she leaves without feeling fooled.

Or worse, feeling hopeful.

She was probably no gold-digger, but better to avoid the awkward last-minute confession and all the complications that would bring. They'd only been on the yacht about half an hour and were already fast approaching the deadline she'd mentioned for her departure. Would it be different if she knew who he was? He hoped not.

She'd fantasised about meeting the owner of this sixty million pound baby – little did she know she'd just slept with him.

'Of course,' she went on, filling Mac's silence, and coming back from that far-away place, 'the high life would be all very well, but it wouldn't mean as much without someone to love – you know, to share it all with.'

'Now where did that come from?' He sat up beside her and pulled her to him and kissed the side of her head. 'You're not going to get all soppy on me now are you, Samantha?'

She frowned and looked away. 'Sorry, did I say that out loud?' She forced a smile. 'Guess it's a while since I've felt this relaxed. You know what I mean though, don't you? After all, this is great, and I'm so glad we got to know each other better, and you are pretty gorgeous.' He was smiling and nodding, waving his hand as if to say 'carry on', so she did. 'And amazing in bed. Incredible, actually. But this place – it's a fairy tale isn't it? Hey, it's the sort of place you'd go for a honeymoon.'

'You can rent it out for honeymoons as it happens.'

'Can I? Are you offering?'

He laughed, but said nothing.

'Gosh, just imagine it, having this to share with someone special,' she said. He didn't answer, so she looked up at him. 'Or maybe, since you've gone all quiet ...' she bit her lip, '... maybe you've secretly already got someone?'

Talk about great minds think alike.

'Hey, we're not supposed to discuss things like that, remember?' He tickled her playfully.

She responded by throwing a cushion on his head. He threw it off and turned over to face her.

'As a matter of fact, I do have someone, right now.'

She looked alarmed.

'*You*! So, thank you, Sam.' He smiled up at her from under his brow and was hit with the sudden realisation that he really meant it. 'Thank you for sharing all this with me.'

Well, it made a change to have 'undercover' sex.

But then, so much about this encounter was different. By now, the old Mac would have been making excuses about having to say goodbye, not willing to hear yet another thrilling post-coital monologue about designer shopping trips and invites to shallow celebrity parties. *Early start, I'll call you* ... and the woman would be sent on her way out the door, panties in hand.

But with this beautiful, ingenuous woman, it felt different, very different. He was eager to hear her opinions, to impress her. And she seemed genuinely fascinated by what he had to say, with no ulterior motives. None. It felt good – more valuable somehow.

And there was, no doubt about it, a connection between them. He'd felt it when she first walked by, and he felt it again now, with her golden tresses flowing over her bare shoulders, lying in his arms, like ... like she belonged here.

He shook himself.

Coming down from a cloud, he thought, *that's all this is. No doubt my body really needed this. I've been working too hard.*

But he liked seeing her reaction to his decor and his floating home – though for the life of him he couldn't work out why it should matter so much that she approved.

He had to really fight off the urge to show it to her some more.

Sadie broke the spell with a question, seemingly trying to keep it chatty – perhaps she sensed the change, sensed there was something awry.

'So, in another life,' she asked, '*would* you want to be rich and famous? And actually own something like this?'

'Is this a test?'

'No, silly, it's "let's play make-believe".'

'Oh, *make-believe*! Famous? No, never. Seen enough of the problems that can cause. Rich? Well, in that case, yes I could probably force myself to spend a summer or two cruising round the world – till the novelty wore off.'

'Hmm … Would it ever wear off?'

'Well, it'd depend on what you did the rest of the time. If you were feeding orphans and adopting chimpanzees, shall we say, then two summers off would be fine,' he said.

'Escaping from the world – doing rich guy things, like swimming with dolphins, fending off pirates …'

'… finding Atlantis …'

She turned to him and raised an eyebrow. 'Now you're being silly!'

'You're the one that said make-believe! But to answer you seriously, yes, that's the clichéd life everybody would love, isn't it?'

'Actually, do you know what?' She looked thoughtful. 'Come to think of it, no. Not really. I honestly don't think I would.'

'No?'

'No. This floating palace is breathtaking for sure, but just think of the upkeep. And what you could do with all that money instead. If you could afford this, think of all those other charities you could help out, not just orphans and chimps. What about scientific studies – research for the greater good.'

It was Mac's turn to raise an eyebrow.

'No,' she went on, 'I think sailing into the sunset once or twice a year would be quite enough – that would keep it really special.'

'Oh, okay, just once or twice a year, eh? Well, I'll see what I can do.'

'Thank you. Wouldn't want to get spoilt. Too much of a good thing and all that? And let's face it, this is not a real home, is it?'

Mac furrowed his brow, just a little. 'I suppose not.'

'And what if I – if a person – had a family,' she went on. 'Kids don't exactly fit in to a superyacht lifestyle, do they?'

'Oh, I don't know, any little rug-rats could always be banished to the poop deck. They'd fit quite nicely in there.'

'Ha-ha. But you don't have a poop deck.'

'I'd build one especially for the rug-rats.'

'Well, don't do so on my account. I wouldn't need one,' she said.

'No crèche, no playpen?'

She shook her head.

Ahh, no rug-rats, he thought. 'Okay, just as well. The *Nomad* is actually used for business a lot.'

'Ahh, business.' Sadie's face came over all reflective for a moment. 'Kids and business don't mix very well.'

Never a truer word, thought Mac. 'Ain't that the truth.'

'And anyway, Mister Deckhand, shows how much you know, 'cos it's not a poop deck, anyway, it's a fly bridge.'

'Oo-ooo! So you *have* swallowed that brochure!'

'No, you can thank Mr Sunseeker for that little nugget.' She laughed.

'He'll be celebrating tonight,' Mac said, leaning over and playing with a tendril of her hair. 'I hear it was sold to a movie star this afternoon.'

'Oh, really?'

'*And* his wife, before you start wanting an introduction to him, too!'

'Cheeky! What kind of a girl do you take me for?'

'This kind,' he said, and pushed her back on her elbows, raised her knees in the air.

'Again?'

'Oh, yeah.'

'I thought you'd never ask.'

'I don't usually ask.'

He came up for a hot passionate kiss, before resting his finger on her bottom lip and, smiling devilishly, slid back downwards, grazing his thigh on her heels.

'Oops, sorry! Shoes off?' she asked.

'Oh, no, shoes on,' he replied, and she moaned, gasping as he buried his face in her wetness, making her throw her head back. Nuzzling, and thrusting his tongue inside her, he looked up from between her legs. 'Definitely shoes on.'

Sucking and kissing her, using his fingers and tongue, he explored every inch of her, as she pulled at his hair and writhed beneath him. Mac found himself delighting in her responses to his every touch, and found that he was even more keen on pleasing her than before. Then he felt the telltale tension and heard the change in her breathing as another earth-shattering orgasm washed over her.

She was speechless, breathless, and just flopped herself back onto the cushions.

He was hard again, but he saw her sneak a look at her watch.

'Would you like a drink before you have to leave?' he asked.

'I could murder a hot chocolate. It's my only vice.'

'Mine too. With cream on top.' He chuckled.

'Yes, and stroodles.'

'Stroodles?' he asked, getting up.

'Yes,' she said, 'curly chocolate shavings – much posher than cheap old chocolate shaker stuff!'

He laughed. 'You do like a taste of the high life, don't you! Sadly there's none available "Chez Mac", unless we wait for chef to come back, or you help me find my way around the galley kitchen. Otherwise … I could get us both a whisky instead?'

She shook her head and smiled. 'You're going to get told off for taking advantage while the Captain's not here!'

'Well, while the Cap'ns away, the mouse will play …'

'Ha-ha, funny man! And bringing strange women on board! He'll have you cleaning the silver when he gets back!'

'Me? Never! He lets me do what I like.'

Well, at least that bit was true.

'Yes, okay then, but I'd prefer a Bailey's if you've got one, with ice, please, waiter.'

Mac draped a tea towel over his arm, and another one comically around his middle and walked towards the elaborate bar in the corner of the lounge. Sam gazed in wonderment and followed him over. She marvelled at the half-dressed Adonis before her, and resisted giving him more compliments about his incredible toned body. She adjusted her clothing slightly to make her own shape as alluring as possible. Some kind of makeshift toga – *yeh, that'll do for now.*

'I think you're really lucky having the run of the place,' she said. 'He's a good boss, isn't he, the Captain? My last boss was a nightmare. That's why I started up on my own, I guess. Easier to keep a grip on things when you're in charge.'

'Are you hard to control then, Sam?' Mac winked, cracking open some ice from the dispenser. A small piece escaped, and he picked it up in his fingers and seductively licked it then offered it to her. Her heartbeat went up a notch.

'Depends on what I'm being asked to do,' she said, rising up on tiptoe to reach the ice. He traced it around her lips slowly as she held her mouth open for him. The dripping cube felt exotic against her full lips, still swollen from kissing him.

'That depends on what's on the menu,' he said, circling the ice around her top then bottom lips.

Sadie sucked the cube into her mouth completely, and then suddenly crunched it, looking up at him wickedly. 'The menu depends on who's doing the choosing.'

In response, he kissed her passionately, her mouth cool, his tongue hot. She melted too, her knees feeling weaker by the minute.

Then Mac ended abruptly and leaned back against the bar. He took another ice cube into his mouth. 'What if *I'm* doing the ordering? What's on *my* menu, Sam?'

Things were getting intense again, and Sadie felt strong emotions stirring in the pit of her stomach. And not just sexual ones. *Oh-oh.*

The passion tonight had taken her by surprise and it wasn't just because it marked the end of a considerable drought. For her own sanity, she knew it was vital now to stay on the right side of the line. *Keep it simple, Sadie, keep the emotions at bay.*

'On your menu? I'd say pretty much anything – a complete smorgasbord if I'm asked nicely. After all, sometimes – just sometimes – I'm quite easy to control.' She raised an eyebrow and smirked.

'Ooooh, there's a thought,' he said as she took her drink. 'Don't start me off again. "Control"… you … Mmmmm,' he said, bringing himself up to his full height and pushing up against her slightly.

'And sometimes,' she purred, taking a sip and placing her

drink down on the counter. 'Sometimes I can't help myself.' She relieved him of his glass then forced his hands behind his back. 'Sometimes I just have to be the dominant one.'

She leaned into his hard body, forcing it up against the bar, feeling his arousal stirring again below her, and reached up on tiptoe to kiss him deeply. He tasted of sex, and whisky. Then, without saying a word, she put another ice cube into her mouth, and crunched it. He did a theatrical flinch.

With her cold mouth she licked his nipples, and chest. He leant back and groaned. Then she pulled his arms behind his back more tightly, while her other hand came round to the front. She held him, long and hard, freeing him from the fabric that imprisoned him, and stroked up and down while she reached up and her tongue explored his mouth. It was hot, and he hungrily kissed her back.

'Your turn,' she said. 'This time it's all about you.'

Suddenly there was a noise from outside.

'Shit,' she said as he moved quickly away from her.

Footsteps – several of them – walking swiftly along the wooden deck towards the steps that led in their direction.

'Shit,' Mac echoed, and Sadie knew her magical evening was about to end. At least Cinderella had the clock striking to warn her.

Straightening themselves up, Mac hesitated, then seemed to make up his mind that it would be best if they weren't seen. *Oh God – is he going to get in trouble? Or maybe ... maybe he's ashamed?*

'This way,' he whispered, and grabbing their things, he led her through another door and through the galley to the other side of the deck where they dressed on the run, in the darkened recesses, helping each other do up buttons, and stealing kisses in between carefully avoiding the returning crew. Suppressing giggles, Sadie went to speak but Mac hushed her with a finger on her lips. They ducked behind some loungers just as Mario sprinted up the gangplank with two big bottles of champagne under his arms. When the coast was clear, Mac turned Sadie towards him for one last, lingering kiss, and pretty soon they were back on the jetty, half-walking, half-jogging along till they reached the street. Sadie hailed a passing taxi, and turned to face Mac, wondering what would happen next.

The answer was a pause.

A long pause.

But he said nothing.

Absolutely nothing.

In that moment she knew it was all over.

Okay, brave face time, thought Sadie.

'I guess this is goodbye,' she said, plastering on a grin. *He must want a clean exit, otherwise he'd have said something by now. Given some sort of indication.* 'Thanks for a lovely evening, and for showing me round your super-boat.'

He smiled. 'It's been a pleasure.'

For the longest time he seemed torn, looking down at her big green eyes, and playing with one of her blonde tresses. The look on his face drew her in, entrancing her and she caught her breath. Time stood still, and for a split second, Sadie's heart leapt as she thought this might not be the end after all, right here, right now.

But after several heart-stopping moments, he just leaned down for the most tender, loving, delicate kiss she'd ever experienced, melting her soul. A powerful bolt of emotion sliced through her from her stomach to her toes and turned her legs to jelly.

Then he kissed her on her nose, and on both of her eyelids. She felt a tear prickling but she shook it off, forcing a smile.

Then, looking deep into his eyes, instead of going back in for a final passionate lip-lock, she flittered feather-light kisses over his lips ... and jawline ... and cheeks ... and chin. He inhaled and shut his eyes and she kissed those too.

'Well, as they say, thanks for "having me".' She laughed, breaking the tension.

'Look after yourself, Samantha Businesswoman.'

'Bon voyage, Mac.' And with one last, brief kiss, she was gone.

The taxi pulled away and she waved back at him through the rear window. He ran his fingers over his jawline and watched. As she disappeared into the distance, Mac almost found himself chasing after the cab, to – what? – explain? Get another kiss? Take her back for another session? Tell her everything? He didn't know. He shook himself and turned to trudge back towards the jetty. The walk down the cobblestones had never been longer. He stood at the edge of the gangplank, by the railings, watching the seawater slap up against the hull.

What a woman.

She hadn't hinted, hadn't whined, hadn't fluttered her eyelashes and said how nice it would be to see him again. Hadn't offered her contact details, hadn't tried to make him feel bad on parting. God, it was so long since he'd been in that situation, he'd completely forgotten his initiative.

But there must be a reason why she didn't want to see him again. One he may not want to find out.

And a man had his pride. If he had asked for her number, she would have turned him down, he knew it.

Wouldn't she?

Would tonight be a night to remember, or a decision to regret, he wondered. *In more ways than one.* Puzzled, Mac stared at the shore. He'd only experienced one other person so willing to walk away from him. Perhaps she did have a secret after all.

A heavy slap on the back brought him back to the present with a jolt.

'Here, matey, this'll make you feel better,' Captain

Wiltshire said, and he thrust a bottle of whisky into Mac's stomach. 'Present from Mimi.'

'Thanks, but I'll take a rain check. I've got some serious training to do in the morning.'

'Well, yes, your technique's not what it used to be. Must be rough, being threatened by all those young bloods.'

'I keep telling you those young bloods don't bother me. If I finish in the top one hundred I'll be happy.'

'No, you won't.'

'Okay, top fifty.'

'No, you won't.'

'Top ten?'

'Hah. Top ten? Good luck with that one. It's an Ironman. If it was "tinman" you might have a chance,' the Captain bellowed, pleased with himself.

'I'll still be out there bright and early tomorrow morning,' Mac replied.

'Well, you'd better be. I don't want to miss our slot to leave the harbour again, even if you do talk the authorities round, like you did last time. Bloody millionaires.'

'Billionaires, Jimmy boy, billionaires.'

'Billionaires shmillionaires! It's only money, Mac, my boy, and you know what they say …'

Mac joined in, chorusing the last line together. '… *The last suit you wear doesn't need pockets.*' Mac shook his head and smiled at the old sea dog.

With a hearty hug and a slow meander back on board, Mac was regaled with the story of that night's antics between one of the crew and Melissa the Aussie barmaid. But had anyone asked him to retell the story, Mac couldn't have remembered a thing. He was cast adrift, lost in his own little faraway world.

Back in the hotel, Sadie found herself unable to think straight, caught up in her conflicting emotions. She fought back the tears, rationalising everything.

It *had been* just one night. She'd always known that. So no point being upset. Focus on the good side. *Was there a good side?* Okay ... how about not having to own up to lying? She found she was surprisingly relieved about that, partly due to having avoided a very awkward conversation about her real name, and partly due to managing to get back to the hotel on time. And partly because she could finally stop holding her belly in.

But above all, there was no denying, she couldn't stop herself having that old familiar sinking feeling. Soon, the wonderful night would be nothing but a memory.

But what a memory.

Sadie smiled dreamily as she took off her make-up in front of the mirror. She too was in her own little faraway world. A world where Mac was on her arm, in her bed and in her life. She allowed herself precisely ten minutes of 'dwelling' then shook herself.

He worked on a boat, for goodness sake. Travelled the world. His life was hardly jet-setting glamorous, but it was full of variety.

Her world was ordinary, full of responsibility and routine. And children.

Men are all the same, she thought, *and he probably has that effect on all the girls.*

But as she settled down to sleep, somewhere deep down inside, a little voice disagreed.

Chapter Five

Sadie knew she'd be late. For the first time in fifteen years, she knew she'd be late.

Why couldn't she have just got going this morning, like she always did, instead of lying in bed, turning over her emotions in her head? The cynic inside her had surfaced with the type of vengeance that only a 'morning after' alone in bed can bring. We've all seen *Bridesmaids*.

He's moved on by now … set sail to the next girl in the next port … didn't ask for a number … didn't want to follow up …

It really was a *one night only*, her traitorous brain kept echoing, *one night only*, *one night only* – chanting the song from the film over and over in her mind. She swung between feeling miffed at how it ended, and thrilled at how it began.

She pressed a final 'eject' button in her mind, and finished getting ready just as the phone in the room rang. Her heart leapt, till she remembered she hadn't swapped surnames, let alone phone numbers.

'Oh, hi, Mum,' she said. It was a quick good luck call from home and she explained about her lack of mobile, promised to get a replacement soon, and to ring with an update as soon as the meeting was over. Then she made her way out the door, with a spring in her step, and her heart in her throat.

Out in reception the queue to leave her luggage at the concierge desk had delayed her by another two minutes, and now as she crossed the road to the swanky hotel opposite for her first ever grown-up investor meeting – *'potential' investor meeting, pardon me* – she'd never been more nervous in all her life.

She'd have run, but that'd be a physical impossibility right now. Whatever made her think it was a good idea to wear the high heels again?

Yes, tall people were more successful in business, but wasn't that just for men? She should have left the 'fuck me' shoes back in the 'lose me' suitcase, but when she'd woken up this morning and seen them, memories of last night had rippled through her, making her feel alive and confident again – after all, they'd been wrapped around Mac's hips not ten hours ago.

Focus!

Straightening her slightly-dated, over-tight but elegant designer skirt suit for the fiftieth time, and breathing through the restrictions of the slimming pants below, she inhaled deeply and asked for her floor. The operator in the smartest lift in town nodded his head politely to her and the other two occupants – an older lady and her younger husband, who was ogling Sadie's backside until the wife slapped his wrist.

Ping. 'Cinquième étage. Fifth floor.' The operator brought the lift, complete with its elaborate wall dressing of fresh flowers – *fresh flowers, in a lift?* – to a halt.

Stepping out Sadie looked up and down the conference floor, smelling the fresh floral fragrance of a hundred huge lilies on the table opposite. She tottered over to register at the business desk nearby, where a snooty-looking receptionist held up a finger while she spoke on the phone. It was in French but Sadie knew it was about her.

'Miss Turner?' she asked.

'It's Ms, actually.'

'Mr Anderson and his associates will join you soon. Please be seated.' The receptionist spoke haughtily with just a hint of a French accent, and waved her to a seat nearby.

Sadie couldn't believe her luck – she was the first one there. She wasn't late. No keeping the investor – *potential* investor – waiting. Thank heavens.

Being on time might be one of my *'things', but it obviously isn't one of his.*

She sat down in an oversized, richly-upholstered chair,

her feet not quite reaching the floor. Her suit – the same one from yesterday but given a good steaming with the travel iron this morning – felt like a straitjacket and she squirmed, adjusting her bra strap. She felt like a kid waiting to see the headmaster.

This guy must live the high life, choosing a place like this for a one-hour nine a.m. meeting. *What was his latest megabucks deal worth?* Sadie tried to remember.

She sighed and drummed her fingers on the side of her leather briefcase, thinking. Attila the Receptionist sent her a look that could kill. Smiling sheepishly in apology, Sadie opened her case to review her notes. She took out a wad of papers – research, printouts and handwritten pages of scribbles – she loved to prep thoroughly, geeky nerd that she was, and never threw anything away until she was sure she wouldn't need it.

She separated a couple of particularly tatty scraps and put them into the bin next to her – or maybe it was some antique umbrella stand ornament – whatever. Then she re-read her initial contact letter from the advisor. It was gnarled at the edges having been pored over so often by Sadie in the past few days.

As well as a trip to Hawaii, as part of her prize for winning the marketing award, she'd been given an in-depth company health check with an expert. She scanned through his introduction email and looked again at the jazzy business card.

Simon Leadbetter. Business Advisor and Chief Financial Officer for Michael Christopher Anderson (MCA) Associates. It was as official sounding as he'd looked in his three-piece grey suit: dapper, impressive, almost smelling of money. If money had a smell. Damn sure Sadie had had a cold for the last couple of years if so, there was so little of it around in her life. The card was embossed, platinum lettering. She fingered it and bit her lip.

Their track record of successful ventures read like a *Sunday Times* Top 100 list. Sadie felt a reassuring wave of calm remembering the encouragement from the older man. Simon had been a true breath of fresh air, and had taken Sadie under his wing somewhat. Even though her prize was for just one session, he'd given more. She made him laugh, a rare thing for Simon, and he'd been impressed with the way she ran her store. And with the neatness of her accounts. He'd even let her tease him about being a workaholic and she smiled, recalling his jokey reply that the boss needed someone to look after him, always had done. There had been a protective look on his face as he said it, which quickly vanished before he pronounced that the love of a good woman was the biggest prize of all – but the right woman. There was obviously a story there, but he refused to be drawn on it. Sadie wondered if Simon had been married or had children but he'd changed the subject any time she got too close for comfort. Then he'd bid her bon voyage and if she wasn't mistaken, there was a hint of that same look on his face when he wished her good luck at the awards.

When she'd rung him from Hawaii buzzing with news of her success and the once in a lifetime business opportunity, he hadn't even seemed that surprised that she'd achieved it – it was a lovely moment for Sadie. To have someone like him have such confidence in her. He was the only person she'd *needed* to call, as he whipped into motion once he heard about the thirty day deadline.

Was it complete pie in the sky – albeit organic, gluten-free pie – to imagine it was even possible to tie up a deal like this within a month? Simon had been straight on the phone and it turned out destiny leant a hand once again – MCA's boss, Michael Anderson himself, had actually just come across the product at a sports event, where he was told how it was helping some athletes achieve personal bests. And, yes, he would be interested to take a meeting. And, yes, if he had to, he could work fast. He'd definitely have to if Sadie was to beat the thirty day deadline. It was now day six. No time to waste.

Simon had even given her presentation the once over before she left for Monaco. Then, in true Fairy Godmother fashion, he warned Sadie it now all rested on *whether Mr Anderson liked her.* He was very much a gut-instinct kind of investor, apparently, *and if anyone can do it, Mr Anderson can. If he feels he can trust you, he can trust the deal.*

Simon's team dug deep and vetted the deal fully too, and it must have passed, otherwise it would have never reached Mr Anderson's desk.

Okay, well it takes one to know one. She'd researched him too.

But despite her attempts to Google him, doing a background check on this elusive Michael Anderson was more difficult than she'd expected. There were all the usual company standard profiles, but very little other detail online, despite several hours on the laptop while 'bonding-with-kids-via-teenage-TV'. Her older daughter, Abi, had even helped her on the Internet, her profile picture looking identical to Sadie's in the photo Georgia had taken of them with their noses in their laptops. Georgia, on the other hand, had the red hair of Sadie's mum, Grace, and the temper to match.

Simon was right, though – the mega-rich must have ways of protecting their profiles. She'd only found a few that weren't group photos with countless diverse females draped on his arms. All with sunglasses, very slick, rich and prickly looking poses, and worlds away from Sadie's life. Couldn't even tell his age. Never mind. Would he like her? That's what mattered.

The enormity of what she was getting herself involved in hit her as she sat there looking up and down the imposing, and still empty corridor. She suddenly felt so nervous she thought she'd implode. *Would it work? Would he hate her?*

Would they be in time? The life-saving commission on offer was so close she could taste it – she'd visualised receiving it – but the doubts were creeping in.

Come on, Sadie, me girl, don't lose it now. You make your own luck.

She only hoped they'd speed up the 'cursory due diligence procedures and usual protracted contract negotiations' Simon had mentioned in his verbose manner. It would be touch and go. Assuming the boss wanted in. *Oh God, please let him want in. Let him like me, let him like me, let him like me.*

Seconds ticked by as Sadie waited, not calmed at all by the occasional superior look from the receptionist. With every passing minute, her anxiety went up tenfold. She was feeling a little hot, and fanned herself with the presentation folder. She would ask for some water but felt sure the robotic woman typing rhythmically behind the desk didn't drink, eat or breathe so would frown upon her even more.

Sadie eyed up the bottle of Frish inside her bag. It was tempting. *No, it's my last one.* Plus she'd had a headache pill before she left the hotel and there was some small print in the literature about the water which made her not want to risk it just in case what they said about it was true. So she just visited the ladies room across the hall in search of water. Stepping inside, an icy blast of air conditioning met her, and she shivered, just as the lift doors opened and a smartly suited man and a small entourage stepped out towards the reception desk.

'This way, Mr Anderson,' said one of the hotel staff, fussing around him. Sadie wheeled around and peeked back out through the closing ladies room door, but couldn't see much, just a designer suit disappearing into the conference room followed by several others.

She quickly finished and re-emerged. A condescending nod from Frosty Felicité on reception meant it was time to make an entrance. Sadie straightened her skirt, smoothed her hair, took the deepest breath she could, and opened the door. It was one of those pivotal moments after which life was never the same again. For Sadie it would be forever imprinted on her mind with the smell of lilies and leather chairs.

Inside the Napoleon Room, Simon Leadbetter stood up from his seat at the head of a large shiny oak table, and greeted her warmly. Freshly-brewed coffee and sweetness filled the air, and a slight buzz of conversation from the other people busying themselves around the room made her entrance less daunting. So far so good.

'Sadie! How lovely to see you. Mr Anderson's just had to step into the anteroom to take an urgent call from his business partner, he'll be with us soon. Good night last night?'

'What?'

'Was the hotel to your liking?'

'Oh, er, yes, lovely, thanks. Lovely hotel.'

'Breakfast okay? Did they look after you?'

'Lovely.' *Just don't ask me what I had.* She'd been too nervous – and too late – to eat any. 'Lovely, thank you so much.'

Lovely? Lovely? Is that all you can manage? Oh goodness, girl, get your brain in gear or they'll be getting a refund on their hour-long room booking, it'll be over so soon.

Simon talked about the weather, her journey over, and the lack of time in Mr Anderson's busy schedule.

'He's flying straight out to yet another sporting event in an hour or so – so do *make every second count.*'

Sadie swallowed. Then nodded. If she wasn't mistaken, even Simon seemed a little nervous.

Her presentation was already being projected into the back wall. Simon had also brought some hard copies, freshly bound, sitting in a neat pile in the middle of the table.

He signalled towards an assistant who was setting up the

laptop and projector. The menu for the presentation came up on the screen, then the front cover. For good measure and because of another paragraph in the small print about jet lag, she'd added a picture of a plane to the images of sports people, celebrities and a hospital patient. She hoped it wasn't too over the top but Simon had said the more eye-catching the better. And if the research proved it to be true, it would be the fastest hydrating water in the world. Big bucks ahead, indeed. *If* the science stacked up.

The lines she'd rehearsed a thousand times went over and over in her mind as it reached overdrive and went skywards. She sipped water through dry lips from the glass someone had kindly put in front of her.

The flunkies were scattered around the room talking in hushed tones, variously rearranging expensive cookies into perfectly straight lines on the silver platter, flicking through documents, tapping at their phones, pouring richly whipped hot chocolate from silver pots into designer porcelain cups, or discussing the information on each other's laptops. One was less flunky and more floozy, giving Sadie dark looks which brightened into a smile when Sadie fully glanced her way. Who was she?

Simon beckoned Sadie over for some introductions.

'Derek and Graham, business analysts.'

'Nice to meet you, Miss Turner.'

'It's *Ms* Turner, Graham,' Simon said.

'Oh, sorry. *Ms* Turner.'

Sadie laughed louder than she'd intended and shook hands with these two younger, geeky looking guys, and then with a few others. The small talk wasn't exactly taxing but her tongue was numb and she felt a little headachy with her tight skirt stopping her breathing properly. She straightened it self-consciously when the next person was introduced to her. The floozy – a particularly nubile-looking young blonde in expensive Gucci – shook her hand.

'I'm Alexis,' she said as if Sadie should know who she was.

'Hi, I'm Sadie,' Sadie said, and immediately felt stupid.

'Oh, I know who *you* are,' Alexis replied. A shudder of dislike emanated from the woman even though her smile stayed fixed. Take away the notebook and the glasses perched on top of her head and she could just as easily grace the pages of *Sports Illustrated*. She looked at Sadie with slight curiosity, eyeing up her navy business suit and shoes.

Oh God, where are my sensible pumps when I need them ...

'Nice to meet you. Quite a coup you have on your hands here,' she said in a West Coast American accent, suddenly beaming again. 'Congratulations for landing the investment of the decade. Mr Anderson will be very pleased.' The girl smiled, opaquely. 'Assuming you can pull it off in time.'

Sadie scrutinised her, but the handshake was strong, and her face was confident. *Staking her territory,* Sadie wondered? But Alexis would have nothing to worry about from Sadie in that department – stealing a billionaire away from someone with *those* looks would be as likely for Sadie as ... well, as ever seeing Mac again.

Damn that man, get out of my head, she told herself, watching the blonde deliberately sashay away, to start distributing the hard copies of the presentation around the top of the table. Sadie hardly registered the names of the other people Simon was introducing.

'That's nearly everyone,' Simon said. 'Unless BJ McKowski deigns to join us – that's Mr Anderson's occasional co-investor. Bit of a character, I'm afraid, but pay no heed. Mr Anderson likes to spread his risk, and BJ's capital is as beneficial as any.'

'Spread his risk?'

'Yes, the mega-rich often do this – much of it is like toy money to them, so they play games with each other – politics about whom to include on the latest "get richer quick" deal they're working on. In this instance, Mr Anderson picked BJ, probably because of the undue influence of Alexis over there.' Simon nodded his head towards the blonde, who was eyeing them from a distance. If Sadie wasn't mistaken, she was scowling.

'Who is she again?'

'Oh, it looks like they're nearly ready,' he said, either not hearing or ignoring her question. 'I'll go check on their progress. Just relax, and ... good luck!' Simon touched her on the arm, then left, taking time on his way out to rotate a large apple in the fruit bowl on a side table so the reddest side showed outwards.

Sadie was so nervous she didn't know what to do with herself.

She breathed deeply, and closed her eyes, looking in her bag for a top up to her lipstick, as everyone took their places around the large table. She stretched down and took out the weighty glass trophy and lifted it. As she did so, she felt a tiny *rip* in the zip of her skirt. *Oh no.* Sadie sat up, looking around her, but no one had noticed. No one except Alexis, who smiled again then nodded her head slightly.

Sadie put the award pride of place where everyone could see it – and she could hide behind it if her skirt demanded it – slap bang in front of her on the table. She whispered some words of encouragement to herself and gave it a little rub for luck.

Suddenly she was aware of a silence that had fallen and a complete change in the atmosphere – a reverence was sweeping around the room as everyone looked in one direction. She followed their eyes. As the door to the anteroom swung open, a smart, tanned, older man who looked a bit like Father Christmas stepped into the room. Not what she was expecting at all – he'd obviously not weathered well. *Still, that's the man I need to impress,* she thought, studying him. Older than his photos, well, the white beard didn't help, but with an unmistakeable air of affluence – chunky gold chains and rings, a huge watch, and an expensive designer suit. *Didn't expect the cowboy hat, but the über rich are a law unto themselves.*

Sadie cleared her throat and stood up.

Then, to her utter surprise, into the room behind him stepped ... *What? Surely it can't be ...*

Oh dear God, what on earth was Mac doing here?

Chapter Six

Mac?

As in McKowski? The business partner?

Sadie felt sick.

Mac looked … well … amazing, having shaved and dressed in an immaculate suit. Taller somehow, but just as attractive, and a definite air of confidence. Her heartbeat went stratospheric. She hardly recognised him at first, cleanly shaven and hair groomed, with designer glasses on his head. But that telltale half-smile was there, and that stance, that confident posture. He was shaking Simon's hand warmly, leaning in to whisper something. Then, turning, he stopped dead.

If anyone ever looked as though they'd been hit between the eyes with a slingshot, Mac did, right now. He did a double take as he spotted Sadie. His eyebrows shot up almost to his hairline, then down again, his eyes narrowing suspiciously, before he regained his composure. All in an instant.

She walked over to greet Simon and the investor, glancing sideways at Mac to give him a quizzical look when he made no move to show he knew her. With just a heartbeat's hesitation, Sadie smiled her biggest smile at the small group.

'Gentlemen, meet Ms Sadie Turner,' said Simon.

'Mr Anderson,' said Sadie. She took the hand of the older guy first, glad of his firm grip since her own hand was shaking so much.

'Sadie, this is BJ McKowski,' Simon continued, and Sadie turned towards Mac, the flush in her cheeks and the glare in her eyes hopefully warning him against any sudden confessions.

'Nice to meet you, Mr McKowski,' she said to a bemused Mac, letting go of the older man's warm hand and going to take Mac's. Simon coughed, and gestured towards Mac.

'Ahem. No, *this* is not Mr McKowski, this is Mr *Anderson*, Sadie.'

'Oh.' *OMG.* She'd never heard her voice sound so small. 'This is Mr *Anderson*?'

Simon continued unabated. 'Mr Anderson, this is the instigator of your latest business opportunity, Ms Sadie Turner.'

Sadie shook his hand, her fingers suddenly completely numb. Her potential investor, the man who could make her business dreams come true was there before her, looking at her with somewhat confused eyes. *The same azure-blue eyes that had gazed up from between her legs not ten hours ago.*

She was still shaking his hand in bewilderment. For a moment, no one spoke and a flicker of confusion crossed Simon's face. He looked at Mac, curiously, then Mac spoke.

'Sam.'

'Sadie,' she said. 'Not Sam.'

'Not Sam.'

'No. It's … Sadie.' She gulped, her hand still firmly in his grip. 'My middle name's Sam.'

'Oh, easy mistake to make,' he said, looking directly into her eyes, without blinking.

'Pleasure to *meet* you, Mr *Anderson*,' she managed.

'The pleasure's all mine.' His face had become impenetrable as he finally released her hand.

Whatever's happening, someone had better let me in on it double quick, Sadie thought, fighting to control her urge to ask him a) what the hell was going on, b) whether she was the victim of some elaborate set up and c) why he moonlighted on big boats fixing small engine parts.

But there were no cameras, and no one had batted an eyelid so Sadie snapped herself out of it. Too much was at stake.

'No, I can assure you,' she said, playing along, 'it's an honour and it's all mine. Thank you so much for taking the meeting at such short notice. Simon tells me you have a very busy schedule.'

'Mac was in town anyway for the racing – he loves fast cars ... and fast women!' BJ McKowski laughed and slapped Mac on the back. 'But don't worry – you're safe. He never mixes business with pleasure!'

Mac winced. Sadie frowned. BJ laughed and Simon looked on quizzically.

'Unless it's beating his rivals hollow. He takes great pleasure out of that. Ha-ha!' Then the big guy leaned towards Mac and lowered his voice. His big belly got in the way so he turned slightly sideways, as he patted his top pocket where his mobile was. 'As Tremain knows only too well. Mac here is smug because he just beat off his arch competitor for my attentions. I told him no-go, I'm in bed with Mac on this one – but maybe next time.' BJ's eyes twinkled mischievously. Mac narrowed his, but didn't reply. Then BJ raised his voice again and turned to Sadie. 'Now, what's this special water you've found us, Miss Turner,' he went on. 'It sure cured my hangover this mornin'!' His southern drawl betrayed his Texan roots, that is, if the bootlace tie and hat didn't. 'Mind you, nuthin' like hair of the dog. Whisky, Mac?' And he headed off towards the drinks table.

'No, thanks, BJ.'

'I think we'd better get started,' Simon said, casting a disapproving gaze at BJ and handing over the laser pointer and remote mouse to Sadie, 'or Ms Turner will be apoplectic with anticipation.' Simon's droll sense of humour lightened the tension.

'And I wouldn't want to miss my flight,' Mac added, coldly.

Feeling the mounting pressure, Sadie stood and walked past Mac to the front of the room. As she passed, he leaned towards her and whispered softly, 'Everything rests on the next hour. Everything. Depending upon what I see, we'll chat after.'

'Yes, yes, of course,' she stuttered and tottered unsteadily away towards the front of the room.

'Nice shoes, by the way,' Mac added, and Sadie blushed.

She began her presentation in the same way she'd rehearsed, using the PowerPoint slides to guide her audience through the various points, each slide filled with impressive images and charts and graphs.

'As you know the new power-water, Frish, is taking the US health food stores by storm. It's produced by the Galloways – a small "mom and pop" organisation, as they call it, based in Hawaii. When Bill Galloway saw my science marketing proposal, he asked for a private meeting, and the rest, as they say, is history.' Sadie paused for a response. None came. You could have heard a pin drop. Or her heart beating. Mac was looking at her like he'd never seen her before, so she forged ahead.

'Word of mouth is creating huge demand, they can't keep up.'

'Especially from people who realise that it makes your whisky more powerful when you mix them!' BJ joked as he sat down in between Alexis and Mac, sloshing his tumbler of drink. Mac gave him a glare. 'What?' BJ asked, indignant. 'It does – doesn't it?'

Sadie cringed. 'Well, according to some anecdotal reports listed in their small print, it would appear that whatever you take with it may well be absorbed faster by the body, yes. But that's phase three or four of our research plan – initially I and my university colleagues ...' *ex-colleagues* thought Sadie, '... will do urgent trials in the Surrey testing facility where I used to work. The Galloways appear to need a massive cash injection to take their Frish to the next phase. With my involvement they believe their expansion can all happen much faster, and that, I'm told, is why they want me involved. This, gentlemen – and ladies – is how we plan to do it.'

Over the next half-hour, apart from feeling Alexis's eyes piercing her like knives occasionally, Sadie became quite confident that she was doing well – with her presentation at least.

If someone had completely erased Mac's memory of the last twenty-four hours, he couldn't have acted more formal and business-like than he did in that boardroom. As Sadie took them all through the slides, her hands gradually stopped shaking each time she pressed the button for the screen to change. And her heart gradually stopped pounding every time she thought of his touch, his body, hot next to hers, his ... *Focus!* He is now well and truly out of bounds, she told herself. Especially if mixing business with pleasure is forbidden. *Well, that's fine by me,* she told herself.

After a wobbly start, Mac looked more and more interested in the deal. He leaned forward, ignored Alexis when she sidled up to him and slid a note under his elbow – which Sadie took ridiculously great pleasure from, especially because Alexis even appeared to pout a little as he just passed her 'vitally important note' over to one of his staff without looking at it. His aides were writing copiously, and he nodded appreciatively as Sadie went through the history of the product, the founders, the anecdotal evidence of better sports performance, and the mixed sales results so far. The company were well-placed for massive expansion, with a new production plant in the offing, and the secret formula had just gained its protection with a new patent.

It sounded good. She warmed to the task and hoped she looked confident. But if anyone studied her closely, they'd have seen white knuckles clutching the laser pointer and a little trickle of sweat running down her neck.

Why? Well, what Sadie *didn't* reveal to the room was that finding an investor for this deal would earn enough commission to prop up her and her little company for the next two years. Longer if she became the sole importer in the

UK. It was everything, this meeting. A step up, a foothold on sanity and a reprieve from staring bankruptcy in the face.

Instead she stared Mac in the face – the man who in less than twenty-four hours had turned her whole world upside down.

Once or twice Sadie held her breath a little too long. Once or twice she lost her place – but only briefly. And several times Sadie caught a sexy-as-hell billionaire gazing intently at her shoes. On one of those occasions, Sadie saw Alexis's eyes following where Mac was looking, and it made Sadie stand even more proudly in front of the room.

Throughout the whole process, Sadie was painfully aware of his gaze. Even though she couldn't tell for sure, she wondered if his eyes were undressing her, and she had to use every ounce of her being to remain calm, composed, and professional. Which she did. Only once did she slightly trip when walking to the other side of the projector, at which 'that woman' crossed and uncrossed her impossibly long legs, tittered slightly and elbowed her colleague then started whispering. If she was trying to put Sadie off, it didn't work. Well, it did a bit. But too much was resting on this so she fought it, kept calm, and carried on. *So far, so good.*

Then came the projections.

In the speedily-prepared but thorough business plan, which Simon had helped her with, an impressive cash flow forecast predicted massive profits in year three, assuming the new scientific studies were published, and the dramatic new claims would finally have enough usable proof to be incorporated officially into the marketing materials. Then everything would explode. But even the preliminary trials could give it a lift. The science was groundbreaking, pivotal, and at the root of what made it so right for Sadie. Everything – the worldwide launch and the international projections – rested on both clever marketing, and on the scientific community buying into the new research which Sadie outlined in full.

It was vital, and without careful handling, the entire rising success of this product could be a mere flash in the pan.

She concluded with a reminder of the deadline.

'The international distribution rights all hinge on getting the research done swiftly. With your investment, Mr Anderson, the new bottling plant can be fully financed, and the studies can begin. And then in phase two, with the publishing of these new scientific studies – assuming my own early results are confirmed – everything changes for Frish. And for us.'

'And for you,' Mac said, and rubbed his chin, stubble-free and clean. Sadie noticed his skin looked perfect, super-smooth. There was an expensive-looking watch in place of the old one he'd worn last night. 'No offence, Sam, I mean Sadie, but I have to ask this question – why you?'

Sadie faltered.

'They ... as I mentioned, they ... they said they were impressed with my marketing expertise, my credentials. But mostly with my crucial contacts.'

'Ah, yes – what does it say here ...' He flicked through a hard copy in front of him. 'In the three major Sports Science university research departments.'

'Precisely.' She could feel her palms start to sweat. 'The, er, studies can be done speedily but still using the applicable methodology. The right way,' she added, when she saw Derek and Graham look at each other, puzzled.

'Yes.' Mac nodded. 'I can see how the results could turn around their whole campaign, once they can back up their claims. And they allowed you this thirty day window to obtain the investment.' She nodded and he asked, 'Why?'

His question was brusque. 'Because I told them I can make it happen faster.'

'And can you?'

'Of course.' She felt hurt.

'How?'

'My connections – plus my PhD in nutritional science.'

'Your what?'

'It's all in the brief, Mac,' said Simon, coughing a little and shifting in his seat. 'You reviewed it as usual, presumably?'

'I, er, was tied up a bit last night. Sorry.' He met her eyes and she looked away. 'So, you're a scientist too, then?'

'Used to be.'

'Simon, you often find me surprises, but this whole thing has to be one of the biggest.'

Sadie blushed.

'Thank you, Mac. It's what you remunerate me for,' puffed Simon.

'Yes, it is. And another question that's been bugging me, Sadie, one that I'm sure you knew I was going to ask.'

Sadie's heart was in her mouth, as she waited for the next question.

'Why the huge rush? Thirty days is an unheard of timescale for a deal like this. I normally wouldn't have given it the time of day, but for … circumstances. What did they tell you about their reasons?'

She felt relief wash over her. 'Only that firstly it would test my mettle, see what I was made of. They informed me, of course, that they had other options, but if I could swiftly bring in the extra investment to cover the studies, it would change their whole business plan.'

'Change their whole business plan.'

'That's what they told me, yes.'

Mac stared at Sadie, and she swallowed hard. Those azure-blue eyes gave her a flashback she knew definitely did not belong in a boardroom. She felt herself begin to glow. And not in a good way.

'They had a plan for expansion, but only for building the bottling plant. When they discovered what I could do, everything changed.'

'Everything changes when you come on the scene,' mused

Mac. Sadie continued trying not to let him distract her. *Was he testing her?*

'Well, I didn't know if any of it made sense, and to be honest I was going with the flow really, and it wasn't until I got back and emailed their original plan to Simon, along with the estimates from the university teams I know, that he thought it was even doable.'

'And is it, then? "Doable"?' asked BJ, swigging on his whisky and wafting himself with one of the brochures. Alexis passed him a tissue, so he could dab his forehead. It was getting warm in here. She went to pass one to Mac, but he waved it away without looking up at the expectant beauty queen, so she got up and went to the thermostat on the wall by the door and began twiddling with it. *I wonder what her real role is* thought Sadie, realising most of the men in the room seemed to be watching Alexis's backside in her tight skirt as she played with the air-con. Except Mac.

'I think, Mr McKowski,' interjected Simon with a cough, 'that we can safely assume that to be the case, considering my involvement. I deduced the feasibility of this venture to be sufficiently ... "doable", to interrupt Mr Anderson's tight schedule and coordinate an update of the proposal with Ms Turner. Isn't that right, Sadie?'

Sadie nodded.

BJ looked confused at Simon's words, and as Alexis walked back past him, she simply patted him on the shoulder. He seemed satisfied. Sadie continued the explanation.

'Plus, Bill Galloway, the CEO, said that if I could pull it off in that time then it would indicate how fast I can work. And prove that he was right about his instincts to trust me. Bill's the inventor ... and, er,' she hesitated briefly. *In for a penny*, 'Well, he told me he was a bit psychic.'

Simon coughed again, this time a tad more uncomfortably.

'And he had a strong feeling,' Sadie went on, 'that I was the one – the one who could make this happen.'

Mac looked blank. A couple of his entourage looked at each other.

'He told me, and the rest of his team, that he knew I was the key to achieving great things with their product. His staff told me I'd struck lucky – right place, right time – because he often makes big decisions based on hunches like that. Apparently he's always been right.'

No one spoke. Sadie felt a flush creeping up her neck.

'Well, anyway, I'm just telling you what he said. Plus they mentioned that if I didn't act fast, there was sure to be another party investing. Hence the timescale. So here we are now, thirty days and counting, well about twenty-four actually, to find the finance. Or they'd be forced to go elsewhere.'

No one said anything. Sadie looked at Mac and he didn't seem to be paying attention. He was just staring at her feet. She shuffled behind a nearby chair and suddenly felt very nervous. *Oh God, less about the intuition and more about the research labs,* Sadie chastised herself, wondering for the first time if she might have actually blown it. Damn being honest about psychic magic water inventors.

Then Simon spoke. 'Derek, I believe you have something to add. Can you shed any more light on the situation, please?'

The young bespectacled Chinese man with sleek, trendy black hair and a garish red tie stood up for his moment of glory, cleared his throat theatrically and spoke with a perfect English accent.

'Our due diligence has as usual revealed some extra information they've been trying to cover up. The timing is indeed due in part to their crippling shortage of cash. It seems they need an injection fast to continue building their new plant. Seems they've overstretched themselves. The new equipment works fine, but the plant is incomplete. Ultimately it could quadruple the output, and halve the staff. But it's become a race against time.' He paused to allow it to sink in then began walking round the table distributing a handout of his own, showing some charts and graphs.

Sadie took one and sat open-mouthed. *They've pulled this together in no time, where on earth do I fit in with a team like this?*

Derek continued. 'So far they've sold off big parts of the family's empire in Hawaii – the local hotel, the helicopter taxi firm. Bill Galloway was reluctant, but the son – Peter Galloway – appears to have pushed it through. There's a chance they'll stall, and they won't be able to keep up with demand for free samples, which the son appears to be handing out to major sporting stars. Top sports teams have begun relying on their performance-enhancing water, and the word of mouth tipping point is within reach. But the freebies – without sales to back them up – well, they're just not sustainable. As the word spreads, and more and more sportsmen are demanding their product, they're – if you'll pardon the pun – drowning in their success. They're going to be on borrowed time before too long, I'm afraid.'

The room went silent for a moment. Sadie swallowed hard.

'They didn't say anything about this in Hawaii,' Sadie said. She felt a bit silly, going on about her unique attributes and a clairvoyant Hawaiian when really the company were in need of financial help as much as she was.

'Don't worry, Miss Turner,' Derek explained. 'They wouldn't have told you. But there's more,' he said. 'Graham has the details.'

'Yes, indeed,' said the similarly bespectacled young man with spiky ginger hair and a very nearly identical tie, standing up and passing Mac and BJ a memo. 'W-we've just heard this morning about who is behind these new d-developments – it may mean a fly in the ointment. A s-spanner in the works, if you will.'

'Please continue, Graham,' said Simon.

'It is our belief that, as of O-two hundred hours, a f-final offer was on its way from another source. An offer that apparently includes a – shall we say – f-financial i-incentive.'

'A cash advance?' said BJ. 'A bribe?'

'I have a bad feeling about this,' said Mac.

'Who is it from, Graham?' asked Simon.

Graham practically glowed. 'We just had it c-confirmed by our operatives just before the meeting. I'm afraid it's the T-Tremain Group, sir.'

'Tremain!' Mac said, incredulously. He sat back in his chair, clenched his fists and looked up at the ceiling.

Sadie was trying hard to keep up with the information flooding back and forth, but she could tell by Mac's face that this Tremain was bad news. She began to feel a little panic in her stomach. *What if Tremain's appearance meant Mac would back away from the deal?*

Mac was glaring at BJ, who was looking out of the window and shuffling slightly in his chair.

'What else do you know?' asked Simon.

'Our West Coast sources tell us that behind the scenes Tremain Group have been putting the p-pressure on. But Bill Galloway hasn't given in yet – he'd rather remain independent of Tremain's demands. But there's a w-weak link – the son, Peter Galloway. He'd sign with Tremain tomorrow, apparently.'

'He's the one in charge of the new plant, and of the complimentary sample programme,' added Derek. 'He's stopping at nothing to get the new machinery operational urgently. Then he can keep signing up every top sports star that comes knocking on their door.'

'Peter Galloway is a bit of a star-chaser then,' said Mac.

'Yes. So n-now that they've had to put the next phase on hold, Tremain's argument is gaining m-mom-momen-m … pace,' Graham continued, standing up to open his briefcase.

Sadie's mouth dropped further and further open at the wealth of information this team had gleaned – certainly not from the Internet – she'd tried. They must have contacts everywhere to gather this many facts, all done in a couple of days.

Just when she realised her jaw was gaping like a guppy, she caught Mac's eye and snapped her mouth closed immediately. He just looked away, turning his back towards BJ slightly.

Now she really couldn't tell whether it was all going terribly well, or really, really badly. She took a swig of water from one of the cut crystal glasses on the table and waited while the latest sheet of charts and graphs was passed across the table for BJ and Mac. Her iPad pinged – everyone had been sent it wirelessly, and it instantly appeared on the projector on the wall too at the next button press.

Mac took the document and frowned. 'Tremain Group – again.'

'But how come they're even involved?' BJ asked, going slightly red-faced.

'Look at this i-inside information. Last week they took a large stake in the biggest health food distributor on the west coast,' Graham replied, 'whose strategy has been w-working. Any product they wish to promote, they assign an aggressive local rep who spends hours p-persuading local stockists to take big supplies of it, then t-talking to customers in-store.'

'Word of mouth,' said Sadie. 'Oh-oh.'

'Oh-oh? What's with the oh-oh, Miss Turner? You can't just say oh-oh, you have to explain oh-oh.' BJ was getting flustered and Mac touched his arm.

Alexis was giving Sadie what appeared to be daggers. Sadie shifted in her seat.

'Elucidate, please, Sadie,' said Simon.

'The advertising authorities don't like it. You fall foul of them, and it's a nightmare to recover from. If there's nothing written, it makes it harder to prove if they've been making claims they had no right to. And twice as annoying for the authorities – which means you're put on their watch list.

Hence Bill's sudden change of plan when he heard about my connection with getting proper studies done,' Sadie replied. 'But there's no denying it can result in fast sales. Just not sustainable, credible ones.'

'Ahh, I see what ya mean,' said BJ, looking a bit more comfortable now. 'A bit like the old days when the travelling salesmen would shout from a soapbox that their potions could cure baldness or cancer, but it was really just snake oil.'

'Exactly that,' said Sadie. BJ looked pleased with himself. Alexis didn't look pleased with Sadie.

'N-nonetheless their sales have as a result been stratospheric,' Graham said. 'Our contact says it's given Tremain reason to be b-bullish about obtaining the contract.'

'More "b-bullish" than usual,' sneered BJ. 'The man's raw beef as it is. Albeit stringy, skinny runt type beef.'

'They're very aware of how weak the Galloways' position is,' said Derek. 'Our sources suspect Peter is sharing more of the patented information than his father would like him to. That's why Tremain Group are pushing forward with this brave new approach.'

'Brave?' BJ sneered.

'Er – enterprising,' said Derek. 'Unethical, but somewhat enterprising.'

'And who would be the recipient of this "financial incentive", this chunk of change?' asked BJ.

'It seems some would be for off-the-record payments to contractors to speed up the new build,' Derek replied. 'And some to the family itself. Young master Peter has a penchant, it seems, for fast cars.'

'And this is the company you're wanting me to invest in?' said Mac, drily.

Sadie gulped. Her mouth was like sandpaper and her mind was racing overtime. *What if, what if, what if ...* She had to speak up.

'Mac, Mr Anderson, listen. All I know is that this product

works wonders. Nothing else in the world has produced such results. When I was in Hawaii I did some preliminary studies, all promising. What's more, my colleagues at the unis – the top three UK sports research departments – are keen to get their hands on it. And Simon seemed to think you liked the product too as you love innovation.'

'Or else we were the first available money men.'

Sadie blushed. They were.

'But tell me, Sadie,' Mac asked, lowering his voice. Everyone around the table leaned in a little nearer. 'What do you really get out of this?'

'Commission – pure and simple,' she replied in a flash.

'Commission is never pure and simple.' Equally as fast.

'Well, in my case, it will be,' she said to him. 'Tranche one for bringing the investment to the table from someone who can help put the plant back on its feet and fund the studies up front, and tranche two when the studies are completed. If there's ever a tranche three it won't come out of your coffers, but from business expansion once the new claims can be made. It should ramp up sales astronomically. And we can follow-up with more studies on hydration and reversion of plasma levels to—'

'Okay, I get it. I've heard enough. Thank you. That's all assuming Tremain doesn't steal this deal out from under our noses – and from what I've heard, and from what I know about Tremain's cronies, they don't see the need for studies so they won't need you. So unless they cut a deal with *us* you're out of the picture.'

Sadie swallowed, hard. The lump refused to budge and she felt a bit sick.

Alexis came round and began whispering to BJ.

Mac leaned forward onto his elbows and pressed his fingers into his temples. She watched him, and still felt torn. But she quashed the urge to go over to rub his shoulders. After all, she wasn't in a Hollywood romance movie.

Right now, however, she wasn't entirely sure that she hadn't stepped straight into a TV drama – it certainly felt that way. With a perfectly-chosen cast – all except her. In fact, most of the last month had felt like she'd been living on borrowed time. Sadie wondered what would happen next. She certainly couldn't tell from Mac's stony face.

Alexis took this moment to step into the spotlight, clearing her throat delicately.

She walked round the table and stood at the other end of the room to Sadie. In fact, she didn't walk, she glided. With a barely-concealed flutter of eyelashes in Mac's direction, she spoke, her West Coast tones making her sound like she should be in some teen reality show.

'But may I make a point? Right now, Bill Galloway doesn't trust Tremain, isn't that right, boys?'

Derek and Graham nodded.

'And how certain are you of this new offer – can we be certain that Tremain will ever win Bill over?'

Derek and Graham looked at each other.

'Our sources do say a m-meeting is imminent,' said Graham.

'But it's not too late? If we can move fast?' she asked.

'It's possible, of course,' said Derek, 'but in all likelihood—'

'In all likelihood maybe we should take this new information with a pinch of salt until we know more?' Alexis snapped. 'Is that possible?'

'Yes, ma'am,' the aides replied in unison.

Then turning to BJ and Mac, Alexis added, 'You've beaten Tremain before, Mac. And from reading those notes, as far as we can tell, Bill's still in charge, and his son Peter's nowhere near ready to take over the reins at Frish. So,' she said with a smile, tossing her hair back with a flourish, 'there's all to play for.' She looked over expectantly at Mac but he didn't even look up. Sadie suppressed a grin.

Graham chipped in, 'Would you like us to do a f-feasibility study?'

'Yes,' said Derek, all fired up. 'We could compare analysis models, and—'

'Not just yet, Derek,' replied Simon, standing up and taking charge of the room. He had a very commanding manner and everyone stopped to listen to him, including Mac. 'Let us first be clear. As far as you have learned, Bill Galloway is a man of his word, and has given Ms Turner here the chance to win the contract fair and square. Correct, Sadie?'

'Yes, he has. He seemed perfectly genuine to me,' said Sadie, 'And he's a scientist himself – an engineer – he would see the value in the studies—'

'And in you, Sadie,' Simon interrupted. He opened his mouth to continue, but BJ piped up. Simon glared at him, but BJ was oblivious.

'And maybe the old man wants to escape Tremain's clutches,' he said, breaking out in a slight sweat. 'Especially if he could be "made aware" that Tremain himself is a … a double-dealer. And other unrepeatable words!' BJ added, nodding towards Alexis, who nodded back and smiled knowingly. BJ winked at her. Mac seemed oblivious. Simon ignored them both and continued speaking.

'So, as I was saying, with Ms Turner as our secret weapon, if you'll pardon the metaphor, Sadie, we may still be in time to come to the rescue of one of the most exciting new products to hit the market in more than a decade. And what's more …' He paused to pour a little more fizzy water from a bottle on the table into his crystal glass and sipped it while everyone waited for his next sentence. 'And what's more, if our camp has faster access to published studies, the marketing – thanks to Sadie – could be our trump card. Ours, not Tremain's. But we have to act fast.'

The information dump came to an end, and Simon wrapped it up, looking at his watch. 'The only question is whether MCA Associates is willing to take on the risk.

Willing to pitch yourself up against Tremain – again – with these odds.' And with that he looked over to Mac. And so did everyone else.

Mac was nodding his head, thoughtfully. Every eye in the room was upon him, awaiting his decision. But it didn't come.

Simon looked a little surprised.

Mac was wavering.

Whoever this Tremain was, his involvement seemed to have taken the wind out of Mac's sails. And they were already at half-mast – Sadie could tell.

She bit her lip, terrified that last night would have blown it.

All her hard work – her family's future – blown out of the water.

But she hadn't exactly lied to him. True, she'd withheld crucial facts from him but only as he had her.

But he was the one holding the cards.

Or rather, he was holding the millions.

Sadie considered the chances that she might faint if she didn't stop holding her breath.

Mac had a quick word with BJ. BJ started wiping his brow again and beckoned Alexis over, who passed him something Sadie couldn't see. He showed it to Mac who whispered to Simon.

Simon then stood up to address the room and Sadie's heart went into overdrive.

'Well done, Sadie. A very thorough presentation.'

'Thank you.'

'Now, will you excuse us a minute, please?'

'Of course, no problem.'

She sat there expecting them to leave, then suddenly realised everyone was looking at her. They wanted *her* to leave the room. Oh God, how embarrassing. Feeling like she was going to see the headmistress, she took her bag and stood up.

She forced herself to smile genially around the room at everyone before stepping out the door, her cheeks burning.

Once outside, she unbuttoned the tight jacket. She let out a huge breath. The receptionist peered at her once again over the top of her glasses and gestured towards the chair.

I'm not sitting there again, Sadie thought, wafting her jacket as inconspicuously as she could, to cool herself down. She paced a little, growing impatient as seconds turned to minutes and she felt the overwhelming urge to pee. Feeling even more nervous than before, she walked towards the ladies room again, to splash some water on her face. God what a mess.

If this is living the dream you can keep it, she thought, *it's more like a living nightmare.*

She was in the stall, taking a much needed bathroom break, when suddenly the door to the ladies' room slammed open.

'Sadie!'

'Mac? Are you in here?' She struggled to make herself decent enough to join him outside the stall then stepped out.

He walked past Sadie with a face like thunder and splashed some water on his face. Sadie washed her hands and did the same.

Oh-oh ... she muttered under her breath. His aura of power made him all the more desirable and she felt conflicting urges – to embrace him – or to run. She smiled politely anyway and tried to pretend they were strangers, as she thrust her hands in the drier. But the sudden whoosh of air and noise made her jump and blew her hair all over her face. *I am such a doofus.*

'Sadie Samantha Turner,' he said, dabbing his face with a towel and coming to stand opposite her. 'We need to talk.'

Chapter Seven

It was a cavernous room, with an over-enthusiastic air-conditioner overhead. It buzzed a breeze through her hair, and Sadie shivered. She wrapped her arms protectively across her body. And it wasn't just because of the chill.

Mac stood facing her, and she realised he was gazing at her chest, at the flimsy blouse betraying her reaction to his being near, her vulnerability clearly on show. A little gap in the fastening seemed to be mesmerising him. Sadie fiddled with the buttons but then gave up, instead just wrapping her jacket even more tightly across her body. Mac focused back on her face. He quickly checked the cubicles and looked satisfied that no one was there, and then licked his lips before he spoke. Alone again with Mac, Sadie felt a sharp pang of desire as he got closer.

'Sam … Sadie. I need to ask you two questions,' he said, hesitantly, and looked deeply into her eyes. 'And I want you to think very carefully before you reply.'

'Two questions? Easy, "Mr Anderson", I can manage *that much*, I'm sure,' she replied.

His eyes narrowed, but he let it go. Taking a deeper breath, he said, 'Okay. Why didn't you tell me your real name? Your first name?'

'For the same reasons you let me think you were a deckhand, I suppose,' she retorted, the indignation in her eyes, but not in her voice. A big deal was at stake here, and while she felt like confronting him on the one hand, on the other she knew that she was treading a fragile line. So, civil and business-like, it was. 'We were *both* playing other roles last night on the yacht, weren't we?'

He flinched a little at her words, made a little shush noise, and double-checked the door to the ladies' room was firmly closed.

'Obviously last night should remain … private.'

'Obviously! Of course! I was just escaping from my life,' she explained. 'So were you, I now find out. All I wanted was to forget about work, and home – the mystery thing, remember? No wonder you were so quick to agree.' She looked at him, disappointed, but he didn't respond. 'Same story? Behind *your* masquerade? Or was it something else?'

He made a face but she couldn't tell what it meant.

'And second question,' he said, poker face firmly in place. 'Tell me honestly, did you *really* not know who I was, before you saw me on my yacht?'

'Oh, *your* yacht? Silly me, of course, it's yours. And it's yours *now*, not "*one day*". So much for playing make-believe with me.' She was clearly offended now, and couldn't help showing it. But he was still waiting for the answer. 'Of course I didn't know! How could I?'

He looked relieved – fleetingly. But then his face became unreadable once more and Sadie felt a bit miffed. 'So was it just a game to you? Was it? Pretending to be a deckhand, pretending to fix stuff?'

'You're the one who jumped to conclusions about who I was. I *did* tell you, if you recall, but you didn't believe me. So I just went along for the ride. And I *do* fix stuff, I don't pretend to.' He put his hands on her shoulders. 'But you've got to admit – it does all seem a little bit too … coincidental? Don't you agree?'

'That's three questions.'

Her mouth stayed firmly shut as she glared at him, until she remembered she wasn't talking to Mac, lying Hot Boat Guy. She was talking to her potential business investor – and lifeline. Letting her shoulders down, and uncrossing her arms, she sighed deeply. 'Look, Mac … Mr Anderson … This has knocked me for six, I've got to tell you. Last night … if I'd known it was you … well, I can assure you, I never … I never would have …'

'Me neither,' he said, quickly, a bit *too* quickly for Sadie's liking. But she detected the tiniest softening in his voice. 'You see it's true about the rule,' he went on, 'about business and pleasure. And it's totally non-negotiable. It's helped me out of a lot of ... "situations", shall we say.'

Sadie raised an eyebrow. 'I can imagine.'

'Look, Sam – I mean, Sadie – last night was ... unexpected. I wouldn't want you to think it would be a regular occurrence. It can't happen again.'

'Mac, I mean, "Mr Anderson",' she said, deliberately. 'What I *think* is that it will never – in fact, never, *ever* – happen again. *Will* it now?' It was as much a challenge as a question. She realised that her whole future depended upon the response. He paused.

'You're right, it won't. Ever.'

She smiled her relief. *There was hope.* If 'pleasure' was out, maybe that meant 'business' was in.

She held up her chin, and thrust out her hand, as if to say, 'deal'.

He looked down at her hand, hesitated, then searched her eyes as if looking for something extra, something unsaid. They were still quite close, in the chilly ladies' room, and she could smell his clean aroma once more, this time mingled with his expensive-smelling cologne. It intoxicated her, firing off a thousand anchors. Powerful memories of last night's most intimate moments came flooding back in. She swallowed hard, hoping beyond hope ...

Would he put last night behind them? Would he give the deal a chance?

'Deal?' she tried again.

Finally he took her hand in his, and she thought she had her answer. His big fingers moved across her palm, and she closed her eyes. The warmth from his hand flooded through her – familiar and comforting – and almost immediately, waves of emotion overwhelmed her as their energies connected like magnets once again.

She opened her eyes and found him gazing at her face. Then immediately, as if someone had suddenly waved a magic wand, a veil came down, and he appeared to go into business mode once more. The intimate moment ended, and the energy disappeared – it actually disappeared, just like that. *God he was good at this.*

Mac gave her hand a firm, formal shake then let go, straightening up and displaying a cool smile. Not the half-smile, not the smile she knew, just a little smile that forgot to reach his eyes. *But a smile nonetheless.*

Huge relief washed over Sadie, the tension left her body and she too straightened up, and began to fasten her jacket again. This time, though, he didn't watch her do it. Instead he looked intently at his expensive watch.

Something's changed, I hope for the better, she thought. But the trial wasn't over yet.

'Sadie,' he said, saying her name like he'd never heard it before. 'It's my team that usually vets a deal. They do everything. I don't much bother with the detail. So the Frish proposal wouldn't have made it to me unless they'd investigated fully and not found it lacking. At every level so far all the due diligence has stacked up behind the numbers.'

She nodded.

'So to save my time,' he said, 'I have to ask you this. Is there anything else that I should know at this point? And, *Miss* Sadie Samantha Turner, I don't have time for games. Your proposal has to be one hundred per cent straight-down-the-line, or we can never do business. If there's anything missing, or anything else I should know … Well, this is the moment to tell me. And if ever things change in the future, I'll need to know – the moment it happens.' He paused.

She said nothing.

Entranced by his blue eyes again, and with her head slightly swimming from the morning's events, she wasn't entirely following what Mac was saying, but kept nodding anyway.

'It's a two way street,' said Mac. 'Obviously Simon keeps a day-to-day watch over business, but I'm accessible at all times by email – via Simon, of course. Just in case anything should need a high level response or if something is urgent. Once I commit, I commit. Twenty-five hours a day, heart and soul. But it's all for nothing, unless there's complete and total honesty.'

'No, I told them everything. It's all there – everything you need to know.'

He looked relieved. 'Good.'

'Anyway,' she said, finding her composure again. 'Your guys seem to have gleaned far more info than I did, about some things anyway. So there's really nothing more to tell. And besides,' she raised herself up to full height, which wasn't very high, even in the heels, 'I'd be very happy dealing with Simon in the future. If that's what you're implying.'

Mac paused for a second looking as though he was considering her comment. It wasn't meant to be a slap in the face, but it appeared he'd taken it as one. His eye twitched briefly. Then the steely veil returned to his face, and the formal smile returned with a vengeance.

Sadie was utterly bewildered.

In front of her eyes stood a distant, cool and efficient businessman – as if he was a total stranger. All totally appropriate for the occasion of course – apart from the fact that they were standing in a ladies' room.

She did wonder though if she'd ever forget the other side of Mac.

Still he pondered.

And then finally he smiled – detached, maybe slightly sad.

But a smile's a smile, she thought to herself, *surely that's promising?*

Sadie's hopes leapt, thinking maybe he was about to give her some good news. She was wrong.

'So ...?'

'I'm not decided yet. I'll think about it,' he replied.

'Oh. Okay,' Sadie replied in a small voice, with barely disguised disappointment. Then she forced a grin onto her face and reached out again to shake his hand.

'Thank you,' she said. 'Whatever your decision. Thank you for considering me.'

He responded this time with a nod, then a final run of the mill handshake, but his eyes glimmered ever so briefly. Skin against skin. Familiarity. His face may not show it, but she was sure his body felt it too.

Like when you meet someone and you feel like you've known them forever ...

He held her hand just a little longer than necessary. As if they were communicating entirely without words, something was happening, and her body responded of its own accord – her nipples began to harden and her breath quickened. His did fleetingly too. And then he pulled her towards him, and kissed her hard on the mouth. His foot was against the door in case anyone should walk in, and Sadie felt her whole body ignite in a glorious union with the desire she'd been quashing since he walked in that door. His kiss was intense, deep, searching, and every bit as passionate as last night. They separated and he looked into her eyes. She was panting slightly and trying to catch her breath.

'*If* we have a deal. This ends.' He said it with slightly narrowed eyes, and she could see the beat of his pulse in his neck. 'And this,' he said, and reached his finger to her nipple, pert through the blouse and brushed it, ever so delicately. Sadie let out a small groan. Their eyes locked and he moistened his mouth. Then he curled a finger under the button of her blouse and flicked it open, pulled her to him with a hand in the small of her back and buried his face in her breasts. His other hand slid under her skirt and up her thigh, coming to rest between her legs almost touching her heat. And then he was kissing her again, his hand slipping around to her bottom and pulling her closer, against his hardness. Suddenly he stopped, pulled himself away as if it was painful and shook his head. Then he came to his senses and suddenly let go of her like a red hot poker and stepped backwards.

'It has to end, you hear?' he muttered and straightened himself up.

Shut down.

She was searching his eyes for something, some clue, some hint. But there was nothing. The glimmer had gone as quickly as it came, replaced by this alien formality once more, and she knew she'd lost him forever.

Sadie pulled herself together again, and felt the first signs of a tear in her eye and a lump in her throat. She fought it with all her might.

'Safe journey back, Miss Turner. It was nice to meet you.' And he was gone.

Sadie was crestfallen.

'It's *Ms*,' she called after him, but no one heard.

Sadie couldn't move for the longest time, the drip, drip of a tap beating time with the pulse in her ears. When she'd finally regained enough composure, she hauled herself to the door. As she opened it she just caught the last glimpse of the entourage at the end of the corridor, bidding the receptionist goodbye as the lift doors closed behind them.

No one was left in the Napoleon Room.

She slumped down in a chair and reached for her glass of water from earlier, draining it thirstily. Then she drained the one nearby, whomever that had belonged to, and the one behind that. She was collecting an apple from the fruit bowl when Simon returned.

She visibly brightened. 'Simon, hi. Has he gone?'

'Yes, the whole troupe has gone.'

'Did I do okay?'

'If you meant the presentation, yes, you did very well, Sadie.'

'Oh, no, there's a "but". There's a "but", isn't there?'

'*But* ... Mr Anderson was ... unusually preoccupied. I'm not sure why. It's most unlike him at final meeting stage. He's usually laser-focused and decides in a split second whether he wants to take a deal or not.'

'And does he? Does he want to?'

'He didn't say at first. At least not till after he went out to double-check those facts with you.'

'Double-check those ...?'

'Your tête à tête in the prestigious surroundings of the ladies' lavatory?'

'Oh.'

Sadie looked dejected and cast her eyes to the floor. She had a feeling she was about to hear bad news. Simon's usual poker face didn't help.

'I don't know what you said to him out there, but ...'

Sadie drew a sharp breath. There was that word again.

'But ...?'

'But it worked.'

'It worked? He said yes?'

'Indeed. As of now MCA Associates and Ms Sadie Turner can be partners. If we can seal this deal, you will earn your commission for your finder's fee, and the subsequent payment for overseeing the studies to publication in peer-reviewed journals. In addition to which, you will become Europe's sole importer of Frish, and hold the distribution rights for the whole of the UK.' He held out his hand. 'If that's what you want.'

Sadie let out a little squeak. '*Do I ever!*' She couldn't help the massive beam spreading across her face. Glad that only Simon was in the room, she finally allowed herself to relax fully, stopped holding her belly in, and took a massive deep breath.

I can't believe it!

She went to hug him, then decided to just shake his hand right off his shoulder.

'May I reclaim my hand, please, Ms Turner.' He grinned.

Sadie smiled into the middle distance.

'Pheeeeeew!' she said, allowing it all to sink in.

'Pheeeew indeed,' he said, putting his hand on her arm, and bringing her back to the present. 'But, Sadie, we have the rest of the company due diligence to go through, before we can sign. And there's more. And I'm afraid it's a bit of a bombshell.'

'Oh hell, what now? I mean, do go on.'

'Mr Anderson has postponed his other appointments due to the pressing nature of the latest turn of events.'

'He has? You mean because of the Tremain Group?'

'Yes – they are arch-rivals, I'm afraid, as you could probably tell. They worked together once – we all did.' Simon looked sad for a split second, then continued. 'Then they fell out, and a while back, he beat Mr Anderson to an executive island. And a chain of health food restaurants. But Mac trumped him on a yacht purchase last year. Tremain's face was a picture, if I recall. They thought they had it in the bag with their underhand methods.'

'This Tremain guy sounds like a piece of work.'

'Indeed he is, as you say, a "piece of work". A big piece. Now his group seem to be intent on stealing away Mac's business at every opportunity. And – sad to say – vice versa.'

'Oh.' *Now I understand.* 'He doesn't like to lose, does he?'

'Not at all. In any capacity. I fear it will be his undoing one day. That's one of the reasons I was keeping my ear to the ground for someone like you, Sadie, for a deal like yours. One he will excel at. One that's perfect for his current situation – he needs to triumph over adversity, shall we say.'

'And I'm guessing Tremain is the adversity. So he'd better act fast then, huh?'

'That is precisely, Ms Turner, why Mr Michael Anderson is travelling immediately to Hawaii.'

Sadie's mouth fell open.

'As we speak, he and BJ are en route to the airport. BJ's private jet will be flying directly to meet the manufacturers in Hawaii tomorrow and secure the deal within two weeks. Even faster than the thirty days they stipulated. Mr Anderson is, after all, a fast worker. One of the fastest.'

'You can say that again.'

The irony was lost on Simon.

'Well, since time is of the essence it seems Mr Anderson wants to cover all the avenues in this one trip – and that includes his chief asset.'

Sadie looked perplexed.

'You, Sadie. Mr Anderson has reserved a place on the plane for you.'

'Is there a phone I can use, please?' Sadie asked, breathlessly, fiddling with her jacket, and checking her newly collected suitcase while she waited. The pretty receptionist in the hotel lobby signalled for Sadie to wait a second while she finished her phone call.

Sadie's mind was racing, and in true fashion, she got clumsier as the nerves kicked in. A yacht yesterday, and now a private jet. *What the hell do you wear on a private jet? Not a business suit, not repeating my Club Class faux pas*, she thought. But realising most of her other clothes needed washing, she just shrugged and reached round to undo the button of her tight waistband. She exhaled properly for the first time that morning, and began fiddling with the leaflets on the counter near the receptionist. The girl raised an eyebrow as several of them cascaded down over her keyboard, and Sadie smiled sheepishly, and pinned her arms tightly to her sides. Finally, the girl finished her call and asked Sadie to repeat her question.

'Bien sûr, madame,' she answered, pointing towards a courtesy phone at the end of the desk. Sadie sprinted towards it.

She could sure use some friendly words from home right now.

If her mother could cope for another few days, Sadie's roller coaster ride was about to go stratospheric.

Simon's words echoed in her head while she waited in turn for the phone. *You've got an hour before we take off from the private airfield.*

She considered her suitcase full of dirty suits, damp shoes and big pants, plus no sarong in sight and only a tiny bit of factor 50 left. Sadie had nearly declined. But there was no way she could miss out on an invitation like this one. The taste of adventure she'd just had, and the desperate need to secure this deal, gave her no choice. Plus there was an uneasy feeling that this was also a test. Another one.

Of course I'll join you.

The taxi to the airport was waiting outside.

Now all she had to do was break it to her mum that it would be dinner for just three again tonight, because Sadie wouldn't be coming back. Having already given up one bowls match to keep an eye on the girls, her mum wouldn't be happy. Sadie knew she was pushing it and she felt like a teenager again as the phone rang in Turner's Health Store.

'Mum, it's me. I've got some news for you and I'm not at all sure you'll like it.'

Chapter Eight

Mac was waiting on the private jet, gazing out on to the tarmac.

The journey to the airport in his chauffeur-driven car had been tedious. Mac wanted time alone to think, but BJ McKowski had insisted on coming along. Never one to miss out on a drama, BJ had promptly cancelled his plans and would now also fly to Hawaii. Usually it was all good banter, listening to BJ go on and on about wine, women and sarongs. But today the non-stop chat had been plain annoying. *Another sign it was time for a change*, thought Mac. Maybe Simon was right. It was too late with this deal, though, so best take advantage of his business partner's private bar, private jet and public liability.

Monaco wasn't as bad as St Tropez for wall-to-wall eye candy, but BJ had still given a commentary on every pair of breasts they'd seen through the tinted windows as they wound their air-conditioned way down the tree-lined avenues, a wavering heat haze visible just above the parched pavements. The day was even hotter than yesterday, if such a thing was possible, and Mac felt a pang of regret. He tried to work out what it was, rubbing his stomach and furrowing his brow.

'You got an appetite for some of that ass? I'd join ya if I wasn't betrothed – you know what women are like when they get a ring on their finger – hold on tight and never let you go,' BJ had said, then stopped. 'Apart from your ... Well, hey, look at those – I swear they're *real!*'

Mac ignored him. He needed some peace and quiet to process the last twenty-four hours of groundbreaking events, but he got neither. In typical BJ fashion, a constant stream of jokes about how Tremain might whip Mac's ass this time filtered past the muzak playing in the back of the limo. The older guy took delight in making Mac bristle with a less-than-PC appraisal of Sadie and her 'assets'. If they hadn't been about to take an international flight together, he'd have jumped out of the car right there and let him continue on alone.

Once seated on the plane, BJ continued his onslaught. 'That Turner gal filled that skirt in all the right places, didn't ya think?' he said.

'Can't say I noticed,' Mac replied, not looking BJ in the eye.

'Come on, Mac, I've known you enough years to recognise when you're enamoured of a lady. You were watching her, more than her presentation.'

Mac hadn't responded.

'Although,' BJ went on, 'I found *her* "PowerPoints" rather intriguing.'

Rolling his eyes, Mac finally gave in. 'Yes, okay, she was quite attractive,' he said, knowing his old colleague well enough to wisely opt for the shortest route to being left alone.

This time, it didn't work.

'There, I knew it. Ya see, I can read you like a book.'

'Business and pleasure, BJ. Business and pleasure.'

'There's always an exception, Mac, my friend. *You* of all people should know that.'

'I've told you before, that was the reason why there's now a rule.'

'Rule, schmule. I remember the rack on that lawyer gal – you must have been gagging for it by the time you got together and did the dirty deed?'

The hiccup had been years ago but BJ had a long memory, and took sadistic pleasure out of reminding Mac of it every so often.

'Leave it, BJ.'

'It wasn't your fault the boy's father had a change of heart, you know. But it's best the child was with his parents – his real parents. You of all people have to agree with that, don't ya? Lucky escape, though – you all but had a ring on that little lady's finger.'

'No, it was fate, BJ, old boy,' said Mac through a clenched jaw. 'Fate and destiny.' *And Mac would have controlled his own fate, if he'd just stuck to the rule.*

'Well, I think it's high time you put down some roots. You're not gettin' any younger.'

Mac resumed staring out of the window. BJ tried a different approach.

'Although you do still run like a greyhound, I'll give ya that. I know how important this deal must be for you. I couldn't believe my ears when I heard you pull out of tomorrow's training event in London. But are you still on course for the big one? How *is* the training going?' he asked, changing the subject.

Mac sighed. 'Not a bad swim this morning. I didn't beat last week's times though, when I had Frish. Definitely helped my stamina.'

'Yeh, if it gives *you* more endurance, it's definitely the right product to add to our portfolios, assuming we can foil Tremain. But here's what I wanna know. Does it also *make "things" last a whole lot longer*, if ya know what I mean?' BJ laughed, beginning to shred Mac's nerves. Fortunately, just at that moment, the stewardess came along with BJ's lunch order.

Mac took himself off to the on board bar to get some water. *What a morning.*

He toyed with his drink, standing at the small bar at the front of the plane. When he'd seen Sam ... Sadie ... in the meeting room, Mac had nearly fallen over in surprise. He was perturbed by seeing her there, but more importantly, by the sudden realisation that the very first thing he'd felt was that old devil – suspicion.

She *had* lied to him, deceived him. But this time *he* was just as guilty. Nevertheless it had still unsettled him.

Old habits die hard.

She'd looked amazing, a total professional, commanding in her sexy, fitted skirt-suit. And 'those' shoes.

But should I have confronted her straight away? Given her no time to think?

No, not with Simon there, let alone BJ and the entourage. Couldn't risk losing face. *I'd never hear the end of it if they found out what had happened.*

That she'd flatly denied tracking him down to surreptitiously bed him was consoling, but not enough to prevent him being absolutely mortified that he'd slept with one of his business contacts – albeit a potential contact. After vowing *neve*r to do it again.

Last time, when it had all gone wrong, Simon had given Mac some wise counsel. *You're both over twenty-one. Either accept it, do the deal and move on, or throw in the towel right now.*

Since Mac chose very carefully when and where his towel got thrown, and whose ring to throw it in, there really had been only one option.

Now as he stood at the bar and nursed his iced water, he felt the pang of hurt deep in his stomach. The damage had still been done.

Mac remembered the rest of that conversation with Simon. How Mac had ranted about living life by his own rules from then on. *No one else in the way, no one to consider.* Turning to extreme sport for comfort, religiously training for the toughest of all triathlons – the Ironman – he'd never missed a session or an event. Yet even his rigid routine was taking a back seat since this Sadie Samantha Businesswoman had arrived on the scene.

What turmoil one woman could bring. He smiled.

But it would all be worthwhile to beat Tremain again. And it would be of some comfort – much more minor of course –

to see the smile on Sadie's face when they signed the deal and Sadie could collect her payment. The one that would save her business. Mac gulped down the drink and pushed the glass forward to the barman for another. He felt the icy water sliding down inside his chest, calming his stomach.

This business opportunity had fired up his juices more than anything he'd been offered in a long time. But it was only being up against his biggest adversary ... wasn't it?

Mac sat down in a plush chair near the bar and flicked through his iPad looking belatedly at the pages of the proposal, responding to the niggly feeling in his gut that he'd missed something. But he couldn't concentrate and found himself skimming through instead of his usual fine-tooth combing. His mind kept coming back to Sadie, struggling to balance the out-and-out suspicion with a feeling of protectiveness and compassion. To see her, so green and new, fired up with a spark in her eye at the thought of achieving something so huge, so unjaded by years in the boardroom ... it awakened a part of him he thought had died long ago. And he was the one who could help her dream come true.

He twinged a little, realising with a jolt that it was that very thought that was bringing the *warmest* glow to his chest. Despite their rocky start. Well, fine, so he was helping a newbie – a single businesswoman in need – maybe he was more into charity work than he thought.

He could only assume her *real* reason for last night's game was exactly what she'd told him at the time – that she simply preferred one-night stands. She was that sort of woman. Well, fine by him, he was no one to talk.

At least with Sadie he was assured that last night would have no impact on their business relationship going forward. She was a true grown up. A dedicated single woman, if he remembered the conversation right, putting business first, so nothing to get in the way of this deal being swiftly finalised. Nothing.

But, hey, a principle is a principle – there could be absolutely no repeat of last night. Pah. '*Plus ça change.*' He'd just leave her behind, like he did all the others. Back to focusing on training for the next important event. He'd simply forget about her. Easy.

He glanced around the plane and felt a little panic – where was she?

'Excuse me, sir, would you be wanting anything from the chef before we take off?' asked Nicola, chief executive-jet air hostess and proud of it, all bright red smile and robotically efficient manner. Mac snapped back to the present and shook his head.

'What's our ETA?'

'Captain says it'll be about fourteen hours – that'll be about midday local time. Mr Simon Leadbetter's confirmed your accommodation and onward transfers. He gave me this message for you, in case you'd switched off your phone.' She passed him a small manila envelope. 'Will there be anything else, sir?'

'Has Miss Turner reported to the check-in desk yet?'

'Not that we've been made aware of, Mr Anderson, but I'll go get an update for you, sir. I'll be back shortly.'

Hmm, not much time to go. Has she got cold feet? wondered Mac.

Sadie's feet were actually clip-clopping across the arrivals hall just at that moment, in pain and fast losing the battle with the clock. With the proposed departure time close at hand, she stopped dragging her suitcase along, kicked off her heels, put them in her tote bag, and put on a sprint.

Oblivious to the strange glances she was getting as she padded barefoot through the plush premier section of the private airport, one quick check-in later and a sprint through what looked like a short cut, and she emerged onto the tarmac a little breathless, with precisely four minutes to make it across to the twelve-seater Gulfstream GV or else she'd be flying back to rainy Gatwick, not to sunny Hawaii.

The hostess returned. 'Warm towel, Mr Anderson? And, sir, I think we can safely say your guest is very close.'

'Thank you,' said Mac, then followed the hostess's gaze behind him, out of the extra-large windows in the private jet. The view that met his eyes was a sight to behold for sure. He walked across to get a better view. Sadie had hitched a lift on the back of a luggage cart, suitcase and all, her bare feet trailing over the side and her hair blowing in the wind. She was completely oblivious to the bemused chauffeur, trailing along in the transfer limousine, just behind the motorised cart. The baggage handler deposited her at the foot of the stairs to the jet, and waved away her offer of a tip. Whatever charm this woman had, it worked on everybody, it seemed. This was going to be a very interesting trip.

Blustering into the cabin a minute later, Sadie found herself in awe of how the other half live, for the third time in twenty-four hours. She settled herself into the seat she was allocated, towards the back of the cabin, unable to see the other passengers as the seats were so big and so plush. Carlo, the air steward, helped to make her comfortable.

'And, of course, more daylight through these windows plus travelling at a lower altitude means less jet lag. And no need for protective face masks as the cabin air is one hundred per cent fresh every ninety seconds.'

'Nice. So if I sneeze, no one will glare at me.'

'Aha-ha. Well, that's all you really need to know about these Gulfstream G5's – not that there are that many of them, Ms Turner. So fast, we will be in Hawaii mid-afternoon local time, with just one stopover – a tech-stop as it's known. Meanwhile, settle in and anything you want, you just have to ask.'

His warm smile and friendly manner helped Sadie feel at ease in such an alien environment. Now her comfort zone was so far out of sight, it was a mere dot on the horizon.

With a tuna salad on the way, and her aching feet being massaged by a vibrating heated bean bag, Sadie lowered her chair back a little, tilted it first one way then the other, puffed up the lumbar support then let it down again, then finally got comfortable and submitted willingly to the high life. Surrounded by luxury, she gave up trying to look up the aisle for Mac. Then the handsome steward asked if she would put her seat back to upright, so she started flicking through the in-flight entertainment folder.

The plane began taxiing for take-off and the comedy show she'd selected started playing before her on the little TV screen built into the side wall next to each seat – a classic about a badly-run hotel. At least that was familiar.

Recounting the events of the last twenty-four hours she had to pinch herself to prove it was real – and it had all happened to her.

It was the stuff of Hollywood movies.

Well, most of it.

Some of it had been like a horror film – like coming face-to-face with the man you'd been down and dirty with the night before, simply to find out that it wasn't only your backside, but your *future* that lay in his hands.

It had worked out so far, thank God.

But deep down inside, something was niggling Sadie, and she just hoped she could work out what it was by the time they reached Hawaii.

'Smooth take off, Mac, man,' BJ said, sleepily, rubbing his face. 'I didn't even notice we'd got airborne.'

'Well, your snoring changed pitch.'

'Maybe that was when my dream reached a juicy part. Want to know what happened?'

'I'm sure I can guess,' replied Mac, mid-email on his smartphone.

'Yes, but this time there were *three* of them. All dressed in —'

'Mr Anderson, there's a call for your guest.' The red-lipped stewardess stood brandishing the plane phone. 'I'm wondering if you'd like me to wake her. It sounded urgent.'

'No, don't worry. I'll go,' Mac said, and before he could stop himself he was up out of his seat, phone in hand, making his way back along the aisle towards a sleeping Sadie. Just taking a break from BJ – *anything to take a break from BJ*.

Even Simon had had enough of the brash Texan – choosing to travel to Hawaii separately. 'One's conviviality can only stretch so far,' the charming English gent had told Mac, before 'bidding him adieu' and setting off to 'rendezvous with some women friends, and do some last-minute business in Monaco' – which Mac suspected was Simon's euphemism for a trip to the casino.

Women friends, thought Mac – hmm.

Women.

Friends.

All his life they'd been mutually exclusive. So far. Well, there's a first time for everything, he thought – and he'd try his hardest to be *this* woman's friend. God knows she needed one right now. Much more than she needed him as a lover. *Ooops, where did that come from?*

He stopped when he reached her seat, his face softening as he gazed upon the sleeping beauty before him. Her golden locks were gently cocooning her face, peaceful in slumber. She looked like an angel, with slightly running mascara, barely-there lipstick, and a tiny blot of balsamic cutely sitting on her chin. The remains of her tuna salad had been cast aside, and her mouth was slightly open. He looked intensely at her lips. The lips he'd been kissing so passionately last night.

The lips that had delivered a very competent presentation in a high-pressure boardroom situation. For a moment he just watched her. The sound of her deep breathing told him she'd obviously gone off to dreamland.

'Sadie ...'

No response. Lifting her headphones gently, Mac whispered her name again, but he was competing with the hypnotic tones of the meditation channel seeping from the plush, noise-cancelling headset. Mac raised the telephone to his ear, turned and walked a few paces away.

'Hello, may I take a message for Ms Turner?'

'Hello, oh, yes, I guess you can. Can you tell her that her mother called back?'

'Er, yes, Mrs Turner, certainly. Is there a message? Anything urgent?'

'It's Mrs Parker, not Turner. Turner's her married name. And if you don't mind, can you ask if she got the earlier message that ... well, that she should ring her mother please, when she can. Are you the steward? Is it a big plane?'

'Er, no, I'm not, and yes, it is quite a big one. She'll be able to call you when she wakes up. I'll pass on the message.'

'Thanks so much. And do give my thanks to the billionaire chappie for looking after her so well. I'm sure she's loving it – we all like a bit of luxury and no mistake! The girls and I are very jealous.'

Mac frowned and ticked himself off for interfering – he should have let the stewardess deliver the message. Serve him right. And now for his trouble, her mother had given him that acid feeling in the pit of his stomach again. *Is the universe trying to tell me something?* If you can make your own good luck, you can also create bad.

'Mrs Parker, before you go, I'm ... Michael, part of the development team. You said "the girls" are jealous? Of going on a big plane?'

'Yes – Georgia more than Abi – but they'd both love to see

how the other half live! Does it have its own jacuzzi too? I do like a good bubble bath!'

'No, no jacuzzi, just the gym.' Mac could feel himself bristling.

'A gym. How decadent. Bet that billionaire chappie sorts his six-pack out that way! Anyway nice to talk to you – better go – the girls are here helping me and they're busy telling a little old lady how to avoid cancer by eating Brussels sprouts. Serves me right for resorting to child labour. Oh, don't tell Sadie I said that! Bye!'

'Bye.' Mac's face was stony. *Okay universe – I get the message*, and he took himself off to the gym double quick, to take it out on the treadmill.

Hours later, Sadie awoke to an 'ohmmmmm' sound. Opening one eye, she gradually realised where she was, smacked her dry lips and lifted up the headphones. The plane noise rushed in, replacing the ethereal chanting in her ears. *It might be an executive jet but it still roars*. Pushing aside the blanket someone had placed over her, she drank down a full glass of water, and looked up and down the aisle. A stewardess was at her side instantly with a warm washcloth, which Sadie gratefully smoothed over her face, followed by an expensive looking face spritz.

Smiling, the stewardess indicated under the eye, and Sadie looked quizzically into the mirror on the built-in vanity right next to her first-class seat unit.

Ooops – panda eyes.

Mouthing 'thank you' to the cabin girl, who nodded back, Sadie then picked out the most expensive-looking teabag she'd ever used – *was that really muslin?* – from a wooden box being held under her nose. She sat back and opened a manila envelope someone had placed on her side table.

One refreshing Earl Grey later, plus a phone call home, Sadie pondered her gung-ho approach. Was it wise to have given urgent permission for yet another expensive school trip? She hoped Mr Rosebery wouldn't find out. But what do they say? *If you build it they will come …* Or something. It's all in the intention, apparently. According to Wayne Dyer, on the meditation channel, what you believe will be true for you. So Sadie *had to* cling on to the belief that everything was going to work out. So it was sorted – permission given.

But a pang of 'bad motherhood' still snagged in her solar plexus. Yes, the trip was another thing she'd forgotten to sort out in the rush to get away. And now her mother would have to forge her signature on the permission form. *Going from bad to worse with the whole 'honesty' thing, Sadie,* she chastised herself. But anything was better than having to suffer the indignation of begging the girls' father to sign it. In any case Stuart and Mum were not on very good speaking terms at the moment. Sadie sighed and got up out of her seat and stretched her arms a little.

Let's focus on something positive.

She stared in wonderment at the plush interior of the jet and began listing things to be grateful for – being on a private jet for one. Going back to Hawaii for the second time in a fortnight, for another. Truly jet-setting – *that's what I'm doing*, she thought, as she ran her hand along the edge of the expensively upholstered seat next to hers, which someone had left in a reclining position. Sadie was amazed – she'd never flown horizontal before, but she was sure as hell going to give it a try.

After a bathroom break.

She stretched, slipped her shoes back on, *ouch,* then immediately took them off again. Remembering she'd unfastened her skirt, she tried, and failed, to do the button back up, so she gave up and just untucked her blouse and grabbed the thin, expensive cashmere blanket from a packet on the seat, and pulled it round her shoulders.

Walking forwards up the aisle to the front of the plane, she passed several luxury seats filled with sleeping aides – some she recognised, and some she didn't, people she assumed worked for either Mac or BJ McKowski. One seat held a sleeping Alexis, who looked like a princess waiting for her prince.

Sadie rolled her eyes and continued on past the first ladies' room, which was engaged, on to the one nearer the front of the plane. One bathroom break later, she emerged to the sound of male voices. She took a right turn, and saw where it was coming from. Leaning against the lavishly-equipped bar, with their backs to her, Mac and BJ were mid-conversation.

'It's absolutely out of the question, BJ,' Mac was saying. 'There's no way I'd ever date Sadie. Now give it a rest please, big guy.'

Sadie's heart immediately began to drum up a tattoo on her ribcage.

'Well, I know she's not your usual type, but you shouldn't hold a few extra pounds against a gal,' BJ exclaimed.

Shit, thought Sadie, and tried to reverse before she was seen. She bumped straight into a steward.

'Ow!' he said and dropped a tray.

'I told you before, I ... Sadie!' said Mac, catching the commotion in the reflection in the mirrored glass and swivelling round. Mac looked aghast. But not as aghast as Sadie. Flushing right down to her toes, she backed away apologetically, wishing the floor would open up and swallow her.

'I'm sorry – I should have ... knocked. Only,' she said, waving her hands in the air pathetically, 'there's no door.' Sadie was embarrassed, suddenly very conscious of her gaping skirt buttons and reached round the back to fasten them, then stopped to grab the blanket which began a slow, elegant slide from her shoulders.

Was Mac really that shallow? Was last night all just an act? Is that what her niggly feeling was? Perhaps he had simply taken her for a complete ride just to get in her pants?

'Anyway, you're obviously in the middle of something.'

'No, we're not. Not at all. BJ's just leaving – *that right*, BJ?'

'Ha-ha – yeah, sure!'

Shuffling off, and touching his hat, BJ headed in the direction of Alexis, leaving Mac and Sadie alone for the first time since the confrontation in the ladies' room.

'Join me, Sadie,' he said. Ordering drinks, Mac looked sheepish, but when he sat down, he didn't even attempt to correct what she'd overheard.

Sadie's heart sank. Her body echoed the feeling and she slunk into a luxurious leather lounge chair opposite Mac. She sat awkwardly, smoothing herself down as best she could, shrouding the blanket around her shoulders. She picked up the mint and ice-crystal-bedecked glass of mineral water, which had a 'work of art' straw-and-cherries creation dangling out of it. Sadie gave up chasing it around the glass with her tongue when she realised Mac was watching her and just sipped it awkwardly out of the side of the glass, ignoring the straw poking her in the temple.

She shifted slightly in her seat – the leather was cold against the backs of her bare thighs as her pencil skirt rode up. Mac watched, then stopped ogling and tore his eyes away. More apologetic glances. *Awkward, awkward.*

Then he found his voice.

'Did you … did you speak to your mother okay? Everything all right?'

'Oh, yes, it was just one of my … my daughters,' she said, swallowing hard. Dodgy subject. *Too late.*

'Ah, yes, your daughters.' He winced. 'I had a very interesting little chat with your mother and she mentioned them. You, however, didn't.'

'Not last night, no, the same way *you* didn't mention a lot of things.'

'I wouldn't say a *lot* of things, Sadie. I'd say *you* "didn't mention" a lot more things than I didn't.' Mac made a face, seeming to realise as soon as he said it how juvenile that sounded. 'I mean, I was just surprised, that's all. I mean, I asked you if there was anything else I needed to know. And you said "*no*". "*No*", you said. "*There's nothing else*", you said. That's what you said.'

'But there *wasn't* anything left out of the presentation. It was all in the pack, didn't you read it?' Sadie got that sinking feeling again and realised finally what the gnawing feeling was.

He never read the details, did he? This was a man whose 'team' did all that for him. He was still looking at her open-mouthed. This man who didn't like business and pleasure obviously also didn't like business and children.

Mac could not believe that an hour's pounding in the gym had done nothing. The angst all came back as soon as she spoke about her kids.

'Yes, but what you said was that there was nothing else to tell me. Nothing else I needed to know,' he said.

'I thought you meant about the deal. Anything that wasn't already in the business proposal.'

He was silent. Staring ahead, rigid. He couldn't think straight.

What was it about this woman that made him unable to think straight?

'Truly, what difference does it make?' she demanded.

He took a deep breath. She'd blindsided him again. Not only was she not Samantha, she also had kids and now she was trying to act like it was no big deal. Worse still, he knew he didn't have a self-righteous leg to stand on when it came to the topic of working mothers.

'But you said you didn't need a poop-deck,' he whispered.

'And I don't. They're teenagers not toddlers, Mac. Well, one's nearly a teenager and the other is fourteen going on twenty-four. They don't get in the way and they fully support me. And their father is—'

'Their father? Oh, yes, you're married as well. Yes, your mum told me she's got a different surname.'

'Their father is a completely useless knob-head, hence my giving up on men, hence my "one night only". If you thought you were *Mister* cynical, meet Missus.'

'Ms,' he corrected.

Impasse.

They sat in silence while he just stared, looking for all the world like he couldn't decide whether to kiss her or kill her.

'Well, at least you can't throw me off the plane,' she said in a small voice.

At last he took a deep breath. 'You realise this is the third version of you I've been faced with, in less than a day?'

'Yes, I'm sorry,' she said, relief in her voice. 'No need to grab a parachute then?' More silence. 'And which version of me do you like best?'

'Don't ask me that,' he snapped. *The one from last night, the one on the dance floor, the one naked on my sofa …*

Eventually he walked to the now unmanned bar, picked up a bottle of scotch, sloshed a shot into a glass and drained it down in one, banging the empty on the bar. He made a face. *Get a grip, Mac.*

'So how *are* the kids? All in order?'

'Yes, they're "all in order", thank you. Everything's fine. Another expensive school trip on the cards and they've both got tests looming.'

So should she be at home? Does she mean she should be at home?

He didn't speak so Sadie continued.

'Mum's sorted out where they'll be for the next day or so now I'm not coming back.'

'Which is where?'

'Why do you want to know? Is it to make sure I'm going

157

to be fully focused on the deal? Because I will be, Mac, I'm a professional. Men will not get in the way of my success this time. And neither will my kids. It's them I'm doing it all for, after all.'

'But what if they're ill, what if something happens, what if somebody else comes into your life who demands that you change who you are, for them?'

'Can I refuse to answer please, Mr Anderson, on the grounds that if this were an HR interview I'd be pulling you up on all manner of employment laws by now?'

Mac signalled to the returning barman, fuming.

'It's not a crime to have kids, you know,' she went on, prising her legs off the leather seat, making a face as they stuck a little, and then standing up. 'And it doesn't mean our deal is in danger just because *you* don't care about children. Perhaps I should leave.'

Her face was pink, her chest was flushed, and her body language spoke of murder. *If only she knew the truth, if only she knew who he really was, and what he was really planning.* Time for a change of tack.

'You're right,' he said, begrudgingly, as the barman poured another scotch. 'You're absolutely right, and I apologise.'

Sadie took a breath, nodded and then slumped back in her chair, pulling her skirt down a little and shrouding the cashmere blanket protectively around her shoulders again. Where she'd been about to take off to, he had no idea, but it looked like her 'fight or flight' instincts had certainly been wound up to the hilt. 'Sorry, you're right.'

'Thank you,' she said quietly.

She picked up her drink, and sipped, staring out into space and swinging her feet like a hurt little girl. His heart went out to her. No, it was his fault for not reading the notes through. *And for pretending to be a deckhand. And for not sticking with his trusty 'disposables'. And his principles.*

He regained his composure.

'And the store? Things have been looking up since the article?'

She narrowed her eyes at him, and then replied. 'I see you read *that* bit. Good thanks, yes, they've been much better. Mum's a saint, in more ways than one. She's been using the last of the money Dad left her to invest in the shop and help me and my sister out. Bless her.'

'Your sister?'

'Yes. Helen was made redundant a little while ago – she's gone off to a yogic retreat to retrain. She's very spiritual is Helen. Except for the shoes.'

Mac coughed a little. 'And your mother? You said your dad left her money. I'm sorry to hear he's not with us any more.'

'No one's as sorry as Mum. He was her world – they had us young. She's funny though, now it's like she's rebelling – the teenage years she never had or something. But I couldn't have set up on my own without her.' Mac just nodded. 'I will buy her back out again one day though,' Sadie continued, a catch in her throat. 'If this deal comes off it may be sooner than she thought.'

'Not if. When.' He smiled. 'What Mac wants, Mac gets.'

Sadie squirmed a little. 'Including me last night?' she asked, glaring at him.

'Come on, throw me a bone here.'

'Hmmm. Well, yes, it would be nice if it's "when" not "if".'

'Very nice,' he agreed.

Another short silence. *Come on, Mac, say something pithy.*

'It must be hard work running a shop in this current economic climate, what with the credit crunch and depreciating value of the pound, you know, less in people's pockets. I guess health food purchases would be regarded as a luxury, wouldn't they? Easy to do without?' Mac heard the words come out of his mouth like some crass current affairs show host, mid-interview. Yep, that confirmed it, this woman definitely threw him off-kilter.

Sadie didn't bat an eyelid. She must be used to this debate.

'For some, but not as many as you'd think. You see, when it comes to something they really believe in, some people are willing to do anything they can to make themselves afford it. Especially for the health of their family. The big drug companies think they've got it all tied up with their claims, and their rules, but the little guys like us are making a stand, and so are our loyal customers. The health food industry is ready for a battle. Sometimes you have to fight for what you know is right.' Defiance lit up her eyes, but her face remained neutral. 'And if you do it the right way, you really can turn the science press to your advantage. It can be very powerful.'

'And very time consuming.'

'Well, yes, but I've done it before and I can do it again.' Sadie looked pensive for a second. 'Anyway, studies have to be scientifically correct, and usually take an age to complete and be published. If you have contacts, it can help speed up that side of things.'

'That's why you think you got offered this opportunity by Bill Galloway? Your scientific mind?'

'Yes. And because he sees dead people.'

Mac's eyebrows raised in surprise, then fell again when he realised she was playing with him. Then she got all serious once more.

'Without the publications in peer-reviewed journals you just can't get through to today's cynical scientific community. And the results on peak power output we've already seen in just two preliminary trials—'

'You're talking just like a scientist!'

'That'll be because I am a scientist, remember? I ran the lab.'

'You *ran* it?'

'Don't tell me you thought I was just a researcher?'

'I didn't … realise.'

More silence. More assumptions. Mac had really gone and done it now. Sadie sighed.

'Well, at least you know, now.'

'There's a whole lot I know, now.'

'Don't worry. Read your document in full and you'll know the rest as well. '

'I'm sorry if I didn't have you down as a proper scientist type,' he said.

'It's not the first time and it won't be the last. It's my fault for being blonde.' Sadie looked hurt, angry and insulted all at once.

'Well, you don't look like the picture in your file, that's for sure.'

'I was fed up of being brunette. Serious businesswomen just don't look like me, huh?'

Mac's heart clenched, and a wave of protectiveness swept over him. *Say something – make it better, make it better. Or get the hell away from here.*

'It's just … you know, no beard or sandals you see. What with you being so beautiful and all.'

Sadie rolled her eyes and pursed her mouth.

Oops, made it worse.

'I'll cope. I always have,' she said. 'Just as I cope with life. I come with my own long list of baggage – which you would have known about, had you done your reading, Mr Anderson. Yes, for the record, it shouldn't really matter what I look like. I'm a single, *divorced* mother, running a business on my own, travelling away from home, taking care of my kids, and even remembering to put the bins out on a Thursday. I do it. I'm a woman – it's hard but I cope.'

Mac caught the mood, and shut up. The silence strung out a little too long for comfort. *Was he reading this right?* He looked around him before lowering his voice and leaning in conspiratorially.

'Sadie, I have a suggestion for you.' He swallowed. He was taking a punt but she had a lot on her plate. Maybe this would make it easier.

'You seem a bit stressed. Maybe it's the sudden extra trip I thrust upon you. Would you like to just go home when we get to the tech-stop halfway? I don't mind. I'm sure Alexis and the team can take it from here.'

Sadie's eyes widened. Mac thought he was onto a winner, so he continued. 'In fact, how about this, although you'll still get your commission – and you will of course help with the studies ... er, manage all the studies – I really don't mind if you want to take a less hands-on role from now on. If you think it's best. Maybe one of your colleagues would be willing to take over the donkey work ...' He paused. 'In the lab, so you have more time to ...'

Sadie bit her lip and breathed deeply.

Uh-oh.

'To be with the kids? Focus on the store? From what you're saying you're needed there really, if that's where your heart lies? You've brought it this far, and there are dozens of professionals in my organisation who've done this type of thing before.'

'No, thank you,' she said curtly. Her lips were pursed and her knuckles were white, her hands were clenching so hard.

'Tell you what, I'll offer you an advance. You could buy your mum out now – that's what it's all about ultimately, isn't it? Sounds like you've got a lot going on, and well, some people may be expecting it.'

'Some people including you? Now you know I've got kids? Well, "some people" are going to be disappointed,' she snapped. 'Don't forget *I'm* the one the Frish people want to run the contract for the studies. Because I can get them the claims they need faster than anyone else on this planet. And what's more, I can front-up the marketing and PR – handle difficult questions and so on. Explaining the new studies to the layman or to ruthless journalists isn't something "one of your people" will be able to do as easily as you think. And don't underestimate me. Why do people always underestimate me? Sorry, Mister Big Shot, thanks, but no thanks. You're stuck with me, whether you like it or not.'

Holding her gaze just a little too long, Mac felt the draw towards her, and the warmth stirring again in his groin.

Dammit, I'm about to lose control.

Sadie, on the other hand, had reached a pinkish shade of purple.

Shit, and now so is she.

Mac ran his hands through his hair.

Sadie was looking at him through narrowed eyes.

'I'm sorry, Sadie, I just thought I'd ask. I was thinking of you – the kids. I'm only interested in the deal working out.' Again that look – only worse. 'But don't worry – your CV stacks up, you were passed by the due diligence team, so if you really think you can handle this yourself, *and* be a mother, then I guess …'

Her big green eyes flared up from beneath long lashes, as she took a sharp intake of breath. Mac continued, sensing that if there had been a window nearby that she could open, Sadie would have flung him out of it.

'I guess that means you're a lucky woman.'

She stood up, whispering. Somehow she seemed more menacing when she whispered like that. 'Well, thank you, *Mister* Anderson, for that vote of confidence. If I didn't know better, I'd tell you to—'

'Mac, we've got an update from … oh, I'm sorry.' Alexis chose that moment to appear, looking fresh as a daisy, with newly-applied make-up and pristine clothes. She was loaded up with files and notes. Mac straightened up. *Enough of this.*

'That's quite okay, Alexis. I think we've said all there is to say. Wouldn't you agree, Sadie?'

Alexis's sideways glance to Mac was met with a brief nod.

Sadie watched as Alexis just carried on, and leaned near him to place the pile on the coffee table. Admittedly it was a bit too near. His face turned to a frown as he caught Sadie's raised eyebrows.

'Sadie, I hope you enjoy the flight. Anything else, the girls back there will help fulfil your needs.'

'And the guys,' chirped Carlo, walking by, winking at them. 'Would you like me to accompany you back to your seat, Miss Turner?'

'It's Ms,' said both Sadie and Mac together.

Mac's self-talk continued later, during his second frantic treadmill session this flight.

Nothing good came of getting too close to anyone he did business with, he knew that to his cost. He'd learnt the hard way many years ago. He tutted and shook his head. *So no romance this trip.* Not with Sadie Samantha Businesswoman anyway. She'd said 'one night' and one night it was.

Whatever. It really made no difference even if she'd been the one to want more after all this – a rule is a rule is a rule.

She was now out of bounds, seriously, completely, one hundred per cent, out of bounds. Even more so since she was a single mother. Bad news. When you walked out you didn't just walk away from the woman – you walked away from the kids as well. *And I ain't going there again.* Ever.

Women could make very good business partners, driven, focused and free from distractions. But it was rare. It was no coincidence therefore, that all of his CEOs were men. He knew it was old-school, but he took no chances.

Yes, you were right to make her the offer – thinking of the deal, always what's best for the deal.

And any more thoughts of pleasure were forbidden. They were not – repeat not – to be about any woman. For the foreseeable future. Dammit – if she could do it, so could he.

Back in his seat, Mac smiled a satisfied smile to himself and allowed one last indulgent reminiscence. Then he shook himself to ward off any further fanciful feelings as far as Sadie was concerned. *Nice to be back on track,* thought Mac.

Totally.

From now on, it would be just him. Women were trouble. And this one was undoubtedly more trouble than most.

Chapter Nine

Nothing could have prepared Sadie for the heat and humidity as she cast her eyes on 'real summer Hawaii' for the very first time now the weather had turned into full-on summer. Unlike her first arrival at Kona International airport two weeks ago for the marketing conference on the big island, Kapalua airport here on Maui was quite stark – apart from some garlands and a colourful Hula girl taking pictures for tourists, and a faint smell of hibiscus.

Sadie breathed in the warm early afternoon air, humid and fragrant, deeply inhaling, and feeling her shoulders relax. Her magical mystery tour was continuing and the next crucial steps were just around the corner. She wouldn't forgive Mac in a hurry though. It wasn't the first time she felt belittled about what she was capable of – by someone who mattered. She'd divorced the last one, but the wounds were all too easily reopened.

Maybe she'd allow herself the tiniest sulk on the way to the hotel.

Sadie was ushered into the waiting minibus along with the staff, while Mac and BJ were guided beneath huge sun umbrellas to their waiting limousine.

The journey wasn't far, but Mac began to wish he'd travelled alone as, despite the cool air-conditioning of the sleek saloon, BJ was like a furnace sitting next to him leaking sweat all over the seats.

Watching Sadie sitting on the back seat of the minibus in front of them, laughing and glowing, his heart filled with derision.

She could turn on the charm when she wanted to, couldn't she?

Especially with her fellow passengers, many of whom she'd befriended during the final stages of the flight, much to Mac's annoyance. He felt a twinge of an ancient emotion – could it be jealousy? Really? Now that would be ridiculous. No, it had to be frustration, that's what it was – frustration at being wrong-footed so badly. Several times. *And all within forty-eight hours.*

When they arrived at the hotel, Mac jumped out of the car with relief but reached the minibus just as Sadie emerged. He smiled – courteously – and held out his hand to help her dismount. She looked like she was about to refuse, but then she glanced at his staff gathering all around them, and seemingly changed her mind. With a gracious smile, albeit not with her eyes, Sadie slid her hand into his and stepped down from the minibus. Her hand felt soft, warm. He held it for only a couple of seconds, but he felt the warmth of it long afterwards. As he watched her rear disappear into the hotel in front of him, without a backwards glance from her, he wondered if he should make sure his room was as far away from hers as possible – or as near as he could get.

Two hours later, Mac returned from the gym and opened the door to his hotel room, wiping down his perspiration with a towel. He stripped naked, then walked into the shower, not noticing a note being slid underneath his door.

After getting dried, he sat with just a towel draped around his waist, and threw open a big vertical trunk. It went almost everywhere he travelled, and had been packed by his valet for the flight – super-fast, as usual.

He reached past the designer suit bags into the back section and brought out an old, battered wooden jewellery chest with rusting black iron rivets holding it in place, and a chunky padlock. Retrieving the key from a concealed pocket in the trunk, Mac opened the chest and looked inside.

His tank watch sat there, plus the thin gold chain with

167

the silver St Christopher that had sat around his neck on the boat yesterday afternoon. He put it back on ultra-carefully.

But before he closed the lid, he hesitated. At the bottom of the wooden chest, right at the very bottom, some old photos and a sheaf of papers cried out to be touched. He picked them up. Perhaps in this state of flux it was the right time – maybe like this he could deal with the distant past. Where he began. Where he reinvented himself. Before any women got in the way or rivals put a fly in the ointment.

This tightly-bound package was the link to his roots – and it was the photos that opened the doorway the widest. An old creaking doorway that unleashed an avalanche of memories filled with pain and regret. He knew he could never forget, but found it difficult to force himself to remember.

Is it time to look? Has it been long enough?

A pained expression crossed Mac's features and he breathed out slowly. Removing the first photo from the stack, he gazed upon a twenty-year-old group shot – a dozen or so raggle-taggle children, all boys, in front of a building in serious need of a paint job. A young Mac stood on the end, by far the tallest, and a smaller, skinnier lad with sandy hair rested his head against Mac's shoulder, his hand covering his face. As it always had in photos. Mac inhaled sharply and shook his head.

No, not tonight.

He delicately replaced the old curled up photographs and papers, then laid the bundle carefully back at the bottom of the chest and locked it. Gingerly he slid the chest back into its resting place in the expensive trunk, and closed it once more.

Towel drying his hair, he walked out of the bedroom and noticed for the first time the small envelope by the door. *What the …?* Opening it, Mac noticed rounded handwriting on hotel notepaper and read the name. It was from Sadie.

Dear Mac

*I know we haven't got off to the best start. But we both
need each other – so to speak – to make this deal work.
I admit I was very offended at your insinuation that my
children would prevent me doing a good job, and you
must have your reasons. But I assure you, I won't let you
down.*

*Can I ask that we be civil to each other, at least? Since
we will be in such close proximity for the next couple of
days? Then, after that, as you suggested, we need not see
each other again – in any capacity – unless we absolutely
have to.*

*I am very sorry for what happened between us, in the
way it did, anyway.*

*Plus, you're very generous to have put your faith in me
and the product, and I want to thank you. I do believe
that we can do great things together. So to speak.*

Either that or drive each other mad. Joke.

See you later at the dinner.

Sadie Samantha Businesswoman.
Smiley face.

Mac smiled. If there was one thing this woman had, it was
guts.

Considering it was early hours of the morning body-clock
wise, most of the entourage had an afternoon nap. Then,
that night, after a bracing wash and brush up in the coldest
shower she could stand, Sadie appeared at the top of a long
sweep of stairs, and felt full of trepidation. Far below, people
were talking and laughing, people she had to impress.

But first she had to get down there.

Several people turned to look at her as she took her life

in her hands and descended. She realised their eyes were following the progress of 'those' heels clacking down the precarious-looking staircase. Slow, slow progress.

'Taking up stunt work?' said a voice at her ear as she exhaled a big breath having reached the bottom step. She jumped slightly, but knew from the cologne who it was – Mac. Dammit, she knew from her body's reaction to the memory of that cologne. Mac's strong steadying hand held her elbow.

'It's a posh do! I had two choices and I didn't think you'd want me to turn up in my Ugly boots.'

'Do you mean Ugg boots?'

'No, I actually mean Emu boots, but I didn't think you'd know the difference.'

'You'd be surprised what I know about women's footwear. I invested in an Australian manufacturer once. You know what? Our first task tomorrow morning, "partner", should be to make sure we buy you different shoes.'

'We? I'll buy my own if that's okay.'

'That's actually what I meant.'

'That's actually *not* how it sounded.' She shook her elbow free and noticed him looking her up and down. 'And don't worry, I'll buy myself a different dress too.' *Damn the man, starting me off again. Damn all of them.* Get the deal done, that's what matters.

'But I like this dress,' he added.

'I bet you do.'

'I got your note.'

'Good.'

'It was under my door.'

'I know. I put it there.'

'I forgive you,' he said.

'Hmm. You do, do you? Well, I'm still mad at you – a bit,' she snipped.

'But you'll let it go, right? *Entente cordiale* and all that?'

'No, I'll have champagne.'

Mac made a 'ha-ha' face.

'Anyway, while you were busy preparing for your Hollywood entrance, I was sniffing around. We might have a problem,' he said, handing her a drink from a passing waiter.

'Oh?'

'Bill Galloway's son, Peter. Apparently he swings towards Tremain's methods of doing business more than anyone knew. Tremain's been weaselling away behind the scenes this last week. Peter now wants his big bucks via the fastest route possible. Could mean trouble. We need to get him on side.'

'Which side would you like me to get him on, exactly?' She arched an eyebrow and Mac looked away. 'I'll do what I can – apart from any more role play,' she breezed, heading off in the direction of the table chart. One quick place setting shuffle, with the aid of the maître d', and Sadie had herself sat right next to the person in question.

Introductions, welcomes and two courses later, Mac found that his initial relief at not having to be near Sadie in 'that' dress and 'those' shoes had been replaced with pure frustration. And a creeping desire to throttle someone tall, dark and then some – Peter Galloway.

At first glance the FrishCo boss's son appeared charming and clever, but anyone listening for a bit longer would realise he was not as charming and clever as he thought he was.

Sadie appeared to be tolerating the young gun's cocksure banter – and elegantly sidestepping his inelegant advances. He seemed to be more keen on her cleavage than her clever conversation.

Mac could hear the boasts from across the table.

'*Miracle*' this, '*ground-breaking*' that, and now, after several refills of bubbly, his magical Frish could even help cure cancer. *Good God.*

He was a danger to himself *and* the project.

He was an unknown quantity, suddenly getting in the way of the deal – in the way of Mac's next triumph. And what's more, he was flirting shamelessly with Sadie. Not that Mac cared, but it was unprofessional.

Mac smiled at one exchange. 'But, Peter, *why* does it hydrate faster than ordinary water? *That's* my point. Where's your proof? We can't just *say* it. Even if it does. Even if anecdotal evidence backs up the claim, you can't just use it. Your new label design is great, honestly, eye-catching, powerful. But it disobeys the advertising rules. They're very strict.'

'That's not always a bad thing. I can imagine *you* being a bit … strict,' the man said, sliding his arm around the back of Sadie's chair.

'When I need to be.' She smiled politely. 'But do you see, even if all this *is* true, you can't just emblazon it everywhere without the proper approvals. They don't like it.'

'Oh, I don't know, maybe you should give it a go – you never know what you might like until you try it. Be daring once in a while!'

Mac could stand it no more. He wondered if the man was being deliberately obtuse or if this was his idea of foreplay. Pretending to listen was never a strong point of Mac's so he went over to join them. He walked around the table and sat next to Sadie, putting his own arm on her backrest, prompting Peter to remove his, and to give Mac a glare.

'Ahh, but sadly we *do* know, Peter,' Sadie continued. 'If you make yourself a laughing stock in the scientific press now at this crucial stage, it would take months to undo.'

'Sometimes years,' added Mac, catching Sadie's surprised look out of the corner of his eye. 'Especially with some of the incredible claims involved here. You'd be crucified by the cynics on the net. Best to wait for the studies, isn't it? They'll be interesting.'

'*Someone* was paying attention,' said Sadie, quietly, to Mac.

Peter grimaced a little at Mac's intrusion. 'Well, I'll tell you something "interesting",' he challenged. 'The sales update yesterday from the West Coast distribution team. Now that was *very* "interesting". You see it seems they've found a way round all that studies bullshit.'

Mac could almost *feel* Sadie bristling.

'Sounds *very* interesting,' Mac said. 'Do go on.' The young man was clearly enjoying the audience.

'In their West Coast health store outlets,' he went on, 'we have just seen a huge jump in the sales of Frish. Stratospheric. Word is spreading about our little company now. Frish has been accepted by more stores in the last week than we achieved in the last three months. And all thanks to a contact of mine. You see, it's not just you in the running, Miss Turner.'

'Tremain,' she said.

Peter looked surprised. 'Yes, Mr Tremain.'

'But – I'm just wondering – is there a reason why your father hasn't accepted his funding already?' she asked.

'That I cannot tell you. But he has more than demonstrated to me how keen he is to help us.'

'I'm confused,' said Sadie, blinking several times, fluttering her lashes ever so slightly. 'Why would your father ask me to get involved if he already had an interested party?'

'If he didn't tell you when you met him last visit, then it's not for me to say. I will, however, make no secret of the fact that if it was my decision, I would have no doubts about which strategy to adopt. And – no disrespect intended – I share Mr Tremain's belief that it would not involve a beautiful woman stalling our progress while she spends thousands of dollars on scientific research we can do without.'

Sadie went to reply, then stopped. Mac could feel her stiffen against the chair back. There was a definite awkward smile before she raised her glass to her lips. Only Mac could see that her hand was trembling ever so slightly and there was a telltale flush creeping up the back of her neck.

Peter took her hesitation as a sign to go on. 'You see – it's like this. His team have simply put reps in each store who *tell* people what Frish can do. That way there is no paper trail. No paper trail, no proof of flouting advertising laws. Foot soldiers – in the stores. Word of mouth sales growth. See? Ha-haaa! The old man might not like Tremain's methods but their aggressive sales cannot be ignored.' He finished off his glass of champagne triumphantly and signalled for another.

Mac's eyes narrowed at this clear disrespect to Galloway senior.

'But the "studies bullshit" is what will stop this being a flash in the pan, Peter.' Sadie frowned. 'Set Frish apart from the crowd.'

'No flash. No pan. Just a whole heap of order forms.'

'It is working now, naturally it would, initially. But when they are discovered – or reported – it could fall around your ears and set you back, far further than if they'd never begun this tactic. Your father was very clear when he last spoke to me that he is keen to avoid ridicule and cynical posts in online forums. Otherwise there may be a backlash.'

'I'm willing to take that risk. And I think you're wrong.'

'You think I'm wrong?'

'Whatever you call it, it's working. We're selling. We're growing.'

Mac scowled. 'Don't you think that's a bit unorthodox?'

'Whatever it takes, I say.' Peter smirked. 'Frish *is* a miracle – we all know it's just a matter of time before we change the face of the water industry. It's just whether we choose to do it the fast profitable way or the slow painful way.'

'But, Peter,' Sadie interrupted, but he was on a roll, drawing attention from the others around him, loving every minute.

'And with my new plant finished we'll be able to flood the sports world with samples until every competitor is having to come to us to buy their own Frish just to keep up. And the media will be raving about it too. Pictures of winning athletes in the press, Sadie, they are worth a thousand scientific words and sadly, dear Sadie, it may or may not involve you. Or your dear friend here. No, I think Tremain's right – simple word of mouth *would* be the fastest way to my … our … fortunes.'

If Peter Galloway had known how much that name riled Mac, and how close Mac was to walking away from him and the deal completely, the young man may not have been so blasé. But seeing Sadie's flush creeping towards her chin, he found himself stalling.

When was the last time I cared this much about a deal, he thought.

Sadie, meanwhile, was putting on a charm offensive.

'But, Peter, let's face it,' Sadie said, her hand touching his forearm. 'A full-scale multi-channel media launch *backed by* double-blind, placebo-controlled studies that have been peer-reviewed and published in the key journals, there's no comparison, surely? You must be able to see how much faster that will improve the bottom line in a solid, long-lasting way. No more struggling for the next lot of investment. No more bowing down to entertain the likes of us. To be truly in charge of your own destiny.' She paused, and Peter said nothing. She must have hit a nerve. 'And just think of the world headlines – think of how the press will be clamouring to speak to you.'

The young man's eyes flashed, and he smiled a toothy grin, looking thoughtful.

God she was good, Mac thought. Sadie certainly knew her stuff, no wonder the Galloways had been impressed with her. Peter was certainly mulling over her words, his dark features brooding and looking straight at Sadie, who appeared to be looking straight back. For all his sliminess, some women would probably call him handsome and fall for his charms, Mac thought. Alexis certainly would have and he found himself wondering if Sadie would. And hoping desperately that the answer was no.

'Well, yes, I have been working on my own versions too. It's not only my father who can create life-changing products. A world platform would generate the highest bidding for my own inventions. Hmm, I suppose you may have a point.'

Peter toyed with his glass, musing, and Sadie patted him on the arm. He shifted a little closer to her until a waiter came along and reached over to top up his glass again. Mac and Sadie both refused a refill.

'Short term, however, it still doesn't help us. Right now is what counts, we are … um … needing to maximise the impetus Tremain's team have created. Those publications take ages,' he said. 'That whole scientific process takes ages. No, to be frank, I'm not sure we can afford to wait that long. My father's … concerned. About timescales. About how long before we get a return on our investment.'

Not as concerned as you appear to be, thought Mac.

'But we're so close, Peter. Why muddy the waters now? My contacts at the UK universities are chomping at the bit to work with you and to make their own mark, fast – with a breakthrough as revolutionary as your water.'

The younger man nodded at her words.

'What's more, we'll *protect* the brand, not damage it. And best of all, when you've got heavyweight backing on board – when someone like Mac's interested,' she said, turning to look at Mac, 'well, let's just say he's one of the fastest movers I know.'

Despite Sadie's dig, her smile was on full beam, aimed directly at Mac and he puffed up with pride.

'What's the timescale we're talking about here?' asked Peter, with a furrowed brow.

'Half the time it usually takes, and half the cost,' she replied.

'And you can really meet the deadline for the funds to be in place?' he said, turning to Mac.

'It's possible,' said Mac, his serious business face firmly in place.

The younger man paused, then nodded thoughtfully. Sadie relaxed slightly, and leant back, brushing against Mac's fingers resting on the chair behind her. She sat back up again immediately.

'So, Peter,' Mac said, standing and offering his hand. 'Let's talk seriously in the meeting with your father tomorrow. I'm sorry he was unable to join us this evening.'

Peter took his hand and shook it.

'Three o'clock, isn't it?'

'Is it? I suppose it is,' Peter said, and winced at the vice-like grip. Mac let go of Peter's hand, and turned to leave.

'So, Sadie, tell me how you actually walk in those heels.'

Mac turned back. '*Actually*, Peter, I'm afraid I have to steal Sadie away. Conference call, I'm afraid, but she'll look forward to seeing you tomorrow.'

'You did a good job in there tonight, Sadie Samantha,' Mac whispered into her hair as he guided her away from the table. She felt a shiver down her spine at his breath on her ear. She smiled graciously.

'Thank you,' she replied. 'But I didn't need rescuing. You don't have to be my knight in shining, you know,' she continued as Mac led her out onto the patio and down some steps towards the picturesque gardens beyond. 'I was quite enjoying the attention, to be honest. He's quite easy on the eyes.' *Where did that come from?* Sadie wondered. 'And I am a *big* girl. As your friend BJ told you on the plane.'

'You heard that? The man's a liability. That's why I share business deals with him, not opinions.' Mac shrugged off his jacket and swung it over his shoulder.

With no one else around them for the first time in a while, she felt the mood become more relaxed and familiar.

'I guess he's okay. I take men like that with a pinch of salt,' she said.

'Yes, albeit a Texan-sized pinch.'

Sadie looked up at him. 'Makes no odds to me. *Business and pleasure don't mix*, do they? So whether you think my bum looks big in this really doesn't matter.' Sadie walked on a few steps, then realised he was looking right at her bum, so she swivelled round and walked backwards.

'Anyway, I'm well aware that it's your alter-ego, Mac the deckhand, who downgrades to "dumpy" once in a while.'

'Who's "dumpy"? Surely you don't mean you? You're curvy, not dumpy.'

Sadie ignored his backhanded compliment. 'And anyway, I'm sure that "Michael C. Anderson – billionaire extraordinaire" will always have an Alexis on hand, you know, to attend to his every need, to attend to his "small print"…'

Sadie knew she shouldn't have said it, but right there on her shoulder there was a little devil licking a finger and striking a 'one' in the air.

Mac didn't miss a beat. 'BJ's "small print", not mine,' he said.

'What?'

'I think you'll find it's BJ's small print Alexis "attends" to.'

That took the wind out of Sadie's sails. 'You mean she works for him?'

'I mean she's his fiancée.'

Oops.

'Oh.' Oh shit. *And with a 'pfffft' the little devil made himself scarce.*

'But I can understand your mistake. BJ was her … shall we say, second choice? But as I keep explaining, I never …'

'… mix business with pleasure. Okay I get it.'

178

'It's more than that, Sadie. She's not my type. I wouldn't *want* someone like Alexis anywhere near my ... "small print".'

Sadie smiled. Small comfort, but comfort nonetheless. And she hadn't even realised she needed comforting. She swivelled back round and fell into step alongside him again.

'Anyway,' Mac said, mischief in his voice. 'My small print's not so small. *Is* it?'

'I take it that's rhetorical.' Sadie laughed, more relieved about Alexis than she had a right to be. They walked on a little.

Well, she got that one wrong. But he was still a playboy. Even if he was a damned sexy one with such gorgeous muscles peeping out from beneath that polo shirt. As they followed the little pathway round the edge of the gardens, Sadie was careful to keep just enough distance away from him so she couldn't feel the heat coming from his body, and more importantly, so that he wouldn't feel hers.

Mac had halted in front of a low veranda looking out towards the sea. The sun had long gone down and the gentle breeze picked up a couple of Sadie's escaping tendrils and blew them across her face as she looked up at him. His hand reached out, then stopped halfway, and she brushed them back herself quickly. She shivered and looked down, and he noticed her nipples beginning to harden beneath 'that' dress. It flooded his whole being with flashbacks. She folded her arms swiftly.

'Come on, let's get you inside,' he said, sweeping his jacket across her shoulders. The movement brought them close again, as he faced her and looked down into her eyes, almost black in the lamplight. *There it was again, that spark.* Electricity crackled between them, creating a perplexing cocktail of emotions. Passion, lust, plus a connection that made him feel like protecting her. More than anything, he felt a strong desire for things to work out for Sadie. For her to be free from the debts and the daily grind.

And free from men like Peter.

And – dammit – free from men like himself.

He couldn't get involved – and wouldn't get involved. It was just the romantic atmosphere of exotic Hawaii and the thrill of another deal in the offing. They always got his juices flowing.

There was a lot to do, and Mac had a hunch it was not going to be the easy ride they initially thought it would be. *Just when he thought he was about to wind things down.*

Might as well go out with a swan song.

'We've got an early start tomorrow. Let's call it a day. It's been a big one.'

'You talking about your "small print" again?' She smiled, and they made their way inside. 'I've booked a cab into town first thing to buy myself some more comfortable shoes. So if anything exciting happens make sure they don't go without me,' she said.

Mac bade Sadie goodnight at the bottom of the stairs, resisting the urge to kiss her, and as she ascended slowly once more, she didn't look back. So she would have missed the fact that Mac had headed off in the opposite direction from his room.

Chapter Ten

The next morning Sadie awoke to an insistent knock on the door. When she opened it, she couldn't believe her eyes. There was a valet standing holding bag after bag after hat box after suit carrier of expensive clothing and shoes. Flat shoes. Plus a brand new top of the range mobile phone.

She couldn't believe it. In her just-woken-up state, she could only stand watching in amazement as the valet wheeled in the bags, saying she should check off on the list the ones she wanted and the rest would be collected later. And that if she wanted all of them just call the number on the side of the form and let him know how many suitcases she would need to pack it all in to take home.

She closed the door behind him and stared, stunned. Suddenly she opened the door and called up the corridor after him, but he seemed not to hear her and just disappeared round a corner.

The clothes were amazing. Not one tight business suit in evidence. Not one prickly jacket. Just lots and lots of loveliness, including several silk negligees and some beautiful underwear. *How did he know my size?*

But Sadie was proud. After much deliberation – and much playing dress up – she put all but the bare essentials that she would need for the few days she would be here back in their packages and with a heavy heart picked up the form, holding a pen. Her hand ticked just a few of the boxes on the list until she reached one pair of pumps – which had a heavy price ticket, but she had loved them so much. She would pay him back, every damn penny, if it was the last thing she did. She couldn't become 'one of his women'. She wouldn't.

Soon after the valet had collected what she didn't need, she got a call from Alexis to meet in the lobby, where everyone was waiting to get on a little coach which would take them off on a surprise excursion. Most of Mac's team were bleary-eyed and rubbing their temples, necks or eyes. Sadie looked around and saw Mac coming from the other direction with Alexis hot on his heels, and BJ hot on hers. She held up a hand to wave at him but Mac didn't see. He just bid Alexis goodbye and went off with BJ.

Alexis strolled over. Sadie noticed she wasn't wearing her usual high heels, but a pair of pumps. When she got closer, Sadie was shocked to see they were exactly the same as her own.

'Oh, snap,' said Alexis, getting nearer and seeing Sadie's shoes.

'Where did you …?'

'Mac's so generous, isn't he?' Alexis drawled. The spark in her eye put Sadie on alert. Was she lying? Or was this another one of Mac's traditions? Does he buy all his female staff shoes in times of need? Whatever. Alexis was talking about how wonderful a night she and BJ had had and how Mac and they had met for breakfast and how she was looking forward to seeing the plant.

'Perhaps you can tell me some of that science stuff,' she cooed. 'I hear you're very good at it? Guys love an intelligent woman, don't they?'

'Sure,' said Sadie, making sure she was sitting as far away from Alexis as possible when they boarded the coach. It pulled slowly away around the huge curved driveway in front of the hotel lobby and Sadie saw BJ getting into a big car, the same black car she'd seen a couple of times before. And Mac standing there bidding him goodbye. As her coach went by, he looked up, and seemingly without thinking, he blew her a kiss, then looked embarrassed and turned back to BJ. Sadie smiled to herself, and saw Alexis two seats down waving and blowing a kiss back towards the car. Or to Mac, she couldn't tell.

*   *   *

Peter had arranged a tour of his pride and joy, the Frish bottled water plant. Plus a token bit of sightseeing, including a trip to a local organisation supported by the Galloways' company, FrishCo.

Peter explained that this tour would be vital in understanding fully the scale of the investment stated in the business plan. Particularly the patented process. Sadie didn't mind – she was fascinated. Knowing that she'd be an integral part of the process to formulate the scientific research plan, she was given pole position on the coach and was kept at the front of the party for the tour of the plant.

Sadie was a little frustrated, however, as she checked her new mobile continuously. Mac had even had her number transferred already. How the hell do the super-rich do stuff like that?

She was awaiting the latest performance results from the early trials on the water samples she'd sent for analysis last week. They were due any moment, before everyone went to bed in England. Her old cash-strapped uni friends had been working on it day and night for her, and in return she'd promised this lentils and tofu brigade a steady supply at wholesale prices. Intellectuals could get very creative with a bit of couscous and some soy sauce. She was envious of them in one way at least – salivating at the thought of getting back to doing some solid research work. She'd missed being a geek.

'Boo,' said a voice over her shoulder. It was Mac. 'Have I missed the floor show?'

'No, you just arrived in time for the star attraction,' Sadie said, annoyed that she could feel herself beaming back at him like a schoolgirl. Before he could reply, the guided tour began.

A bottled water plant tour was a new experience for Sadie, but she kept being distracted by Mac who was catching up with several employees as they walked around. Sadie started taking notes and making observations, taking it all in. She casually looked around as they stopped once more at the next point of interest and saw Mac, looking like he was dictating some business letter or something to Alexis, who had been trotting along beside him. Sadie hung back a little, and pulled at the frumpy net cap covering her hair – standard issue for the sanitised interior of a plant like this. An oversized, starched white coat had also been issued to each of the group – compulsory wear for everyone stepping inside the plant itself.

Sadie squirmed awkwardly, conscious of how glamorous Alexis had somehow made hers look. Like a forties siren. Even in lab gear and the identical flat shoes, the damned woman looked stunning. Sadie contemplated also turning up the collar and rolling up the sleeves slightly, and cinching the white coat in at the waist. Then she remembered that her waist and the word 'cinch' had parted company years ago, and decided just to stew a bit more instead.

There she goes purring along at Mac's heels like a hungry tabby cat.

But Alexis could purr all she liked – Mac's 'small print' would still be out of bounds.

Hah!

And anyway the woman was supposed to be engaged to BJ who had apparently taken the private jet back to his next charity function in California, leaving his 'fiancée' behind to tie up any loose ends and what-not. Right now, it looked like it was Mac's loose ends she was trying to tie up, and she almost certainly had her eye on his what-not.

Still, what do I care? Business, not pleasure … business, not pleasure.

The plant and machinery hummed in the background, and the group trotted along obediently amidst a quiet buzz of conversation, but Sadie wasn't quite far enough behind Mac to be out of earshot.

'So did you agree with my choices for our local area visit, Mac?' Alexis said.

'Yes.'

'Hope you approved.'

'They're fine.'

'You see Bill Galloway gave us some options and BJ said you'd probably want to go see the children's home, so I requested a detour – even if only to show your face.'

'You don't just "show your face" at a children's home, Alexis, but, yes, I approve.'

'A-ha-ha, of course.'

Mac just sighed and nodded and glanced back towards Sadie, who suddenly took an inordinate amount of interest in endless rows of empty plastic bottles whizzing along past them at high speed towards the filling station.

'And, Mac, I sent for your surfing gear just in case you fancied having a ride out yourself. I gather you've been missing out on some of your important training so I took the liberty. I did it to ... please you.'

'Well, I ... okay. Thanks.'

'Well, you did enquire about local surf times yesterday,' she said, coming round in front of him and walking backwards, to talk more confidentially. Sadie found herself masochistically inching closer to listen.

'And it has been a while, hasn't it? Since we went surfing?' Alexis said, leaning in towards Mac, who instantly leaned back slightly, so she had to raise her voice just a little louder than she'd intended. 'It's been ages since you bared that chest of yours, and it's so worth baring.' With that Alexis caught Sadie's eye, and merely smirked. A smirk that could only mean one thing.

What the ...?

He's slept with her!

After *all he said* about business and pleasure, the lying, cheating so-and-so had slept with her.

And he's *bothered about* me *bending the truth,* Sadie thought. Waiting for the reply that never came, Alexis had continued to blabber on. Sadie stopped walking, her jaw falling wide open.

A couple of the others overtook her. She shut her mouth but began to flush a little.

Mac was scouring the group looking for something, then he saw Sadie watching. He smiled and jerked his chin towards her. *Come here?*

Sadie looked around her as if to say *who me?*

He did it again.

Bloody cheek.

Indignant at the summons, she rose up on her newly-purchased comfortable pumps and trotted towards him like a dog in beg position, hanging out her tongue. When she reached his side, and stood there panting, Alexis backed off a little, giving Sadie a weird look.

'And today, we are being ...?' said a bemused Mac, walking on.

'Can't you tell? Today, "we are being" summoned by the master. Obviously. *Pant pant.*'

Mac furrowed his brow. 'Who *are* you and what have you done with Sadie?'

'It's like you say, *what Mac wants, Mac gets*, right? You called, so here I am. Obedient pet. *Pant pant.*'

Mac looked bemused and went to reply, but just then the local plant manager walked up to them.

'Hello, Kaha'i, is it time for lunch yet?' Mac joked.

'No, Mr Anderson, not even, how you Brits say, elevenses. Just to let you know that the information you were asking for will be sent to your room at the hotel by tonight.' He was a genial, white-coated chap with a kindly face, and eyes that smiled even when his face didn't. They all looked like a happy bunch of workers, noted Sadie, apart from when Peter was around.

'Thank you so much. I'll get back to you once I've read it,' said Mac and Kaha'i left. Mac saw Sadie was looking quizzical.

'He said he'd find out which of the competitors in my next Ironman were being supplied with Frish,' teased Mac, a sparkle in his eye, but before he could continue, a loud, pompous clapping noise sounded from a small gantry in front of where the group had come to a stop.

'Oh God. Cue the sermon,' Mac said.

Peter Galloway, pumped up and full of self-importance, stood on high, holding his hands up for silence. Then he raised his voice so he could just be heard above the rising whir from the two huge stainless steel cylinders behind him.

'And this, my friends, is where the magic happens. It is here, in these very chambers that we produce our fabulous life-giving water. It's here with the addition of our top secret ingredient, we create a miracle ...'

'Does he think he's preaching to a congregation?' said Mac, leaning so close to Sadie that his breath tickled her ear. He smelled fresh, intoxicating and his hand had slid to her shoulder blades in a gesture of intimacy. Or was it just to be heard more clearly? *Despite* herself, the corner of her mouth quirked. Then she remembered she was miffed with him for lying – again – and unquirked it.

Then she remembered that it doesn't matter. *Men don't matter, Sadie Turner.* Not for now.

Then she remembered to breathe.

'They contain the secret process that changes ordinary water into Frish ...'

'All Praise Father Peter for he hath created a miracle,' Mac whispered, nudging Sadie. She elbowed him back. Peter looked down in their direction.

'A-hem!' Alexis said from just behind them, tut-tutting. Sadie snapped back to the real world and slid away from Mac. She moved to the front of the group to listen more carefully to Peter, who then directed his 'sermon' at just her for the next few minutes.

'Ten thousand litres an hour, filtered to zero milligrams per litre, then energised to seventy electron volts higher than usual at room temperature. This, my friends, is no ordinary water …'

Mac joined Sadie again. 'You understand all this, boffin?'

'You obviously don't, numpty,' she whispered back.

'There we go with those school nicknames again. I thought you'd—'

'Shhh! I'm trying to listen.'

'We use reinforced PCP with a lower migration factor and then finally we pack our masterpiece into double-boxing, drop-tested to twice the normal standard …'

Sadie was fascinated, admittedly loving the science, but not as much as she was loving Mac's attention. 'Kaha'i already explained most of this,' he whispered in her ear.

'Shhh, Mac.'

'Did you know Kaha'i means "the one who tells"?'

'No, I didn't. Shush, Mac.'

'Hawaiian names are very meaningful, they—'

'Mac, please!' Sadie said, trying not to giggle, and moved slightly away, play-acting annoyance with him. Peter was now explaining the purpose of the big cylinders, and Sadie was back in her element, lapping up the science as she listened to him going on about 'cavitation'. She was, however, not too engrossed in the commentary to feel Mac's mood suddenly change.

She felt the frostiness from a foot away.

Oh, no, have I overstepped the mark? Shit.

But when she turned round she saw why Mac had stopped joking around. He was looking into the distance, stony-faced. Following his gaze across to the entrance of the huge chamber, she saw a thin, designer-suited executive-type in heated discussion with Bill Galloway. And it wasn't Simon.

'Tremain,' growled Mac. 'What's he doing here?'

Peter was just ending his spiel, and waved his arm to begin the filtration process. As the cylinders whined up to maximum volume, a high-pitched whirring sound filled the huge plant with noise and vibration. As he stepped down from the gantry, Mac was waiting for him. He shouted something into Peter's ear. They both looked over to the new arrival, Mac shaking his head and saying something that *didn't* look like '*good speech mate*'. Then both men stomped off towards the entrance, where the new arrival was waving away a white coat from a lab technician and standing in a proprietorial pose, arms folded, braced for Mac's onslaught. Sadie couldn't see much of Mac's adversary, but she could tell by his walk that this meant trouble. But before Sadie could react, Alexis was at her elbow.

'I'll go,' she said to Sadie. 'You stay here and follow the tour – it's more important that you don't miss the science, right? I'll take care of Mac.' And she set off hot on their heels, leaving Sadie with the plant manager, Kaha'i, shrugging his shoulders then holding out his arm to say 'shall we continue' on the final part of the tour, including a reluctant Sadie whose arm he took while he continued the running commentary.

Sadie could only look over to the commotion, longing to know what was going on. She saw more arms being waved, knew there was something heavy going down, but had no choice but to stay with the rest of her group, all of whom had noticed the furore in the corner.

If Alexis hadn't already trotted along so keenly, Sadie might have been tempted to go over there. But she had to keep things in perspective. Mac was a womaniser and a playboy billionaire and she was a cog in a wheel. That's all. A bloody irritated, frustrated, curious cog, but a cog nonetheless. She wasn't even high enough up to look after anyone's small print. So better let them get on with it – she'd have to wait for the update from Mac later. So she plastered the smile on her face once again and continued the tour, and another hour of watching boxes whizzing round in a cling-film machine, hearing about hermetically sealed purification technology rooms, and listening to more water jokes from their guide in sixty minutes than she'd heard in a lifetime.

Slumping in the back seat on the coach again, she thought of home, wondering how her girls were getting on. She'd called from her room this morning, around their suppertime. Abi had been fine, busy with her work as ever, but Georgia had used four minutes fifty seconds of her five-minute allocation to moan about Nana. First for cooking food the 'wrong' way and mixing up chopping boards. Then 'dumping' her and Abi with a neighbour while Nana went to dinner 'with some stupid, boring, old grey guy'. The final whinge was that Nana had been refusing to help her revise for a 'really, really, like super-important test' the next day. *'And then, Nana told me that she thinks German is a stupid language and I'll never need it anyway.'*

After saying goodbye, a powerful pang of missing home had hit Sadie hard. Guilt crept insidiously under her skin, creating a *'bad-mother'* cloud hanging somewhere between her shoulders.

It sat not far from the *'jealous ex-lover'* puddle that had just taken up residence in the pit of her stomach.

And quite near the *'broken family'* millstone, ever-present around her neck.

She shook her head, unscrewing the bottle of Frish she'd been handed on the way out of the plant and drinking it straight down. The coach started up but there was no sign of Mac. No Alexis. And no Peter. What on earth was going on?

Oh God, this had better not be bad news.

This was the biggest, most important deal of her life, and if it didn't work out, she didn't know what she was going to do.

* * *

Half an hour later, the diminutive local guide was playing the role of Pied Piper to the MCA group, winding their way along a clean, white corridor. Sadie was totally distracted, lagging behind. They were at the children's home, and there was still no sign of Mac. She wasn't really listening to any of the information the guide was relaying, as she was too concerned about Mac. What *was* that commotion she'd witnessed back at the plant? She hated being out of the loop.

'So without the steady supply of public contributions we could not have provided the care needed to help so many unfortunate orphans, especially following the 2011 Tsunami,' the guide was saying, as the entourage turned a corner and disappeared from view. Sadie, however, did not follow them, because something had caught her eye through a window – something that had her heart pounding once again.

There, out in the yard in the middle of a makeshift soccer pitch, with beaten up metal goalposts and a battered old football, a heated game of soccer was being played. A dozen boys and a few girls of different ages were running rings around a tanned, shirtless older guy who kept falling to the floor when tackled, laughing and rolling about in the dirt.

Mac!

Sadie ran outside into the heat. Mac kept playing. She kept watching. Finally he patted the winning team members on the head, and handed out candy to everyone from his rucksack. And, Sadie noticed, a few coins on the quiet.

He saw her, smiled briefly, then got sucked back into a maelstrom of arms and legs. The raggle-taggle children were jumping on his back, tugging on his arms and pulling on his belt. He must have been playing for some time, given the state of his surf shorts, red face and sweating torso. It was late morning, the sun was beating down, and still the 'man who hated children' continued to jostle with the kids from Maui Waikoloa Children's Home in a way that took Sadie by surprise.

There was clearly more to Mac than meets the eye. Now it was her turn to be wrong-footed about him. There she was, labelling him as a cold, self-centred, womanising businessman – a playboy billionaire – and here he was looking every inch like someone's favourite uncle. A hot one at that. She wished he hadn't taken his shirt off. But the lads had no shirts on, so he'd just joined in. One of them.

Every time he tried to get away, a gang of them gripped his clothes and pulled him to the floor.

'Did you win?' Sadie called, above the hubbub.

'Actually, I ...' but he was whisked away before he could finish that sentence.

Finally he threw a handful of sweets into the yard, escaped, and came over to join her.

'Sorry about that. To answer you, no,' he said. 'I never win. Works better that way.'

Sadie found herself lost for words. So many questions, but where to begin. There was a pause.

'I just—'

'So, did you—?'

They both spoke at once.

'Sorry, you first,' said Mac, as he bid the kids a fond farewell and walked back inside the building, dusting himself down.

'Everything okay?'

'Yes. Did you enjoy the tour?'

'No, I mean, you know.' Sadie looked at Mac quizzically but he obviously didn't know. Or didn't want to say. 'I just wondered if you found out why that Tremain guy was at the plant?'

Mac chewed his lip briefly, looking around him. A couple of people walked by.

'Sadie, don't take this the wrong way but I'd rather not discuss it right now. Is that okay?'

'Oh. Sure. Probably spoke about it already with Alexis, huh.'

'Sorry?'

'Nothing.' There was a silence. 'Nice to see you out there enjoying yourself with the children.'

They walked a few paces as Mac shook his dusty shirt then put it back on and picked up his jacket from reception. There was a definite air of tension returning to his shoulders, and he forced a deep breath and then smiled.

'Two of them remembered me. Still here though, poor kids.' He seemed lost in thought for a second.

'You've been here before?'

'Yes. I was visiting the home a year ago when I first sampled the water. Bill Galloway was here at a fundraiser. Told me all about his dream of a new plant and worldwide distribution. Took it with a pinch of salt. Thought it tasted good but that was all. Never realised it would take-off so fast.'

'Ahh, you knew him – and the water. Which is why you were so quick to accept the meeting.'

Mac just nodded, and pulled out a chequebook from his rucksack. He started writing.

'And why Simon got in touch so quickly with me when I returned? He told me he'd heard on the investment grapevine, but they were already on your radar.'

The receptionist appeared and took the cheque.

'Just an extra, Laiana. As I said, buy a new football post and fix the sprinkler system, okay?'

'Thanks, Mr Anderson.' She disappeared again.

'So you donate too? What brought you to this kids' home then, Mac? I thought you were based in LA?'

'I'm based wherever I need to be based. Hence the "boat".'

She grinned and looked downwards, recalling their first encounter. *Ahh, the 'boat'.*

'Don't you mean the superyacht?' she said.

Mac paused, then changed the subject, and Sadie was glad, before too many memories came flooding back.

'Your first time on a tour like this?' he asked.

'Yes. The kids seem well looked after, don't they? Well fed? Quite happy? Nice that the Galloways support the home so well, isn't it?'

'Yes, they and many others. Bill's a good man.'

Another silence fell on them both. Sadie biting her tongue to stop herself firing a million questions at him when he clearly wasn't ready to talk.

'Listen,' he said. 'I think I'll let you go on ahead with the others. I'll give the rest of this trip a miss. I've got to go tidy up before the meeting this afternoon, but there's something I've got to do first.'

Sadie put on her best pleading face, ensuring he at least told her what it was.

'There's a surfboard with my name on it waiting for me after my run, down at the beach.'

Sadie made a perplexed face. *Add 'enigma' to the list of names I can call you,* she thought. She opened her mouth then shut it again.

'Don't worry, I'm pulling out all the stops to overcome the obstacles being thrown in our way and I *will* get this deal. I can't talk about it now but leave it with me. I'll see you at the meeting, okay?'

'Okay. Will Alexis be going surfing with you too?' *Dammit – why did that woman still bother Sadie so much? Gut instinct? But the words were already out of her mouth.*

'No. No idea where Alexis is. Did you need something? I can ask her to call you if you—'

'No, no it's not that, I just—'

'What?'

'Nothing.'

'Sadie, I wouldn't usually say this to a normal business partner, but I suppose you're not ... ahh ... a normal business partner. If there's anything troubling you, you would let me know?'

Sadie looked into his eyes, a mixture of concern and troubled waters. *So much she needed to say, so little she'd allow herself to admit.* Anyway, now was not the time.

'Mac, the deal's still got legs, right? Nothing's changed?'

'Now who's being paranoid? No, nothing's changed – not if I have anything to do with it. Only my determination to see this through and do what's right. And I don't just mean this deal. Trust me.'

Sadie searched for a clue as to what the hell was going on, but the receptionist appeared again with a receipt and so did Mac's full-on poker face. A practised player, aloof once more. Just then his face cracked into a wide smile but his gaze wasn't on her – it was looking behind her.

She turned around to see a little brown-faced girl, flushed from playing football, running up to Mac holding the hand of a smaller boy, who was hiding his face behind her arm.

'Mister Anderson, Mister Anderson!' she squealed. 'Lee spoke! My brother – he spoke! He tried to call you when you went off with the lady. Lee, say what you said to me. Mister Anderson wants to listen.'

The little lad emerged from behind his sister's arm and looked at the floor.

Mac left Sadie's side and knelt down next to the boy, who could have been only about three or four.

'What is it, Lee, what did you want me to hear?' Mac said with a softness to his voice that caught Sadie's breath in her throat.

He looked up at his sister ruefully and crinkled his little brow, chewing his cheek and digging the toe of his battered trainers into the floor.

'What is it, little man?' Mac said more confidentially, and held out his arms. The boy did the same and Mac lifted him up and wandered slightly off to the side. The little girl followed. Sadie looked on in wonderment.

'Say it, Lee, say it,' she said.

'You …' the youngster began, looking Mac straight in the eye and taking a piece of grass off Mac's chin. 'You pick me next time? Please? You pick me?'

Mac swallowed hard. Sadie saw the impact that question had had on his face.

'I—'

'He means the team! He wants to be on your team next time,' Sadie said.

'I be …' said the little boy, '… I be big enough. Next time. You come back, right? You pick me?'

Mac let out a breath and laughed. 'Yes, I pick you next time. When I come back.'

'When you come back, Missah Anderson pick me! Missah Anderson pick me!' The little lad beamed, showing a gappy smile. Then he held out his hand for his sister, and Mac put him on the floor, gave them the rest of the bag of candy, and said goodbye. They scampered off into the yard again with the candy, and were met by a cheering group of kids. The look on Mac's face said it all.

'It's definitely not about just showing your face, is it,' she said, tenderly.

His answer was a crinkle in the corner of his eyes. 'See you later, Ms Turner.'

'We'll chat later, right?'

He paused. 'Right.'

'See you later, Missah Anderson.' She smiled.

He went to kiss her on the cheek, then thought better of it as she turned awkwardly, reaching instead for his hand as if to shake it. He ended up patting her arm. They stood apart, slightly embarrassed.

'Get your glad rags on this afternoon. The ones you kept. I guess the ones you sent back weren't so glad.' He looked at Sadie with a sideways glance. She made a face at him.

'I will be paying for them myself, thank you. And the,

er ... phone. Will be just a loan. For now. OK? But I'll make my rags look perfectly adequate, don't you worry.'

'You *wow* that Bill Galloway and it won't matter *what* his son thinks.'

'I will, Mac.' A beeeeep sounded from outside.

'Looks like the bus is leaving. Hurry.'

She rushed to the door and waved back. But he was gone.

As Sadie was lining up to get back on board the coach, the air filled with a loud thudding, and a helicopter taxi appeared in the sky overhead. The whole yard was suddenly full of windswept, cheering children, rushing to wave to the helicopter as it rose up into the sky from behind the trees, and disappeared in the direction of the beach. Mac was at the window and waved back at them, and, Sadie thought idly, at her too.

Up in the helicopter the children were now just diminishing dots hundreds of feet below. Mac let his face go, and immediately it became furrowed once more. He turned away from the window.

Another home, another wrench to leave them.

It wasn't a question of saving them all – even Mac's pot wasn't bottomless. And often it wasn't just about the money. These kids needed love. But he wasn't the one to rely on for that. Whatever money he could give, however, he would, and he'd keep on giving for as long as he knew he could make a difference. Giving his time was another matter. It meant giving of himself. And some parts he just wasn't ready to give.

But in a year's time, if all went according to plan, all that would be different.

He gave a command to the pilot to descend towards the beach a few miles in the distance, the sun glinting off the golden sand and vivid blue water. He felt a pull in his stomach and he closed his eyes. *Children's homes.* Each time it drained him, as much as it energised him.

Too many memories, too much pain. Twenty years ago one of those kids would have been … Snapping his eyes open again, he shook away the chains anchoring him to the past and looked out the window.

The helicopter pilot began his descent and Mac felt adrenaline start to flow. Nothing helped him escape the past more than his extreme sports – except they'd had to become more and more extreme over the last few years to satisfy the growing emptiness within. Surfing some waves would have to do for now – he had to find some way to clear his mind. And get some serious sea swimming in, so that his training didn't go completely to pot.

He'd revealed a little more of himself than anyone ever saw today. To Sadie Samantha Businesswoman. So, most of all, he needed to clear away the image of Sadie's face, soft in wonderment, watching him hold the little boy. And he definitely needed to banish his innate instinct to hold her too. 'Cos that just wouldn't do. Wouldn't do at all.

Besides, he needed to focus. Because in about three hours it was make or break time for the deal, and possibly for Sadie's future. And what he hadn't told her was that after this morning, it could go either way.

Chapter Eleven

Sadie got back to the hotel and showered for the second time in five hours. Humidity had a lot to answer for. It had been a busy morning – all that science and seeing Mac's soft side all before lunch.

An hour later, she was still in the bedroom, with two half-finished cups of coffee sitting beside her. She was sitting on the bed with her legs up, her chin on one knee, checking for any messages on her new mobile phone. There they were at last – the latest performance results from the early trials on the water samples. She read them through, then sent a quick text home, and left the phone to charge.

Still no word from Mac.

She'd at least expected a heads up. Still, she reminded herself, it was probably Alexis who was getting the briefing from him right this minute. Probably somewhere in the hotel. Maybe even just the two of them, alone in Mac's room, she was probably …

Brrrrrrrinnng.

The room phone rang and she nearly jumped off the bed to answer it.

Mac!

'Daaarling!'

'Oh, it's you, Mum. You're up late.'

'Yes, well the girls insisted on watching the TV with me and George.'

'Mum! I told you about—'

'Darling, we have news. I did leave a message earlier, at least I think I did. But I've got you now. Anyway, Georgia passed her Greek! I mean German! All on her own! See how clever she is? Yes, you are my smooch-coochy … what? They're not *your* cheeks, they're your mother's cheeks – and mine by proxy, so I'll pinch them if I want to! Anyway, go to bed, you can talk to her tomorrow. If she finds out I let you watch the late movie she'll ... oh, here you are then.'

The plaintive voice of Sadie's youngest came on the phone. 'Mum?'

'Hello, darling. Told you you could do it. Did you use that verb conjugation I told you about, and—'

'Mum ...'

'What?'

'We miss you.'

A lump in Sadie's throat just about stopped her saying 'Nana driving you nuts again, huh?' Instead, she said, 'I miss you too, darling.'

'Mum ... if ... if you can't afford to pay for the trip. We spoke about it. We'll give up the places. If you need us to.'

'Let's see, my lovely,' Sadie replied, then got onto small talk as quickly as possible for a couple more minutes before Georgia gave her a big 'mmmmmwah!' good night kiss, and handed her back.

'Sadie, are you still there?' said her mum.

'Yes, Mum.'

'How's it going?'

Sadie slumped onto the bed. 'To be honest, I don't know.'

'What? Haven't they given you an answer about signing the contract yet? Will it be long? Can I buy my sports car yet?'

'Mother ...'

'Well, it's nice to have something to look forward to darling, that doesn't involve George and bowls.'

'I thought it was Herb.'

'No, Herb's gone off with Greta. Anyway less about us and more about you. When *will* you hear, then?'

'I really don't know, Mum.' And Sadie went on to have a quick word with her other daughter, who was unusually quiet. Sadie's creeping guilt began to make its way once more into her psyche. She badly missed home. But this trip was so important. And she needed someone to talk to about it all – and with her sister, Helen, incommunicado for a week or so, she decided to update her mother on everything that had happened. She normally wouldn't share everything with her in such detail, as it usually came back to haunt her, but Sadie felt lonely so it all came tumbling out. She had to admit she did feel a little better afterwards.

'Well, don't forget we all love you. And think you're amazing and clever and all those things a mother should say to a daughter.' Sadie's mother paused. 'And so often doesn't … I don't … Not often enough, darling.'

Sadie choked up a little at her words. Her mum went on, 'Abi and Georgia understand, too, by the way. A big bill arrived this morning – one that wasn't on your list. So I had "the chat" with them earlier this evening.'

'The chat?'

'That the latest school trip had better be a no, after all, since it's just out of the question given your budget right now, and the extended deadline was yesterday, so they've both decided to turn it down, and agreed to tighten their belts too, till this is sorted.'

'That explains a lot.'

'Well, I told Abi being the only one in the class not to go to China is character building. And Georgia can stay with her friend, Suki, whose parents are getting a divorce so she can't go either and at least they can share each other's pissed-offness. After all, we've all had our fair share of disappointment in our lives, haven't we? I said haven't we, darling? Sadie?'

Sadie couldn't speak – she felt the lump grow exponentially bigger in her throat. Her eldest was going to miss out on the one trip she'd been talking about for a year. No wonder she was quiet.

Sadie felt the tears prickle and shook herself. *Just a little longer – so close now, so close. Think positive, think positive.*

'Well, it's bedtime now, for us at least. We'll talk again tomorrow. Nice to hear from you. Glad you're back in mobile communication. I'll give the girls the news that they can harass the hell out of you again now, instead of me. Plus they can slag me off via the wonders of social media. Like those trawls.'

'Trolls mum, you mean trolls.'

'Whatever. Goodnight, sweetheart. And I'm sure it'll all work out, you'll see. Glass half full and all that. Now talking of glasses, where's my Chardonnay.'

Sadie said goodbye and dabbed her eyes with a tissue. She really wanted to go home but this was it now. At the big meeting this afternoon the heads of terms should be signed, and her future secured. At least Mac seemed sure it would. But her initial excitement at the cut and thrust of being thrown into the middle of a business battle had been replaced with a sense of anticlimax. Especially now she hadn't heard a word from Mac. She had a funny feeling in the pit of her stomach. And she desperately hoped he'd be in touch soon. Unless something was the matter.

She got up, showered yet again, got changed and ready to go out, and was about to walk out the door when there was a knock.

Mac?

'Hello, Sadie.'

Bill Galloway stood at the door.

'I was wondering if you'd join me for a brief spot of lunch?'

Over lunch the old man looked troubled, but he carried on a conversation with Sadie nonetheless. She remembered him mentioning that he'd have liked a daughter once upon a time, and she had to admit, he reminded her just a little of her father.

As they ordered drinks, Bill quizzed Sadie about her work.

He wanted to know her opinion of the plant, the science and more about her planned studies. Then Sadie told him about Peter's speech from the gantry – and that he only needed to break some loaves and share some fishes to complete the image.

'You make me laugh, Sadie. In some ways you remind me of my late wife, God rest her.'

'I bet she would have been proud of Peter and of what you've achieved.'

The old man hesitated, his smile fading. 'In some respects, I'm sure she would.'

The subject turned to his support for the children's home.

'Yes, when Peter's mother was alive we made many visits.'

'The children are well looked after there, aren't they?'

'Nowadays the homes are great, yes, but it wasn't always that way. My wife, she grew up in a home – it never left her. Kindred spirits, she said. We often went to visit the children together – especially in the early days.' The old man's eyes were wistful. 'She always loved children but we were too busy back then. What with starting up the hotel, and everything.'

'So the hotel came before you set up the first air taxi company here?'

'You've done your homework.' He chuckled. 'Yes, and the little mineral water plant, and the local bakery. Most of them have gone now though.'

'Wow, it's a wonder you ever found the time to have children at all.'

'Mmm,' Bill said, uncomfortably.

'And the invention of Frish? Was that after Peter came along?'

'Yes, I was always dabbling. Thelma – that's my wife – used to complain I spent too much time out in my den. It was only the garage, but I'd turned it into a lab. Helped me cope with the pressure of all those businesses. Once a scientist, always a scientist, but then you'd understand that, right?'

Sadie just smiled.

'Ahh, yes, those years were the best. Little Peter always wanted to help me, always wanted to be involved, but he was quite an accident-prone young lad, always breaking things and knocking things over. Found him using my expensive equipment to make his own concoction once. Had to lock the lab door in the end.'

'Well, he seems to have turned out fine.'

'More credit to his mother than to me, really.' Bill looked skywards. 'You see, Thelma, Peter's all down to you!' He chuckled and sipped some of his wine. 'No, I was too busy selling Frish. Just making enough to sell locally to our friends. We had queues around the block back in the day, you know.'

'Yes, I do know, you were telling me the story when we met at the Awards Ceremony.' Bill looked blank. 'Two weeks ago? Where we met? Remember?' Sadie explained. Surely he remembered, it was only a fortnight ago.

'Er, oh, yes, yes, of course I do. Occasionally get a bit foggy nowadays, I'm sorry, my dear.' Bill opened a bottle of Frish and glugged it down.

'You said they came from far and wide to sample it. Miracle water, you said they called it! You must have been very proud.'

'I was. It made a lot of people better. But it wasn't enough to save Thelma.' Bill gazed into the distance. 'All the years of hard work to make it all a success. But by the time it was at its peak she was very ill. So Peter and I fulfilled her legacy, took it commercial after she passed on. Built a plant, then another plant. Now we must continue as best we can. We must expand to keep up. "Run before you can walk", Thelma would have called it. Now we have to find a way to do it properly – that's where you come in, Sadie.'

'I hope so. Gosh, you've been a busy man, Bill.'

'Maybe too busy. Life goes by, you know? There's only so much you can do. Peter fights me. He doesn't agree, you know, with my offering you the chance to raise the funding we need.'

'So I gathered.'

'I'm sorry, Sadie. He is headstrong – only young still. He's only in charge of the plant, and cannot wait to be in charge of it all. He means well, but he's in too much of a hurry.'

'Headstrong kid, huh? I've got two of those!' Bill patted her hand and Sadie felt a pang of missing her kids. She decided not to elucidate. 'So does that part of him come from you – or his mum?'

'Me, I'm afraid. Thelma was always the sensible one, a calming influence on both of us.'

'And who does he look most like?' Sadie added, keen to distract Bill from a topic that obviously caused him some angst.

'Ahh, well, you see, neither of us.'

Sadie looked perplexed.

'It's not widely known but … we couldn't have children, in the end. Left it too late, you see. Peter was a special child – chosen by us.'

'Not from the home?'

'Yes. It was a natural step. It's not something he likes to talk about, however. Just like Mr Anderson.' The old man sighed, and poured some dressing on his salad. 'They should get on well really.'

'I'm sorry, what do you mean?'

'Well, you know, when we found out Mac also grew up in a children's home, I felt it was fate. Destiny sends us these connections, you know?'

Sadie did her best to swiftly digest what she'd just heard. *There's another surprise – no wonder he showed such affinity with the kids this morning.*

'Like my winning that competition, only to come here and meet you? And having the scientific connections you needed right at that time for the product to be taken seriously?'

'Exactly, my dear!' said the old man, and clinked glasses with Sadie.

'Well, they say everything happens for a reason.'

'One of my favourite sayings. Oh, you are indeed another kindred spirit, I knew you were. My instincts told me we would work well together. I just wish my son felt the same. He has ... ahh, issues. Always has had. Mind you, without that there would be no Frish.'

'Really?' asked Sadie, leaning forward and putting her elbows on the table. 'Tell me more.'

'He always seemed more calm and in control when he'd drunk enough water instead of rubbishy sodas. We banned them – long before people knew about these things. Then I just kept going till I found a formula he didn't mind drinking lots of.'

'Why did you call it Frish?'

'Frish was what Peter called it. He said it made him feel that way.'

Sadie laughed.

'Said he'd never ever felt "frish" when he was at the children's home. Made me and his mother laugh. And the name stuck.'

'Well, I think it's the name of a toilet cleaner back home,' she joked, making Bill laugh out loud.

'I'm sure that won't matter, once our Frish is as big as we're hoping it will be. If Peter has his way it'll take over the world.'

'Does Peter ever go back to the home? To help out?'

'Never. He has been too busy, what with his science degree he's continuously studying for. Or that's what he calls it – studying. I think he's been a bit too distracted by the trappings of success. You need to be dedicated, like me. Like you, Sadie.'

'Thank you, Bill. If nothing else, I'm dedicated for sure.'

'If only Peter were too. But he is a good boy. Most of the time, anyway.' Bill's eyes clouded over a little. His half-hearted attempt at eating a forkful of salad was interrupted by a call from across the lunch hall.

'Father, there you are!'

'Talk of the devil.' The old man winked at Sadie. 'Thank you, Sadie. You are a good listener.'

'Anytime,' she said, and briefly placed her hand over his.

Peter rushed over to join them both and made a great show of signalling to the pretty waitresses. He put a bottle with a red label prominently on the table in front of his father, who picked it up and examined it, then put it back down again.

'My usual, please, Huaka, my darling,' Peter said loudly, reading from her name tag.

'I'm sorry, sir, and what might your usual be, please?' the girl replied.

'The same as you ordered me yesterday. Don't you remember? Kalua pig with cabbage.'

'Apologies, sir. I was not here yesterday. But I will bring it for you as soon as possible and I will remember in the future.'

'Too right you will! Or I will be having a word with the new management,' Peter snapped.

The poor girl took his drinks order, refilled Bill and Sadie's water glasses, and left.

'Excuse me, Sadie, may I have a word with my son,' said Bill. And he stood to one side but not so far away that Sadie could not hear what was going on. Sadie made a great play of sorting out the walnuts from her salad.

'Peter, there's no need to be rude,' she heard Bill saying.

'Father, you're too soft. That girl was mistaken – she definitely took my order yesterday.'

'They are not our staff any longer, remember your place in our community. Her father or brother may work at our water plant – we do not want repercussions from your actions – not again.' Peter made to reply but Bill held up his hand to finish. 'Not when we rely on their goodwill to do all the extra hours. Now come eat.'

They re-joined Sadie at the table where she had almost finished her meal. A small pile of walnuts lay on one side of the plate.

'Apologies, Sadie. We were just talking ... shop. I am sorry to interrupt your tête à tête but I had to see my father,' said Peter, sitting himself down and shuffling his chair a little too close to Sadie's. 'I do hope you enjoyed your tour of our plant this morning?'

'Illuminating,' replied Sadie. 'It was just—'

'Now I must steal my father away,' he interrupted. 'I have something to show him and I'm sure you must have preparations to make for this afternoon's meeting.'

Cross at being so thoroughly dismissed but unable to do anything about it, Sadie said her goodbyes. He was right, there was a very important meeting to prepare for – and a certain person to track down. But no matter where she looked, or who she asked, Mac was nowhere to be found. So in the end Sadie gave up and, feeling just a little bit frustrated, returned to her room and went through her own notes one more time to double check her new proposals – the ones she was planning to go over with Mac, *had he deigned to show his face* – then went to freshen up. It was nearly time for the meeting.

Outside the boardroom the mood was tense. The mahogany doors were tightly shut – but they should have been opened twenty minutes ago. Mac was late, as usual, and Sadie – now in her best suit again, minus the killer heels – was pacing a little. The other members of Mac's team had arrived, and were talking in a low hum. She approached a small group of them.

'Are you well, Miss Turner?' asked Graham, turning towards her, his garish green tie the first thing that caught her eye.

'It's ... Oh, just call me Sadie,' she said. 'Yes, very well thanks. Any idea what's keeping us? It's twenty past three, isn't it?'

'When? Now? Oh, yes it is. Three twenty two precisely. Yes, they are running a little late. No idea why I'm afraid, we just turn up with our due diligence and reports as requested, and just wait till we're called.'

'Thanks.'

'But maybe Alexis will know something more.'

That's all I need.

Sadie turned and was met with yet another cover girl creation. This time perfect hair and perfect teeth combined with pink lipstick and matching nail varnish and tailored pink shift dress. Sleeveless, *natch*. And if she wasn't mistaken, it looked like Alexis had been sunbathing a little. *Or surfing* ... Sadie tried to blame the pang she felt in her stomach on nerves.

Sadie raised her chin to signal hello, and smiled.

'Oh, hello, Miss Turner. Simon's emailed me over some new projections. I've taken the liberty of adding them to your PowerPoint. FrishCo have already been given them to study in advance of the meeting at Mac's request. Simon said to tell you the proposals your friend emailed at lunchtime for the university studies were spot on. Timing-wise, it dovetails neatly into our three-year plan. Simon's added the new costing to the forecast.'

'Oh, but I would have happily added those—'

'You weren't around. I did knock on your room, but I figured you'd need all the time available to get yourself ready. It's not a problem, honestly, that's what I'm here for. Here's your copy to bring you up to speed.'

'You've been busy.'

'Yes, a woman's work is never done. Ha-ha.' And she swept off across to the rest of the team.

Sadie smiled curiously. She still felt like she'd been stung, but at least Alexis was a bit more friendly. Maybe she'd given up scoring points and this was her attempt at some female bonding.

Soon after the big doors to the boardroom opened finally and the group were beckoned inside. Some of them stopped in surprise.

At the far end, Mac stood already in deep conversation with the Galloways – both father and son – and seemed to be even less relaxed than when she'd last seen him. He didn't look up. Alexis joined them, to Sadie's displeasure, and handed a blue file to Mac. Soon everyone was seated around the table and the crucial talks began.

Two hours later, Sadie had done her part and Mac had put up a splendid show of solidarity, he and the team providing an utterly convincing case as to why the contract could *only* work with MCA, including one vital ingredient – Sadie.

Sadie had sat through all of it swinging like a pendulum – one moment wanting to give him a piece of her mind for neglecting her, and the next, wanting to wrap her arms around him for being so imposing, so commanding, so impressive.

Giving her a big build-up, he'd then handed over to Sadie to present her brief summary of the latest business plan, including all the newly-updated research proposals and, vitally, their impact on the likely future success of the marketing campaigns. Everyone leaned forward and you could hear a pin drop as they all sat hanging on her every word, as she listed the claims the company would be able to make just as soon as the studies were published. Claims that would indeed – if they came off – be not only groundbreaking, but should hit the headlines around the world. That's when the fun would start.

'So the full trials should concur with the confidential pilot test results – they should show that blood plasma volume reverts to normal around sixteen times faster than it does compared to giving dehydrated athletes ordinary mineral or tap water. And as we all know, an optimally hydrated athlete is a winning athlete.'

A small murmur went round the room.

'Then, every competitive sportsman in the world will be looking for a steady supply of Frish. And those tests can begin within three weeks of the contract being signed, according to my contacts in the UK sports science departments in all three major universities. They're clearing their decks as we speak.'

'And MCA's "NewCo" will be there, fully funded, to push through those studies, and to make sure the world has its supply line,' added Mac. His voice was strong, controlled, but something in his eyes was amiss.

The meeting came to a close, but instead of massive handshaking and popping champagne, instead of much back-slapping and a joyful buzz, there was a dull stillness in the air, an odd lack of oxygen she could only liken to the calm before a rainstorm.

No hearty handshakes? Does that mean no deal? What on earth was going on?

'Thank you, gentlemen, ladies,' Peter Galloway said, standing up in place of his father to bring the meeting to a close. Sadie looked over to Bill Galloway. His face was downcast, he had a faraway look in his eyes. What on earth had happened since lunch, merely two hours ago?

Peter then announced grandly and dramatically that the decision 'whether to go ahead with MCA's proposal' would be made within the next twenty-four hours.

Whether to go ahead? What the hell …?

'So enjoy the facilities until then, and we'll reconvene this time tomorrow afternoon.' He didn't even look over at his father, not for confirmation, not a smile, nothing.

Something definitely had not gone according to plan.

She could see it in Mac's stance, the wooden way he was shaking hands. It had to be connected with the sudden appearance of Tremain on today of all days, and she narrowed her eyes recalling Mac's reluctance to talk about it. She watched as Mac turned away, talking quietly on his mobile. Then she picked her moment to go join him.

'Mac, I—'

'Sorry, Sadie, got to pop out. I'll come find you later.'

'But, I—'

'I'll tell you everything when I see you.'

'Promise?'

'I promise.' But she noted that he said it with his words, not with his eyes.

Sadie watched him disappearing towards reception and frowned. A voice at her side suddenly made her jump.

'I would imagine he's off to consider how to raise the stakes, given how friendly Galloway seems to be with Tremain,' said Alexis.

'I thought Bill Galloway hated Tremain.'

'I mean Peter Galloway. He's been a busy little bee behind the scenes and no mistake, he's the one that's put a fly in the ointment somehow. Certainly unethical, letting Tremain turn up like that today.'

'It was all Peter's doing then?'

'You've probably already heard this from Mac, but yes. Flew in early this morning, the heli-pilot said.'

Of course, Alexis would just have to be the one to know all this. Sadie's eyebrow flickered slightly.

'From what I could tell, anyway,' Alexis continued, 'Peter Galloway likes to feel in control. He was telling me this morning before the tour that he's always been in the shadow of his father. Hard to live up to. So bringing in Tremain is his perfect opportunity.'

'But we were so close to signing.'

'Honey, at this level of the game, nothing's a "done deal" till the deal is done. Ain't nothing signed till the ink's dry.'

Sadie's shoulders slumped. 'Dammit.'

'But you know,' the leggy, blonde, 'small print-handler' continued, a glimmer of something mischievous in her eyes. 'If only there was some way to convince Galloway junior. Why if I wasn't engaged, I'd give that man an offer he just couldn't refuse ...' and she pointedly looked at Sadie, before sashaying away.

Sadie watched her go.

'Oh, well, could be worse,' said Graham suddenly joining her, with Derek close behind. 'If you ask me, it looks like they just want time to go through the new proposals in depth.'

'Yes,' agreed Derek. 'Could be the liquidity ratios, could be the ...' He kept on talking but Sadie's mind had stopped listening, and was working overtime running through the facts – but nothing added up.

Bill Galloway should have been pleased – just the final due diligence and the first vital funds would be made available well within his thirty day deadline. *That was what he'd asked for, wasn't it?* But Bill's face too had been unreadable and instead of signing the heads of terms for the deal, as everyone expected, he'd disappeared right after the meeting, walking straight off, even ignoring Mac. Sadie didn't get a chance to say one word to him, let alone shmooze him.

Peter Galloway, the renegade son, however, was loving his moment in the spotlight, holding court and spouting off as if he'd already usurped his father. And he was now coming towards her across the room. Next to her, Graham and Derek were having a debate about equity splits and Peter gestured for Sadie to join him.

Looking around, Mac was nowhere to be seen, and Sadie found herself thinking the unthinkable.

Was there anything she *could do?*

It had to be worth a try.

If, somehow, *she* could get Peter Galloway back on their side, his father would maybe follow. It was now or never. She wouldn't do what Alexis was implying, but what could she do?

'Peter, take a walk with me,' she said, holding up her arm and beaming at him.

'Funny, I was about to ask you exactly the same thing.' They went out into the flower-filled gardens for an early evening stroll before dinner.

Chapter Twelve

Mac returned just as Sadie's back was disappearing out the door.

'Graham, Derek, where's Sadie going?'

'Just gone outside to take some air with young mister Galloway, I believe, Mr Anderson.'

'With Peter Galloway?'

'Yes, sir.'

'Take these notes, lads. You've got some urgent work to do.' Mac passed over a blue folder to Derek, who immediately brightened. 'Simon will explain everything.'

'Yes, sir. It's all systems g-go again then, is it, sir?'

'Just read the notes and get cracking. There's no time to lose. Ask Simon about any further questions you have. He's jetting in urgently this evening.'

'Yes, sir, of c-course, sir.'

'Excuse me,' said a bellboy as the lads left. 'The limo is ready and waiting for you at the front entrance.'

'Thanks, please tell them to wait. Ms Turner and I will be there shortly.'

Mac followed Sadie outside along the flower-filled, fragrant garden paths and was very careful to stay in the shadows some way behind. He trailed her into an ornamental garden, before getting close enough to hear snippets of their conversation from an alcove behind a big bush. He stood there, frowning. *What the hell is she up to?*

He was about to find out.

'The thing is, Sadie, I am glad of what you tell me but your UK scientists *should* be impressed with their early results – it's no big news to me. Of course, if you actually provided me with full copies of their impressive preliminary tests, that would be even better.'

'Sorry, Peter, it's not protocol.'

Their voices were very close together, and Mac strained to see through the branches of the bush. His fears were confirmed. Peter Galloway was arm in arm with Sadie, walking slowly round a little ornamental pond. *Too close for my liking,* he thought. *Maybe there's a whole other side to Ms Sadie Turner.*

Sadie's shoulders were slumped and it looked to Mac as though she'd been hoping for a different outcome to whatever conversation they'd been having – he'd only caught the tail end.

'Hmm, I understand. They are keen to do the research – as they should be. It will be an accolade for them.'

'Yes, but they need to know they're dealing with a bona fide operation, not a bunch of mavericks who may undermine their chance at conducting proper research,' said Sadie.

'And whom would you be referring to?'

'Just from what you said about how it's currently being sold in the stores … by Tremain's people …'

'If you're looking for a maverick, turn your eyes to Anderson's camp. You need to research your ally a little more thoroughly, Sadie. You might be surprised at what you find.'

'Mac's been nothing but straight with me,' Sadie said, lifting her shoulders.

Mac smiled behind the bushes.

'Are you quite sure about that?' Galloway asked, a sinister tone to his voice. 'I've seen the way he looks at you. Just as he looks at all other women.'

Sadie blushed.

Damn the man. Mac gritted his teeth. He watched as Galloway turned to face her and held her arms.

'He's a playboy, Sadie. People like you are playground fodder for him. Don't be fooled, he's not in it for you. He's in it for the money, just like Tremain. At least Tremain is up front about it.'

'Peter, I never thought I'd say this, but you may be right.'

Mac blinked, amazed at her response. *What was he hearing?*

'I am right.'

'But that raises a very important point,' she went on. 'And that point is who's the most likely to follow through? To do it right? This is business, after all. Don't underestimate Mac's determination – he's already recompensed the research teams for their early work – without even a contract. They're already happy to work with him.'

'If the UK team don't do the studies, we will find others who will. Others who could be more easily … persuaded … to work *our* way, shall we say.'

'Hang on, who said anything about—'

'Don't worry your pretty little head on the matter, Sadie,' Galloway smarmed.

He probably shouldn't have said that, thought Mac. Sadie's eyes had narrowed.

'I *worry my pretty little head about it*, Peter, because your father asked me to. Because he had faith in me – that's what he told me. He said he "saw" me working with him, being involved in setting up the deal.'

'Ahh, my father's visions. Yes, Sadie, I've listened to them all my life. Sadly, they are not as strong as they used to be – the local police stopped coming to him for help with their unsolved cases some time ago. And he has been suffering lately – he gets tired. And you see, what with the latest developments, it might mean that the other … options … on the table may now be preferable to ease cash flow.'

'But your father was very clear he wanted to give me a chance first.'

'Well, there are some offers that are too good to refuse,' Galloway continued. 'As your precious Mac has probably told you – Tremain's offer may change everything.'

Sadie looked confused.

'Ahh, he didn't tell you, did he?'

Goddam.

Sadie ignored Galloway and just crossed her arms, shaking free of his grip.

'The commotion in the production plant this morning?'

'Yes, indeed. That "commotion" may well bring my father – and our business – exactly what it needs, and all because of me. And if it does, my father will know that I am the one who has made this deal happen, not – with all due respect to you and your talents – one of his infamous "hunches". He thought I couldn't do it, but he was wrong.' Galloway was ranting now, pacing a little in front of Sadie. 'You brought Anderson, with all his due diligence, red tape and cronies. I brought Tremain himself, with proven sales, and a new offer that's hard to refuse.'

'As is Mac's. Not many people would be able to fund the deal so fast.'

'Well, not even Mac can do what Tremain has offered.'

'Which is?'

'Tremain has moved the goalposts. He is offering up-front royalties to FrishCo if my father agrees to do the deal with him, not Anderson. In cash. Now.'

Sadie frowned. 'A bribe?'

'A legitimate incentive, Sadie. Unusual, but not unethical. Royalties based on their future sales of Frish, that's all, but paid out way before they're due. It reinforces just how confident Tremain is of success. And it's very timely. With the pressure off cash flow, it allows my father to think things over. He has gone to lie down.'

'Is he okay?'

'It is time for his medicines and he just needs to rest. In fact, he needs to step out of the limelight for a while. A man of his age finds it exhausting.'

'He seemed okay at lunch.'

'Nevertheless, one day he will step down permanently. And I will, of course, be standing by.'

'Of *course* you will,' Sadie snipped. 'So, let me get this right, the race against time is off?'

'Exactly.'

'So no more thirty days?' Sadie looked incredulous.

'No more thirty days. You didn't know? You didn't know that either?'

Sadie looked away. Mac shrunk back further into the bushes in case she spotted him straining to hear.

'And may I ask what Bill himself has to say about all this? I'd like to hear it from him.'

'You will, my dear Sadie, if this evening's meeting goes according to plan, you will.'

'Who with? Tremain? He's meeting Bill tonight? After everything we did this afternoon?'

Now it was Galloway's turn to shrug. 'I can't possibly reveal.'

Mac swallowed heavily. He looked at his watch. *No time to lose.*

'You may not know this,' Galloway continued, 'being so new to the game, but the world of business is cut-throat. It takes a special kind of person to understand the rules.'

Sadie's eyes narrowed to a slit.

Oooops, thought Mac.

'Well, no one's quite as "special" as you, Peter, are they? *Do* tell me more.'

Oh oh. Mac smiled, but Galloway continued, oblivious to Sadie's sarcasm.

'Our product is a phenomenon. It will take the world by storm. Whatever the outcome of these initial negotiations.' His voice was rising, and he turned Sadie round by the arms to face him, placing his hands on her shoulders and getting a little too close for Mac's comfort.

'Don't you see? Money men get a taste of this water and what it can do, they see the numbers, and they want part of it. They can smell the success, feel it in their bones. Tremain has *seen* it first-hand too. He's a money man through and through, and money men, by their nature, will stop at nothing. Why do you think Anderson agreed to turn this around so fast?'

'Mac's certainly got a one-track mind where business is concerned,' she said.

Mac shook his head a little in disbelief, his eyes wide open. *What was coming next?*

'And where you're concerned,' Galloway added.

'Hardly.'

'Anderson needs you much more than you need him or his money.' The young man's voice was filled with spite. 'And after you hear what I have to say next, you might agree with me.'

Sadie cast her eyes downwards. 'I'm not sure I want to hear.'

'Listen to me. Your loyalty is commendable, but how long ago did you actually meet? He is a loner, and does his own thing. Do you know his full story?'

'No, I—'

'You are a family person. We are a family business and we need solid family people. Like you. That's partly what appealed to my father about you in the first place.'

'You may be right, Peter, I haven't known Mac for long. But it's irrelevant. We're getting off the point. For Frish to work there's a strict protocol involved.'

'I am sorry,' he replied, stiffening up. 'I do not mean to be facetious, but we are reinventing the protocol. We are already spreading the word, and achieving great sales, are we not?'

Sadie visibly bristled. 'But we discussed this at dinner, Peter. Frish needs to be handled carefully, very carefully.'

'Very well, my dear. Let's say the studies will definitely happen – if they are indeed so crucial. But as for who does them? Well, it *could* be you. Imagine the kudos. Would you like that?'

'I think you know my answer to that one.'

'Ah yes – once the eager little scientist, always the eager little scientist.'

Mac watched for Sadie's cutting retort, but she was keeping her calm.

'Why do you think your father gave me this chance?'

'A hunch. Intuition. Who knows.'

'It's because of my credentials. I can cut years off the process. If you go with Tremain you may ruin everything. Everything.'

'Leave behind this mask of righteous indignation, and listen to what I have to say. I have some news for you. After our long discussion today, I persuaded Mr Tremain that because of the results of your preliminary studies – which I told him were confidential and could not be shared yet – it appears they may be more valuable and more speedy than anyone imagined. That's what I told him.' Peter smiled – the irony wasn't lost on Sadie.

Sadie looked incredulous. 'So why are you—'

'I listened to you, Sadie the scientist. And I used it to my advantage. He is now taking your involvement seriously. Very seriously. All because of me.'

'Well, I …' Sadie wasn't sure what to say. Galloway cut her off again. Mac was still behind the bush straining to hear and going redder and redder with anger.

'And your studies and your scientists will now become an integral part of *his* offer to my father, to FrishCo. Sure, he also told my father this morning that unless he seriously considered this new offer, he was going to put an immediate stop to all current distribution and delay the payments due.'

'He what?' she asked, suddenly understanding why everything had gone so very 'not' according to plan today.

'Tremain is a businessman. He drives a hard bargain, what can I say? One day when I run FrishCo I will take his lead and be just as ruthless. God knows those lazy workers deserve to be taken down a peg or two. And as for you?' He moved closer towards Sadie and she stood her ground.

Mac nearly burst trying not to miss a word.

'Well, *Miss* Turner, we have an offer for you. And I would advise you to accept what I am about to give you. It will pay you – literally – to keep on the right side of Philip Tremain. And Peter Galloway.'

Mac thought his heart might stop as he waited to hear what was next.

'And if I don't like his offer?'

'Oh, a woman like you is sure to *like* it.'

Again, no reaction from Sadie. *What the* ...? Mac's heart began to pound out of his chest.

'You can indeed choose to accept Tremain's offer, or refuse it. If you refuse and Tremain gets the contract anyway, if your precious university contacts accept their offer too, then we will consider our options. Your currency will be worth much less then. For my father, you were essential. For me you are "nice to have" – in more ways than one, Miss Turner.'

'You make it sound as though I'm disposable. What happened to Bill's prediction?'

'It seems Tremain's offer may help him "see" things slightly differently.'

Sadie looked dejected.

'And I?' Galloway continued, nudging Sadie's chin back up with his finger. 'I'm not so sure we couldn't just get a local laboratory to do some simple studies and have done with it. That way you and I could have a slightly ... different ... arrangement.'

Mac leaned forwards to get a better view through the bushes and saw Galloway play with the ends of one of Sadie's blonde locks. His gut wrenched.

'I do hope you're not talking about mixing business with pleasure, are you Peter?' Sadie said, her tone neutral, unreadable.

'Would that be so bad?' Galloway said, with a mock pout.

'Oh, yes. Yes, very bad. Best to keep business and pleasure separate. Always.' Her voice was flat, uncompassionate.

Now it was Mac's turn to glance downward. He bit his lip.

'We shall see. And now, Miss Turner, I have the offer for you.'

Mac pushed himself into the bush as far as he could and stopped breathing.

'Sadie,' Peter Galloway was saying, 'Tremain has said if I can persuade you to work for his team, it will be ... ah ... lucrative ... for me too. It will be, shall I say, big.' He handed Sadie something.

She gasped.

'And who knows, you and I may have some fun along the way.' He twirled Sadie's hair towards his face and smelt it.

Mac nearly jumped out of the bush at him. *The smarmy, double-crossing ...* But he had to hear Sadie's reply.

'This is what they're proposing to give me? Me? Now?'

'Yes, right now, as soon as you agree to jump ship.'

'Let me think about it, Peter. This is a lot of money.'

Mac's jaw dropped.

'And double that will go immediately to your university friends to begin their work.'

Sadie looked up at him, as if in shock. She bit her lip. Mac held his breath.

'This is sudden,' she said.

'Anderson is not the only one who can act fast.'

'I don't know what to say.'

'Say you'll accept.'

'Tremain does drive a hard bargain. It's a tempting offer, for sure.'

Mac's blood ran cold and he froze in his tracks. *What the ...?*

'It is, and you're right to take it. Don't fret over Anderson. He's a big boy. It's not like you have any strong allegiances already. He's rich, sure. But he's a fly-by-night. Chancer's blood, by all accounts – too much time with the ladies. Not a serious businessman like Tremain is. Like I will be when I get to take over the company.'

'Hmm,' said Sadie and turned away.

Hmmm? thought Mac. *Is that all she can say?*

'What if it's Tremain who isn't true to his word?'

'Sadie, we are people of the world, you and I.'

Mac winced as he squinted through the bushes and saw Peter make Sadie turn around to face him once more, bringing his body near hers. But they had moved further away from the bush and Mac felt twig marks creasing his face.

'You might not get another chance like this. Anderson's team are straight down-the-line venture capitalists. They would never offer you what Tremain is willing to offer us – to offer you.' He held her hand up, brandishing the note in it.

'This is all so unethical, Peter.'

'That is why I am coming forward in secret right now. Bu-u-u-t, it has to be said, Tremain is not a patient man. He knows Anderson will bite back.'

Sadie was standing still, nodding.

'So Tremain will not wait around to be beaten. I need – you need – to give him a decision soon. It is essential. I have a contract waiting.'

Sadie stood staring at the note in her hand. Mac willed her with every ounce of his being to do the right thing. *Give it back, give it back.*

'Sadie, imagine the freedom it will buy you. Freedom for – who is it – Georgia and Abi, yes? Think of them if not of yourself.'

I don't believe it, thought Mac. Sadie faltered.

'Sadie, take my advice, take the money now. The offer would cease to be valid if, shall we say, my father no longer ran the company. He will one day hand over the reins to me, and tell me the patented formula for the secret ingredient. My own version of Frish – Red Frish – will be unbeatable once I have them both. Then I will have no chains around my neck, no obstacles to my own plans.'

'But that won't be any time soon, surely?'

'Ahh, he has his good days and bad days. And I have to tell you, sweet Sadie,' he said, lifting Sadie's hands to his mouth and kissing her fingers. 'There are already other university researchers who can be more easily bought than your team in the UK. Your value may not be a window that's open for long, you see.' Mac watched Sadie recover her composure and smile sweetly, pulling her hands away from his and stepping slightly backwards.

'I appreciate your offer, Peter, really I do. That amount of cash—'

'Tax-free bonus up front …'

'Would help my shop and my family, of course. That can buy a lot of school trips. But I have to do it the right way, using the science to our advantage, not being slaughtered by the scientific cynics and buried before we can truly take-off. I'd be a laughing stock in my industry. You understand, I have to do things correctly?'

'Of course.'

'Of course?'

'Of course.'

'But if I accept – if Tremain wants me on board that badly – it means his team have to stop their current marketing tactics. Till we can make the claims officially, on the back of the new studies.'

Mac's heart dropped through his stomach. He swallowed heavily and his shoulders slumped. *No.*

'Look, if that is the deal breaker you need, let me go talk to him. He may choose to do as you wish, in order to cut the bullshit and get you on board. He will also almost certainly want to meet you. Soon. And in return for this boost to your family's fortunes, he will tie your sweet little ass up in a contract immediately.'

Sadie smiled limply.

'And it is a sweet little ass.' He moved towards Sadie and pulled her to him, grasping her backside. Much to Mac's dismay, she didn't slap him, just pulled away gracefully.

'I will still have to think about it,' she said. 'But if I choose to go ahead, yes I will happily meet with him. It may be interesting to see what he has to say. But you need to go and tell him that tonight before he meets with Bill.'

Oh my God, thought Mac.

'Good, Sadie, good,' said Peter Galloway. 'And till then, don't trust Anderson.'

'Peter, have you thought that Tremain may be using you too? Just like he could use me for my contacts and then cast me aside. I know as much of him as I do of Mac.'

'You are right, but much of what you have heard about Tremain has come from what source, huh? Anderson himself.'

'Hmmm,' she acknowledged.

There it is again, Mac fumed.

'There will be a contract between us, one that will give you what you want, or no deal. Have you got one with Anderson? A full one?'

Sadie just chewed her cheek. Mac strained to hear more clearly, they had moved a little further away.

'If I can make that happen, like I can make so many things happen, what then?' Galloway asked her. 'Can we seal it with a kiss?'

Mac closed his eyes and sat holding his breath, willing Sadie to give the answer he so needed to hear – or the sound of a hefty slap. But it never came. He waited and waited some more, then realised they had both moved out of earshot over the other side of the pathway.

Panicked, he took off around the side of the bushes and set

off stealthily in search of Sadie and Galloway. He tried to pick up her scent on the breeze, he tried to listen out for voices, but the wind was getting stronger and the gardens were full of fragrance. He picked a path and took off down it.

He had to find out what she had said. Would she stay with him and his team?

Or would he lose her forever?

Sadie let go of Peter Galloway's arm as they made their way back to the main reception. She was more confused than she'd ever been. But deep in her heart, she knew what she had to do. When they reached the entrance, Sadie held out the note for him to take back.

'I'm sorry you choose to take this route,' Galloway said.

'Peter, I'm not saying no. I'm just not saying yes. Yet.'

'It's a shame as I was looking forward to our first celebratory kiss.'

'I'm not sure that would have been part of any deal I'd want to do with you, Peter, I'm afraid.'

'Come now, Sadie, I've seen the way you look at me, the way you flirt with me. Anderson may have the hots for you but I know his ethics – you will never have him all the while you are in business with him. Now come over to Tremain's side and you'll find that I won't have that problem. Then maybe we could do a little double dealing of our own – and if you're not in business with him after all, maybe you would still be free to have your Mac.'

His words were making her skin crawl, but she had to play him along for a bit longer. And the temptation was huge to pay off her mum and her mortgage, pay for all the school trips and holidays and more for the rest of the girls' student lives, and have enough left over for a substantial trust fund for them all in one fell swoop.

But who are you, Sadie? Are you losing sight of who you are?

227

She was thinking of her girls and their faces if she'd brought that much money home in one go, when all of a sudden Galloway was kissing her.

'No!' She broke away immediately. Pushing him away slightly, she refused his further advances, but as she turned around, all she saw was Mac getting into the waiting limo and taking off.

'Mac!' she called, and waved. But he'd already gone.

'Hah. I'll see you later. You know where to find me when you change your mind.' Galloway beamed, and left, strutting like a peacock, even though the woman he'd just stolen a triumphant kiss from was wiping her mouth with the back of her hand.

No sooner had Galloway gone, than Alexis sidled up, looking like the cat that got the cream. 'Oh, Sadie, Mac was looking for you to accompany him,' she said, waving towards the departing limo. 'Something about an urgent meeting. But it seems as though he's decided to leave by himself, since I pointed out you were … otherwise engaged.'

'Oh, shut up, Alexis,' said Sadie. And she stomped off back to her room.

Behind her, she did not see a new arrival pulling up at the hotel entrance in a black Mercedes with darkened windows. Inside was the same person who had been watching them on the hillside in Monaco. And had followed them out to Hawaii. If she had known what had been happening, everything Sadie did from then on might have been different.

To say Sadie was disgruntled would have been an understatement. She made several calls and left express instructions with Derek and Graham to get Mac to contact her at the hotel. He wasn't answering her calls or texts. *Mac, I need to see you, urgent.*

This was unbearable.

She needed to find out what he'd seen in the gardens – and hopefully it wasn't much. Then face-to-face she'd explain what had happened, then find out if there was any truth in what Galloway said. Whatever Mac's reaction was to her news would help make up her mind on what to do next.

Chapter Thirteen

Half an hour and a hot shower later, there was a knock on Sadie's hotel room door.

Mac! She thought, hopefully.

'Ahh, Sadie,' said a smarmy-looking Peter, trying to push into her room.

'What do you want, Peter? I haven't made my decision yet,' said Sadie, blocking his way, but he still managed to lodge himself just inside the room. She kept the door open.

'I wanted to offer you dinner tonight, by way of apology.'

'I'm afraid I don't yet know my plans for dinner.'

'If you mean you are awaiting news from Mac, I have to tell you the hotel staff have informed me he hasn't returned since he took off in the limo some time ago, and sadly they don't have anything on their schedule for bringing him back again tonight.'

Sadie blinked hard and her shoulders dropped. *Where has he gone? And why isn't he answering me? I don't even want to contemplate that Peter is right.*

'So, allow me to take you to dinner. We can talk further about your studies and you can explain to me how they will change everything.'

It was tempting.

But it was Mac whom she really needed to talk to. Plus, she still had to be wary of rejecting Peter too strongly, in case it hampered the deal. Whatever deal ended up being done. All that mattered was her children's future. Wasn't it?

'If I am free, then perhaps.'

'Well, I will call on you in an hour then. Until then let me ask you something.' He produced a bag and took out two half-litre Frish bottles but they had a red sticker covering over the usual blue label. Brandishing them as though he'd caught a ten-foot fish, he offered them to her.

'What are these?'

'Prototypes for a new upgraded version of Frish,' he replied. '*My* version of Frish.'

Sadie sighed. 'Upgraded, how?'

'More effective than standard Frish.'

He was giving nothing away, anticipating more questions about his marvellous new invention, but Sadie wasn't in the mood for games. So instead she brushed him aside and indicated the door.

'Okay, leave them there.'

'But ... well, try some and perhaps we can discuss your thoughts on it later when we meet for dinner?'

'*If* we meet for dinner ... I'll see what I can do. See you later, Peter.' She closed the door behind him and found that curiosity was getting the better of her. She picked up one of the bottles and opened it, sniffed it, then sipped it.

Just as 'thin' and easy to drink ... nothing special. After half a bottle, Sadie made a 'so what' face, put the lid back on and headed into the bathroom to freshen up.

Almost as soon as she turned on the tap there was another knock on the door.

'Peter, what do you ... Mac!'

Mac stood at the door looking troubled.

'A robe? And you're expecting Peter, clearly.' He looked at her suspiciously and walked past her into the room. 'And you got me instead. Sorry if that disappoints you.'

'Great. I've been trying to contact you,' she said, ignoring his little dig. 'I needed to let you know what's been going on.'

'There's no need to explain,' said Mac coldly. 'I made it clear to you that there could be nothing between us, so you're free to invite whomever you like into your hotel room – even low-lifes like Peter Galloway. Kiss whom you like, too, for that matter.'

'He wasn't "in my hotel room". He was just delivering those bottles over there. And if you saw what actually happened earlier on, surely you'd know that *he* kissed *me*, Mac? You're being totally unfair.'

'Am I?'

'Yes. I would never want Peter Galloway. I want ...' The words were so nearly out of her mouth. She stopped mid-sentence, biting her tongue.

She may want Mac, but Mac didn't want her.

And now she came to think about it, what *did* he want? She knew so little about him. Peter Galloway's words resounded in her head.

'I want to know the truth,' she finished.

'About what?'

'Everything. About you. You don't know what he told me.'

'Actually, I think I *do* know.'

'How?'

'I have sources.'

Sadie was incredulous. 'What is it with you businessmen! You're all secretly watching one another. It's so unethical. Can't anyone just be straight with each other any more?'

'You tell me! Because you and I haven't been straight with each other since the start. You never told me who you were – nor me you. I didn't know about your children, you didn't know about my money. I'd say we're both able to withhold the truth.'

That hurt.

'What are you saying, Mac? That you think I'm just in this for your money?'

'Not necessarily, but—'

'Not necessarily?'

'Sadie, let's be honest, we don't know anything much about each other, do we? A one sheet resume is little more than useless.'

'Especially when you don't read it.'

232

He winced. 'And given the note you slipped under my door, it's unlikely we *will* get to know much more.'

'Especially given your stance on mixing business with pleasure.'

'One that's worked for me for a long time. It pays not to sleep with my colleagues.'

'Apart from Alexis.'

'That was *before* she was a colleague.'

'So you *did* sleep with her ... Oh!'

Mac was silent and looked down.

Sadie flushed.

She turned away and felt like she'd been kicked in the stomach. The pain stopped her speaking for a second.

God she was so stupid to believe him about his 'small print'.

Mac reached out for Sadie's arm. 'Sadie, it was *before* she was a colleague.'

Sadie gently shook away from him and turned her back, then took a deep breath. He was still the boss.

'Anyway,' she said, finally, 'it's none of my business if you did or didn't, is it?'

'Well, actually, if we do this deal, no it's not.'

'Well, "actually", even if we *don't* do this deal, it will still be absolutely none of my business. Ever. Will it.'

The implications of what Sadie was saying hung in the air like a storm cloud about to crack open.

Mac nodded his head slowly.

'Business *or* pleasure, you see?' Sadie said, cynically. 'So I'm right, about our ... options? You and me?' She turned to face him.

It was obvious what she was asking.

He took a breath, and looked at her, but his face had become that impenetrable mask – a practised face. One he used post-coitally when dealing with his many clingy females, no doubt.

Damn Peter Galloway for putting doubts in her mind.

'Why would we not do the deal?' He sidestepped the issue. 'You wouldn't have had a better offer by any chance, would you?'

Sadie couldn't believe her ears. Were they all spying on her?

'Who have you been …? How did you know …?'

'Because I followed you, Sadie.'

'What?'

'I'd come back to get you, as it happens, to come with me to a crunch emergency meeting – to find Bill Galloway and get him on his own. But you'd already gone off arm in arm with his son, as soon as I was out of the room.'

'You spied on me?'

'I'm not proud of it, but I'm glad I did, considering what I heard.'

'Yet you didn't have the decency to come and ask *me* about it? You didn't give me the benefit of the doubt? You obviously think *very* highly of me.'

'Actually, I do. But that's precisely why I came *back* here, to ask you just what had happened with the slimy toerag. Just in time to find he's been to your room!'

'I told you he was just—'

'Save your breath, Sadie.'

She flushed. This was a full-scale lovers' tiff. And they weren't even lovers. Not any more. She picked up the nearest bottle of water and walked across the room, glugging it back. Almost trembling, she closed the open door Mac had flounced through. She rested her back against it and wrapped her robe around her body defensively.

'I thought—'

'Sadie, it doesn't matter. I've got to be honest with you. I heard and saw quite enough today. There's no doubt in my mind *what* you thought. What were your words again? "*It's a tempting offer, Peter … no, I don't really know Mac at all, do I, Peter?*" I heard it all, Sadie.'

'There was ... a reason for that.'

'What reason could there possibly be for being tempted by that scumbag? So you could play him along? Just in case my deal didn't work out for you after all?'

'No, Mac,' she said softly. 'I did it for us – for you. In case there was any chance I could make some difference that would maybe persuade him that ours was the best option. That *you* were the best option.'

'Sure. You say that now. From what I heard it sure didn't sound like it.'

'Well, eavesdrop correctly next time and you'll know I didn't accept.' Sadie was flushed but calmer now, the full heat of the argument had passed. She was mortified he'd overheard her – it removed any chance of a proper explanation. But she felt aghast that he'd been spying on her. And angry he hadn't come to find out her side – what was one of her favourite sayings?

'Seek first to understand then be understood,' she told him.

'You didn't accept?' he said, quietly.

'You're not much good at stealth work, are you? Next time get the professionals in.'

'I do only have your word.'

'Are you calling me a liar, Mac?'

'A liar? You?' His eyes narrowed. '"*Sam*"?'

Sadie went red, and said nothing. Counting elephants wouldn't help now.

'And sure, maybe you didn't say yes. But did you tell him "*no*"?' he pressed.

She hesitated and bit her lip.

'Did you tell him where he could stick his offer? Did you tell him no?'

Ouch.

Now it was Sadie's turn to squirm. No, she hadn't told him no.

'Not yet. I told him "not yet" —'

'Not *yet*?'

She froze and felt like a rabbit in the headlights. Sadie hated confrontation. She'd known why she'd played Peter along, but now it just came out like she was betraying Mac. How could she convince him? She opened her mouth but nothing came out.

'Your silence says it all.'

'Well, what it *doesn't* say is that I was only trying to convince Peter about the implications of the early trials – it's even got a slightly different *boiling* point, for goodness sake! And that we need to do it right. If we do, we could change the face of hydration around the world.'

'Very noble. Spoken like the scientist you are. So?'

Sadie could feel the angst rising up like bile in her throat, she was making such a hash of this. She knew she had to get him to understand. She went over and took his hand. He didn't move.

'Mac, I was trying to get him on our side – to explain how important my studies will be in all this.' Sadie stood in front of him and looked pleadingly into his eyes. So close, the energy between them rose up again like the elephant in the room. He took her hand and pointedly removed it from his.

'How important *you* are in all this.' Mac turned and walked away from her.

'I ... I didn't know that. It's not my fault he offered me that bonus.' She was downcast now.

'It's a bribe, Sadie, not a bonus.' He almost spat the words out.

Again his vehemence cut through her like a knife.

'I didn't take it,' she said in a small voice, and sat on the edge of her bed, sipping some more water. Mac strode over and kneeled down in front of her. For a split second her hopes rose. Then he opened his mouth and spoke.

'Look, I can't stop you. If you choose to go over to

Tremain's side on this deal, that's completely up to you. I'll lose out, but there will be others. Like there always are.'

'Deals? Or women like me?'

He paused. Went to reply then stopped. Then he spoke. 'Either.'

Her eyes welled up and she turned away, gathering her thoughts. She began to feel just a little bit sick.

Dammit. Why were the words so quickly out of his mouth? Habit. Mistrust of beautiful women. The need not to commit? The need not to seem too keen? Or was it just being around this particular beautiful woman that made him act completely out of character.

A woman whom, if he opened up his heart and was truly honest with himself, he just wanted to scoop up into his arms and reassure it would all be okay. The burgeoning bubble of heat in his heart threatened to swamp him, to stop his breathing, to make his head burst. He hated this, hated it. Wanted to just hold her. Despite the fact that she'd nearly betrayed him. *If she had.* God, he wasn't used to being this indecisive.

But he didn't know her, not really, so how could he be certain? There were others in the past he'd been adamant about. So sure they wouldn't hurt him, despite warnings from friends. But still he'd been burned.

Now this one comes along and turns his certainty upside down. Looking into her green eyes, welling up with tears and anguish, he felt so bad. It shouldn't be like this. Not with her. Of *course* he knew her. Deep down, he felt like he had known her all his life. That they should be together. *Wow, where did that come from!*

Mac stood and walked to the window, thinking. It was simple really. If he did the deal, being together would be impossible – because of his own stupid rules.

Or would it?

Was Mac too long in the tooth to change? Was it too late?

Was it too late to pay heed to his instincts, to his gut, which was crying out *stop, stop!*

But what Sadie did next gave him his answer. She held her head up high and stood up.

'Mac, can you please go to your important meeting, you have business to attend to. You stick to your principles and I'll stick to mine. I'm on your side – and always have been. A part of your team – for as long as you want me there. I will inform Peter Galloway he can go stick his bribe, and if you can persuade Bill before it's too late, you will have your deal. Assuming he hasn't signed up with Tremain already. But you'll have to help out with funding probably more than you realised, because of what he's been threatening to do to Bill and the company's cashflow.'

'What are you talking about?' Mac asked, feeling confounded once again.

'Go find Bill. Peter told me they're meeting Tremain tonight. Presumably you're out of the loop on that one.'

Mac frowned.

'Not nice, is it?' Sadie added. 'To be kept out of the loop.'

Ooh that was a dig. And it hit home. But he didn't respond, so she continued.

'But don't worry, it's not my business. I'm a minion. I'm a Derek or a Graham. I'm not even an Alexis, am I?' she said. 'Small print or no small print.'

She was on a roll, gesticulating and walking around flashing her thighs in the robe. Mac just listened. 'I won't ask you to explain it all to me. Who am I but a ditsy woman? No, you can rest assured I will not get in the way of your business any more. Now it's time for you to leave.'

And with a dignity Mac had never seen in someone he'd just hurt so badly, she walked elegantly to the door, head held high, and opened it for him.

'Sadie, I—'

Mac stopped when they saw a bellboy appear at the doorway, holding a delivery. Sadie made an 'excuse me' motion, and closed the door again. They both dropped their voices.

'I think we've said enough to each other, don't you? You go do your business, I'll do mine. And after this, we can both keep out of each other's way and live happily ever after,' she snipped, in a tone he'd not heard her use before.

He went to say something else and thought better of it. 'You're one hell of a woman. You deserve much better than me.'

'I'm also a mother, Mac, so *you* need someone other than me.'

She opened the door and he left.

Sadie closed the door behind him. Immediately, she rushed into the bathroom to throw up.

Outside, Mac was leaning back against the door, chin in the air, eyes looking skyward. *Dammit! Should I just walk away? Or go back in?*

He angrily pushed himself upright, and went to leave. Then stopped and turned back. *Goddam women. Goddam Galloway.*

'Room 241?' said the bellboy coming back up the corridor now the coast seemed clear. He held out a small box. Mac nodded.

'Delivery for Ms Sadie Turner from Mr Peter Galloway? There's a message on top.'

'Thank you, I'll take it back in,' said Mac, tipping the lad generously as he scrawled on the receipt, and then taking the box from the bellboy who skipped happily away towards the lift.

Mac considered the parcel before him. He raised his hand to knock on the door, but curiosity got the better of him.

He was about to be unethical again. But dammit, there was more than just a business deal at stake here. And the biggest of snakes had sent it.

Walking a little way away from the door, he peeked inside the envelope attached to the top of the box.

Sadie

Please reconsider my offer for dinner.

I'll keep asking until you say yes. We could meet at nine? I want to know what you think about my baby – my own Red Frish. Here are some more in case you run out. I think my version is much better than my father's formula, and it would give me great pleasure to hear you say so.

And to kiss you again.

More importantly, regarding what we discussed earlier, Tremain would indeed like to meet you. I have some urgent business to attend to, but I've written his number on my card. Call soon. It may be just the news you're looking for.

And I hope to see you later.

Yours affectionately
Peter xx

Mac shuddered. Unprofessional, a slimeball *and* persistent. Or maybe there's something going on after all. A bubbling fury began to boil inside him and he knew exactly what to do. He turned tail and headed off swiftly down the corridor, dumping the bottles of Red Frish in a trash can.

It was make or break. Time for some straight talking.

Peter Galloway stood at the window of his father's office, fidgeting. He peered through the blinds and watched as

240

the rear view of an ambulance disappeared out of sight, its lights flashing. He had beads of sweat on his upper lip and forehead, despite the noisy air-conditioning unit overhead being on full blast. It was a balmy night.

Moments later, the figure of Mac came in sight, bounding up the steps towards the office door, taking two at a time, seemingly impervious to the humidity outside. He seemed composed. Unlike Peter, who had a slight tremble in his hands as he wiped his forehead with a handkerchief.

Before Mac's knuckles reached the door, it opened, revealing Peter Galloway's smiling face. In fact it was more of a sneer.

'Where's your father? He's agreed to meet me. And that doesn't include you.'

'There's been a slight change of plan, Mr Anderson, I'm afraid. You see we all knew my father was ill—'

'The ambulance. That was him? Is he—'

'Yes, he will be okay, but he has had one of his turns. Quite a serious one this time. They've been more frequent these last few days. It's the stress, you see.'

'You didn't go with him?'

'No, he took his assistant, Makini. I wanted to be here when you arrived. To give you the news.'

'What news?'

'It is with regret, but my father has decided to go with the offer from Tremain Group.'

'Well, with regret, and with all due respect, I can only accept that from your father.'

'Ahh, but that may prove a little difficult, seeing as how my father is incapacitated. Before he had his funny turn, he made me the acting head of the company.'

Mac couldn't believe what he was hearing. How suddenly fortunes turned.

'He what?'

'I have this signed affidavit.'

Mac took it from him and saw it had indeed been signed by Bill, and witnessed by the assistant. Mac took out another piece of paper from his pocket and put them side by side. It may have been a more shaky version of the old man's signature, but it matched the one on the note Bill had sent Mac earlier that day.

Mac turned towards the window and ran his hands through his hair. His body ached from tension and lack of exercise. His mind ached from the maelstrom of the last few days.

And his heart ached too – but he refused point-blank to dwell on it.

Peter continued, 'So you might as well ship out now. It's over, Anderson. Tremain has won.'

'And Sadie?'

'She is meeting me for dinner tonight – a feisty one, for sure – but with you out of the picture, I'm certain I will find that, like most women, she will turn her attentions to where her bread is buttered, as you English say.'

'If I find you are lying to me about any of this—'

'Yes? What will you do? Your threats are idle. Tremain holds all the cards. Tremain is the one who will make our miracle water – *my* miracle water – a success around the world. And, yes, including the studies – and if Sadie will not do them our way, well, we shall just replace her.'

'You might find she's not quite the pushover you imagine her to be. Dinner or no dinner.'

'Ahh, you are speaking from experience, I can tell. Well, my own methods of "convincing" a woman may be slightly more effective than yours.' And with that, Peter picked up a tumbler of whisky and swigged it down. He slammed the glass back on the desk triumphantly and smacked his lips, reaching for a top up. His hand accidentally knocked over several medicine bottles – tablets and herbal remedies, and an empty bottle of Red Frish. Peter saw Mac looking at it.

'You are curious about my own creation, are you not? Well, in time it may be even more successful than my father's. Too bad you won't be a part of it.'

Mac turned towards the door, his head reeling.

'Now, before you go, no hard feelings, huh? The best man won! Join me for a drink and we can part amicably. You never know, with your sports event not far away, we may even be able to sponsor you and give you some free water ... *my* water.' Peter poured another huge tumbler for himself and a second one for Mac. But when he turned back round holding the drinks, it was too late. Mac was gone.

Outside Mac was already on the phone. His head hurt, his heart ached, and more than anything else, he could feel a building desire to run. He wasn't used to losing. He wasn't used to being pushed away by a woman. And he wasn't used to this throbbing feeling gnawing away inside of him, one he couldn't ignore. No matter how much he rubbed at his stomach, his chest, it continued unabated. In fact, it was only getting worse. There was only one thing for it.

'Alexis?'

'Mac, at last. I need to see you.'

'Well, first get a car to take my surfing gear to the beach for me.'

'Surfing, Mac? At night? Skinny dipping again? If I remember rightly, last time you and I did that a certain lady had just broken your heart. History repeating itself again, is it? Anything I can do to help, Boss Man? You know you can count on Alexis.'

No wonder she'd never look after his small print again.

'Not now, Alexis. But there is something you can do for me.'

Chapter Fourteen

Back at the hotel, Sadie had started packing. It was half-hearted, as she kept putting things in the case then taking them back out again. Throwing up in the bathroom wasn't helping – the stress, she supposed. She wiped beads of perspiration from her forehead. Then her new mobile rang.

'Mum? ... Oh, Simon!' she said, and suddenly she found herself brimming up with tears. A friendly voice. He'd be there soon, so hold fire ... and had anyone seen Mac? Sadie quickly filled him in on what had happened so far, Peter's jumped up ideas about Red Frish and how she'd fallen out with Mac. He then left Sadie to continue packing, but very soon he was back on the phone to her again.

'There's something you should know,' Simon said.

He told her what no one else had, revealing Bill's sudden hospitalisation, Peter's coup and the fact that Mac had gone missing again, and suddenly at least one part of the puzzle began falling into place. And now Sadie knew what she had to do – if time permitted.

But where *was* Mac? He wasn't answering his mobile – neither was Alexis. Sadie grabbed her bag and rushed out the door. Were they together? *God forbid.* She didn't know. She didn't know about a lot of things right now, but it was time to find out.

The waves usually worked his troubles away. The effort, the pounding against the body, the extreme coordination of muscles and mind. Usually surfing left Mac satiated, spent – like good sex. But *without* the annoying 'morning after'.

This time, however, he felt nothing.

Mac stopped. Gave up. *It wasn't working. Nothing was working.*

No matter how hard he tried, no matter how many waves he caught, no matter how much he tested his body with sheer physical effort, he could not shake the sickening feeling in the pit of his stomach.

Losing to Tremain.

Beaten by slimeball Peter Galloway.

Worried about Bill.

But most of all a mixture of concern and disgust over Sadie.

'Women,' he said out loud, hauling himself and his board up the beach.

But the hut wasn't empty. Inside, Alexis sat waiting. She'd also been swimming and was drying herself down. She threw her damp towel at him and it landed squarely around his face. She laughed. Mac didn't.

'Mmmm. Seems that six-pack is even more defined than I recall. Still looking good, Boss Man.' And she reached out to trace her fingers along his stomach, which was dripping wet as he breathed deeply from his exertion. He caught her hand and pushed past it, throwing the wet towel aside and heading for the little shower behind a screen at the back of the hut. Mac grabbed a fresh towel and placed it on the hook, then disappeared behind the screen.

'Okay, so what's the news on Bill? Did you get through at last?'

'Sure, it's not good, Mac. He's had some kind of seizure. It may be something he ate. Or one of his kooky Hawaiian herbs. His assistant was very worried about him. Said it's touch and go. He's in isolation until they get the test results, in case it's something more serious. No visitors. Even you.'

Mac was behind the screen, removing his shorts.

Alexis went on, 'But the assistant, what's she called ...?'

'Makini.'

'Yes, I knew it was some weird name.'

'They're all weird to you, Alexis,' he said, popping just his face back out from behind the screen as he threw his shorts on the ground.

She wrinkled her nose at him, but he ignored her.

'Well, anyway, she *did* witness the signing. Bill *did* sign over the company. She's confirmed it. Peter's in charge.'

Mac heard it all, but didn't respond, just turned the shower on full, directly onto his face.

'Sorry.' She stood and picked up the wet towel and hung it over the top of the screen. Then took a step closer towards the shower area. 'I'm sorry it didn't work out, Mac. A deal ain't done till the ink is signed, huh. Just a shame it was the wrong ink this time.'

'Thanks,' Mac replied.

'Anything else I can do? For you? Boss Man? Like ... anything?'

'No, but thanks for your help. You can go now. There's no phone signal here, so you can get my driver to take you if you like. Tell him to come back for me afterwards. He's up in the car park waiting in the limo.'

'Yes, I saw him. Waiting to make sure you were safely out of the water. Someone's always looking out for you, huh, Mac. Thanks, maybe I will. Or ... maybe I have my own plans.' She got up and sashayed over to look out at the ocean. 'What's it like always having to be babysat, Mac? Simon's like a nanny, isn't he? At least BJ is his own man.'

Mac ignored her dig. She and BJ had never cared for Simon.

And, yes, Simon took care of Mac – he was always taking care of Mac. Always giving strict instructions to ensure Mac's safety. Another few months and that wouldn't be necessary – the tight schedules and stressful deadlines would all be over.

Well, maybe it can happen sooner, now ...

Mac stepped further into the shower and gasped as the hot water hit his body. He contemplated his options. At least this next step was obvious – and the pounding of the shower spray was just what his body needed. He rubbed his chest and washboard stomach under the running water, feeling the tension in his muscles dissipate slightly.

But the tightness inside his gut was still there.

Turning the shower off, Mac realised he still had a bit of soap in his eyes, and started to rub them but only made it worse, so he kept them firmly shut. But when he reached around to feel for his towel, it wasn't there. It must have fallen onto the wet floor.

'Alexis?'

There was no reply. She must have gone. Probably just as well. Last time he'd been this low, this vulnerable, she'd also conveniently shown up and had preyed on his weakness.

Damn women.

They were all the same.

Weren't they?

Who knows. Who cares? Maybe it really was too late for Mac to change.

Now where's that towel rack?

Feeling along the wall to the shelf where the towels were kept, he finally felt the fluffy edge of some towelling, and pulled it towards him. But what he actually did was pull Alexis's dressing gown wide open. She hadn't gone at all. Instead, she'd undressed, and was standing up close to him, naked underneath it.

'Alexis!' Mac retreated back behind the screen and washed the soap from his eyes with water. 'You're the limit, you know that.'

'I gotta shower too, Boss Man. Sure you don't wanna come back in with me?'

'No, I don't, and cover yourself up. Those days are long gone. Hand me a towel, please.'

She reached for one round the corner, and he watched her in the mirror, peeking past the screen just far enough to make a 'wow' face at his naked rear view. He caught her and scowled. She shrugged, handed him the towel, and retreated.

Then Mac emerged with it wrapped around his middle, she'd given him a small one – only just long enough to reach round. You could see the muscular thighs peeping out from the slit at the front. He pushed past Alexis and grabbed another towel for his hair.

'Shower's all yours,' he said. 'I'm out of here.' *Be civil, Mac, be civil.*

'Need me to do that?' She moved in closer and started rubbing his hair, but he suddenly stopped and pulled her roughly to him by the arm. She offered her mouth to him. But instead of kissing her, he just held her still, trapping her arms by her side.

'Ancient history, Alexis,' he snarled. 'I told you before. You know my rules. You know how to behave if you want to stick around.' He glared into her eyes, daring her to respond. She did so, by freeing up her arms and immediately throwing them tightly round his neck.

Mac's towel started to fall and he tried to grab it. As his arms stopped pushing her away, Alexis thrust her naked body up against him and reached up once more for a kiss. In the tussle his towel dropped to the floor, leaving Mac naked with Alexis skin-to-skin, her dressing gown wide open. But before Mac could react, there was a noise from the doorway.

'Sadie!' said Mac.

She was standing there open-mouthed, shocked.

'The driver said you were in here … Oh for God's sake, Mac!' Sadie cried, and ran off.

'Wait!' he called. 'It's not what you think!'

'Mac leave her! The heli-taxi's been ordered for her. She's leaving on the late night flight. She's the one that's outta here. I, on the other hand, am right here in front of you.' And she stepped forward and thrust her rounded bosom into his chest. He just shook his head, stepped backwards, and turned away, reaching for his clothes.

'How did she know to come here?'

'A gal's gotta do what a gal's gotta do, Boss Man.'

Suddenly Mac got it. 'Get away, Alexis. Get back to BJ before I tell him everything.'

'And lose your best funding buddy? I don't think so. But I'm going anyway. It just got kinda dull around here.' She pulled her dress over her head and grabbed her bag. 'And you just got kinda boring. Usually *this* body doesn't need to beg.' And she stomped off towards the door.

Mac chased past her after Sadie but the wind was picking up and she was almost back to the car park. He went to shout, then changed his mind.

'Dammit.' He stood on the darkened beach, the warm Hawaiian night breeze blowing his damp hair around, looking like a shot from one of those calendars, but with no one there to appreciate the view.

Alexis was off to take his limo. Way in front of her, Sadie had already reached her waiting cab.

If she looks back …

But she didn't. She got straight in, and they pulled away without a backward glance. He watched the cab disappear slowly out of sight, taking Sadie with it. Mac felt frozen to the spot. The ache in his chest doubled. Now it actually hurt. What was that ache? Maybe he'd pulled something.

A minute later, Mac's limo also whisked Alexis away, leaving an empty car park – apart from one other brave soul sitting in their black Mercedes. *I wonder if he's got woman trouble too,* Mac thought.

At last, he turned and walked back to the beach hut, kicking up the sand angrily as he went. Well *this* trip had been a turn up for the books and no mistake.

Maybe it's for the best, he thought.

He had, after all, taken Sadie halfway round the world on a gigantic goose-chase. And Mac didn't know how to handle 'goose'. Usually everything just worked out – so smoothly, so efficiently, so predictably. *What Mac wants, Mac gets …*

Except this time.

Mac finished dressing and sat staring into space for a while.

Once again, Mac was all alone.

There was a growing battle in his head and it refused to be quashed. And right in the middle of the maelstrom, was his conscience.

Yes, he should try to contact Sadie. He needed to explain about Alexis. He shouldn't have to, but he felt the need to. Why, God only knows.

But then what good would it do? She wouldn't believe him, and in any case, he'd done exactly the same and not believed her about Peter earlier on. The irony wasn't lost on Mac. *Touché*.

What a mess. A right royal botched up mess.

Proving once and for all, that women had no place in his business life. Especially this woman – in fact, she had no place in his life for either business *or* pleasure.

But no sooner had he thought it than the same angst-ridden feeling was gnawing at his gut once more. His head was saying 'let her go'. But his heart was telling a different story.

Finally, he sat on the steps of the hut, swigging a beer and feeling the warm wind on his face, feeling more down than he'd felt in years. It hit Mac like a sledgehammer that even now, after all that had happened, there was only one person in the world he would have wanted to be with right now. And in that moment he knew that was precisely why he had to let her go.

It wasn't too late to charter a private jet – better get the hell out of here, before he changed his mind.

Chapter Fifteen

Back in her hotel room, Sadie's case was open and clothes strewn all over the bed. The run back to the cab in the humid air had made her need yet another shower, and she calmed herself beneath the bracing spray.

Seeing Alexis and Mac in the beach hut had been such a shock. All thoughts of finding Mac and telling him her theory about Bill had gone straight out of her head. Instead, all she kept seeing were flashbacks of Alexis's perfect ample boobs pushing up against Mac's washboard stomach. She felt sick, she felt angry, and she wanted to punch something.

As she stomped through reception, she'd seen Graham and Derek, who were bickering amongst themselves about an email from Alexis. They too had been booked unceremoniously on the next plane back home. Sadie wasn't sure why, but she soon found out. Before she bid them goodbye, the guys had made the bottom drop even further out of Sadie's world, by announcing to her that according to the email MCA were giving up on the deal, that was it, game over. And they told her Peter Galloway's definitive triumph. Derek and Graham were miffed about the last-minute changes, but they already had their next assignment for BJ.

Now back in her room she was resolute. Soon the heli-taxi would whisk Sadie away to the airport for the late night flight, and a day later she'd be home. *What a difference a day makes.*

Her mind was racing. Just what was Mac's game? She was sick of it.

Men!

When will you learn, Sadie, me girl? When will you learn?

Give them a wide berth till the girls are grown – that was

the plan. Stick to the plan. It's a good one. Then you can't get hurt. *Yes, good plan.*

Coming out of the shower, she noticed the light flashing on the phone on her bedside table. Her heart pounded as she pressed the button to listen to the message, then chastised herself for still hoping beyond hope that it would be Mac.

But it was Peter's smarmy voice that began talking.

'Sadie, they said you're packing but don't leave. Not just yet. I need to see you, but I have some important business to attend to first. It's true, things have changed, but … there's more to tell. Don't leave. I will contact you later.'

What the …?

Would he repeat his offer? Should she complete her alienation from Mac by jumping ship? For the sake of her own fortunes? Or just pack her bags once and for all and go home back to her everyday life once more?

She wished she could ask Mac his advice. But he was the last person she'd be able to talk to right now. Not after what happened on the beach. Maybe Bill could have advised her. In any case, Sadie didn't want to leave without at least saying goodbye. And if he was able to just listen, thank the old man for giving her such an amazing opportunity – even if it hadn't worked out. If she could sneak past the hospital militia to see him.

She sat in her dressing gown, thought it through, then made a few calls.

Peter Galloway was not answering. Sadie chose not to leave a message.

And she tried Simon a dozen times but he must still be in transit.

She was missing her daughters enormously, and her mum, she admitted begrudgingly. Although she'd probably get a right 'told you so' for going off gallivanting and it not working out. What would she do next? Maybe one more call to Peter, just in case … But she felt the pit of her stomach fall away at the notion of 'going over to the dark side', along with a huge wave of guilt that she'd been away from home for so long. *What a mess.*

She wasn't really hungry but her tummy seemed to have recovered enough to nibble something, and for the first time this trip she thought *what the hell,* and ordered the most expensive item on the menu to go on Mac's bill.

Serves him right, she thought.

A knock at the door had Sadie scrambling for her robe, calling as she did so.

'Just a minute!'

But it wasn't her chateaubriand at the door.

It was Mac.

'Oh,' she said, the sight of him immediately making tears prickle at the back of her eyes. Suddenly she couldn't breathe. 'What do you want?' she asked. Her chin was proud, her face strong, but her resolve was weak. If he'd taken her into his arms right then and there, she would have had him back – *back! What are you talking about? You never had him in the first place.*

'I wanted to explain,' he said. 'I needed … to explain. I owe you an apology.'

'There's no need. What you and Alexis get up to is totally your affair.'

'We weren't getting up to anything. She is very persistent, she was trying to kiss me, and my towel slipped.'

'How very convenient.'

'Sadie, there's no need to be like this,' Mac said.

'Oh, but there is. Doesn't this sound familiar, Mac? You didn't believe me about Peter. And this is no different.'

'Well, it is a bit,' he said.

'Okay, yes it is. He tried to kiss me in public, fully clothed, and Alexis tried to kiss you in a private beach hut, stark naked!'

'Sadie, I'm sorry. Okay, it works both ways. Let's … let's

forgive each other and at least leave on good terms. I had such high hopes ...'

'Yeh because *what Mac wants, Mac gets*, right?' She turned away from him and began clearing some of the mess into her suitcase.

He just smiled, closed the door, and walked towards the window. Sadie pulled her robe around her more tightly. Being suddenly alone in a room with Mac again, with next to nothing on, made her senses heighten.

'Did you see the sunset?' he asked. Her window looked out over the ocean. 'It was the most amazing cacophony of crimsons and oranges and deepest yellows.'

The sun had also all but set on one of the most eventful days of Sadie's life. She joined him at the window and sighed.

'Yes, I saw it.'

'Amazing, wasn't it?'

Nothing was said for the longest moment, and then Mac broke the silence.

'Sadie, don't go.'

'What?'

'I said I don't think you should go.'

'Mac, I don't know what to say,' Sadie said, feeling brighter, despite her best intentions to be angry with him. 'I was—'

'I failed. With the deal.'

'I know.'

'But it's not over yet. Peter is likely to make you an offer – you might not have missed out after all,' Mac went on.

Sadie's shoulders dropped. *So that's what he came to tell her.*

'Peter may be full of shit, but if I know Tremain he'll investigate this need for scientific studies before he agrees to do what Peter wants. Especially if there's money changing hands up-front for bringing *you* on board. And if he knows what's good for him – and I think he will – Tremain will want you as part of the deal.'

Sadie looked at her feet. Mac continued. 'He's here, in

town. Don't you see, that means he's really serious about this? Whatever he is, as a businessman he sees things through. Don't miss out – don't miss out on the offer just because it wasn't with me.'

'Oh,' she said.

'It's not your fault everything changed. Your part of the contract could still go ahead. If you want it to. You'll just be in business with Peter Galloway and Tremain, not me.'

'Oh.'

'Is that it? Just "oh"?'

'I thought you were going to say ...' her eyes searched his, azure-blue, with dark, dark pupils, and for a moment – a fleeting moment – she got caught up in his gaze. 'Oh, I don't know what I thought,' she said at last.

He was silent for a moment, and then took her hand. 'You thought I was going to say "now we're not in business any more, let's have mad passionate sex. Just for one night"? Didn't you?'

'Mac!'

'I'm joking! I was ... I was trying to make you laugh.'

'Huh. Some joke.'

They stood for a while longer, with Mac still holding her hand. Sadie's body and mind couldn't get a certain image out of her head – one from a moment that seemed a million miles away, on a yacht somewhere in the Mediterranean. Mac seemed to sense it.

'I'd better go,' he said at last. 'I need a drink. Hot chocolate with stroodles ... or maybe a Baileys.' He smiled. Sadie flushed at the memories he evoked and spoke quickly to stop him noticing.

'I'd offer you one but I only have this other bottle of Red Frish – and that doesn't seem like such a good idea considering who created it.'

'Yes, Simon's filled me in about Peter's little brainchild.'

'You spoke to Simon?'

'Yes, I got a phone call the second I left the beach. No signal in the hut. He wasn't impressed at how long I was incommunicado.'

'It doesn't appear as though much impresses Simon!' Sadie joked.

'Well, you did,' Mac said. A silent wave of knowing passed between them again. Mac let go of Sadie's hand and picked up the Red Frish.

'Simon's been busy,' he said. 'He discovered some interesting information from some of the staff here – people who also do shifts at the water plant. The word is out that Peter's been beavering away late into the night at the plant, working on this little brainchild of his. But Bill never gave it any importance.'

'Of course, his own little effort at getting one up on his father. It's not as nice. I tried some earlier but didn't finish it. Don't know where he's going with it, but it needs careful testing.'

'Oh?' asked Mac.

'Well, from what I can tell, it acts slightly differently from regular Frish if my visit to the bathroom earlier is anything to go by.'

Mac looked surprised.

'Ooops, sorry. Too much information,' she said.

'Actually, not enough. Tell me more. That's the other reason I came to see you. To discuss what I saw at Bill's office.'

'What did you see?' she asked.

'First tell me about how this water works.'

'Well, I can't say much more, but I've asked one of the guys in the lab here to liaise directly with my uni friends and compare testing results so I might have more news soon.'

Mac took a little taste of the water in the bottle as Sadie continued. 'But it's a good job I only drank half a bottle of the stuff with my senna tablet. You know, to help …' Sadie waved her hand around. Mac looked quizzical. 'You know, like … it's for constipation. Felt like I'd taken two instead of just the one.'

'Interesting,' said Mac. 'And slightly disturbing.'

'Too much with the sharing again?'

'Little bit,' he said, smiling. 'And not in the least bit of a turn on.'

Sadie shrugged and smiled. 'It wasn't supposed to be.'

'I know,' Mac replied, warmly. 'And I'm learning it's just the matter-of-fact way your brain works. It's who you are. It's good, who you are, Sadie. Don't let anyone ever tell you otherwise.'

Sadie's breath caught in her throat and she swallowed hard. 'Glad my geeky brain came in useful for something,' she said with a half-smile.

'Sadie,' he said, crossing to her once more and touching her arm, 'You're not a geek. You're only half a geek.'

She couldn't help but laugh, glad of the tension breaker. 'What's the other half then?'

'Mother? Super-hot lover? Successful businesswoman?' he said.

Sadie didn't know where to put her face. She squeezed his hand.

'Hardly successful businesswoman. Seems I'm not that lucky, after all.'

'You make your own luck. Remember?'

So the gloves were off. Not only off, but in the process of being sent to long-term storage. Mac was playing nice guy.

'It's that knowledge of yours, Sadie. That *super-brain*. Time to use it.'

'I thought I had been. Fat lot of good it's ever done me.'

Mac put his finger under her chin and raised her face towards his. 'So what if you had to leave the research lab when you had the kids. Some of those ex-colleagues of yours will be green with envy when you get the commission for this. You'll have done it all on your own. You just have to play along a little longer, that's all.'

'Like a game.'

'Exactly.'

Another game. Sadie sighed. 'Is that what all this is to you? A game?' She turned away slightly.

'That's not what I meant.'

'That's exactly how it sounded. And I don't play games, Mac. Not any more.'

Mac took a deep breath. He turned her to face him, and she fought back the tears once again. Feeling his hands on her arms, the heat from his body only inches away, she felt the pangs of longing begin to course through her body.

All that stood between them was a plush robe and a million miles of misunderstanding.

'Sadie, listen to me.' He looked at her in earnest now. The blue eyes searching her own green ones, sincere, genuine.

Just like he'd stood with Alexis not two hours before.

Sadie felt like she was going to kiss him – or kill him. She just couldn't decide which right now. She cleared her throat. Listen to him? She could at least do that much.

'Yes?' She tried to make her voice impassive. To make her heart impenetrable.

'Sadie, you deserve happiness. I thought for a brief moment that it might be through me – through our deal. A deal I wanted, too. But I've realised something – and it's something big for me – that I just want you to be happy. If I'm honest, that's the main reason I was working so hard – being so hands-on – to try to make this deal work.'

'Really?'

'Really.'

'So you think I should still go for it?'

'Yes.'

'Peter did call. But I wasn't going to do it, Mac. It felt like I was betraying you.'

'No more than I betrayed you, by putting my principles before my ...' Then he stopped.

'What?'

'Nothing.'

'You were going to say ...?' she asked.

'Nothing. Forget it, Sadie.' Mac walked away from the window and looked dolefully at her half-packed luggage. 'Nope, it looks like fate has other plans after all. God knows you deserve a bit of luck. If you do this thing now, maybe some of your heart's desires will come true. But it might be a one-off chance. So do what you think is right. Do it, Sadie. The opportunity may never happen again.'

'Do it?'

'Yes.'

'Do what I think is right?'

'Yes,' he said.

So she took two steps towards him, reached up, and kissed him. Hard.

Mac acted surprised at first, but then he kissed her back. Hard.

Sadie's arms flew round his neck, as her lips touched his and he responded by taking her up into his arms and lifting her bottom in the air. Sadie wrapped her legs around him as the kisses intensified and he backed her against the wall, still held high in his arms.

Just like last time. Only so, so different.

This time she knew she loved him.

Don't say it, Sadie, don't say it.

His tongue was exploring her mouth and her lips, kissing her cheeks and jaw and neck. Her hands were in his hair. Sadie felt a level of intensity she'd only glimpsed on the *Nomad* in Monaco. This time, there was history. She knew the man. She knew his soul. She knew his heart. She knew ... that he was only doing this because they were no longer in business together. *Hang on a minute.*

Abruptly she stopped, and looked at him.

He made a face. 'What?'

'I'm sorry, I shouldn't have started something I can't finish.'

'What the ... hang on a minute, Sadie, what happened?'

'You wouldn't be kissing me back if the deal was still on, would you? Answer me that.' He paused. 'Tell me, Mac?'

'If the deal was still on, no I wouldn't be kissing you back. And you wouldn't be kissing me in the first place. If the deal was still on we'd be downstairs celebrating.'

'Well then, put me down, because I'm not going to be one of your disposables.'

Mac raised an eyebrow.

'Yes, I know what you call your women. Derek and Graham were a little too free with their conversation after dinner the other night.'

'You'd never be one of my disposables. If anything, *Ms* Turner, *that's* exactly how you made *me* feel!' He was still holding her in mid-air, her legs still around his waist, his arousal still obvious for her to feel. The air thickened and he looked at her mouth as he spoke, his face only inches from hers. '*One night only* – your words – remember?'

'Yeh, well, maybe. But that doesn't mean we should have a repeat performance.'

Neither of them spoke.

'It doesn't?' he whispered, as their pulses throbbed in time, as did their breathing – getting heavier – and a deep ache began to connect their very cores.

'No, I'm afraid it doesn't,' she said, with a tinge of sadness, resolute.

So he set her down upon the bed, gently enough to remind her how strong he was, but just rough enough that her robe separated slightly. *Oh-ohh!*

Sadie made no move to close it. She followed his eyes as he cast a glance downwards, despite himself, and unconsciously licked his lips. Then Mac looked at her face, a look that Sadie knew meant just one thing. *Do what you think is right,*

Sadie, his words resounded in her ears. And in that moment, she couldn't stop the words coming out of her mouth.

'Hypothetically though …' she said.

'Yes?' he asked, dropping to his knees in front of her. Her heart was pounding out of her chest and she could see the pulse throbbing in his neck.

'Hypothetically, if you did … if we did … well, say there had been a second night.'

'Yes?'

'Tell me what … what would have happened?'

'Only if you tell me how it began first.'

Sadie's heart felt like it was in a vice. Battling with her body, which badly needed Mac's. Right now. The deal was over. And soon they would be gone. One more night. *One night only.* Second time around.

She took a deep breath, exhaling out all the 'Sadie' angst and emotion she'd built up inside. Then inhaled a huge lungful of 'Samantha'. She focused for a second then felt a smile creeping across her face. Maybe this bit was going to be easier than she thought. Because if she gave herself to him now she joined the ranks of his disposables – meaningless, nothingness sex. *Then it would be easier to say goodbye.*

'So you want me to remind you of our second night? Our "hypothetical" second night? You mean you've forgotten already? Tut tut.' She teased.

He nodded, and rose up on his knees, getting slightly nearer. His pupils were turning black with desire.

'Jog my memory,' he said, and gently rubbed her knee with his thumb.

Game on, Sadie thought.

'Let me see if I can,' she said, and she slid to the edge of the bed. 'First you surprised me by turning up unannounced when I'd just taken a shower. And as I was sitting on the bed, you slowly reached for my robe.'

Mac slowly put both hands on her robe.

'And then you pulled it back.' Her eyes met his in a knowing moment of no return.

'Like this?' he asked, drawing her robe back to reveal her thighs, stopping just short of revealing her completely.

'Almost.'

'You mean …' He breathed deeply. 'Like this …' And he kept looking into her eyes as he gradually drew back the edges of her gown the extra crucial inches.

'Yes, just like that,' she whispered, and nodded, urging him on and laying back onto her elbows.

His eyes left hers and looked slowly down her body to where she lay, completely exposed. He breathed deeply, closing his eyes and moistening his lips ever so slightly.

'Did I touch you?'

'No – no you didn't.'

'Fortunately.'

'Unfortunately.'

'Would you have liked me to?' he asked.

'I've not *stopped* wanting you to touch me.'

'And I've not stopped *wanting* to.'

With that, Sadie sat up and took his face in her hands. He kneeled up higher to face her, and looked intently at her mouth. They were up close again, and the electricity was starting to spark between them once more.

Undeniable, indefinable, unavoidable.

She kissed him on the nose. Then the eyes. Then the cheek. She dwelt on the side of his face where, without the benefit of stubble, his scars were more visible, and she kissed those too. Sadie felt a tear prickle and blinked it away. If this was going to be goodbye, this would be a proper send-off. One he'd remember. And one she'd never forget.

Then she continued kissing. By the time she got to the corners of his mouth, he was parting his lips ever so slightly, and closing his eyes.

He wants me. We're really going to do this.

She lay a delicate butterfly kiss right at the very edges of his mouth, and he turned his face slightly so that their lips met. Neither of them moved. They just stayed there, breathing each other in, and feeling the passion stirring their bodies to life. He ran his tongue across his own lips, fluttering onto hers as he did so. She moaned ever so slightly.

'Mac.'

'Sadie.' And he climbed onto the bed with her and took her into his arms – powerful, longing, and full of desire – and his kiss had never been more deep, intent, and meaningful. They pulled each other close, and finished the kiss with a long embrace, holding each other as the seconds ticked by, neither wanting to move.

'You were quite the dominant one, I can tell you,' she said at last.

'Oh?'

'On our second night.'

'Oh.'

'I thought you were going to make me do something we'd regret!' she said.

'What?'

'You really want me to remind you?'

'I really, really do.'

'Well, see if this helps.' And with that, she lay back on her elbows once more. 'I was here, like this and you were there.'

'Down here?' he said, and moved off the bed to kneel on the floor once again.

'Yes, right there.' She moved so that her legs were either side of him. Despite the fact that this would undoubtedly change everything, again, the feeling of doing what she shouldn't be doing, considering everything that had happened – that he'd made happen – just heightened the excitement of the moment. She felt herself getting wet and ready for him once more, and his arousal was also obvious, but she closed her robe across herself, just covering up once again.

'And then what? What happened then? What did we do?' he begged.

'You want me to tell you this, why?'

'I like it when you tell me.'

'Well, then hold my robe open.' Parting her legs, the edges of her gown drew apart, tantalisingly slowly this time, until inch by inch, she revealed herself to him once more. He drew a sharp breath.

'You know the rest.'

Then Sadie gave herself up to the moment, and lay back fully on the bed. Mac moved closer. She could feel his hot breath getting nearer her body, and when she looked up his mouth was only inches from her mound.

She knew what she was getting herself into but she was powerless to resist.

'Yes. And now, you. You tell me. What did we do?'

'I think I would have done this,' he said, lowering his face until it was an inch away from her. 'Then this,' and he opened his mouth and exhaled slowly, onto her sensitive skin. She groaned. 'And then,' he said, breathing around her in a small circle, 'and then I think I would have done this.'

He opened his mouth as wide as it would go, so his lips covered her, then his tongue came out flat and he licked her, all the way up.

Sadie let out a long, low moan.

Then barely touching her, he flicked his tongue again from the very bottom to the very top of her, inserting a tiny bit further in, just as he reached the top. Then he breathed out heavily – hot, tantalising, teasing. She writhed a little beneath him. Sliding his tongue into her crevice at the very top, he slid it inwards, deep into the wet slickness, stopping just over her most sensitive nub. He paused and Sadie could feel the pangs of passion shooting up and down her body.

'Would you?' she said, panting. 'Is that what you would have done?'

'Yes.'

In that moment, Sadie resigned herself to the fact that her last memories of Mac would be similar to her first.

'What else?'

'I would have done this, and you wouldn't have stopped me.' And he teased her lips slowly apart, pulling them upwards so that her nub became exposed. He kissed it, tenderly, as if it was her mouth. So tenderly. She groaned in earnest. He did it so slowly, so skilfully she thought she would burst. Then he curved a trail around her hot centre with his tongue, then pulled it into his mouth.

'Oh God, and I wouldn't have been able to stop you,' she groaned.

'No you wouldn't.' And with that he slid his two fingers inside her, and she bucked beneath him, as he resumed kissing and sucking her at the same time.

And suddenly he was bringing her to the peak again, and she was rising and rising, then suddenly falling over the top into an abyss of amazing light, and sensation, and then darkness. Her panting slowed slightly and she opened her eyes and saw him looking at her face, and her body.

'But then what?' he asked. Sadie couldn't speak, so she just smiled. 'Well, I can't pretend I wouldn't have done this,' and he rose up and started to undo his belt.

'Oh, yes,' she said, reaching up to help him free himself, 'and maybe, accidentally, I'd have let you do this.' She pulled him out of his trousers and sat herself up before him on the bed. 'Oops … But most importantly I would definitely, absolutely, *never* have done this,' and she kissed the very tip of him and slid out her tongue to circle him.

'Oh, Sadie,' he groaned. 'Oh my God.' And he tried to make her stop.

'Hands behind your back this time. This time, it's all about you.'

'Oh … God.'

And with that, she ran her tongue down to the base one side and back up the other side, and then took him fully into her mouth – a deep long stroke that had him touching the back of her throat, in and out, in and out. Then she took him in her hand and stroked up and down, providing a tightness at the base as her tongue and mouth provided a soft cavern, caressing him at the tip. Over and over again, she swapped between sucking him in deep and teasing him with her tongue. He bucked beneath her deeper and deeper until suddenly he withdrew, before it was too late. She grabbed him again and sucked.

'But – ohhhh – you see, I don't … think I *could* have stopped you,' he whispered huskily, moving his hips back and forth against her mouth. 'Because it wouldn't have been long before ultimately,' he said, kneeling up, and pushing down his trousers, with her hands helping him, 'I did this.'

He leaned down over her till the edge of him was touching the edge of her. He looked into her eyes and she nodded. And then, slowly, slowly, without taking his eyes from hers, he moved inside her. Deeper and deeper. He was huge. Her groan was as deep as he was within her.

With him fully inside, she took his two hands above her head, his chest lowering down onto hers, their stomachs making contact, and he rubbed his chest slightly against her body. He groaned, so she opened her legs wider still, then brought them up vertically either side of his hips, so his penetration was even deeper.

'Well, I'm afraid – there would only be – one outcome …' and with that his pace increased faster and faster until she had to bite her tongue to stop herself from screaming out with pleasure. Higher and higher she climbed, and then he was losing all control, making love to her like his life depended upon it, until they fell back down to earth together in the most incredible, emotional, irreplaceable ecstasy.

And silence.

There was just silence.

They'd done the inevitable, but now what? More silence.

Sadie bit her tongue – never had '*I love you*' been such a gamble. It felt like she should say it. The words were all she could think of. But she couldn't take the risk. *Everything they'd just done pointed towards a declaration of love – never had it felt so right.*

Do what you think is right Sadie … do what you think is right.

So Sadie did what Sadie always did. She gave the guy an out. *Would he take it?*

'Well, good job we *didn't* actually end up having a second night then,' she said.

Always the one to make light of it, pave the pathway for a hasty retreat.

Mac didn't react at first. Then she heard him sigh, felt him move, watched him pull up his trousers. She felt a bit strange, watching him as he looked around the room. She couldn't breathe. *What's he going to say next?*

Mac noted her luggage again. Her words resounded in his head. He looked over at her and past her, caught sight of the picture of her daughters on the bedside table. Her chin was moving gradually into that proud Sadie pose, and it all pointed to one thing. He felt a resolve stirring inside him.

'You were ready to go then?'

'Go home, yes. Of course. That's what I was told to do,' she replied.

'Is that what you want?'

'Of course it's not what I want! I want the fairy tale. I'm "that girl", remember? The type you can't deal with.'

Mac bit his lip. *Had he made a mistake? Is she brushing him off?*

'Sadie, there's another reason I came to say goodbye.'

'Goodbye – so you *did* come to say goodbye?' she asked.

'Yes, but—'

''Course you did. Of course. Okay.' The chin went higher. 'Well, what was the other reason?'

Mac saw a flicker of emotion enter her eyes, but just as quickly it disappeared again and she smiled.

She's smiling.

'Well, Mac? What might that be?' She sat up, pulling her robe protectively back across her. Covering up. *In more ways than one?* he wondered. *Oh, well, here goes.*

'I wanted to let you know, I've been thinking about you and your ... situation. And I've arranged with Simon to cover your expenses, your time in coming here. It's only a few thousand pounds, but it'll hit your bank account in the next day or so. Whatever happens with Tremain. It may help.'

'And why would you do that?' she asked, visibly starting to bristle. 'That was never part of the deal.'

'Well, if you must know, it was Simon's suggestion. He said it would be "pertinent and proper to help to reimburse the opportunity cost of Ms Turner's time away from her business", or something like that. You know Simon and his big words. Think of it as costs.'

'As long as *you* aren't thinking of it as "services rendered".' There was an edge to her voice. Mac frowned.

'Sadie don't be stupid. I never have and I never will. With anyone – least of all you.'

'I'm not sure if that makes it better or worse,' she said, feeling a churning anger in her stomach. 'You wouldn't have sex with me when it was business and you thought you could make money out of me. And now there's no deal, it should be pleasure and yet you're trying to pay me. It certainly *feels* like services rendered.'

'I don't know what to say.'

'Tell me what this really meant to you,' she cried.

And there it was, right there. The challenge. *I hate it when this happens* he thought. Mac looked at her and paused. His

268

breath was ragged, his face flushed and he opened his mouth to speak, taking a deep breath and closing his eyes.

'I'm saying this to help you, Sadie. To help us both move on.'

He moved back to kneel before her, looked at that proud face, tears threatening to fall at any moment, but her chin still held high.

No, he just couldn't do it to her. Couldn't risk hurting her.

So he spoke the words she probably hoped not to hear. Practised words. Words he'd said many times before. Words that came far too easily from his mouth.

'I'm not a good bet – I'm never going to make anyone a good husband. I'm one of those guys that loves being single. So, no romance for me. I love the fact that if I want to go to Cuba today – or Paris, or the Antarctic – I just bowl up at the airport and buy a ticket. No bags, all I need is my passport. Is that bad? I guess I'm selfish, or maybe I'm just honest. Oh, I flirt. Oh, I make love. Oh, I do dinners and walks and sleepovers … and all that gooey stuff, but only with people who know where they stand with me. Not that I've made any offers recently … You understand, Sadie?'

Then he paused, and looked expectantly and somewhat sheepishly up into her eyes. And smiled his default smile – the one that never quite reached his eyes. It was kinder this way. She didn't deserve any less.

So this is it then.

Sadie's heart was yearning to allow the tears to flow, but she kept a poker face to rival the best she'd ever seen Mac make.

'Great monologue. Scripted – almost rehearsed. Guess you've said *that* a few times before.'

'Sadie, here's the thing. I love being in control of my own life. I just do. Been single too long – that's who I am. And I don't think I can ever change.'

Sadie didn't move. Her smile plastered on her face. 'Well, if you think you can't, then you won't.'

'Sadie, I'm sorry.'

'Me too, Mac, me too,' she said. 'So I guess that makes us equal.'

'What do you mean?' He looked confused.

'We're two peas in a pod, you and me. I'm on a man ban, remember? So, no harm done. Now go. Go back to your superboat, or whatever—'

'Superyacht.'

'Or whatever. Go back to your Ironman, and to your single life.' She paused. *Oh, what the hell.* 'But one day, just one day, don't turn up on my door saying you got it wrong, 'cos if you do, you'd better bring a handwritten retraction to that stupid, rehearsed, clichéd monologue you just gave me. A retraction *in fountain pen, in triplicate*, 'cos if I *am* the girl for you, believe me, buster, *this* is your moment. And there ain't gonna be another one. Not like this one. Not ever again.'

Mac seemed to hesitate. Sadie breathed deeply and slowly, to ward away the palpitations threatening to make her faint. But to no avail, because, with a final sigh, he pulled himself together, stood up and kissed Sadie on the forehead. She pulled away.

'Goodbye and good luck, Sadie Samantha Businesswoman.'

Sadie held her head high. The least she could do was keep it amicable. So she saw him to the door.

'Bye, Mac.'

And he was gone.

In his place, standing at the door, was her steak dinner. Sadie held it together just long enough for the waiter to place her room service on her bed. And as the latch closed behind her, the floodgates opened.

Out in the corridor, Mac didn't know what to do with himself or where to go. So he set off as fast as he could away from her room before he changed his mind. But after several paces, he stopped, stood still like a statue and took a few strides back the other way. Then seeing the waiter coming out of the room, he turned back for the last time and headed for the lifts.

He made a quick call to his valet, instructing him to have his belongings shipped back home. Wherever that would be – this week, next week – always somewhere different. It was time for the next Ironman – then he'd find another event, and another, on the other side of the world from where Sadie was, if he knew what was good for him. It was what he knew best. It was all he knew.

Besides, he didn't even own a fountain pen.

Then Mac the billionaire made straight for a chauffeured limousine and the nearest airport, wanting in that moment to get out of town as fast as possible.

Chapter Sixteen

Sadie sat in her room feeling numb, just staring at the tousled bedclothes, and feeling very, very used. Feeling dejected. Feeling ... old.

The tears had fallen, and then finally run out of steam as she realised Mac was right. He was living the life of a playboy, being single suited him. How could a playboy billionaire ever want to be with a small-town single mother of two feisty teenage girls, with a hippy grandma in tow, and a barely-solvent health food store to run.

Different league.

Different world.

Different life.

But that life must go on. If there's one thing Sadie had learned from her years of being let down by men, it was that.

Or '*Morgen ist auch ein tag*' according to Georgia's last homework. A huge pang of missing home flooded her body. And that's when the crying began again in earnest. Only this time, it was for lost opportunities, missed moments and 'if only's. And for the slap-in-the-face reminder that, in this life at least, she was destined to be on her own.

Ah, well – *c'est la vie*.

She looked down and realised that Mac had left his socks behind when he speedily fled her room. She smiled and threw them in the trash bin.

Twenty minutes later, Sadie was sitting on her bed, feeling empty. She'd been busying herself with a copy of the latest scientific research to arrive from the UK, but decided to call it a day after re-reading the same paragraph for the ninth time. Now she was just staring at her feet, more specifically her right foot and even more specifically, at Mac's sock. On her right foot. Retrieved from the bin – just the one, mind.

Wearing one of his socks is allowable, it's wearing both of them that's sad, she told herself.

Her phone made a noise, making her jump, and a text popped up on the screen, snapping Sadie back to the present. From Simon. She read it aloud.

I do hope you will accept our offer of recompense for your time and troubles. And you should still explore the offer from the dark side, aka the Tremain Group. Let me know if you would appreciate my assistance with anything, even if merely to ascertain whether Peter Galloway's promises are more than idle. Call me if you need anything. S.

It made Sadie feel a bit better. If he put it like that, she didn't mind accepting the 'recompense'. From Simon. When he put it like that.

At least she knew there would be something to keep them ticking over when she got back, even for a short time. She had a feeling that Peter's promises would turn out to be *so* idle, they were virtually stationary. So she wasn't holding out much hope. She texted back.

Thanks, Simon. But Peter made it clear that if he was in charge, my value went down. Thanks for caring.
Will give it some thought.
SST.
Ps thanks for the offer to reimburse me. Gratefully accepted. x

She added the 'kiss' at the end, then deleted it, then added it again and pressed send. The trip won't have been totally in vain if she could at least pay some bills when she got back.

Sadie began to re-pack her things for the final time, mulling over the reactions of all those people in her past who had doubted her. She'd so wanted to see their faces when she told them about having landed the big one. Oh, how close she'd come to the big one.

At least she had the award. And she'd had an adventure. But she also had a nagging feeling in the pit of her stomach.

She picked up her pumps – the ones he'd bought her – at least she liked to think it was him, not flaming Alexis bitch-face. She shrugged then threw them in the bin. Then she tried to fold a particularly fiddly blouse, then gave up and screwed it into a ball, shoving it in her case and sat on the bed. She took some deep breaths. Everything was changing again, and it was happening so fast. She went to look out of the window at the amazing gardens once more. Bright, vibrant colours, and when she opened the window a little, the most amazingly fresh air filled her lungs. This magical island, with all its scenery and waterfalls and views. And she'd only had the chance to walk round one garden and she'd be going home again.

It had been only a few hours since she last heard there would only be one offer coming her way – from the slimeball that was Peter Galloway. But an offer was an offer. And with Simon to help her … Hmmm.

Galvanized by the text, Sadie decided it was time to talk to the devil. But there was no answer on the number he had given her, and when she rang the front desk, no one knew how to find him at this time of night.

He was no doubt holed up somewhere right now, meeting with Tremain, and deciding how to split up Bill's empire. *But where exactly would she fit in now?* She had to get some answers, and not only from Peter Galloway.

Sadie's nagging feelings were often grounded in truth, and as she relived her words to Mac earlier on, plus what she'd picked up today, an awful realisation began to dawn on her. *I wonder…* Sadie did a little more research on the notion that had just occurred to her, then a call to the lab followed by another to the hospital confirmed her suspicions and a massive penny suddenly dropped.

Oh my God, thought Sadie.

She knew exactly what she had to do.

Simon wasn't responding, so she left a message with him. Then, after pondering for a while, she decided that yes, she would send just one last text to Mac, just in case she caught him in time. It was losing face a little, and taking a risk, considering how he'd made their parting so final. But what the hell. It was now or never.

Then she set off for a date with her destiny.

The lift down to the hotel lobby couldn't go fast enough, and Sadie rubbed her stomach. There was a lurching feeling inside her and she knew it wasn't hunger. It was that same feeling you get when you lose your diary, or your hard drive crashes with all your family photos on it. Or when the doors close in front of you and you're one minute too late for the last train home. It was time to take the biggest chance of her life. After all, she knew what she was doing. She had confidence in herself even if it felt like no one else did.

'Taxi?' she asked the concierge.

Sadie pulled up at the hospital and raced inside. She was met by Makini, Bill's assistant, a jolly, mid-forties woman still dressed in her smart but plain office attire, who led her down a private corridor past the hospital staff to a small stark room.

Sadie walked in, and there was a pale-looking Bill. He was attached to a ventilator mask and a drip. The regular bleep, bleep from the nearby machine seemed reassuring, but according to the last doctor's visit, it was still touch and go.

'Okay, Makini, listen to me. We have no time to lose,' Sadie said, and pulled out of her bag something which she hoped would be the solution to Bill's current condition.

275

'Are you sure?' asked the assistant. 'The specialist said nil by mouth for now.'

'I've never been more sure. Trust me.' And Sadie and Makini went in search of a doctor to try Sadie's plan.

Meanwhile, outside the hospital, a black Mercedes pulled up. Its occupant got out, entered the hospital, and then the car drove away again. Through the hospital corridors the feet strode purposefully, until they paused outside a doctor's office door. After no more than ten minutes the car drew up again at the hospital entrance to pick up its passenger. Then left, at speed, in the direction of the water plant.

Two hours later, just as Sadie was about to drop off to sleep, her head resting on the back of Bill's hand on the bed, he stirred.

'Hello, Sadie,' he muttered, and smiled weakly at her.

She smiled back.

'What brings you here?' he asked, taking small, shallow breaths through his mask. 'Makini, I ... sure as hell ... need a bed pan.'

Makini was close to tears as she ran out to fetch the nurse, and Bill groaned a little as he moved to get more comfortable. Hopefully all would now be right in his world. As right as it could be with a son like Peter.

When Bill had had his checks, and the nurse was satisfied and left them once more, Sadie touched his arm.

'Bill, I have to ask you a few things,' she said to the old man. 'Take your time.' He gripped her hand feebly. 'Can you remember what you drank and what medicines you took today?'

Bill looked troubled, as though he was struggling to recall. Then he signalled to Makini and coughed a little.

'Mr Galloway wasn't able to recall what happened earlier today,' said the assistant.

'Not yet,' whispered Bill. 'Trying.'

Makini just touched his hand and made a motion as if to say '*it's okay*'. 'Sadly, for me, Bill can't remember,' she said. 'However, happily, for you, I can.'

Not long after a concerned-looking Simon also arrived at the hospital. But the one person who wasn't there was Mac. He must have gone. Sadie put him out of her mind – there were other more important things right now. *Forget and move on.*

'So I told the doctor about the latest findings from my colleagues at the university, and the tests from the lab here,' she was explaining to the kindly face of Mac's still-suited advisor outside Bill's hospital room. 'And we gave it a try. He just hadn't been responding the way they'd hoped.'

'Well, it seems Bill Galloway may owe you the proverbial "one",' Simon said. They looked through the window in the door at the old man, now weakly sipping some soup. 'How did you persuade the hospital to allow you to administer more of the renegade son's poisonous potion?'

'You could say I had some inside help,' she replied, nodding towards Makini. 'And when I knew that Red Frish was the catalyst, I examined the new findings and they all pointed towards the equal and opposite reactions. Red Frish had to make it better again.'

'How so?' asked Simon, eyebrows raised.

'So, you know we had already found that it gets into the cells superfast, right?'

'If you say so, Sadie. Science was never my strong point at school. Too busy chasing girls.'

'Oh!' she said.

'Just introducing a little jocularity into the occasion. Do go on.'

'Right, of course.' Sadie smiled. Simon was funny. 'But it also gets ... stuff, impurities, contaminants ... *out* of the cells too. I tested it on myself back at the hotel and within half an hour I knew the studies were right. So I rushed here with my remaining bottles to see if it worked. And sure enough the overdose in Bill's body was speedily cleared by Red Frish too.'

'Faster than anything they'd ever seen, the doctor said,' Makini added, stepping out of the room to join them. 'Fast in, fast out.'

'Dangerously fast,' added Sadie.

'Remind me to try it with my nightly tipple,' said Simon, with a twinkle in his eye. 'It may save me a fortune in Special Reserve. And possibly my other little blue supplements.'

'It might be more intense but … endurance, shall we say, won't last half as long, so maybe not,' chipped in Sadie, joining in his teasing, and Simon uttered a little polite guffaw.

The joke was lost on Makini, who was clearly still concerned. 'I liked Bill's Frish in my first coffee of the day,' she said. 'Extra caffeine hit. But Bill is a man of habit – same drink, same meds, same time of day. How could I have known this red label bottle was so different? I wouldn't have given him it, but I couldn't find any of our office supplies of regular Frish.'

'Don't blame yourself, my dear, the son probably swapped all the other supplies,' said Simon. 'There's more to the machinations of man than meets the eye, and you were not a perpetrator, merely a bystander in the sorry saga.'

Makini looked at Sadie.

'He means you're not to blame,' Sadie told her. Makini nodded. Simon patted her arm.

'He thought he was having a heart attack,' the assistant added, taking a weary breath and pushing her shiny but untidy black hair back out of her eyes. 'I came into the office and there he was, collapsed on the floor. It gave me such a fright. It frightened Peter, too.' Sadie put her arm around the middle-aged lady, and she felt her give in and lean towards her slightly. *Bless her.*

'I'm sure it did,' Simon said. 'But Bill is in good hands, my dear. Both here and when he gets back to the office – with you.'

'*If* he gets back to the office. It may be some time before he has recovered. Maybe Bill would prefer to take it easy for a while. It may be time.'

'You think so, Makini?' Simon asked, an interesting look on his face.

'Perhaps it's just as well his son is taking over after all,' she went on. 'Maybe it's time Bill took a break. A holiday. He hasn't been away for such a long time. I could go with him. I could …' and the jolly face quivered a little and she was unable to talk. Sadie handed her a tissue. Then Makini took herself back into the room to tend to Bill.

'Must be wonderful to have someone care for you that much,' said Sadie to herself, wistfully.

'Now, Sadie, here is that little matter we discussed,' Simon announced, somewhat officially. He put an envelope in one hand and folded the fingers of her other hand over the top of it, tightly, then paused and looked at her sincerely. 'And now I have to go. There is a venture capitalist I need to track down,' he said, and he held out his hand to shake Sadie's, then while she was fiddling with the envelope, he changed his mind and rested his hand on her shoulder.

'Sadie, I have no idea where our paths will cross again, but I am very aware that this is an important time in Mac's life. Things are changing around him. Do not think badly of him.'

'I don't, Simon. He stuck to his principles, you have to admire that in a man. At least he's honest. But I know he and I will never be more than – ahh – friends.'

'He could do with more friends like you, my dear.'

'Thank you, Simon. He has my number, he knows where to find me.'

'He certainly does, and so do I,' he said, and leaned down to kiss Sadie formally on the cheek. 'But I have had one last request from him – that I talk to Mr Philip Tremain. I responded that it's the least we can do to effect an introduction for you. It's probably best to deal with the horse, rather than the rear end. I will be in touch.'

Then with one more squeeze of her shoulder he left, purposefully marching off towards the lift, punching in a number on his mobile phone. Sadie went back in to Bill's room.

Bill was sitting up in bed, looking just a little bit brighter. Makini had clearly been apologising again.

'It's okay, Makini, truly … you weren't to know,' he reassured her, in short measured gasps. 'You see, my boy … he was experimenting for months … with the formula. He told me that Red Frish was only a tweak … It shouldn't have had that effect … It must have been an accident.' Bill looked over at Sadie. 'You know I have to believe that, Sadie, don't you?'

'I don't blame you, Bill. You have to do what you have to do,' she said, covering his hand with hers.

'He is … family. So I can only assume he had no idea what he was doing.' But speaking just made the old man start to cough a lot. A little blood was in the tissue as Bill continued to cough, and the nurse came rushing in, ushering both of them out of the room. There were so many questions Sadie had bubbling over in her mind, but none of them could be answered here, so she left Makini arguing with the nurse about remaining with Bill, and bid them goodnight.

In the limo Simon had booked for her, Sadie was churning things over and over all the way back to the hotel. Bill was okay, that much was true. But what would tomorrow bring?

Sadie returned to her room and phoned home. The girls had just got in from school and the latest instalment of 'jeggings-gate' filled her head and made her feel grounded again – back to normality. It wouldn't be long and she'd be home. She examined the contents of the envelope. Proof of the transfer. More than she'd expected.

Turner's Health Store had a reprieve, even if it was only for a while.

Sadie remembered Simon's words in his note – '*ascertain whether Galloway's promises are more than idle*,' and from the hospital, '*I can effect an introduction for you*'. But the way Sadie's luck was going it would amount to nothing. At least the bribe was off the cards now Peter was taking the deal to Tremain anyway.

Nonetheless, Simon would be true to his word and no doubt let her know once she was back in the UK whether Galloway and Tremain wanted her to help with the studies. She hoped so. But she'd lost the commission for bringing in the investment to FrishCo. And with it the chance of any more school trips in the near future. The girls would not be impressed. *Perhaps it's time their father started pulling his weight anyway.*

Sadie kicked off her shoes, pulled on her comfiest shorts, and suddenly felt starving hungry. She realised she hadn't eaten since the 'Red Frish plus senna tablet' saga. Downing another whole bottle earlier that evening to flush everything out again, just before her dash to the hospital, had left her starving. Sadie discovered that steak dinner was almost as good when you ate it cold.

As she lay in bed trying to rejig her thoughts to incorporate the latest turn of events, she knew there was nothing more she could do here. A whirlwind adventure, gallivanting halfway round the world, and still she'd be back to arguing with Stuart about seeing the girls at the weekend, selling alfalfa sprouts and searching the Internet for any more tempting marketing competitions with superb prizes.

Sadie climbed into bed and read one final text that had just arrived, before turning her phone on silent.

We don't mind if you can't bring home the bacon, Mum.
Really.
Just come home soon. Please.
G and A.
Ps as you always (keep) telling us (LOL) –
'You make your own luck', &
'You will never know, if you never give it a go' ; -)

She shook her head, smiling at the girls and decided she'd take them shopping when she got home. The money from Simon could at least stretch to some new jeggings each. But whatever was in her future, the one thing she wouldn't have was the one thing she wanted most – the man she loved.

What was that? Yes, the man she loved.

Then she set the alarm and turned off the light. Sadie was so exhausted she was asleep as soon as her head touched the pillow.

Just as the first light of dawn began to dapple through Sadie's curtains, the shadows of two figures appeared on the pathway leading to the front entrance of the FrishCo production facility. In the early morning sunlight, they crossed the paving stones and reached the door. Then a hand produced a swipe card, and they entered the building. One went to turn on the lights, but the other stopped him. Then they set off towards a door marked 'Private'.

A few hours later a note was slowly pushed under Sadie's door. And another text arrived on her phone. It just sat there flashing away until she awoke the next morning. When all of a sudden everything changed all over again.

Chapter Seventeen

'I got your text last night,' said Sadie, looking a bit bleary-eyed having rushed down 'urgently' to meet Simon for breakfast. When she'd spotted the note under her door she realised that this man never sleeps. And never leaves anything to chance. He raised his finger to her.

'Oops sorry!' she said, as she got near enough to see that he was yet again on the phone. But he put the caller on hold while he stood up to pull back her chair.

'Ahh, Sadie, good morning. I took the liberty of ordering you some coffee. Do catch your breath.'

Sadie plonked herself down on the chair and inhaled the morning breeze. Another day, another twist in this Hawaiian paradise.

'Thank you, Simon. And there was I expecting to be on a plane home by now,' she said, making herself comfortable at a smart table covered in breakfast paraphernalia. She squinted in the sunshine and pulled her sunglasses down onto her eyes.

'I do hope you're not disappointed I asked you to postpone your flight?' he asked.

'I knew you wouldn't do something like that unless it was "of extraordinary import",' she teased, breaking the corner off a warm, crusty bread roll and sipping some freshly squeezed orange juice. He raised an eyebrow and indicated the phone.

'Yes, well I just have to …'

She nodded. He stood and walked a couple of steps away to finish the call.

Sadie was usually a morning person but today she felt very heavy-headed. She produced a bottle of Frish with the red label on it and opened it. Simon raised his eyebrows at her, mid-sentence.

But instead of drinking it, Sadie merely sniffed it.

'Felt a bit crap this morning. Thought I'd give myself a super-strong caffeine hit,' she explained, but seeing the look on Simon's face, she put the cap back on. 'Perhaps not.' Then she drank two glasses of table water with a squirt of lemon juice in them, to get her system going. That worked.

Sadie's cappuccino arrived and she sat back, looking around the fabulous terraced café of the hotel. It was covered in planters filled with multi-coloured blooms like the beautiful fragrant native yellow hibiscus. Lawned gardens stretched into the distance to a golf course, where tiny golfers and caddies drove miniature buggies over manicured greens hundreds of yards away. The weather was glorious as usual and the wonderful aromas of freshly-baked breads, grilled meats and fresh coffee filled the gentle breeze. But Sadie's mind was elsewhere.

It must be nice to have a father as forgiving as Bill, she thought, downing the rest of her orange juice in one. Four drinks. Made her think of Mac.

Stop it, Sadie.

Simon strode back over to her and handed her the phone.

'It seems we have some news. There's someone who wants to talk to you.'

Once again her heart skipped a beat … *could it be?* But it wasn't.

'Bill!' she exclaimed as the old man greeted her warmly.

Sadie listened as he explained what had taken place since she left him last night. Her eyes got wider and wider. Eventually she spoke.

'You're rescinding the affidavit? It's really not legal?' asked Sadie, putting the phone on speaker so Simon could hear and mouthed her thoughts at the incredible news. '*Oh my God*!'

'Correct,' added Bill, coughing a little. 'It certainly isn't legal, not in the way it was signed. And I'm sending out a search party for my poor stupid son.'

'So Red Frish wasn't an accident, eh? How did you find out?' asked Sadie.

'Remember the man who showed you around the plant? Kaha'i? Been with me for years. Three days ago Peter asked him to step out of the lab on an errand. When he came back, Peter had created another new batch of Red Frish.'

'The batch he gave me,' she said.

'And me. Last night Kaha'i was informed about my being rushed to hospital, and went immediately to investigate the records at the lab. He didn't want to speak up in the past, for fear of trouble.'

'From Peter?'

'Sadly, yes. My son has not been the best boss. But the lab records prove it – together with that useful information from your uni contacts, Sadie. Peter altered the formula deliberately. So it appears he's not the best *son* either.'

'I'm so sorry, Bill. So was it his plan all along? To take over the company?'

'It looks that way. Seems he was so desperate to prove that his Red Frish was a far superior product to my Frish that he got rather carried away.' At that, Bill began to cough a little. Sadie could hear Makini's muffled voice in the background.

'And now it's backfired.'

'Yes. Until early this morning Philip Tremain thought he had been in negotiations to take over FrishCo, but little did he realise that Peter has no power – no power at all,' said the old man, and he began coughing again. When he stopped he apologised.

'Take your time, Bill,' Simon interjected on the speakerphone.

'Well, let's just hope Mr Tremain doesn't part with any cash before he realises the truth,' said Sadie.

'Let's just hope he does,' said Simon quietly, and indicated for her to end the call.

'Good luck finding Peter,' said Sadie. And she bid Bill Galloway goodbye and turned to look at a smiling Simon.

'So what now?'

'Sadie, I think this little twist in the saga may turn everything on its head once more.'

'Of course,' Sadie said, twiddling her hair, wide-eyed. 'So, back to plan A or what?'

'Or indeed C,' said Simon, raising his eyebrows and seeming in no rush to tell her more as he cut himself a piece of pineapple. Sadie stopped waiting for him to speak and took out the note he'd left her that morning. She perused it, then read from it out loud.

'You didn't get hold of Mac, right? Cos it says here ... *valet confirmed he had left for an important event* ... erm ... blah blah ... *But I may be able to broker an unexpected deal between you and Mr Tremain – a legal one.* So what's the unexpected, then? Who's in charge now? Bill again? Does Mac know?'

'The players may be changing but the deal is indeed still on the table,' Simon replied, dramatically popping a piece of pineapple in his mouth.

'Just who are you going to broker a deal *with,* Simon?'

'Well, it may seem a little unbelievable, but ... our deal is going to be tweaked to include someone I never thought we'd be doing business with in a million years.'

'What do you mean?' Sadie asked.

Simon's phone bleeped and he looked at it and then said, 'I think there's somebody else who would rather explain all that,' and he pulled back his chair, stood up, and looked over at the doorway.

There, across the patio, stood Mac, holding his phone. Bold as brass, smiling, and looking fantastic in a white shirt and khaki shorts.

Sadie's heart stopped. It just stopped.

'Mac,' she whispered.

'Sadie, good morning,' said Mac, striding over with a spring in his step. He kissed her lightly on the cheek, dwelling just a little longer than normal.

'Ahh, you're just in time, Mac,' said Simon, shaking hands warmly. 'I was just about to update Sadie with the news about the newest NewCo,' he added, looking pleased with himself at the wordplay. He was ignored by Mac, who only had eyes for Sadie. Simon smiled and went back to his pineapple.

Mac sat down heavily in a chair and signalled to a waiter.

'Kona coffee, please.' Close up, he seemed a bit tired, but strangely at peace. There were shadows under his eyes but he looked a lot less stressed than when Sadie saw him last. *Then again, her eyes had been filled with tears when she saw him last.* She swallowed, trying to calm herself down.

He was back. What did it mean?

Mac sipped the coffee, which the waiter had brought him, taking his time. Simon seemed amused. Sadie was just about bursting, willing him to speak.

'In the light of recent events it seems an opportunity has opened up.' Mac took another slow sip, savouring the strong aroma as he swallowed his Americano.

Sadie was just about falling off her chair in anticipation. *Stay cool, Sadie, stay cool.*

'I am about to take on a business partner,' Mac said.

Sadie was all ears. From the way he was looking at her expectantly she felt urged to guess. Suddenly a light bulb came on.

'Not ... the dark side?'

'Yes. One Philip Tremain. All thanks to Simon.'

Simon raised an eyebrow as he dabbed the corner of his mouth with the crisp white linen napkin. He shrugged one shoulder as if to say 'naturally'.

Sadie was speechless. *Whatever next?*

Mac continued. 'When I left you last night, I just couldn't

leave. I had to take steps I probably should have taken years ago.' Mac glanced at Simon, who raised his eyes skywards. 'So we went to try to speak to Tremain. He'd just finished with Peter and was … surprised, shall we say, to hear from us.'

'I'll bet he was. Especially after the row you'd had yesterday morning at the plant.'

'Ah, yes. Yesterday morning at the plant.'

'You never did tell me what happened,' Sadie said, quietly. He wasn't her boss any more, so in for a penny. 'What did happen, Mac?'

'Yes, well, everything was kicking off and I didn't like not being in control. I wanted to wait till I'd sorted it so I could just bring you good news.' He touched her arm lightly. 'Anyway, after I left you at the children's home, I got the Galloways alone, and I told them that they were about to lose me if they didn't act professionally. I threatened to walk away from the deal.'

'Well, that worked. Not.' She smiled.

'Usually that works. But there's a first time for everything.' Mac didn't look up at her, just sipped some more coffee. 'It was a gamble. I hoped they'd see sense – they were due to hear our full presentation at the afternoon meeting. We *were* the best offer. With you on board it should have been a formality, a done deal. Signed and sealed Heads of Terms by teatime.'

'So what went wrong?' Sadie asked.

'Peter Galloway had thrown a spanner in the works. Last night, Simon discovered what he'd told Tremain – and later told Bill. Peter claimed that he'd already bought your services with a bribe and that you were ready to jump ship.'

'Shit,' said Sadie, feeling regretful about talking to Peter at all.

'Don't worry,' Mac went on. 'That was even before you had your chat with him in the garden.'

Sadie felt embarrassed and looked at the flower arrangement in the centre of the table, which had suddenly become very interesting.

'I'm sorry,' she said. 'And when I went off with him ...' she tailed off.

'You weren't to know,' Mac said, and squeezed her hand a little. The warmth from his fingers was filtering through her, bringing back that old familiar feeling of connection.

She made herself look up into his eyes. They were staring straight at her. Could see right through to the heart of her. And they were as blue as the sky. And then that emotion was back – with a vengeance – *like when you feel you've known someone all your life.*

She bit her lip, glad of her sunglasses. He took his hand away again.

'I had to backtrack and pray that Bill would give me another chance to state my case,' Mac said. 'I arranged to meet him in private. But when I arrived at his office, he'd been rushed off to hospital. Peter Galloway was waiting. I should have filled you in last night, when I came to see you ... but I was ... er ... distracted somewhat.'

'Mmmm,' mumbled Sadie, now examining the tiniest insect on the minutest part of the smallest bloom of the flower arrangement and feeling a flush creeping up her neck. Simon was attacking a kiwi fruit.

'But after you said goodbye to me, I assumed you'd left the island, Mac. Everyone did. We thought you'd gone.'

'I nearly did. I got all the way to the airport and then turned round. I had unfinished business here. And I don't do unfinished business.'

Hear him out, Sadie, don't get your hopes up.

'When I checked all my messages, I heard Simon's complete update from the hospital. About the discovery you'd made, about what you'd done for Bill – and I was so glad I hadn't got on that plane. That's when I decided to get to the bottom of what Peter was up to. Tremain, of course, was intrigued. He agreed to meet with me first thing this morning.'

'Hoping he could gloat a little,' chipped in Simon, stirring his coffee.

'Wow,' Sadie said. She forced herself to breathe.

'Remember Kaha'i, the guy from the plant?' Mac went on.

'Yes, yes, we were just talking about him,' Sadie replied. 'He was the one who ... wait a minute. It was *you* who told him about Bill?'

'Yes. When I opened up to him, he told me some things that had been troubling him for some time. His suspicions about Peter and his Red Frish. It was me who went with Kaha'i to the plant last night. After that, it was vital to get to Tremain urgently this morning. While I was there, Bill rescinded the affidavit, and it put me and Philip Tremain on the same side for the first time in our history.'

'That must have been weird.'

'Yes, completely. But you know something, for me it couldn't have come at a better time. What I've agreed with Tremain and Bill will tie in with what I have to do for my future – for my sanity.'

'You mean your "important event". That's where you were going off to last night, wasn't it?'

'I was,' he replied. 'I did ... I am.'

He smiled at Sadie and she blushed.

'I can't believe you met up with Tremain,' she said.

'I wasn't sure about it at first, considering his immediate reaction when I got there. Thought he'd triumphed, with the ink still wet on his deal for Frish and Peter in the bag. Then his tune changed. He's a businessman, what can I say.'

'The rest, as they say, is history,' Simon chimed in.

'So the deal is on?' Sadie asked.

'Yes, Sadie, the deal is on. A new deal. A good deal. We did it. But I made him guarantee that the new contract would look after you. Simon and I will make sure of it.'

'Thank you,' said Sadie. 'My goodness, you so nearly walked away.'

'But thanks to you, I didn't need to. You got to Bill in time. It was fate …'

'… and destiny,' Sadie finished.

They both looked at Simon who was peering cynically over the top of his spectacles at them. They both coughed and shifted in their chairs.

'Well, anyway,' said Mac. 'I got my new direction. And you got your deal. All in the nick of time.'

'Not quite soon enough, however, to prevent Tremain being relieved of about one hundred thousand dollars by one Peter Galloway,' added Simon, unable to suppress his glee.

'How come?' asked Sadie.

'Tremain wasn't a happy man when he found that Peter had purposely endangered Bill's health in order to take over the company, but the bribe money had already been handed over,' Mac said.

'The last we heard, Galloway was en route to Mexico,' added Simon. 'In fact, I'm off now to dot some i's and cross some t's on that new contract. It will be interesting to see Mr Tremain again. I'm very much overflowing with anticipation at the encounter. I will see you both later. Don't get into too much trouble while I'm gone,' he said and winked at Sadie, then he stood, kissed Sadie on the head, patted Mac's shoulder, and left.

'He's a good guy, isn't he, your CFO?' Sadie said to Mac, suddenly aware of being alone with him once more. She began toying with the spoon in her half-finished coffee. Mac moved his chair a tiny bit closer to Sadie's.

'Yes, he's one of the best. Always looking out for me. Always did, always will. More than anyone would know.'

'I'm glad. It's good to have someone to look out for you.'

'Very true. Like you've got your mum. And Abi and Georgia. And your sister, Helen.'

'Ahhh – someone's been doing his research.'

'Better late than never.'

Mac looked at this beautiful woman in front of him. She was listening intently, and a smile lit up her face as she lifted her sunglasses on top of her head. He held her gaze, pausing only briefly and then continued speaking. 'And you'd be proud of me. I read up on Peter's notes at the lab. Now at least they know why Bill kept getting those funny turns. Peter must have been planning it for a while, he's very sly. Upping the dose gradually and trying different formulas.'

'Formulae,' she said. And then laughed. Mac realised she was teasing and joined in the laughter. He pushed her elbow off the table playfully and she prodded him in the arm.

'Anyway, I'm so glad Bill's on the mend,' Sadie said. 'He's a good man.'

'He's actually on the warpath, not just on the mend. And Bill's stuck to his guns about you. He always wanted you involved, Sadie.'

'And I wanted you,' she said. He paused and looked at her intently, waiting for the next word. 'Involved. I – I mean, your deal. I wanted to work with you. On your deal.' She pulled her sunglasses back down over her eyes, poured some water from the Red Frish into a glass then popped a wilted flower stem into it

Mac hesitated. He looked pensively out across the lawns.

Sadie marvelled at the sight before her. His hair was recently showered and it fell naturally over his eyebrows, youthful, fresh. Every now and then the breeze caught it and he looked for all the world like the father from one of those 'happy family' holiday adverts. Then he looked at her suddenly and spoke.

'Do you still?' asked Mac. 'Do you still want … to do business with me?'

Sadie beamed. 'Absolutely!'

At that, Sadie held out her hand as if to shake Mac's. *Deal?* He looked at it strangely.

'It doesn't seem right – shaking hands. Not with you,' he said and left her hand hanging there. Sadie's fingers began to go numb and she felt herself begin to shiver slightly, even though the sun was warm overhead.

'Oh,' she said, and tucked her hand into her lap and looked away.

'No, I mean it feels too formal,' Mac added.

Sadie exhaled. She looked up at Mac and he looked awkward, like he was about to hug her. Then stopped, then took her hand from her lap and shook it anyway.

'Doesn't feel right, does it? Maybe we should hug.'

'But we can't, Mac. Can we?' she stated, simply. 'If I hear you right, we're about to go into business together. So we … just can't.' Her resolve was being tested, but she stuck to her guns – stuck to what she'd told him as he left the room last night. *Speak now …*

'Anyway, you must have a reason for not ever wanting to mix business with pleasure and I'm sure when you're ready, you'll tell me what it is.'

Mac looked thoughtful and finished his coffee. 'Come with me,' he said, taking her hand and leaving a handful of dollars for the waiter. They left the table behind, along with the little wilted flower which had already begun to stand erect in the glass.

Mac led Sadie back in the direction of his room. He let go of her hand as they entered the hotel, and she trotted along behind him trying to keep pace while not appearing too out of breath. For someone who hadn't slept all night, he was certainly full of beans. They didn't speak all the way to Mac's room.

Entering his luxurious suite, Mac once again reached out for her hand, and led her over to the massive vertical trunk in the corner of the room. He sat her down in a chair and opened the trunk, pulling out the old wooden chest and the framed photo of the guys on the *Nomad*. He removed the tiny picture from inside the back of the frame and gave it to Sadie to look at.

'That was Ryan,' he said, as Sadie gazed upon a slightly younger Mac holding a small dark-haired boy. She looked up at him expectantly.

'When?'

'Several years ago. Ryan's mum was a solicitor acting for the other side in a high-powered deal we were closing. Late nights, long hours, high-pressure meetings – and I ... I got too close.'

'To her?'

'To the boy. She and I would have probably been a fling, but for Ryan. Once she let me into their lives it was hard not to become attached to the little lad.' Mac played once again with the St Christopher around his neck. 'You see I had a brother once who ... died. Ryan reminded me very much of him. I thought, with me in his life, he might come out of his shell. I'd get a chance to be there for him – I was determined to do it right. To be a good dad. Stepdad.'

'I'm so sorry, Mac.' Sadie reached out and touched his arm. He didn't move it away. 'And what happened to Ryan?'

'His dad came back on the scene – a devious character. Shortly afterwards Ryan's mother left town. But not before she'd fleeced me of as much as she could in the process of our split.' Sadie stayed silent. 'The father helped her – they disappeared and took Ryan with them. I never saw him again. It was my own fault – I shouldn't have got involved.'

'So from then on, you didn't?'

'It was just easier to close myself down completely and keep my two worlds apart. I began living the bachelor life with a vengeance. My life became all about me.'

'You're not really that person though, are you, Mac?'

He shook his head slightly. 'It's a hollow way to live. It

was just an excuse – an excuse that suited me for a long time. Until you came along.'

'Yes, I understand now,' she said, leaning closer to him.

'You do?'

She nodded.

'I just thought it would be better to avoid anyone who already had kids – but not 'cos I don't like them,' he said.

'Quite the opposite. I get it. It was in case you lost them, too?'

He looked away, and Sadie saw again that tender persona – the glimpse of a compassionate side of him she'd only seen once before.

'Well, no wonder you didn't want to get involved with me, then. Not that you'd have found *my* girls so "adorable". But I knew you weren't a child-hater, Mac. When I saw you at the children's home. The way you are with those little ones, so understanding.'

He nodded, looked thoughtful and then opened the jewellery chest. At the bottom lay the crusty old photos and papers, and he pulled them out and separated them.

'First time I've looked at some of these in years.'

'What are they, Mac?'

'This is where I grew up,' he said, handing her the group shot and pointing to the small ginger boy on the end, leaning against a very young Mac. 'That's Shauny, my brother. And that was St Wilfred's Children's Home. They did the best they could with us – with all of us – but it was a rough place. Shauny had asthma and wasn't very good at sport. Always being bullied. I got into several fights with the local lads, trying to protect him. Including one where they had knives.' He rubbed his face. She reached over instinctively and touched his cheek. He looked up at her and an understanding passed between them. Sadie felt closer to him now than when they were in the throes of passion.

'Go on.'

'I couldn't protect him enough. I should have been able to protect my only brother. But I lost him.'

'Oh, Mac, I'm so sorry.'

'Lost a brother and gained these scars. I deserved them. My own private memoriam. They always remind me of him every time I look in the mirror at them.'

'And this?' she asked, touching his neck chain.

'The St Christopher was his. The chain was all we had left from our mother.'

She reached over and kissed his cheek. He rubbed his eyes and stretched.

'It was a long time ago. A lot has happened since then. You see, they have to learn how to defend themselves, these kids. It's never enough, but I do what I can. I run a programme for them – funding classes in children's homes all round the world.'

'Self-defence classes? That's what your charity is, isn't it?'

'Most valuable lesson – better than donations that might be squandered on new furniture for the staff, when the kids were left sleeping on broken beds and dirty mattresses ...' He tailed off.

Memories, obviously hurtful memories – *no wonder he didn't talk about it much,* thought Sadie. She just rubbed his forearm gently. He didn't react, so she stopped it.

'Tell me about your brother,' she said.

'Shauny was a shy kid. Had a stutter. His childhood name for me was "Mac", 'cos he couldn't say "Michael". Then it kind of stuck.'

'That's nice,' she said.

'He loved boats and we always used to dream about travelling the world when we were rich,' he said. 'That's what drove me in the first place, my promise to Shauny. But it couldn't bring him back. I'd let him down, Sadie. I couldn't protect him, and I felt my heart would break when he died. Part of me died with him.'

Mac seemed lost in thought. Sadie stayed quiet, allowing him his memories. After a minute he spoke. 'That was the reason I buried myself in work, made my millions, and why I kept making them. Then I could run the programme, help kids like Shauny to protect themselves. And meanwhile I traded up and traded up until one day I could buy my dream "boat", as you would say.' Mac was pensive again for a moment. 'For a long while I loved living the way I did – a nomad.'

'The way you *did*?'

'The way I do. But who knows, maybe one day soon it'll be time for a change.'

'Change where you live?' she asked.

'Change everything.'

He looked into the distance, lost in thought and Sadie felt a burning question making its way to her lips.

'Well, it may be a bit inappropriate for me to say this, but ... Mac, if things do change, and you're no longer my boss, will you ... keep me informed? I mean, if we're not working together any more, then ... everything would be different ... wouldn't it?'

'And why would that be, Sadie Samantha?'

'Wouldn't it? Oh gosh, sorry, there I go jumping to conclusions again!'

'Well, I'm not sure it would be that different.' His voice was small, and Sadie mentally chastised herself.

'Oh.' She wished the ground would open up and swallow her. *Serves you right for getting the wrong end of the stick again, idiot.*

'Sadie, tell me something. If we were no longer working together what *would* you like to happen?'

'You're not dropping me from the project are you?' Now she was really not thinking straight. She panicked a little.

'No, it's okay, stay calm, I don't mean that at all. I just mean, if I wasn't your boss, if we weren't involved in *business*, then what would *you* want to happen?'

'You mean …?' Incredulously she gazed into his eyes. Finally the penny dropped. 'If not business, then …?'

'Would you still want me, like you said you did?' he asked, and he raised her sunglasses to look deep into her eyes. She felt herself melt in the middle as his fingers stroked her cheek.

Sadie felt an overwhelming relief course through her veins and she took his palm and guided it through her hair, pushing her head against his hand, closing her eyes. He took it from there, and when she opened them again, he was inches from her face. He pulled her head towards him and she inhaled as their lips almost met again. *Almost.*

'I hope that doesn't mean only pleasure and no business?' she said. Always the pragmatic one. *Can't you resist being sensible, just for once?*

Mac drew back and held out his hand. Sadie's heart was pounding out of her chest again.

'Shaking my hand?' she said breathlessly. Then perked herself up. 'Okay, then it's business?' she asked, as she accepted his gesture and he shook her hand firmly. 'That's good,' she said. But her words disagreed with the way her heart was feeling and the way her shoulders were drooping.

'Not exactly,' he replied. 'Sadie, everything's different. So much has changed so quickly.'

Sadie looked up as he went on.

'I'm not sure where this is going, but —'

'But what?'

Out of his shorts pocket, he produced a folded up envelope. He unfolded it, and passed it to Sadie.

On the front, in handwritten fountain pen, it said *Ms Sadie Samantha Businesswoman, PhD.*

'See,' he said, like a little boy all pleased with himself. 'It says *Ms*.'

'You know technically, it's Doctor.'

He laughed, and indicated for her to open it. Her hand was shaking as she gently pulled on the edge of the envelope and teased out the letter inside it. Her eyes filled with tears as she read the contents out loud.

Dear Sadie, I do hereby revoke and retract my ubiquitous monologue and shall henceforth consign it to the history books. I am not, according to fate and destiny, supposed to remain a single man till my dying days, after all.

She laughed, a single tear spilling down her cheek as she looked up at him.

'It's lovely,' she said. He took a deep breath, then went to kiss her but she stopped him. 'But I can't accept it,' she added.

His face was a picture, looking unsure as to whether she was joking. He soon got his answer.

'After all, it's not in triplicate!' she said.

'Oh, Sadie.' He laughed, and took her in his arms and kissed her, long and deep. They fell back onto the bed and just held each other. *Like when you've known each other forever, like everything else has just been a rehearsal …*

'I *am* willing to give it a go – just try me,' she said. He kissed her again, and then looked serious.

And suddenly he was on his feet, a spring in his step, leading Sadie by the hand all the way out of the hotel to a waiting heli-taxi, making her promise to be silent the whole way and not ask questions. Soon after, they were in the air, and still Sadie didn't know what would happen next.

Far below them, a black Mercedes sat in the car park, the window wound down. The occupant's head appeared, and a satisfied smile crept over the face at the window, looking gleefully up at the sky. The face was old, wise, and from the jubilant look, was allowing himself the indulgence of being just a little bit smug. The two people in the helicopter, taking off to one of the most romantic spots in Hawaii, had been brought together by fate and destiny, sure. Plus an intimate knowledge of the confirmed playboy billionaire, bachelor, and dear friend, who desperately needed a change. Add a little bit of behind-the-scenes mischief and a sprinkling of luck, and then helped along with whatever influence he could muster, all leading to this moment. Or something like this moment.

He knew Mac needed someone like Sadie in his life. *And someone like BJ – and Alexis – out of it.*

For months now, the person in the car had been quietly supporting a complete change of direction for Mac – and after his first meeting with Sadie, hoping that she would be part of it, and that nothing would get in the way. And now with the helicopter disappearing from view, the implications of what was taking place meant it was all about to pay off and the man in the Mercedes smiled triumphantly.

His final *coup de grâce* was approaching Philip Tremain on the quiet, and sowing the seeds for a momentous about-turn and a new era. A solid foundation for an arch-rival to work alongside Mac from then on. It removed the last possible driving-force, keeping Mac's nose to the grindstone. It was tricky, and very hard work, but it had been worth it.

Hell, even the fountain pen had been his.

Yes, as the helicopter became a tiny dot and disappeared out of sight, Simon Leadbetter closed the window and instructed the driver – Kaha'i – to take him to the nearest bar for a little personal celebration. Today had been a good day. A very good day indeed. And it would be the first of many more to come.

As they flew over Hawaii's dramatic landscape, Sadie watched in wonder and awe. From the desert scenery near the volcanoes, craters so vast it seemed like they could be on the moon, and beaches of black volcanic sand ... to the lush tropical rainforest, full of vibrant colours and unspoilt greenery, with the occasional clearing that revealed amazing waterfalls and colourful birds, Sadie knew she would be in love with Hawaii forever.

Eventually they began their descent, and Sadie followed Mac's pointing finger towards a small helipad next to a sprawling white villa. They landed, he took her hand, and they sprinted towards the entrance.

When Sadie finally got her breath back, they were several hundred yards away from the villa, approaching a small enclosed veranda which lay right next to a beautiful blue pool. Inside the veranda were fluffy towels, and a side room with a shower and relaxation area, sauna, steam room and outdoor hot tub.

'Whose is this place?' she asked.

'It's a holiday rental.'

'Some holiday!' Sadie said. *God how I need one of those.*

'Come with me, Sadie,' said Mac, and he led her into the changing area, where several choices of brand new bikini awaited her, plus a tankini 'just in case', he explained.

'For a single guy you seem very clued up as to what a woman needs,' Sadie told him.

'You ain't seen nothing yet,' he said, taking her in his arms and – finally alone – beginning the most intense kiss yet.

'Now, change, and come with me – there's a waterfall.'

'Oh, but I thought you weren't supposed to swim in them in Hawaii, there's all sorts of nasties like lepto—'

'Excuse me, Doctor Scientist – I think you'll find it's a *man-made* pool, with fresh filtered water. Trust me! Come on,' he said with the biggest playful smile she'd seen. He looked somehow ... lighter, and definitely happier. And if *he* was happy, *she* was happy. Soon they were out in the water. It wasn't too cold, and after a few seconds, they started swimming towards the beautiful little waterfall, surrounded by all kinds of brightly-coloured foliage and flowers. The water droplets from the spray created a halo rainbow, which arced above them. Sadie stopped and gazed in awe.

'Shall we see if we can find the pot of gold at the end of it?' he asked her.

'Or see if there's a little cavern behind it!' she said, her eyes glinting with excitement and wonder.

'There is,' said Mac.

'How do you know?'

'Saw the picture in the brochure,' he replied, and she laughed as he pulled her towards the falling water, and they ducked underneath it and through the shallow depths to the man-made alcove behind.

'Mac, I ...'

'Sadie, I ...' they both began to speak at once.

'You first,' he said.

'Mac, if I forget to tell you later, I had a really nice time today.'

'And Sadie, I have to tell you – you had me at hello.'

They both giggled playfully at the film references, but the meaning was sincere. Mac cleared his throat and pulled her closer into his arms. He gently pushed away the hair over her eyes and she caught his gaze – an intense, deep gaze. *I look in his eyes and see myself,* she thought, as they shone a spotlight into her soul.

'Sadie, I love you,' Mac said, and she inhaled sharply.

'Oh, Mac, I love you too,' she replied, as she began covering his face and neck and forehead with kisses, and he returned the compliment then kissed down her neck, across her breasts and kept going, as her hands buried themselves in his hair. And she realised once and for all the truest meaning of 'making love'.

A little later, they were reclining on the veranda, having sampled each of the spa rooms and taken a little nap and a spot of lunch – tropical fruit salad was all that remained

– and Sadie languorously held up the grapes to Mac's lips, while he finished an amazingly skilful shoulder rub behind her.

'I'm so glad you walked onto my gangplank, Miss Sadie Samantha Businesswoman.'

'I'm so glad we got ourselves a deal, Mr Michael Anderson. And it's Ms,' she said.

'Well, we'll have to see about that, won't we?' he replied.

And as they fell into each other's arms, Sadie knew at last that for the final time everything was about to change, this time for good.

Epilogue

Six months later

Sadie couldn't remember a time when she'd been more happy. Gazing out on the hazy Mediterranean sea from the bridge of the newly-equipped *Nomad* superyacht, she smiled at her two teenage daughters as they stood on the rear deck, pushing each other for pole position in the queue for the next jet ski. And at Captain Wiltshire, who was supervising procedures, under the watchful eye of his new assistant, whom he respectfully called 'Mrs Parker, ma'am'. Sadie's mum. Even sister Helen's luck was on the turn and she and Sadie had patched up their differences. In fact, Helen was due to join them soon – with her own tale of adventure. Life couldn't be better. Or could it?

'Fancy a pina colada, darling?' said Mac, sidling up to Sadie and kissing her bare shoulders. 'God you look sexy in this thing.'

Sadie giggled. 'The girls might see,' she said, leaning into him and pushing him away playfully. 'Not that their feet have touched the ground since you won them over with that party. Has Jim forgiven you yet for inviting forty teenage girls onto his precious superyacht?' Her sarong blew gently in the wind and her golden tan gave away how long she'd been sailing round the coast. She was overjoyed that after the initial scepticism, both daughters had taken to Mac big time.

'No, but if I'm happy, he's happy too.'

'Same as Simon – you've got some good men around you, haven't you?'

'And so have you now. Mi Cap'n', su Cap'n – mi financial advisor, su financial—'

'Ha-ha! I get the point. Your jokes are still crap. Good job you're handsome, you'd never be a comic.'

Mac laughed and kissed her lips briefly. 'What about a bartender – fancy that pina colada?'

'Em, no. I'll have a virgin colada though, thanks, Mac.'

'Well, funnily enough I took the liberty of bringing you one,' he said, beckoning a steward who arrived with a tray. Mac passed Sadie a cocktail with a garish umbrella and bright red cherry on top. She spied the tray.

'And what else?'

'Okay, you know me too well – an orange juice, a water and a cappuccino,' he said.

She laughed and kissed him warmly, loving the man he was becoming since they got together six months ago. They'd barely been out of each other's company since.

'Another congratulations card. From Hawaii this time,' he said, handing her a couple of elaborately-decorated greetings cards.

'How's Bill doing?'

'He's well. Hasn't been drinking any of his errant son's concoctions for months now, so he's regained full health.'

'Who would have thought it – his own son,' said Sadie. 'I'm glad they made Peter repay what was left of the money, but I can't believe Bill's not disowned him.'

'Well, I guess putting him in charge of the charity division under the watchful eye of Kaha'i amounts to the same thing,' Mac said, and she smiled.

'He's a good man is Bill, even if his son managed to fool him he's still being magnanimous. A wise man, and a lovely man,' Sadie said.

'He's also a very fair man,' Mac added. 'Bill's repaid Tremain the balance. And by all accounts, he has well and truly cut Peter down to size.' Mac was reading the brightly coloured card. 'He's made him drive a Mini.'

Sadie laughed. 'Sounds about right!'

'Hey, have you seen this? Simon sent it through.' Mac

showed Sadie the front page of the latest *New Scientist* magazine.

"*Wetter water – superfast hydration?*" read the headline.

'Wetter water? Who on earth writes this stuff?' Sadie chimed. 'You can't have wetter water. Superior cell membrane penetration maybe but—'

'Sadie, you made the front cover, does it matter?' Mac smiled as he pushed a lock of hair out of her face.

She beamed and flicked open the magazine. 'I'll get straight on to it as soon as we get back from honeymoon. I'm sure Christine at the lab will be able to come up with something in layman's terms that will make it a bit more accurate than that.'

'And a bit more ethical?' Mac teased.

'Okay, Mr Cynical. I get the message – no more geeky stuff for now.'

'I don't mind you being a geek – you're the most sexy geek I've ever met. And in return, you can humour me with all my Ironman-training-shenanigans for this last event, then that's it. After next month, I'll just join you on your power-walking round the grounds at home. But I might have to elbow in on your personal trainer once in a while.'

'Oi! Kieran is mine! He's already been eyeing you up enough as it is. And asking me about your abs!'

'And I only have eyes for yours,' he said, bending down and kissing her exposed tummy.

'Well, funny you should say that,' she said, biting her lip.

'Oh oh, you've got that look on your face again. What does that mean this time? Last time it was a new house. Mind you, it was worth it just to see the look on the girls' faces.'

'And the look on Stuart's the first time he came to pick them up from there! It was such a picture!'

'Don't piss him off – at least I get you to myself when they're staying with him.' Mac reached down and gently kissed the base of Sadie's neck and she shivered with pleasure.

'You're too good at that. You see, you'll probably be wanting to keep a close eye on my belly for the next – ooh, seven months or so?'

'Seven? Why seven, do you—'

Mac stopped dead, stood bolt upright and took her hands in his. For the longest moment he didn't speak. Then he swallowed hard. 'You mean you're …'

'Yes, darling. You are pleased, aren't you? We'll be older parents but—'

'Oh my God, Sadie, I'm delighted. Of course I am.' He took her into his arms and kissed her with all his heart.

'What will the girls think?'

'They'll be very happy about it. Happier if it's a boy tho' – less competition for borrowed jeggings and hair straighteners.'

'I'll buy them their own.' Mac laughed

'Don't worry, maybe Bill Galloway can predict a little boy.'

'That'd be amazing.'

'And you can choose a name for him,' she said. 'And I'm sure I know what you'll pick.'

Mac was speechless, he just held her tight, waiting for her answer.

'Philip!' She teased. 'Or BJ. Or P—'

'Don't say it!' he said, tickling her playfully.

'Or else the girls might insist he should be named Justin, or "Will. I. Anderson" or Jazzy A or something.'

'Wow,' Mac said. 'What a gift you've bestowed on me.'

'I guess I found the one present I can safely give the man who has everything.' Sadie smiled.

'I do now. Thank you, Mrs Sadie Samantha Anderson Businesswoman.'

'It's my pleasure entirely,' she replied. 'And it's still Ms.'

About the Author

Debbie is a QVC Home Shopping Channel presenter. She started her career as the first girl in the hot seat on children's BBC TV, replacing Phillip Schofield in the Broom Cupboard. Then she shared a couch with Eamonn Holmes to help launch BBC Daytime TV. Years later, she hosted her own BBC1 game show (Meet the Challenge) and has co-presented and reported on numerous other live magazine and entertainment and news shows.

She is the author of short stories for children's TV (Buena Vista, 'Rise and Shine'), and published a semi-autobiographical weight-loss book called *Till The Fat Lady Slims*. She has previously self-published her trilogy on Amazon. Her first novel and debut with Choc Lit *Take a Chance on Me* reached the final of the top ten 'Best 100 First Words' competition at York Festival.

Debbie lives in Dorking, Surrey and has two grown-up children and three feisty Labradors.

Follow Debbie on:
Twitter: https://twitter.com/debbieflint
Facebook: https://www.facebook.com/
DebbieFlintQVCFanpage?
Blog: http://www.debbieflint.co.uk/

More from Choc Lit

If you enjoyed Debbie's story, you'll enjoy the
rest of our selection. Here's a sample:

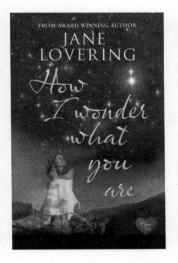

How I Wonder What You Are

Jane Lovering

Book 4 in the Yorkshire Romances

**"Maybe he wasn't here because
of the lights – maybe they were
here because of him ..."**

It's been over eighteen months
since Molly Gilchrist has had a
man (as her best friend, Caro,
is so fond of reminding her) so
when she as good as stumbles
upon one on the moors one
bitterly cold morning, it seems like the Universe is having a
laugh at her expense.

But Phinn Baxter (that's *Doctor* Phinneas Baxter) is no
common drunkard, as Molly is soon to discover; with a PhD
in astrophysics and a tortured past that is a match for Molly's
own disastrous love life.

Finding mysterious men on the moors isn't the weirdest
thing Molly has to contend with, however. There's also those
strange lights she keeps seeing in the sky. The ones she's only
started seeing since meeting Phinn ...

Visit www.choc-lit.com for more
details, or simply scan barcode using
your mobile phone QR reader.

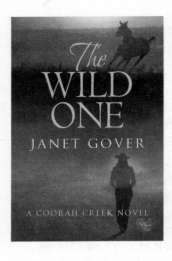

The Wild One
Janet Gover

Book 2 in the Coorah Creek series

Can four wounded souls find love?

Iraq war veteran Dan Mitchell once disobeyed an order – and it nearly destroyed him. Now a national park ranger in the Australian outback, he's faced with another order he is unwilling to obey …

Photographer Rachel Quinn seeks out beauty in unlikely places. Her work comforted Dan in his darkest days. But Quinn knows darkness too – and Dan soon realises she needs his help as much as he needs hers.

Carrie Bryant was a talented jockey until a racing accident broke her nerve. Now Dan and Quinn need her expertise, but can she face her fear? And could horse breeder, Justin Fraser, a man fighting to save his own heritage, be the one to help put that fear to rest?

Sometimes, the wounds you can't see are the hardest to heal …

Visit www.choc-lit.com for more details, or simply scan barcode using your mobile phone QR reader.

Sweet Nothing
Alison May

Book 1 in the 21st Century Bard series

Is something always better than nothing?

Ben Messina is a certified maths genius and romance sceptic. He and *Trix* met at university and have been quarrelling and quibbling ever since, not least because of Ben's decision to abandon their relationship in favour of ... more maths! Can Trix forget past hurt and help Ben see a life beyond numbers, or is their long history in danger of ending in nothing?

Charming and sensitive, *Claudio Messina*, is as different from his brother as it is possible to be and Trix's best friend, *Henrietta*, cannot believe her luck when the Italian model of her dreams chooses her. But will Claudio and Henrietta's pursuit for perfection end in a disaster that will see both of them starting from zero once again?

This is a fresh and funny retelling of Shakespeare's Much Ado About Nothing, set in the present day.

Too Charming
Kathryn Freeman

**Does a girl ever really
learn from her mistakes?**

Detective Sergeant Megan
Taylor thinks so. She once lost
her heart to a man who was too
charming and she isn't about to
make the same mistake again –
especially not with sexy defence
lawyer, Scott Armstrong.
Aside from being far too sure
of himself for his own good,
Scott's major flaw is that he defends the very people that she
works so hard to imprison.

But when Scott wants something he goes for it. And he
wants Megan. One day she'll see him not as a lawyer, but as
a man … and that's when she'll fall for him.

Yet just as Scott seems to be making inroads, a case presents
itself that's far too close to home, throwing his life into
chaos.

As Megan helps him pick up the pieces, can he persuade her
that he isn't the careless charmer she thinks he is? Isn't a
man innocent until proven guilty?

Visit www.choc-lit.com for more
details, or simply scan barcode using
your mobile phone QR reader.

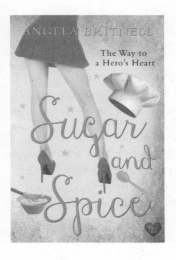

Sugar and Spice
Angela Britnell

The Way to a Hero's Heart …

Fiery, workaholic Lily Redman is sure of two things: that she knows good food and that she always gets what she wants. And what she wants more than anything is to make a success of her new American TV show, Celebrity Chef Swap – without the help of her cheating ex-fiancé and producer, Patrick O'Brien. So when she arrives in Cornwall, she's determined to do just that.

Kenan Rowse is definitely not looking for love. Back from a military stint in Afghanistan and recovering from a messy divorce and an even messier past, the last thing he needs is another complication. So when he lands a temporary job as Luscious Lily's driver, he's none too pleased to find that they can't keep their hands off each other!

But trudging around Cornish farms, knee deep in mud, and meetings with egotistical chefs was never going to be the perfect recipe for love – was it? And Lily could never fall for a man so disinterested in food – could she?

Visit www.choc-lit.com for more details, or simply scan barcode using your mobile phone QR reader.

Introducing Choc Lit

We're an independent publisher creating
a delicious selection of fiction.
Where heroes are like chocolate – irresistible!
Quality stories with a romance at the heart.

See our selection here:
www.choc-lit.com

We'd love to hear how you enjoyed *Take a Chance on Me*. Please leave a review where you purchased the novel or visit: **www.choc-lit.com** and give your feedback.

Choc Lit novels are selected by genuine readers like yourself. We only publish stories our Choc Lit Tasting Panel want to see in print. Our reviews and awards speak for themselves.

Could you be a Star Selector and join our Tasting Panel?
Would you like to play a role in choosing which novels we decide to publish? Do you enjoy reading romance novels? Then you could be perfect for our Choc Lit Tasting Panel.

Visit here for more details...
www.choc-lit.com/join-the-choc-lit-tasting-panel

Keep in touch:
Sign up for our monthly newsletter Choc Lit Spread for all the latest news and offers: www.spread.choc-lit.com. Follow us on Twitter: @ChocLituk and Facebook: Choc Lit.

Or simply scan barcode using your mobile phone QR reader:

*Choc Lit
Spread*

Twitter

Facebook